"Kathryn Mackel can weave a story like no one else. As compelling as *Lord of the Rings*, *Trackers* is more than a riveting and suspenseful read—it's also a subtle picture of how God's goodness triumphs over evil. The characters, warts and all, lingered long after I closed the last page. I'd love to see this in a movie."

— COLLEEN COBLE,
author of *Fire Dancer*

"*Trackers* is rich in imagination, invention, and wonder. In this worthy successor to *Outriders*, you'll face heart-stopping perils and encounter stunning plot twists that I guarantee you won't see coming. I'm a confirmed Kathryn Mackel fan—read *Trackers* and you will be too!"

— JIM DENNEY,
author of the Timebenders
series

"Kathryn Mackel's inventiveness sparkles! *Trackers* is a highly imaginative tale of a world recovering from wars eons past, where evil reigns and genetically engineered monsters do battle against God's appointed warriors. The ending is guaranteed to catch you off guard!"

— DOUGLAS HIRT,
author of the acclaimed
Cradleland Chronicles series

TRACKERS

TRACKERS

The Birthright Project: Book Two

Kathryn Mackel

WestBow
PRESS
A Division of Thomas Nelson Publishers
Since 1798

visit us at www.westbowpress.com

VISIT WWW.BIRTHRIGHTERS.COM

Published in Nashville, Tennessee, by WestBow Press, a division of Thomas Nelson, Inc.

WestBow Press books may be purchased in bulk for educational, business, fund-raising, or sales promotional use. For information, please e-mail SpecialMarkets@ ThomasNelson.com.

Scripture quotations are from HOLY BIBLE, NEW INTERNATIONAL VERSION. Copyright © 1973, 1978, 1984 by International Bible Society. Used by permission of Zondervan Publishing House. All rights reserved.

"Glorious," copyright © 2004 by Victoria James; "That's What You've Done," copyright © 2005 by Victoria James; and "For Always," copyright © 2003 by Victoria James. All used by permission.

Publisher's Note: This novel is a work of fiction. Names, characters, places, and incidents are either products of the author's imagination or used fictitiously. All characters are fictional, and any similarity to people living or dead is purely coincidental.

Library of Congress Cataloging-in-Publication Data

Mackel, Kathryn, 1950–
    Trackers / Kathryn Mackel.
        p. cm.—(The birthright project ; bk. 2)
    ISBN 1-59554-040-7
     I. Title. II. Series: Mackel, Kathryn, 1950– Birthright project; bk. 2.
PS3613.A2734T73 2006
813'.6—dc22   2006012431

Printed in the United States of America

06 07 08 09 10 RRD 5 4 3 2 1

To Pastor Richard Woodward and his family,
Martha, Patricia, Paul, Isaac, and Meghan.
Thank you for your faithfulness.

I consider that our present sufferings are not worth comparing with the glory that will be revealed in us. The creation waits in eager expectation for the sons of God to be revealed. For the creation was subjected to frustration, not by its own choice, but by the will of the one who subjected it, in hope that the creation itself will be liberated from its bondage to decay and brought into the glorious freedom of the children of God.

ROMANS 8:18–21

TIMOTHY CROUCHED IN THE GRASS, HIS HEART HAM-mering as he crept toward the Wall of Traxx. His attention was fixed on danger, but his heart was intent on Dawnray, the lovely village girl on the other side of the wall—held captive in the royal palace. He was ready with a plan and had almost accumulated what he needed to make it all happen.

One thing stood in Timothy's way, and it wasn't the deadly wall of thorns that surrounded the stronghold. The voice of his camp leader, Brady, who was off somewhere with fellow outrider Niki, nevertheless nagged at him in his head.

What most annoyed Timothy was not that the outrider's voice was imaginary, but that it told the truth.

What're you doing, mate? Can't go off on your own like this.

Timothy argued in his mind. But Alrod's holding her prisoner, and he intends her for his own use. You know what that use is, Brady. She needs help.

We can't rescue everyone, Tim.

But we save some. That's part of why we're here. You've led countless rescues, and you've taught me how to do it.

Why this girl and not some other? Is it because she's lovelier than the serving lass in Alrod's kitchen?

"It's because I love her," Timothy whispered, more to assure himself than to convince the voice in his head. Easier to sneak through a wall thought impassable than to deal with a leader who wasn't even here.

A patrol of Alrod's strong-arms approached, and Timothy ducked out of sight, though the strong-arms never looked his way. Two of these patrols guarded the wall, riding its perimeter from opposite sides, but Timothy knew they spent more time trading barbs and spiced rum than searching out intruders. They assumed that no intruder would dare try to breach the dreaded Wall of Traxx. But Timothy knew the wall wasn't impassable. He'd been through it several times just this past week.

Twenty paces high and a hundred deep, the Wall of Traxx ringed the stronghold with a vast stretch of flowers and thorns. The flowers bloomed on the outside—tiny but profuse blooms of roses, lilies, sunflowers, daffodils, and flowers even an experienced tracker like Timothy couldn't name, all infused with intoxicating fragrance. But beyond the blooms lay a maze of thorns the size of a strong-arm's lance and briar thickets that a mogged rhinoceros couldn't pass through. Many men—indeed, full armies—had been fooled by the wall's enticing exterior, only to be impaled by the thorns and die tangled in the briars.

Timothy waited until the patrol was out of sight, then ran up to the wall and began to sing.

Can you hear the distant thunder?
Can you feel the tremble of the earth?

In response, a bent-over creature shuffled out of the flowers, black eyes staring out of a leathery face. Timothy's heart ached for the little fellow—born as a man, but transmogrified by the sorcerer's potions into a turtlelike slung, destined to spend his life inside this wall. Like his many brothers, he feared open spaces and had only one love—music.

"Bask! Thanks for coming." Timothy sang the words, and the little creature's eyes narrowed with pleasure at the sound. "May I enter?"

The slung's answer was to turn and push into the flowers. Grabbing the back of Bask's rock-hard shell, Timothy followed him, singing the whole time. To stop singing was to be abandoned among the thorns.

To be abandoned here was to die.

Within three paces, the flowers gave way to woody growth. With ease, the slung broke thorns twice his size and flattened tangles of bramble that could kill any invader foolish enough to try to breach this wall. Timothy ducked low and followed closely, feeling new thorns and brambles already growing in behind him, lingering occasionally to fill his bag with globs of sticky resin that dripped from the thorn vines. The slung didn't seem to mind, just pressed on steadily. Timothy followed through malodorous muck that sucked at his boots and offended his sensitive tracker's nose—it was always a challenge to keep singing but not gag at the smell. All day and all night, the slungs lugged in buckets of manure and moldy vegetables to feed the living wall—and it was said that Baron Alrod fed this wall with the guts of his enemies as well.

Sheltering behind the slung and longing for the moment he would break through into the fresh air and sunlight, Timothy sang to survive.

But when he finally reached Dawnray's window, Timothy would sing his love . . . and more.

Dark thoughts. A place where the master sorcerer of Traxx was quite at ease.

But today a void haunted Ghedo's mind—a dream he could not achieve, an accomplishment beyond his grasp. Anyone could wreak death. All it took was a sword, a knife, a rock, even a hard fist or an iron skillet. Slash, jab, slam, whack, and death had its way.

Death was simple.

But how long would the secrets of life elude him?

As he trailed after his warlord employer, Baron Alrod, even this glorious day mocked him. The plains of Traxx were lush with summer grasses and blooming wildflowers. A profusion of life that came in its course whether Ghedo willed it or not.

To speak birds into flight and to call men back from the dead was surely not out of the reach of the greatest sorcerer who had ever lived. But how could he grasp the goal when the baron kept wasting his best efforts?

On these plains, for example, Ghedo's greatest achievement now rotted for all to see. He had finally succeeded in transmogrifying cobblers and farmers and fishwives into great, hulking gargants—an unstoppable army of giants. Just a few weeks ago, he'd presented his gargant troops to Alrod, who quickly turned what should have been an amazing triumph into a military debacle.

The gargant corpses now lay scattered for leagues, their limbs almost picked clean by buzzards and their bones bleached white by a blinding sun, a ghastly memorial to Ghedo's prowess and Alrod's folly. And Alrod, ever resourceful, now used the massive rib cages as gallows, stringing their ribs with his own failed strong-arms as easily as a woman might adorn her ears with dangling jewels. Rather than hanging them from their necks, the baron had ordered them bound tightly around the chest. They would bake in the hot sun for days until death finally came.

Cloaked and veiled, Ghedo was forced to stand with Alrod and watch the hangings. In his thirst for vicious revenge, the baron had not grasped this irony: by executing what was left of his army, by hanging them inside the remains of a greater army, he was advertising his monumental defeat for all to see.

After the last strong-arm had been strung up, Alrod walked briskly to the command tent, a good league away from the killing fields. Ghedo followed, breathless with the exertion. He preferred his underground lair to the open sky. His gifts were not of a physical nature.

The baron was the warrior. His lean frame was muscular, his jaw hard, his eyes hungry. That his hand rested on his sword told Ghedo that the execution had not slaked his thirst for revenge.

Alrod's valet Sado met them with mugs of mulled cider. An holdover from Alrod's grandfather, the ancient retainer was bent and gnarled, with a constant moist wheeze that set Ghedo's nerves on edge. As with a beloved dog, Alrod would not put him out of his misery.

"I need meat, Sado," Alrod said. "Spiced and roasted, but with the juices still running."

The servant shuffled out. Ghedo locked the door behind him. He slipped off his cloak and veil so he could breathe freely. Only Alrod had ever seen him without the cloak—or had even seen his face. Ghedo avoided the entanglements of the flesh that the baron thrived on. Celibacy had its virtues—a clear mind among them. And the cloak was a key to his power—almost as important as his cache of transmogrifying potions.

The purple cloak was the most feared—and thus revered— symbol in the stronghold. When Alrod ascended the throne, Ghedo had seized the cloak of the master sorcerer from his father. It was now embroidered with entwined snakes, fangs ready to strike. One symbolized his late grandfather, the other his deceased father.

There would never be a third snake—another memorial to a deposed father by an upstart son. Ghedo had no sons, no need for the kind of immortality men seek by fathering children. He had successfully transmogrified the wall of thorns so that it could regenerate itself immediately, and he had recently achieved similar results with a worm. Surely the regeneration of human life—even his own self—was within reach.

If he could keep his energy up. Ghedo was bitterly tired of cleaning up after a man who could not control his fury. "Alrod."

The baron slumped onto a stool and tugged off his boots. "What?"

"The army is running thin. We need every strong-arm that still breathes just to protect our borders. I'm speaking to you as a friend—perhaps you could cut those men down after a couple of days and restore them to the army. Your anger is understandable, but perhaps you would be wise to vent your frustration on the commoners."

Alrod was on him in a flash, the tip of his dagger against Ghedo's throat. "Perhaps I could spare the commoners and vent my wrath on the friend who betrayed me."

Ghedo held himself motionless. "How have I betrayed you?"

"By your incompetence."

"I would die for you."

"Perhaps you should."

"After all these years? All I've done for you? After all we've done together?"

"If you continue to disappoint me, what choice will I have?" Alrod's voice cracked as he lowered the dagger. "I need a sorcerer with the skill to match my ambition."

"I am that sorcerer, as I always have been. You know that."

"Do I, Ghedo? Do I really?"

The bell clanged. Ghedo shrugged on his cloak and pulled his veil into place before he freed the latches to let Sado in.

A sudden burst of light exploded behind the servant, followed by a blast of frigid air that sucked the door shut. Before Alrod could grab his sword, Ghedo had flung his knife into the intruder's heart.

The man didn't even flinch.

Ghedo grappled for his sword, but Alrod stayed his hand. "Were our visitor a threat, we'd both be dead by now."

The intruder bowed, a strangely formal gesture given the knife in his chest. Cloaked in a shimmer of gray and gold, he too hid his face behind a veil. Beside him, Sado stood as a statue, tray in hand and mouth open. The valet's chest did not rise, and yet he did not fall over dead. Had he been struck with a fast-acting potion that turned him to stone?

"I am honored to be counted worthy as an adversary. But I come as a friend." The intruder's voice was deep but not harsh, with an odd accent that lowered in tone at the end of each phrase.

"Friends do not come masked," Alrod said. "Show yourself."

The intruder unlatched his veil and dropped his hood. Ghedo swallowed back shock at seeing his own face on the intruder. "A trick," he muttered. "Some sort of mog."

"Baron Alrod has suffered a very costly defeat," the intruder said. "To emphasize this point, I wear the face of the genius who engineered the debacle."

Cold snaked through Ghedo's ribs. "Very clever. You must be very popular in many courts. The baron, however, has plenty of jokers at his."

"Are you sure you know your master's mind, sorcerer?"

"That is my privilege and my joy."

"Then surely you must know what is uppermost in Alrod's mind?"

"To raise another army," Ghedo said.

The intruder leaned close, his breath so sweet as to be nauseating. "To find another master sorcerer."

Ghedo spun to face Alrod. "Is that true?"

"I . . ." Uncharacteristically, the baron was at a loss for words.

"Would you replace me? The genius behind your hoornars, the master who gave you gargants, who created the wall of thorns that protects your stronghold? No sorcerer in the world has a craft superior to mine."

The intruder laughed. "Your superior craft results in stupendous failures, Ghedo."

Alrod's brow creased. "It's true. You haven't advanced my stronghold one league. In fact, Traxx is in mortal danger—"

"—from your diminished army and loss of the hoornars," the intruder said. "Not to mention the humiliation wreaked by those peasants with plain swords and sparkling armor."

Alrod would normally have killed any man or woman who dared interrupt him as he spoke. But now he simply turned back to the intruder. "Who are you?"

"I would invite you to know me as Simon."

"And where do you come from?"

As Simon smiled, his chin squared and his eyes darkened to violet, dissolving any imitation of Ghedo. "Here and there."

"A sorcerer without a kingdom?" Ghedo sniffed back the derision in his tone. He wouldn't be able to break headfirst through whatever spell the stranger had cast on Alrod. Best to step back and evaluate the threat.

"I roam at will, practicing my craft the same way."

"Cunning words but empty," Ghedo said. "What can you do that I can't?"

Simon looked to Alrod. "May I demonstrate, high and mighty?"

Alrod shrugged. "Why not? We could use a little bit of amusement."

Simon grabbed Sado's jaw. Breath returned to the old man, and he struggled to get away. "Don't fight it," Simon said. "I can do nothing without your permission."

"Sado, relax," Alrod said.

"What if I could make it so that your back was strong and your eyes sharp, your hands quick and your feet swift? What would you give for the privilege of being young again so you could serve Alrod as heartily as you served his father and grandfather?"

"Anything," Sado croaked.

Simon jerked Sado's jaw, breaking it with a loud crack. Sado's short scream was cut off by a loss of consciousness.

"I will have your head if you don't restore him," Alrod said.

Simon shoved his hand down the servant's throat, suddenly tall enough to straighten his arm from above. Sado's neck popped like a swift blast of thunder. More pops followed as the hump in Sado's back straightened.

Simon would leave the old man as a bag of bones, fit only for the dogs in the street. "Stop this, Alrod," Ghedo said.

"No," Alrod said. "Too late now to do anything but stay this course."

Simon was up to his armpit in Sado's mouth now, eyes intent as if searching for something. The old man's heart, Ghedo realized.

And sure enough, Sado's eyes filled with blood. Simon slowly pulled his arm out of Sado's throat, his free hand caressing the old man's face as a mother might her child's. The wrinkles relaxed into smoothness. Simon threaded his fingers over Sado's speckled scalp and brown hair sprouted, lustrous and thick. The valet blinked as consciousness returned, then blinked again as he became aware of his transformation.

In only mere minutes, the servant's youth had been restored. Sado stood tall and straight, his shoulders broad and his muscles taut. The only evidence of Simon's violent ministrations was the red surrounding Sado's eyeballs. What of his heart? Had Simon crushed and restored it? Or had he replaced it with something hidden, something surging with new life?

Ghedo's mind roiled with questions he would never ask. To ask was to be beholden. In his own time and his own way, he would discover the secret of Simon's power and seize it from him.

Alrod circled his valet, his eyes sparkling with delight. "What have you to say, Sado?"

The servant bowed deeply. "I am thrilled to serve you more ably."

"As am I, high and mighty," Simon said. "In any capacity you'll have me."

Alrod looked meaningfully at Ghedo, his intentions clear.

"No," the sorcerer whispered.

"Give Simon your cloak."

"Alrod, be reasonable. This is some trick. You don't know this man."

Alrod curled his lip at Simon. "My sorcerer says this is a trick. What do you say?"

Simon stared at Ghedo. "I say that Ghedo of Traxx will neither discover such power on his own nor seize it from me." He turned, smiling at Alrod. "I will not beg, nor will I impose. My offer stands: I will serve you in any capacity you wish."

Alrod snapped his fingers, a gesture meant for drudges and not for friends. "Now, Ghedo. I won't ask again."

Ghedo's mind spun. Surely there must be some way to oppose—

Go quietly, Ghedo. Or become the third snake in your cloak.

Simon's voice had bypassed his ears, gone straight for the inside of his eyes. How—

It's a shame to waste your admirable longing, but with no throne, you are of little use to me. Still, you have served me well, so I will let you live.

I've never served you, Ghedo answered in his mind. *I don't even know you.*

But oh, how I know you. You have served me and will continue to do so, for this is my will for you.

I will oppose you with everything in my power.

Should you do that, I will reveal your deepest secret.

No.

And under that secret, your deepest longing. Would Alrod be delighted by such a longing? Shall I ask him now?

Ghedo clutched his head. "Stop it. Stop it!"

"Give Simon your cloak, or I'll cut it off you," Alrod said.

"That won't be necessary." With a sweep of his hand, Simon's own cloak deepened to purple, an exact replica of Ghedo's, even down to the detail of the entwined snakes. But these snakes were truly alive, continually twisting around each other and snapping their jaws.

Panicked, Ghedo wanted to flee, but his feet were fixed to the ground. His cloak began to fade, and he feared he would fade with it.

I have use for you, Ghedo. Don't fight me. Honor me, and your secrets are safe.

Ghedo's cloak shimmered, no longer the glorious hue of a master sorcerer, but a radiant, fine-spun gold.

"Ghedo has worked hard for you, high and mighty. He's due some time off to relax and restore. Time in his lair, to work his potions," Simon said. "You'd like that, wouldn't you, Ghedo?"

Ghedo nodded, his bitter frustration warring with a soaring awe. Hadn't it always been like this for him? Mountains and rivers and plains, hawks and horses and men, wind and rain and snow. All objects of his lust, yet so far beyond his own making that he hated whatever power flung the mountains into the sky and drove horses to thunder the plains.

Simon put his hands possessively on Alrod's shoulders. Men had been killed for such familiarity, but the baron smiled. "Shall we get to raising your army, high and mighty?" Simon continued. "Since you've exhausted the near lying villages, we shall need to make a trip south to find some fresh material."

"Indeed. But first I have something to do," Alrod said. "Something I've put off far too long."

"Indeed," Simon echoed. "Go plant your heir in that lolly of yours. And then we'll be off."

Two

"ALROD'S BACK IN THE PALACE," CARIN WHISPERED.

Dawnray clutched her throat, unable to breathe. "He was supposed to be gone for another week. Are you sure?"

Her maid nodded, blinking back tears. "He's got a new sorcerer, they say. And a new manservant—named Sado like the old man, but nothing like him. Young and strong, he is. And handsome, except his eyes are all red like they're filled with blood." She made a disgusted face. "Anyway, this new Sado scurried into the kitchen demanding that hot water be brought to the baron's wash chamber. A strong-arm rushed forward, thinking an intruder had broken into the palace. And the new man blocked the sword with one arm and snapped the strong-arm's neck with the other. The crack was so loud, it shook the dishes. Needless to tell, we were all shaking too."

Dawnray rubbed her arms. She had seen much evil since being kidnapped, but each day seemed to bring new fear. *Lord, I am trying to trust you. But I am slipping . . .*

"The boys carried huge pots of hot water upstairs," Carin said. "The housemistress had me bring the scent tubs for the new man's inspection, and he's just as picky as the old one. Sniffed each one until he was satisfied, then dumped it into a tub that looks like it's plated with gold."

"I'm sure it is pure gold. Alrod wants for nothing."

"The new Sado said we had to move quickly, that the high and mighty one had urgent business with a—" Carin pressed her hands to her mouth.

"What?" Dawnray asked, though she knew. *With a lolly. With me.*

"I'm sorry, m'lady. We may all be drudges, but no one has the right to speak about any human so coarsely."

Dawnray's skin lost all feeling. Her body resolved to sense nothing at all rather than bear the touch of Alrod. "*Right* has no meaning to these—"

"Listen. Friend, listen!" Carin interrupted, clutching Dawnray's hands. "Oh, do you hear it?"

From outside, a tender song rose on the breeze.

> *Everything was nothing until you came my way*
> *Now everything reminds me of you.*

Carin's eyes widened. "It's the golden-haired minstrel, singing his way into the courtyard again. Your Timothy."

Dawnray went to the window. There were no bars because the ground was impossibly far below. The music pierced her heart, though she couldn't spot the singer.

> *Forever I'll love you,*
> *Forever you will see.*

"He's not my Timothy," she whispered. "He can't be. Tell him to go away."

"No, no! I'll tell him your time is short and he must rescue you. It's in his heart to do it—he's told you himself. We just thought he had more time. Maybe we can—"

"Stop it, Carin."

"You can't give up hope just because—"

Dawnray squeezed her shoulders so tightly that Carin cried out. "Tell him that a swift plague seized me and I died overnight. Tell him my body is already cold in the ground. No, tell him they burned my body. Yes, tell him that . . . and to go away and never come back."

"I don't know. I just don't know." Carin ran to the door, her fists pressed to her temples. She knocked and the guard let her out, leaving Dawnray alone.

She gazed around at the spacious bedchamber, as big as her father's silversmith shop back in the village. The crown moldings were edged in silver finer than any she had ever refined, creating a halo of light but no warmth. The down bed was blanketed in satin and tossed with silk pillows. Over the bed hung a tapestry brocaded with the silver and gold Traxx insignia—a hornet, curved to sting.

Some might think it a great privilege to be allowed in the baron's marble tower, an amazing opportunity to be the object of his desire. Dawnray saw the luxurious chamber for what it was. A prison.

She crossed over to the window and looked down, straining her eyes for a glimpse of the minstrel. The royal suite, including her chamber, topped a broad tower that loomed high above the palace. The baron and baroness's windows faced the palace courtyards, where the view glittered with luxury and excess. Dawnray's windows looked out over service yards where servants and drudges labored, hidden from the eyes of the royalty they slaved for. And where the golden-haired minstrel had found sufficient privacy to sing to Dawnray on his previous visits.

Beyond the palace walls lay the glittering streets of the stronghold where pampered fools shopped, gossiped, and lived in lavish excess. The plains of Traxx stretched beyond the wall of thorns. When Dawnray was brought here, the fields had still been fallow and winter brown. Now their emerald abundance gripped her heart so tightly she almost cried out.

She went to the window and looked down. She could end this nightmare in an instant.

She breathed hard, drawn to the thought against her will. Back in the village, she had been taught that suicide was wrong, a breach of God's plan. But how could submitting to Alrod bring Him any glory? Yielding her purity just so she could take another breath—could that be an act of obedience?

The minstrel's song grew louder. He had sung his way into the washing yard. From there he would scale trees to hop the last security wall and come under her window.

Carin rushed back into the room, her face stricken. "The baroness is coming to dress you for her husband. I am so sorry, friend. But time is short."

"Promise me you'll tell the minstrel to leave."

"He'll find a way up here. He said he was working on a plan."

"No. Tell him I'm dead so he can live. Promise me."

Carin studied her face, then reached out and clutched her. "Yes. I promise. I'll go to him."

"Tell him I died with his song held in my heart," Dawnray whispered.

The door flung open. Baroness Merrihana strode in, her haughty face a mask of efficiency and . . . something else. "It's time, lolly."

Carin sat atop the wall, flittering like a baby bird that has fallen from its nest. "There was this plague, and she died—"

Timothy's heart skipped a beat before resuming with a heavy thud. "No. I would know if she were dead."

She sighed and gave up the pretense. "You will be dead if Alrod catches you. He's going in to Dawnray today. Soon."

Soon? The kitchen staff had told him the baron would be gone for another week. "How much time do I have?"

Carin glanced around. "He's not one to primp, but he's taking time to be clipped and clothed. Maybe an hour."

"Tell her I am coming and she has nothing to fear from Alrod. Off with you now."

"But—" She hesitated, started to speak, then changed her mind. She disappeared on the other side of the wall.

Timothy pulled a bag from his belt and checked inside. *Not enough—but it will have to do.* Each time he had passed through the wall surrounding Traxx, he had mined the sticky resin from inside the lance-sized thorns. He had not yet filled his bag, but he had run out of time. He'd have to make do with what he had.

He hitched a rope about his waist, winding it so none dangled. Fingers that had never trembled on the highest cliffs or most stubborn trees shook now. *You're a tracker,* he told himself. *Think of Dawnray as a collection.*

Timothy scrambled over the last wall that separated the service yards from the palace. From high above, Timothy heard her anxious plea. "No. Go away. I beg you."

He looked up, drinking in the sight of her. Though Dawnray was too far up for him to see clearly, every detail was imprinted on his heart—her hair the color of cherry wood, her eyes a deep blue like the sky at dusk. A village girl, she was strong of build, but moved with the grace of a dancer. When she smiled, the dimple in her cheek deepened.

She had no smile for Timothy now, only a pale dread he could feel even at a distance. "I beg you to go before someone sees you," she called down. "You'll never make it up here. It's impossible."

Timothy eyed the polished marble of the tower's outer walls. It was thought to be impenetrable either by scaling or assault. If flying mogs like Slade's buzz-rats could make it through Traxx's aerial defenses, they would be lanced by the crown of spikes that topped the tower. There were no windows except those at the very pinnacle, where the baron and his wife had their quarters, along with the baron's essential servants and his favored lolly.

Lolly. He winced at the word. For any man to denigrate any woman in that way was wrong. To apply it to a pure, lovely girl like Dawnray was unthinkable.

We can't rescue everyone, mate.

"Shut up, Brady." Surely God would not have let this love seize Timothy's heart if he weren't meant to act on it. And act he would. Trackers excelled at moving one step at a time, oblivious to the danger about them. The first task was the tower, but if

Timothy encountered Alrod, he would kill him. He couldn't believe that Brady had let him escape in the Bashans.

The tracker would not fail where the outrider had.

Timothy pulled on his gloves and mask, woven from silk and shroud. He tied a length of shroud around his neck to form a makeshift cloak, comforted by the familiar faint burn of the shroud against his skin.

What a gift shroud was, with one side a soft cloth and the other side out-of-time. Heaven-sent provision for a divine mission. What would birthrighters do without it? Collections were stored in shroud, wounds bound with shroud, rookie birthrighters wrapped in shroud to ride in the belly of a whale from the Ark to this world. Shroud laced with metal and silk made an excellent and flexible armor. Birthrighters even used shroud to store perishable foods, wrapping them with the out-of-time side against the food to keep it indefinitely.

Today, with the out-of-time side of Timothy's cloak facing outward, light would deflect to some other movement. A strong-arm on a hoornar or a tradesman in the service court would think the shimmer was a trick of sunlight and not some fool scaling the tower in broad daylight.

Timothy kicked off his boots and wrapped burlap around his feet, tightening the strips so that the fabric was like a second skin. After gumming his hands and feet with the resin, he threw himself against the wall.

He stuck and began to climb.

But the resin dried quickly on the slick marble and lost its adherence. Each time Timothy lifted his hand or foot to move upward, he had to dig into his bag for more. He glanced up, dismayed at how far he still had to go.

Retreat is not a sin, lad.

Can't turn back now. He thought of Dawnray. *Won't turn back . . .*

Timothy was less than halfway up when both hands let go.

He arched backward, the force of his body pulling off his right foot with a loud ka-lurp. He hung upside down from his left foot, in plain sight because the shroud cloak hung off his shoulders. Carefully, so as not to force an abrupt jerk, he scooped two hands full of the resin.

Ka-lurp! Too late—his foot let go and he tumbled.

In desperation, Timothy lunged for the wall. He stuck upside down, facing inward. The out-of-time side of his shroud cloak brushed against his head and made his hair stand on end. He could push off the wall, roll into the shroud, fall into the out-of-time, and thus be spared.

But that would leave Dawnray to Alrod.

He inched the bag forward until it hung from his neck in front of him. He had to act quickly—the thwup-thwup sound meant the resin on his hands was drying out. He stretched his knee up past his shoulder, arching his back outward to make more room. When did his legs get so long?

The resin stretched but continued to hold.

He pushed his foot forward and dug his heel into his bag. Just as the resin on his right hand let go, he jammed his heel against the wall. He scooped gum for his left heel and stuck that to the wall as his left hand pulled away.

Head down, he was no closer to Dawnray.

Carin's voice carried out the window with deliberate volume. "M'lady. They've reported that the baron has finished with his bath and is getting dressed."

"Go! Save yourself!" Dawnray called from above.

Timothy flung himself backward, his right arm extended. His right hand caught, with his left hand still free. He pulled away his left foot, gummed it, and pushed upward. When he had moved up half a body length, he pulled his hands away and repeated the sequence.

"Hurry," Carin whispered.

"Go back," Dawnray countered.

His bag was empty by the time his head cleared the window-sill. Facing outward, he couldn't reach up and pull himself in.

Dawnray leaned over his shoulder, her hair brushing his cheek like a whisper of silk, "He'll be here any moment. You've got to—"

"Quiet, please. Let me attend to my business. Take the rope that's looped around my waist. Find something heavy to attach it to, something that will bear the weight of two. Do you know how to make a decent knot?"

"Yes. Should I fasten it under your arms?"

"It's looped on my waist already. Just anchor it somewhere."

He heard the door open. "Just Carin," Dawnray whispered. "She checked the hallway."

"That new Sado came out of the baron's chambers, looking all important-like," Carin said. "The baron will be along quickly. I have to go—they ordered me to leave."

"Tell her to meet us at the bottom," Timothy said. "I'll get you both free of this place."

The rope tugged at his waist as Dawnray anchored it.

"It's all set. You can—" Something cold pressed against the back of his neck.

"Who dares invade my domain?" Alrod, knife to Timothy's spine.

Focus, tracker. You've only a split second to choose a course of action.

Anchored by the rope, Timothy could fall and, in seconds, be free of this man. Disappear into the alleys of Traxx and fade into the wall of thorns. He could leave Dawnray to her fate because, surely, a birthrighter couldn't rescue everyone.

"No!" Timothy twisted, kicking upward so hard he felt muscles in his abdomen tear. He tumbled against Alrod. Together they rolled into the chamber.

Timothy took a fighter's pose, eyes narrowed, short blade at the ready.

"Well, well. If it isn't Brady of Horesh," Alrod said. "We meet in the most interesting of places."

Brady? Timothy blinked. Of course—Alrod had noticed only the shroud mask and had assumed the invader was his sworn enemy. The ruse could be useful in protecting Timothy's identity, and it wouldn't hurt Brady one bit. The outrider already held preeminence in the dark of Alrod's heart. All Timothy needed to do was not look straight on at Alrod, for Brady's eyes were so strange as to be memorable.

The baron drew his sword, a razor-edged rapier. "What is it you seek, outrider?"

Timothy deepened his voice. *Sound like Brady. And think like him—find a way around the obvious confrontation.* With his short blade lowered, he bowed deeply. "To bring this young lady back to her home and family. They miss her mightily and have asked me to collect her for them. You are a gentleman, sir. Surely you would grant them the delight of having her home with them. Will you accept my apology for this unorthodox approach and consider my request?"

"I have need of her here. My bed is cold."

"A good-looking man like you has many women. You surely could spare this one."

Alrod laughed. "I could—but I won't. She will serve me in any way I command. Do you hear me, outrider?" His upper lip curled. "*Any* way—"

"I'll cut that smirk right off your face." Timothy lunged, all strategy forgotten.

Alrod parried and slashed, his blade slicing through Timothy's tunic and gashing his side. Timothy spun and jabbed, angling the broad of his back to Alrod so the shroud cloak would offer some protection and Alrod would be less likely to notice his eyes.

This bizarre dance went on for what seemed forever—Timothy jabbing and spinning, Alrod slashing and laughing. Strong-arms rushed into the chamber, but Alrod ordered them back into the hall. The man was many foul things, but he was not a coward.

Dawnray threw her hairbrush, a tray, and a vase, all of which Alrod ducked without taking his eyes off his opponent. When she climbed the bed and crouched to leap onto Alrod's back, Timothy warned her off. The baron never glanced her way.

Alrod laughed. "You're a buzzing gnat, Brady of Horesh," he spat. "But you'll wear down."

"I shall not," he vowed, more for Dawnray's benefit than Alrod's. His legs felt like putty.

He spun and struck, the clang of short blade against rapier echoing off the marble walls. His arm began to numb, an ominous sign of fatigue. A sword fight had not featured in his escape plan.

Two veiled men entered the room, the first wearing the purple cloak of a master sorcerer. Too tall to be Ghedo, with eyes so dark above the veil they seemed to give off no light. Was the one in the gold cloak Ghedo? But why—

With no preface, the purple-cloaked sorcerer said, "Wouldn't it be more amusing to use the girl instead of your sword, Baron?"

"You're right, Simon. This fly-swatting is a huge bore." Alrod grabbed Dawnray around the neck. She kicked and flailed. He squeezed her neck. Her eyes rolled back.

"No." Timothy almost forgot to keep his eyes downcast. "This is between us. Leave her alone."

"As I told you, outrider. I can use this girl *any* way I want." Alrod let up on the pressure and Dawnray gasped for air. "Here's an interesting idea: I could cut off her limbs. Her legs first? No, maybe her hands. It might be fun to watch her run to the door and have no way to open it. I'd have no more worries about getting crowned with a vase, but her womb would be intact. Yes, the more I consider it, the more sense it makes."

"What do you want? Name your price and you'll have it."

Alrod laughed. "Your head for hers, Brady. You submit; she keeps these lovely arms, which will soon circle my neck, and these lithe legs, which will wrap around my—"

"Stop it. That is no way to speak of a lady."

"Have you not comprehended my complete authority over her? It is in my power to declare *what* she is. And I declare she is a lolly. Submit, or I'll throw her hands in your face. What say you, Brady of Horesh?"

"He's not Brady," Dawnray wheezed. "You're—"

The baron squeezed, and she went limp.

Timothy would gladly give his life for hers. But if Alrod discovered that he was not Brady, his sacrifice would be a useless gesture, and Alrod would vent his rage on Dawnray. His youth pressed on him like a stone. He was too inexperienced to summon a plan out of thin air as Brady always could.

He sheathed his short blade. "Fine. Let her go."

"Give me your weapon."

Use the weapon at hand, lad. At your feet.

Just this once, Brady—thank you for not shutting up.

Timothy unstrapped his short blade, fumbling to disguise his slipping the knot on the rope. He bent to put his weapon on the floor, pulling out a length of rope in his left hand. He straightened, kicking the short blade at Alrod hard enough to cause a clatter. The baron's gaze instinctively went to the sword, giving Timothy the split second he needed to lasso the rope about the man's head.

Alrod dropped Dawnray and fumbled for his neck. The guards rushed back in. "Stand back, or I'll break his neck," Timothy said. "One hard yank, and it'll snap like a twig."

"Do as he says." Alrod's eyes burned with fury rather than fear.

How he hates Brady, Timothy thought. *And I've just added fuel to that fire. It's wrong of me to bring my comrades into the matters of my heart. But Lord, surely you see that I can't help it.*

"Clear the room," he told the guards. "And lock the door."

"Out," Alrod growled.

The strong-arms obeyed immediately, but the sorcerer stood his ground.

"You, too, sorcerer."

"I think not."

"Simon, do as he says." Alrod's voice cracked.

"I lean back, and the baron's neck snaps," Timothy said. "That simple."

The sorcerer raised his hand, palm out. "I think not."

An unseen force slammed against Timothy's chest and catapulted him through the window. Instinctively he gripped his end of the rope, felt it jerk violently.

There goes Alrod's neck, Timothy thought. His own sorcerer just murdered him.

Suddenly the rope let go, cut from above.

Timothy fell with one last regret. *I've died for nothing.*

Three

"KILL THE GIRL," ALROD SAID.

The lolly's eyes flooded with tears. *Even bound and beaten, she was beautiful,* Ghedo thought. This girl was a pawn worth keeping, if only for her effect on Simon. After disposing of her rescuer, the sorcerer had left in a hurry, giving the excuse that he needed to recover the body. But the hunch of his shoulders meant something else was at play here.

Somehow the girl had distressed Simon so deeply that he couldn't look at her. She must be kept alive so Ghedo could discover the source of her power.

"High and mighty, would that not be a waste?" he said. "Of all your lollies, she alone has the fine bones, good skin, and full health that are needed in the mother of your heir."

"I am the mother," Merrihana hissed. "She's simply a breeding cow."

"A *tainted* cow. I'll have nothing to do with her," Alrod said.

The girl lunged at the baron. "I'm tainted? You're filthy through and through."

Merrihana raised a hand to strike her.

"Not the face," Ghedo said.

The baroness shoved her against the wall. Even as she slumped to the floor, Dawnray's eyes burned with defiance.

"Altogether a nasty piece of work," Ghedo said carefully. "But she is of strong spirit. Merrihana's son would benefit from such."

Alrod motioned Ghedo aside. "I cannot touch a woman who has belonged to Brady of Horesh."

"It appears that this was the first attempt on the tower. And you foiled it marvelously." Alrod was vain enough not to contradict the lie. That Simon had cast the outrider through the window and saved the baron with just a touch was something Ghedo would need to puzzle over later. "Why not wait a couple of weeks to ensure that she is not with child, then continue on with your plan?"

"Can't you just get me another?"

Tell Simon *to find you another virgin,* Ghedo wanted to shout. Instead, he smiled. "Certainly. If you are sure that's what you want."

It certainly wasn't what Ghedo wanted. He needed to stay at the palace and devise a plan to depose Simon. *Or*—he realized with a start—*I could depose Alrod.* That would solve both problems. Hadn't he planned for this eventuality all those years ago?

Alrod yanked the girl off the floor. "Such lovely hair, like rich silk. The sorcerer begs for your life. What say you, girl?"

"Kill me."

Merrihana leaped forward, a jeweled dagger ready to strike.

Alrod laughed as he waved her back. "The moment I need my wife to defend my dignity is the moment I leap headfirst from this tower."

He locked his mouth to Dawnray's. She tried to bite him, their teeth clashing with loud clicks. Alrod covered her mouth with his and pinched her nose, waiting for the fight to go out of her.

Ghedo watched the struggle with both satisfaction and frustration. This was the man Ghedo honored. A man who gained power not by sweeping aside the weak and helpless, but by subjugating the strong and proud. The kind of man Ghedo was proud to call friend. Yet in a fit of bewitching, Alrod had rejected his friendship.

"I'm glad to see you granting her wish, husband," Merrihana said.

As usual, a word from his wife was all that was needed to sway Alrod. He released the girl from his forced kiss but kept his arm around her waist. She closed her eyes in the same denial Ghedo had seen in the subjects of his sorcery. *This can't be happening. Maybe this is all a bad dream. Maybe I'll wake up.*

But oddly, her lips were moving. Ghedo had seen this response a few times before in his trips to the villages. What did they call it. Praying? Not that it ever made a difference . . .

"Ghedo, put the tower on war footing," the baron said. "Even if Simon finds the outrider dead, there could be other attempts."

Windows barred and strong-arms in every hall could be a status that could work in Ghedo's favor. He bowed low. "I will make sure your commands are carried out."

Alrod released the girl. She dropped at his feet, covering her face with her hands. "By the time I get back, it will be clear whether or not this girl has been tainted. If she is, then we'll cut Brady's child right out of her. If not, I will use her as originally intended."

"Strange hobby you've taken up," Taryan muttered as they threaded their way through the crowded market. "Tower climbing. Wouldn't recommend it."

Still a little dazed, Timothy stared at his tracker friend. If not for her, he would be broken into a hundred pieces and rotting in some Traxx sewer. The net she had strung at the base of the marble tower had saved him. Taryan had also had the foresight to offer drugged sweets to the guards and to hang a rope ladder so they could make a quick exit from the palace proper. Now that they were on the streets, they had to slow their pace so as not to draw attention.

Finally Timothy caught his breath. "What are you doing here?"

"The question is: what are *you* doing here?"

"I asked you first." A childish tactic, but he needed to find out how much she knew.

"Brady is looking for you. I said I'd fetch you." An angry red scar marred the front of his comrade's neck. During the battle of the Bashan Mountains, she had been stung by one of the mogged wasps called hoornars. Kendo had had to cut her throat open so she could breathe. The wound was healing, but the mark would remain.

"How did you know I was here?" Timothy persisted.

"It's my job as your elder to know what you're up to. I've tracked you since the second day you came here."

"Have you told Brady?"

"I'll let you do that."

He pressed Taryan's hand to his heart. "I didn't plan this."

"No one does, mate. We've got to keep moving here."

"I need you to understand—I'm not betraying our mission."

"Tell me," Taryan said. "Tell me how you're remaining true."

"I don't know where to start."

"Then tell me about this girl."

"When I came to court with Brady last month, I sang for the baroness, but my eyes were caught by the girl next to her. A girl Alrod had kidnapped for his own use."

Taryan smiled. "She must be very beautiful to captivate you with one look."

"She is lovely. But that's not it." The flush rose in his cheeks, and Timothy once again regretted the fair skin that showed every feeling in his face. "I knew—and I can't tell you how—that she was a good woman. A godly woman. And now I know that is true, because I've gotten to know her on these visits."

"You scaled the tower more than once?"

"No. Only in thought and song. But my heart—Taryan, my heart soars when I see her and speak to her and hear her voice."

"You need to tell Brady."

Timothy covered her hands with his. "The builders expect us to remain celibate."

"Real love demands self-discipline," Taryan said. "Surely you know that. And since none of us is married . . ."

"But that's my point," he said. "The builders expect us to *remain* unmarried."

She pulled away and walked faster. "We need to keep moving."

Timothy trotted to keep up. "But that's it—*keep moving* is what the builders don't understand. What I don't think Brady will understand."

Taryan sighed. "Tell me. And then we really need to get the horses and get away from here."

"He doesn't understand that, despite our devotion to our mission, our minds and bodies and spirits have kept moving. We're growing up, Taryan. You're what—twenty? I'm almost nineteen. God gave me this heart that loves. And I truly believe He's given me this woman to love. Brady's not going to understand that."

She turned, a flush rising in her own cheeks. "Mate, Brady understands that more than you can realize. Now let's go home."

Alrod's suite resembled a military command center more than a royal resting place. The trappings of power—his own weapons and battle plans—were what relaxed him. He sat on the edge of the desk and stretched out both arms.

Ghedo clasped his forearms, and the baron clasped his in the deepest gesture of friendship in Traxx. "Can I trust you?"

Ghedo kept his voice even. "I serve with my life, Alrod."

"Then watch out for the stronghold in my absence. Will you do that?"

Merrihana waited, foot tapping like a common fishmonger. "You banish him from your side, and you think he will serve you?"

"Ghedo knows his place."

"Like your lolly does?" Merrihana's husky voice cracked. With black hair that flowed like the night and pearl skin that shone like the moon, the baroness was the beauty that royals of five strongholds had pursued. Alrod—with Ghedo guiding every move—had won her. Their children would have been spectacular—if not for her foolish vanity.

It was almost twenty years ago that Ghedo had refused to give her cat eyes. "Mogging could make you sterile," he had told her plainly, "or the mother of monsters." But she would not listen to his warning. She had gone to some backwoods sorcerer for her beautiful topaz eyes, mogged with a feline potion. Able to see in the dark, Merrihana could track Alrod's nocturnal encounters with precision. The price she paid was her fertility—all she could spawn were deformed children. To keep her husband, she had no choice but to support his plans to father an heir through someone else.

"The lolly will serve when her time comes," the baron told her now.

Merrihana's response was edged with contempt. "Just tell me how I can serve you, husband."

Ghedo remained, privy to their marital skirmishes as usual. Would Simon be allotted such privilege, assuming he even returned?

"You, my dear, will teach the lolly all she needs to know to please me."

"Alrod, grant me a boon," Merrihana pressed his hands to her heart. "Let me try one more time."

"You have been pregnant eight times. Each child a—" Alrod glanced at Ghedo.

To speak *monster* aloud was unnecessary. Of those who survived birth, one infant had four arms, another was legless. The third of her progeny had looked perfect until they turned him over to find a row of tiny skulls growing down his spine.

Each time Merrihana had labored and hoped, and each time Ghedo carried the child off for disposal. For such intimate loyalty, Alrod had cast him aside in the space of five minutes for a grandstanding stranger named Simon.

Alrod took her hands, kissed her palms. "The child will be yours to raise and mine to train."

She clutched at his chest, desperation twisting her smile. "Swear this."

"You have nothing to fear from a lolly. But"—Alrod brushed her lips with his—"since you need reassurance, you may kill her yourself. After our son is born."

"No."

"No? I thought that was your wish."

Merrihana pressed against him. "My wish is that *you* kill her in my full sight."

"If that pleases you, it pleases me."

"I intend to hold you to that, husband."

Ghedo suppressed a smile. The baroness was a fine politician. Perhaps she had been humiliated too long. Perhaps she'd be open to a change.

FOUR

NIKI AND BRADY TRAVELED SOUTH, THE BIRTHRIGHTER camp of Horesh three hours behind them.

They maintained a leisurely trot, passing by Slade strong-arms watching from high towers. Across the water, Traxx strong-arms brandished fierce weapons from their own guard stands. This was business as usual on the long border between the two warring strongholds.

Niki's attention was set on a question that Brady had yet to ask. *Wasn't there another letter, Nik? Surely there had to be.*

She could lie or she could tell the truth. Either way, her heart would be torn in two.

"These fools spend a tremendous amount of energy staring each other down," she said, her tone light. "It never occurs to them to give it up and just form an alliance?"

Brady laughed. "You ask that every time we come this way."

"And every time we come, they're still stupidly pointing spears at each other. So I stupidly wonder why. Is that a crime?"

"Their stupidly pointing spears? It's a blessing. Baron Alrod and Prince Treffyn with fangs bared at each other is far better than two rats sharing a cheese."

"And my stupidly wondering why?"

"Don't know about a blessing, gal. But it sure is funny." Brady ducked before she could cuff the back of his head.

Niki nudged her horse, Tekk, into a trot. Brady caught up to her and yanked down her hood, laughing as the ribbons Jayme had braided into her hair unraveled.

"Stop it," she snapped. Bad enough they had made her wear a velvet cloak, but the mouth paint and hair adornments made her want to scream. A woman on horseback with a sword strapped to one leg and a short blade to another would draw considerable interest from the border guards. It was either cover her weapons with finery or leave them back at camp.

Niki pulled out the rest of the ribbons and let them sail away.

"Shall I fetch your silks, m'lady? The wind certainly has no need of them."

"Who are you to advise me of fashion? What did you use to style that hair of yours—donkey teeth? You look like a dog that's picked one too many fleas."

"Speaking of canines . . ." Brady's eyes shifted to the line of brush that edged the river—and the swish of a canine tail.

Niki sighed dramatically. "I told the wolf to stay back at camp."

"He obeys well, I see."

"He knows his role—to be by my side. What's wrong with that?"

He turned in his saddle to look at her. "What are you saying?"

"Nothing."

Her stomach ached with what she was *not* saying. The scene from a week ago haunted her. They had stopped for the night. With the three newest rooks, not even three weeks off the Ark, fast asleep in their blankets, Brady and Niki had sat together by the fire. "Got the letters, Nik?"

"Sure. Hold on, pal." Niki had stepped behind him for modesty, lifted her shirt, and unbound the letters that the rooks had brought from the Ark. The package included personal letters from families and friends they would never return to, as well as coded lists of species to be collected and instructions for the camp leader.

Niki had prepared for this moment, leaving one page bound to her back instead of her side.

Brady had set aside his own personal letters with the ones for his comrades. His practice was not to read his until the others at

Horesh had theirs. He'd glanced at the collection lists and instructions, his jaw tightening. Rustling the pages, he'd scanned them again, then once more.

When he finished reading, Brady had wrapped all the letters in shroud and bound them to his chest. Niki remembered wincing at the prominence of his ribs. He'd been in two major battles in the past week, fights that had spent him. He pulled his blanket around his shoulders and sat in silence.

He knows, she had thought then, and she thought it now. The elders on the Ark always answered their queries. Yet Brady still had not uttered the words she dreaded: "Were there any other letters for the camp leader, Nik?"

How often she had practiced her answer. "Is something missing? When I was dumped in the river, I may have lost more than I realized. I'm sorry." Much as she dreaded the lie, she was prepared to say it.

She knew the words of that letter by memory, had read them so frequently they were seared on the underside of her heart. "After much prayer, we do authorize you to marry."

In a weak moment, Brady had asked permission, and in a weaker moment, the builders had granted it. But what did the people on the Ark know of this world? They had all been born under the ice and could only guess at the steady danger, the absolute need for focus and commitment. A birthrighter could not allow his or her heart to stray from the mission. To lose focus was to die. And what would marriage be but a loss of focus?

Marrying would put Brady in grave danger and therefore was not in his best interest. Niki had believed that a week ago, and she believed it now.

"Nik." Brady reined Thunderhoof to a stop, coming around so he could face her.

She said the first thing that came to her mind. "You've never brought me to meet Dakota before. Why now?"

He studied her, his green-brown eyes taking on the gold of midday sun. "Arabah."

A full birthrighter camp, trapped in a soul-stinging darkness that their prayers and swords could not penetrate.

"So we're doubling up on precautions?"

"Aye, gal. What I know, you have to know."

"Such as how to find Dakota."

He nodded, eyes fixed on hers. "And what I decide, you must agree to."

"Makes sense." It was good that Brady would put more on her shoulders. He carried a heavy burden. Only twenty-two, his hair was already laced with silver.

"Which means we can't do missions together," he said.

Her stomach flip-flopped. "Not fight side by side? Is that what you're saying?"

"I'm afraid so."

"No!"

"Yes. I can be tempted as easily as anyone in Arabah must have been. As Ajoba was, and as you could be. You have to be my check, and I will be your balance." He grasped her hand, his fingers slipping through hers.

"Isn't that the way it's always been?"

"Yea, gal. Sure is." Brady gave her that sudden, sweet smile, and the decision was made.

For Brady's own good, she could not give him the letter from the Ark. To be distracted was to die, and though Niki would die for Brady, he must not die simply because he thought he needed a wife. Taryan was a fine tracker and a nice girl, but she would dampen his fire, slow him when he most needed to fly.

The matter resolved, Niki urged Tekk faster. Lush with the smell of new grass and coming summer, the wind on her face refreshed her. Brady kept up, his face impassive, awaiting some signal that he laughingly refused to share.

"You need to see it to comprehend how Dakota works," he had said. "I send out a hawk with the time I want to meet and tell him what direction I'm heading in. Dakota does the rest."

They rode in merciful silence until something stung her. "Ouch! Stupid wasp." She swiped at the side of her neck.

Brady scraped a stinger from her skin and showed it to her. "Good thing you're not a tracker, gal."

"So it's a honeybee, not a wasp. Let the trackers study their insects—I know my swords. What more is there to know?"

Brady smiled. "Know this, Nik. Dakota has found us."

Anastasia rolled over, pulling her blanket tight around her neck. Made of the richest wool, it had none of the rough weave of the tunic she had been given to wear *out there*.

Maybe *out there* had been a dream after all.

Maybe she hadn't ridden in the belly of a whale, been coughed up on the ice, and traveled in a wicked and dangerous world. Everyone said she had an active imagination. Her dreams had seemed so vivid—fighting off mogged oxen, cutting through tangled seaweed, climbing high mountains. Huddling in a darkness that she had never known on the Ark, where the lights always burned.

Her stomach rumbled. Anastasia jumped out of her bunk and went out into the corridor, wishing her family's quarters weren't so far from this sector's dining hall. The air recirculation pumps hummed overhead, and the wall vibrated with a slow thud as familiar as her own heartbeat.

Something wet bounced against her cheek.

A tiny bubble of water glistened on the ceiling. It swelled into a half sphere, elongating until it dropped square on her forehead.

One drop became ten, ten became thousands, coming so hard that her face was soaked and she could hardly breathe. "Leak," she screamed. "The Ark is leaking!"

Anastasia clutched the wall as the water swirled about her

ankles. Her pleas for help were mere bubbles, burst by the crush of cold sea as it breached the walls.

"Stop it, Anastasia. Stop. Wake up."

A dark-skinned girl with almond eyes was shaking her by the shoulders. Water pelted from the sky in steady sheets.

Sky—not ceiling.

World—not Ark.

"Shush, it's all right," the girl said. "It's only rain."

Anastasia sat up, blinking. "Who're you?"

"Ajoba. Two classes ahead of you."

Brady had spoken of this girl to Niki in hard-edged whispers: *Ajoba's disobedience bordered on betrayal.* Anastasia scooted back, worried that this was not someone she should befriend. A small man followed her, dark-haired and wiry. His eyes were intense, and he wore a tool belt on his waist. He nodded at Anastasia. "I'm Kendo. And you're one of our rooks, I presume."

"Yea. I mean, aye," Anastasia said.

Kendo turned to Ajoba. "You know you are not to leave your hut. Do I need to shackle you?" His tone was stern, though Anastasia saw kindness in his eyes.

"The rook cried out in her sleep," Ajoba said. "I could not let her go on like that."

Kendo turned back to Anastasia with a courtly nod. "You dreamed you smacked a wall with a wrench, and that place so near and dear to our hearts sprang a leak. Am I right?"

"Something like that."

"We all have those dreams. A month back, I dreamed about racing the halls with a bucket in hand, trying to bail. But there's no place to put the water, eya?"

Anastasia rubbed her arms. "It seemed so real."

"Don't let it trouble you. It's just the rain that's brought it on." Overhead, the curtain of shroud that hid Horesh had taken on a gray sheen. Drops of water snaked through, striking the rocks and the water with a steady rat-tat-tat.

"Shouldn't the shroud stop it?" Anastasia asked. What an

idiot she was, falling asleep out in the open. The rush of the river had been so soothing, and every cell in her body so exhausted, she hadn't even made it to the women's hut to bed down.

Ajoba opened her mouth to answer. Kendo frowned a warning. "The shroud is hung in strings, not as a tent," he said. "Otherwise, if it came down on Horesh, it might trap us all. Can't have that now, eya?"

"Guess not." She stood up, shaking out sleep-drugged muscles. "I think I remember you from back there. But you were smaller . . ."

Kendo smiled. "I'm not so big now. Would you like to come see the gargant with me?"

"The what?"

"A man, transmogrified into a giant," Ajoba explained. "His name is—"

"Enough from you." Kendo glared at the girl.

"I thought you—we—weren't allowed to have mogs in camp," Anastasia said.

"This is Brady's doing, girl. You'll get used to his ways. Come along now." Kendo turned back to Ajoba. "As for you, back to your hut."

"Let me go with you," Ajoba said. "If Jasper wakes, he'll be looking for me."

He looked at her with something like regret and shook his head. "Unlike you, I obey orders. Brady said you're confined, and thus you are confined. Now I'll ask you to go."

"He also said I may come out to exercise. The trip downriver can be my outdoors time. Please."

He considered. "Come, then. But please, no talking."

Ajoba looked down at her feet. "Aye."

Kendo walked off, his pace so brisk that Anastasia broke into a sprint to keep up. As they followed the river downstream, the ground grew more uneven. The rain made the footing slick, yet the outrider moved like a goat.

Move as one with the ground and not as one assaulting it.

Her tracker training kicked in, and Anastasia smiled as her feet found a way where her eyes could not. Ajoba stayed at her side, silent. The Grand River roared by in a steady din. Hundreds of feet over her head, Anastasia heard the wails and cackles that gave the Narrows the reputation of being haunted. Strong-arms and commoners feared this stretch of the river, frightened senseless by wavering lights and the screech of cleverly-placed noisemakers.

The Blunt Cliffs rose on either side like silent sentinels, so tall that Anastasia had to crane back to see the tops through the veil of shroud that hid them from the upground world. They traveled on the livestock side of the river, where the horses were stabled and the goats, cows, and pigs raised.

Just this morning, she, Kwesi, and Cooper had followed Niki and Brady on horseback down here through a winding succession of caves, some naturally formed and some hewn from solid rock. "Make note of the route, rooks," Niki had snapped, and so they had. No one wanted to be trapped in a dead-end cave with a strong-arm on their tail.

Kendo pointed to a thatched shack under a rock overhang. "There's my shop. A bit more primitive than what you're used to, I'm sure."

The Ark's labs were full of gleaming glass and steel. Out here, they could only make do with what this world provided. But Kendo was famous for what he could do with that provision. Stories of him performing pyrotechnics from dung and fish oil were near legend back in training.

Anastasia gazed curiously into the shack. Back on the Ark, she'd been pretty good herself in the laboratory, especially with chemicals. *Maybe Kendo will let me* . . . She realized he and Ajoba had already moved on around a bend. Red-faced, she hurried to catch up.

The river was bridged by a natural stone arch. Swinging bridges hung overhead, structures of rope and twine that looked almost impassable. Kendo noticed her gawking. "For emergencies. Always have more than one way in and out of a situation."

Anastasia's chest felt heavy. No way out of this. Once birth-righters left the Ark, they could never go back.

Kendo drew his sword. "Be alert now. We're coming out from under the shroud. In this haze, we shouldn't be spotted, but I'm sure Niki has drilled into you how to be careful. You got your short blade?"

"Yea. I mean, aye." Within an hour of being delivered by the whale, Anastasia had received her short blade. She would have to earn her sword.

"Jasper is my friend," Ajoba whispered.

"What did I say?" Kendo's dark eyes widened in exaspera-tion. "I swear, I'll make you a tongue shackle."

Ajoba flushed. "Sorry."

"Where exactly is the giant—I mean, the gargant?" Anastasia asked.

"Stashed in a cavern. No room for him under the shroud." Kendo whistled through his fingers and waited for a return whistle. "Kaya shoots first and asks questions later. Two years back, Bartoly came too close without signaling. He took an arrow right in the backside."

When they arrived at the ridge overlooking the cavern, Anastasia was stunned to silence.

Below was a gargant—a man who had been transmogrified to almost three times the size of normal. His feet were as long as she was tall. His chest heaved with ragged breaths, and his skin reeked with infection. A woman with long black braids and sleepy eyes stood guard, a bow in one hand and a sword in the other.

Ajoba scampered down the slope. Murmuring words of com-fort, she dabbed the gargant's brow with a wet towel. He moaned but did not open his eyes. One eyelid was sunken and horribly scarred. *The eye has been cut out*, Anastasia realized.

"If this poor fellow doesn't prove that those stronghold rats and their dog sorcerers will stop at nothing—I don't know what does," Kendo said.

"But why?" Anastasia said. "Why do this to another human being?"

"Because they want to be God, that's why." Kendo spat, his eyes black with fury. "This is the world you volunteered for, rook. Better get used to it."

He's got no scars, Niki thought when she first saw Dakota.

Outriders rode out to face trouble, and trackers clawed into the unknown. She was so used to seeing bumps and nicks on her comrades' faces and hands that to meet a birthrighter without scars was a shock.

A scout's job was to serve as the eyes and ears for the camp he or she served and to locate species most likely to suffer imminent extinction from the lingering effects of the Endless Wars and the depredations of the strongholders. To carry out their mission, the scouts wandered, unattached, avoiding notice. They even trained singly on the Ark so they would become used to the isolation. Under ordinary conditions, only the camp leader had contact with the scout attached to the camp.

These days, nothing was ordinary. After the past few weeks, Niki knew that well enough.

After being stung, she had followed Brady and the bees into a small patch of woods. A man slipped through the scrub pines as if he were a wisp, standing so silently that it was the wolf—fangs bared—and not she or Brady who first noticed him.

"Dakota's a friend, old man," Brady had said.

The wolf now sat at Niki's side as she studied Dakota. Tall, with narrow shoulders and spindly legs, the scout seemed inclined to silence. Perhaps living on one's own without annoying rooks, dangerous strong-arms, and rampaging mogs calmed one's nature.

Brady lounged near the creek, his voice singsonging as he memorized the locations Dakota had recorded. Horesh's missions were based mostly on requests from the Ark, but a scout's list always took precedence. After Brady learned the list, Niki would do the same. No musician, it was action that spoke to her. She would have to find a spot in this stunted forest where she could pace.

"Did we know each other on the Ark?" she asked Dakota.

The scout shook his head.

"So how do you do it?"

"Do what?" Dakota's voice was surprisingly deep for a slender man. His eyes were brown, almost black, though his skin was pale. His head was shaved in a style one might see in Slade. But while Slade royalty adorned their bare scalps with tattoos and jewelry, Dakota's only ornamentation was a burlap hat with a floppy brim.

"How do you find species that are so rare as to be almost extinct? It seems a contradiction."

His only reply was a raised eyebrow, leading Niki to blabber on. "Our trackers have enough trouble finding common species, let alone rare plants and animals. So how can you?"

Dakota reached over to touch the welt on her neck. The wolf growled, his fur bristling.

"Shush, wolf." Niki scratched the wolf's nose and he quieted. "A bee stung me there."

"If I had known two were coming, it wouldn't have happened. I'm sorry."

Niki scratched her own nose, strangely disoriented. "I don't understand."

Dakota stood and offered his hand. She jumped up without his help and followed him about twenty paces into the brush. How could he not be scarred when he seemed to prefer traveling through prickly tangles and not around them? A hum rose about them. Niki's sword was in her hand before she even willed it.

"Put your blade away, outrider. It's not a buzz-rat." Dakota pointed. Overhead, a roiling swarm of honeybees hung from a branch.

"I don't follow," Niki said.

"Horesh has its swallows and hawks. I have my wasps and bees."

"That's how you tracked us?"

Dakota nodded.

"When the birds do our bidding, they mimic our words, but they don't understand them. How could your bees find the creatures and plants you tell us about?"

He nodded quietly, took his time answering. "I show them what to look for. From the Ark lists."

"You're not making this any clearer," Niki said.

"It's easier to show you. Watch."

Dakota dug up a clod of dirt. Kneading it like clay, he swiftly molded a butterfly with wings so thin it was impossible that they should hold their form. Niki held her breath, watching as he brought out a tiny brush, along with a narrow leathery strip so vibrant that it seemed to have been cut from a rainbow. Dakota spat on the strip, causing the colors to flow. Paint, Niki realized.

When he finished, the scout held his hand to her face so she could see his work. The butterfly was so perfect, with its orange-slashed wings, she expected it to take wing. "Now what?" she said.

His smile was shy. "Be still."

The hum increased. Not the swarm this time. Dakota's cheeks vibrated so fast that Niki barely saw the movement of his skin. A shadow descended on them. Once more she grasped her sword but kept it sheathed, understanding that what was about to happen was beyond her understanding and therefore beyond her ability to oppose it.

The swarm circled their heads. But even though bees bounced against her skin, they did not sting.

A fat honeybee landed on Dakota's palm and walked in a jerky motion around the butterfly. "The queen," he whispered.

Darkness engulfed Niki as the swarm wrapped around them.

The buzzing was immense, not as sharp as a buzz-rat's—those infernal mogs of Slade—but pure. These creatures were as they were created—a force to be celebrated rather than destroyed.

Just as Niki feared her lungs would burst, the swarm lifted, and a line of bees headed off to the west. Dakota followed them, crashing back into the brush with Niki and the wolf at his heels. They passed into a clearing ringed with delicate birches, their oval leaves a soft green, and their graceful trunks a variegated white. The open ground was grassy, with clumps of wild irises waving in the breeze.

Dakota walked behind Niki and put his cheek alongside hers. She drew in a sharp breath, about to warn him off when he whispered, "Look." Slowly, he turned her head with his until she saw what he had already spotted. A butterfly poised over a blossom, the real-life version of Dakota's butterfly, its fiery wings catching sunlight and flashing a gold finer than any forged by the hand of man.

"Oh," was all Niki could say.

Dakota turned her face to his. "If you ever need me, just do this." He puffed his cheeks and buzzed through his teeth.

"Just that?" The sound was far simpler than the whistles for calling the ravens or the squeaks for the sparrows.

"Just that. If you need me." Dakota turned and pushed back through the brush.

Niki frowned, then ran after him. *I won't*, she wanted to cry, but the words caught in her throat.

FIVE

BRADY'S VERDICT WAS PROVISIONAL, BUT IT SHREDDED Ajoba's heart.

"You will no longer be Horesh's teacher. You will no longer spin. You will no longer be trusted to serve alongside your comrades." Though his voice was dry, Brady's face flooded with tears. Niki stood at his side. The rest of the camp's elders sat stone-faced.

Why couldn't they see that her mistakes had sprung from inexperience and not disobedience? Eager to do what was right, she had been deceived by a demon who claimed to be an angel.

"We'll go to the teacher's hut now for the testing." Brady nodded to Ajoba. "You'll stand by me, and you will not speak. Do you understand?"

She nodded, her own tears finally coming.

An hour later, almost everyone in Horesh had sat at the wheel to be tested as teacher. The teacher's duty was to teach villagers and outlanders how to read and help them work through the Scriptures. And the role was determined not by patience or amiability, but by the heaven-given ability to spin shroud.

Tylow had been Horesh's first teacher, having come off the Ark in the first-ever group to leave. Brady, Niki, and Kendo were also first-evers, but Tylow had carried the spindle. He had woven the shroud they had been wrapped in during their own transit.

Tylow had died a year ago, requiring Horesh to test for a new teacher. On that night, Ajoba had sat at the wheel, expecting nothing. She'd been only sixteen years old, just a few months past her own transit. But she's never forgotten what happened that night. Glint, like tiny stars, had crossed her palm, the wheel had spun, the spindle had filled. And so she had become the camp's teacher and spinner. From the thread on the spindle she wove shroud.

Spinning shroud was a precious gift, given only to a camp's teacher. It was horrible to lose the respect and affection of her comrades, but to be denied this privilege broke Ajoba's heart. Just as her disgrace would break her parents' hearts.

Brady had already written a letter to the Ark. Soon the builders would know how she had endangered Horesh by taking the spindle out of camp. Only heroic action by Brady and the others had rescued her and recovered the spindle from Alrod. During the battle of the Bashans, Taryan had been stung by a hoornar and almost died. All because of Ajoba's foolishness. A fresh wave of misery swept over her as Brady motioned Anastasia to sit at the stool. The rook was the very last person in camp—except for Ajoba—to be tested.

Brady placed the spindle in the rook's left hand and turned her right hand palm up.

Taryan squatted next to her. "The glint will appear on your palm. You guide it to the wheel. When it turns, the spindle will fill."

The air was thick with sweat. The birthrighters had labored hard all afternoon, preparing for the next round of missions. Grain and dried meat had been loaded on carts, weapons sharpened, saddles and halters repaired, clothes and boots mended. The heart of Horesh beat with vigor. To be excluded from its flow tore at Ajoba.

A minute passed. Another minute and then a third. Someone coughed. Niki shuffled her feet. Kendo carved wood, beating out a phip-phip rhythm with each stroke of his blade.

Something growled. Jayme whirled, her dagger poised to strike.

Kendo whacked Bartoly who, though he stood upright, was sound asleep. "Stop snoring, mate. You're making the trackers nervous."

Bartoly stretched, his meaty hands whacking the roof. "This is a waste of time, eya?"

Brady nodded, his face grim. "Thank you, Anastasia. You can get up."

"What do we do now?" Taryan said. "We need shroud for all these missions."

Ajoba risked a touch to Brady's shoulder. "Please, would you test me? If it's not right, I won't be able to spin."

He shrugged off her touch. "Taryan will go teach for now. As for the shroud, we'll make do with what we have."

Bartoly came fully awake. "For six tracker crews? It's not enough, mate. Anyone can see that it's not enough."

Like puppets, all heads turned to the storage shelves. Before a mission, they were filled with shroud—some patches as small as a handkerchief, some as large as a tent. Ajoba had just started spinning for the new missions when she left camp to track the gargant into the Bashan Mountains. Only two shelves of the fifteen were filled.

Brady folded his arms. "It will be enough."

Kendo leaned in to Brady, his voice low. "I don't like it any more than you do, but you'd better let her try it."

"No," Brady said.

Ajoba tugged at his arm. "I know I was wrong, but I didn't mean it for harm. It won't happen again. I swear, Brady. Please, let me try. I won't be able to spin unless I'm meant to be teacher. If I'm not, the glint won't come. But if I am still Horesh's teacher—surely you need me."

Niki stared at her with such ferocity that Ajoba wanted to beg her to look away. "He said no. Now shut your mouth, or I'll shut it for you."

"As I was saying," Brady continued, "we will make do with what we have. Back to work, everyone."

Her comrades filed out one by one. Brady, spindle in hand, was the last to go.

Leaving Ajoba with nothing to fill her wheel except her tears.

Timothy and Taryan had returned to camp in time for the *gathering-in,* when reports were given, letters from the Ark handed out, the rooks introduced. Timothy saw none of it, his vision still filled with Dawnray crumpled on the floor. The baron was almost certainly dead—Timothy had tightened the noose himself and felt the telltale jerk on the rope before he fell. But what if he wasn't? And if he was, what would the sorcerer—or Merrihana—do with Dawnray?

Though all were expected to stay until the testing was complete, Timothy slipped out after he had sat at the wheel. He wandered upriver for almost a league, picking his way through the dark until he reached the cascades where the Grand River erupted out of the mountains. The roar of the water over the ragged cliffs was a whisper compared to the groan of his heart.

He sat for what seemed like an eternity, desperately wondering if God would hear the prayers of someone who had disobeyed the mission to serve his own heart.

But who had put this love in his heart, if not God? Timothy had traveled these lands for two years, seen women more beautiful and far sweeter than Dawnray. Yet she had latched onto his heart in an instant and clung there.

"Timmy?"

A rook had crept up on him, her eyes now stunned at the dagger he pressed against her throat. "Didn't they teach you to whistle before approaching? You could get yourself killed."

"I did whistle. Maybe the river was too loud."

Timothy sheathed his weapon with a glare he hoped would send the girl away.

"Don't you remember me? It's only been a couple of years. Stasia, remember?"

Their families had lived in the same sector. He remembered her vaguely from training, more clearly from earlier days when they had raced about on roller skates and platter skids. "You're thinner. That's why I didn't recognize you."

Anastasia laughed. "Can't be a tracker if you're wider than your horse, eya? Your mom and dad are doing really well, by the way." She went on with details of his parents' work and stories about his twin siblings, Gina and Beth, who had entered training last year, and his brother, Logan, who was in his third year and itching to leave the Ark.

As welcome as the family news was, Timothy was in no mood for conversation. "Thanks. I'm glad to hear all this. But if you don't mind, I need some time alone."

Anastasia sat down next to him.

"Are you deaf? I said I wanted to be alone."

"I always used to be able to help, Timmy."

She had been the chunky kid, not given to active games, and she'd liked to sit with him as he made up songs. He had forgotten about her and the hundred little confidences he had shared. "We were little children."

She grinned. "I'm still little."

"Look, you're new to all this. You'll get used to your comrades needing time apart. And you'll be courteous enough to grant it."

"Yea. I mean, aye." She put her hand on his shoulder, a touch so warm that it tugged at his heart. "I never told anyone your secrets. I won't start now."

He opened his mouth to protest, but the words tumbled out. *Stop*, he told himself. But as long as her hand rested on his shoulder, his tale flowed. Finally, he reached the end.

"You killed Baron Alrod?"

He nodded. "I think so. Stasia, please—you can't tell anyone."

"But—"

"You said I could trust you. Are you going back on your word to a comrade?"

"No, no." She dabbed away her tears. "Timmy, what're you going to do?"

He helped her up. "First of all, my name is Timothy. Or mate, or even fool. But not Timmy. That little boy is long gone."

Anastasia nodded, thoughtful. "But how will you get back to her? Brady has us all going south and west on collections. Traxx is to the east, correct?"

"I am a tracker, not a traitor. I'm called on mission and I'll go, even if it shreds my heart."

"Make a way to get back to her. That's what they teach in training. Make a way where there is none."

"I can't stay back. The Ark said that if Brady couldn't track down Arabah, Horesh should do their collections along with our own. Apparently we were sent their old lists, along with new lists for us. We're all going out—even you rooks."

Anastasia clutched his arm. "Make Dawnray a mission."

"What? I don't follow."

"Find a way to include her in a mission."

"Stasia, that's just . . . just—" He broke off as a thought occurred. There was one mission to Traxx that Brady would condone.

One mission that would bless Horesh . . . and give Timothy a chance to return for Dawnray.

Six

Timothy found Brady at the campfire. The elders—Taryan, Niki, Kendo, and Bartoly—were discussing what to do with Ajoba while they were all out on mission.

"We can't leave her at camp," Kendo said. "Look what happened last time."

Ajoba hung her head. "Please, let me serve a mission. I haven't forgotten how to track."

"But you have forgotten how to follow orders," Niki said.

"We've got double the work. We need all the help we can get," Taryan said.

"Fine. She'll go out on mission." Brady snapped a fireplace log as if it were a twig. "You will ride with me, Ajoba."

"Thank you." Despite Ajoba's upbeat tone, her eyes betrayed her terror at Brady's anger. She hurried away, giving Timothy the opportunity to step forward.

"Need something, Tim?" Brady asked.

"I'd like to change my assignment."

Kendo snorted. "Don't do this to me, mate. I spent all day figuring out the crews."

"Hold on, Ken. Let's hear the lad out. Will it affect the missions we've set up?" Brady asked.

Timothy glanced at Taryan. She stared back, fingers tapping on her knees. "Can we talk about this in private?"

Brady motioned him into the pantry hut. The long shelves held packages of potatoes, yams, carrots, apples, grain, sweet cane, and dried meat. The shroud sacks kept everything fresh until

Magosha, one of their camp deacons, was ready to cook. Jars of honey and cider were stacked in the corners, and herbs hung from the ceiling. Loaves of fresh-baked puff-bread and flatbread were piled to the ceiling. A camp full of birthrighters was a ravenous place.

Niki came in, the wolf slinking behind her.

Brady pinched his nose. "Gal, there's got to be a limit to where that wolf of yours can go. This is our food, after all."

"He's a comrade. You anointed him yourself."

"Don't know about your comrades, but mine bathe on occasion," Brady said.

Laughing, she dug through a sack until she found an old bone. The wolf went outside, his prize firmly clenched between yellow teeth.

"I thought we were speaking in private," Timothy said.

Brady munched an apple. "You don't trust Niki?"

"Of course I do. I just . . ." He lowered his eyes, scuffing the floor with the heel of his boot. "She'll laugh at me."

"Me? Laugh?" Niki widened her eyes in mock surprise.

"I'm about to volunteer for a mission I'm probably not suited for." Too sheepish—they knew him better than that.

"Get to it," Brady snapped. "I could use a night's sleep sometime in the next century."

"Taryan told you I've been going into the stronghold of Traxx?"

Brady glanced at Niki. She shrugged, shook her head.

"No, she didn't," Brady said. "Should she have?"

"I'm glad she's letting me explain for myself."

"Oh, this should be good," Niki muttered under her breath. When would she learn that Timothy had tracker's ears and heard most of her jibes?

"I'm waiting," Brady said.

"After the battle of the Bashans, you were gone to"—He paused, thinking. It wouldn't do to remind Niki that she needed rescuing along with the rooks—"to help Niki. Kendo was busy caring for Taryan. Bartoly had responsibility for the gargant."

"What has any of this to do with you entering Traxx on a nonsanctioned trip?"

A genuine anger rose in Timothy's chest. "That pig Alrod has the piece of shroud Ajoba made while she was off with the gargant. That's not right."

"So you risked your life to rescue a piece of cloth?"

"I risked my life for the integrity of the Birthright Project. The longer Alrod and Ghedo have that shroud, the clearer it will be that it contains a power far beyond any they've experienced. And there's nothing that drives those dogs harder than the lust for power."

"Aye," Niki said. "Lad's got us there."

Brady tossed a chunk of cinnamon bread to Niki. He ate the rest of the loaf, washing it down with a mug of cider. Outriders were notorious for their appetites. Trackers preferred to stay thin, the better to slip into tight places.

"Your proposal, Tim?" Brady said when he had eaten his fill.

"We need to get that shroud back before Alrod and the others realize its uniqueness." The fact that Alrod himself was probably dead—his neck broken by Timothy's rope—was not something he needed to bring up in this moment.

"Agreed." Brady clapped Timothy on the shoulder. "Thanks, mate. Niki, I'll ask you to head up the retrieval crew."

She nodded.

"But I thought . . ." Timothy swallowed back his protest. *Not too eager, now.* "I thought a tracker should go. Specifically, me."

"Why's that?"

"Because I'm experienced at going in and out of the stronghold."

"You think I'm not?" Niki said.

Why had he foolishly assumed he and Brady were the only ones who had passed through the thorns? Taryan, fresh off her sickbed, had had no trouble following him all the way to Alrod's courtyard.

"You can't just storm the place," Timothy said. "You need a plan."

Niki opened a crock of pears and drank the juice before starting on the fruit. "And you have one?"

"I might."

"Let's have it, Tim," Brady said. "I am weary to the bone."

"Niki and I would have to work together on this."

She snapped her fingers. "The plan?"

"You need to sell me, Niki," Timothy said.

"What?"

"Alrod knows me as Brady's minstrel—that's how we presented it the last time we went to Traxx." *When I met Dawnray. When she captured my heart.* "You can say that I escaped Brady and you caught me."

"Why would anyone care?"

Brady smiled. "Word is that Merrihana is quite smitten with our boy."

Timothy swallowed back his irritation, kept his tone even. "You leave me at the palace, I search until I find the shroud, then you get me out. If we do it quickly, we'll have plenty of time to catch up with our assigned missions."

"That's insane," Niki said. "You expect me to just waltz into Alrod's court?"

Timothy smiled, confident that he finally had the opening to reel her in. "Brady did it. Why not you?"

He only waited a minute or so before Niki punched his arm. "Sure, why not me?" she said. "It would be my pleasure to sell you like a sack of potatoes, tracker."

Brady loved the time of gathering-in, when all the camp's birthrighters came together to celebrate missions, to share stories, to sing, to rest. Nothing was sweeter than seeing that everyone who had been sent out had come back alive.

Ordinarily he also loved the *sending-out*, when crews were dispatched to track species, to protect people, to share the gospel.

Brady had dreaded this particular sending-out.

Nothing was right about it. The doubling of tasks as they took on Arabah's collections meant respite was canceled. As the senior camp—and apparently the closest camp—to Arabah, Horesh would assume their duties, at least until a camp could be formed to replace them. Trackers and outriders who had arrived in from mission only days earlier had to turn around and ride back out again. Training for the rooks was canceled. Kwesi, Anastasia, and Cooper had to be assigned to a crew instead of being given time to learn to survive in a world that the builders, for all their good intentions, could not imagine.

Shroud was scarce, and the assigned collections would be immense. Was Brady wrong not to let Ajoba spin? Did his refusal spring from obedience or stubbornness? He honestly couldn't tell.

The six crews had received their assignments, packed their weapons, gathered their supplies. Each crew had been given Dakota's latest information on possible travel routes. They had tended to their horses, checked their tack, and oiled the wheels on their carts. Huts and personal belongings had been secured and Magosha and Manueo—the camp's caretakers—properly hugged.

All that remained was the farewell.

Each birthrighter of Horesh now came before Brady and Niki to be blessed. Jayme stood before them now, her dark eyes glowing with excitement. Niki hugged her and whispered, "Serve well," then released her to Brady. He cupped his hands on Jayme's head and prayed the blessing.

The rooks trembled under Brady's touch. Timothy straightened, steely determination in his eyes. Dano towered over Niki as she wrapped him in her hug. "Serve well," she whispered.

Brady—tall himself—had to reach up to press his hands to Dano's forehead. He prayed a blessing on the tracker, his heart aching as it always did. Who would come back safe? Who would come back injured?

Who would not come back at all?

Brady had dug Tylow's grave himself, high in the Bashans. He had written five letters to the Ark—"Your beloved child and our treasured comrade has gone home to the Lord"—and hoped never to have to write another.

Niki hugged Taryan with trembling arms. What was that about? Had something happened between the two women that Brady didn't know about? She released Taryan, who stood before him, slender and clear-eyed. He pressed his hands to her forehead. "May the Lord bless you and keep you, Taryan."

"Thank you," Taryan whispered and stepped away so Bartoly could be blessed. He scowled, the one birthrighter ordered to take respite. Someone had to stay back at camp to protect their home and to be available should Niki and Tim need help in Traxx. Nursing a swollen knee and three cracked ribs from the recent battles made the big outrider the logical choice.

Kendo came next, their fellow first-ever. Six long years ago, four youths had been spat up onto the arctic ice into a corrupted world that even their great-grandparents on the Ark had never walked in.

Tylow, Kendo, Niki, and Brady had been sixteen years old. Three of them had lived to twenty-two, an ancient age given their mission.

Brady pressed his hands to Kendo's forehead, Niki's hands on both their shoulders. They knew that one day the three first-evers would be two, one, none. This was a dangerous world, and they took on the danger headfirst.

Niki knew it too. He met her eyes and was surprised to see them filling with tears. She had never been one to cry. But all that had happened to her on her last trip north, especially her time on the mountain with that demon of darkness, had changed her. As it had changed him.

"May the Lord bless you and keep you, Kendo," he told his other comrade.

"You too, mate." Kendo hugged him, squeezed Niki's hand, and stepped aside.

Niki took Brady into her arms. "Serve well, pal," she whispered.

Brady circled his arms around her with a tender squeeze. "Serve well, gal."

She pressed her hands to his forehead. "May the Lord bless you and keep you, Brady." This too was different—the way she said the words she had spoken so many times before. She had finally found faith on that mountain.

He pressed his hands to her forehead. "May the Lord bless you and keep you, Niki."

"Amen," she said, the signal for Horesh to ring with amens.

Then they gathered to depart with their various crews—trackers to track, outriders to guard, all to serve.

As Horesh emptied her heart into the world, Brady prayed it would fill again very soon.

We know that the whole creation has been groaning as in the pains of childbirth right up to the present time. Not only so, but we ourselves, who have the firstfruits of the Spirit, groan inwardly as we wait eagerly for our adoption as sons, the redemption of our bodies. For in this hope we were saved.

ROMANS 8:22–24

SEVEN

TIMOTHY AND NIKI STOOD AT THE MIGHTY GATE OF
Traxx awaiting interrogation and, they hoped, admission to the
stronghold.

"I wonder how Anastasia's making out," Timothy whispered.
They had spent the morning teaching her how to pass through
the thorns. Her task was to sneak their weapons into the stronghold and get them into the palace. It was a huge task to assign
a girl right off the Ark.

"I wish we had Kendo with us," Niki said.

"He had to guard a crew. Bra—" Timothy stopped himself,
then glanced around. *Brady* was a name he dared not say here.

Spies abounded at the entrance portal of the Mighty Gate,
the only way into the stronghold. Those whose golden neck-
bands identified them as citizens were admitted without question. Strangers were inspected and interrogated. Even if found
not to be a threat, visitors with nothing to offer were turned
away. Timothy's voice was the special ware that would get them
into the stronghold—and into the palace.

Niki frowned. "Kwesi would have been better than Stasia."

"He's lanky and long. Not good for tight places."

"Cooper, then."

Timothy laughed. Niki stomped his instep, reminding him
that drudges do not laugh at the expense of their mistresses.

"He's the size of a boy but his feet are as big as a horse,"
Timothy whispered. "Anastasia was the right choice. She's small
and agile."

"She's a pampered princess. If you only knew the whining and pouting I put up with during her transit." Niki raised her pitch in imitation. " 'Don't we have any soy left? I'm allergic to walrus blubber.' "

Timothy smiled. "We're all a nuisance at first."

"I wasn't."

"Rewriting history?"

"Telling the truth." Niki tugged at ribbons Taryan had woven through her curls.

"Stop it."

"I hate this finery."

"You're supposed to be a lady. You need to act as such."

"I'm supposed to be your owner. You keep nagging at me, and I will act as such and beat you silly."

The line inched forward. Dandified men and gaudy women clustered about, hoping to join the city's elite social circle. Merchants with fine wares vied for the opportunity to sell in Traxx's marketplace, where gold coins were known to flow as freely as water. At the front of the line clustered a full company of actors who hoped to entertain Merrihana and reap a little of her bounty.

At the front of the line, a threadbare sorcerer begged for an audience with Ghedo. He likely had inherited one ancient cell line—thought by these ignorant fools to be magic potions—that would be capable of transmogrifying some poor plant or creature through its embedded genetic manipulators. The cell lines had not only survived the Endless Wars but had been enhanced by the toxic radiation and viral weapons unleashed during those chaotic times. That their true scientific nature had been lost in the darkness that followed was just another sign of how corrupted the earth had become since then.

The fondness of stronghold princes for fighting wars and gaining fame through their mogs was the reason a new Ark had been commissioned. The creation that God had long ago declared to be very good was being degraded and transmogrified almost to the point of no return. Once again, as in even more ancient times, Esau had despised his birthright. And the birthrighters had been sent from the Ark to salvage whatever could be salvaged from the resulting mess—whether it was original, unmogged species or human hearts that could be turned back to the One who made them.

That's what I'm here for, Timothy reminded himself, and his stomach clenched to remember the other purpose that drove him. Try as he might, he saw no resolution to his dilemma. To have Dawnray, he would have to give up being a birthrighter. To continue as a birthrighter, he'd have to live without the woman who had seized his heart as readily as if she had thrust her hand into his chest.

Niki poked him. "Smell that?"

"I smell a lot of things." His tracker's nose was continually assaulted with the sweat of the people in front of them, his own anxiety, the cardamom that the man at the front of the line offered the gatekeeper, the heady perfumes of those who aspired to court life. And under it all, though a protective screen blocked the view, the seductive blooms on the wall of thorns.

"Change places with me," she said. "You'll see what I mean."

He moved to where she had stood. A sudden aroma of sewage and burning flesh forced bile into his throat just as a loud creak announced the opening of the exit gate. Two men on magnificent horses stopped for a word with the head gatekeeper. Cloaked and hooded in brown wool, the men looked like lesser merchants. The smell emanated from one of them, though no one else seemed to notice it. The commander of the guard bowed deferentially.

Timothy gasped. "That's Alrod."

Niki's hand automatically went to her hip. If her sword were not strapped to Anastasia's back and on its way through the thorns, she'd be chasing the baron right now. She pressed her hand to Timothy's and used the finger language they all had learned on the Ark. *Who with?*

Not Ghedo. Timothy responded. Too tall.

The baron's here. Kill him now.

No weapons.

With my hands.

"Keep the line moving," the gatekeeper bellowed, and Timothy realized they had reached the head of the line. A short man with a prosperous paunch, the keeper looked them up and down. "State your name and where you're from."

They would have to be wary, a difficult task with Alrod a few paces away and his companion stinking up the air they breathed.

Niki spoke up confidently. "Nikolette of Upper Finway. My father owns a thriving farm on Mount Zion."

"What is your father's name?"

"Yahweh."

Alrod's companion jerked his head around. His ordinary face faded, the skeleton underneath becoming clear, bones robbed of their marrow until all Timothy could see was a cloaked darkness.

Though Alrod rode away without ever looking their way, the creature raised his arm at the birthrighters in an empty salute.

Anastasia had just emerged from the wall of thorns when a pile of dung attacked her.

She had walked right by it, thinking the mound of steaming manure had been left as fertilizer. When the pile leaped on her, she realized it was really a Traxx strong-arm with a grip of iron and a mask woven from onion shoots.

"Surrender, tramp," he growled as he tossed her short blade away. She heard it clatter on the pavement. *I'm going to die before I even complete my first mission.*

The bag of weapons that she carried were useless. Timothy's sword, along with their short blades and daggers, were bundled tightly in burlap. Niki's sword was strapped to her back, but it was heavy—and wrapped too tightly to be useful.

Be your own weapon, Anastasia had learned in training. She dipped her chin, measuring her attacker's torso, looking for a point of vulnerability.

"You be a fine prize," the strong-arm said. "Bit thin, but got clean flesh, all your teeth. Will bring some coin when I'm done with you. Might be a bit worse for the wear but worth a goat or pig from someone."

"No. Please." She didn't have to fake fear—her body shook with it.

He pressed his face to the side of her neck and kissed her, oblivious to the dung on his own lips.

Now. Anastasia feigned a faint, the weight of her body pulling the strong-arm sideways as her knees buckled. He instinctively let go with his right arm to balance.

"Yi-eee!" Anastasia took her chance and drove her elbow into his gut. She tore from his grasp, diving for her short blade.

The strong-arm slashed at her, dung dripping from his arm and blade. And all swarming with germs, no doubt. Anastasia shivered. Birthrighters couldn't be transmogrified because they were inoculated to lock their DNA before leaving the Ark. But they could catch the same plagues that anyone else could, and she doubted she had resistance to whatever was on this strong-arm's weapon.

She circled, trying to keep her focus. Why had Niki and Timothy assumed she could come through the thorns on her own?

Because they had not expected a trap inside the wall.

"Maybe I'll bring your liver to the baron," the strong-arm was saying. "That will be worth a gold piece and a barrel of rum. Or maybe I'll bring you to 'im in one piece. He like 'em young, he does."

She fumbled with the pack on her back, trying to get to Niki's sword. The attacker had picked up her short blade, holding it as if it were a silly toy. As if Anastasia was a silly little girl.

Which she was, of course, she realized as an unexpected calm washed over her.

A silly girl with a mighty God.

"What does the Baron fear from a commoner?" she said, stalling for time.

"I saw you come out of the thorns. You think me stupid?"

"Stupid I cannot judge. That you stink like a crushed toad left in the sun—that much is clear."

Think, Stasia. Make a way.

There was one place she could go safely that he could not. She started back in on the tune Timothy had taught her, lowering her voice to the tenor pitch that the slungs liked.

> *Can you hear the distant thunder?*
> *Can you feel the tremble of the earth?*

The strong-arm's eyes glittered. "You be seeking a roll with me, tramp?"

"Not if you insist on trying to kill me."

He lowered his sword, lust clearly warring with his good sense.

"Would you give me one moment to adorn myself?" Anastasia ran her fingers through her curls, bouncing them coquettishly as she worked the lacings on her pack. Niki had insisted her sword be tightly bound.

"This be a trick?"

"Nay. But would you romance me like this?" She leaned against the flowers in the wall, feeling the lure of their scent, reminding herself that their song was a sweet lie.

"Watch it, tramp. Those flowers be deadly!"

"Really? I think they are absolutely wonderful." Praying for the strength to swing Niki's heavy sword, Anastasia twirled, its blade cutting a swathe in the flowers of the wall.

The strong-arm leaped at her, his own sword swinging for her head. She aimed high because Niki's heavy weapon put off her aim. Their blades clanged, and the attacker backed off, reassessing the threat.

She spun again, cutting away enough blooms so she could see the branches—and deadly thorns—beneath.

"Enough of play time. Say your good-byes, little girl." Sword raised, the strong-arm charged.

Anastasia dove into the wall. The flowers closed behind her, trapping her in a dappled prison of bramble. Where was the slung? It would only be moments before the fast-growing branches sought her out, thorns pressing against her chest to impale her.

Tiny black eyes glittered through the woody growth.

"Slung! Bless you!" Grabbing the back of his shell, Anastasia interrupted her song just long enough to scream in agony. Let the strong-arm think the wall had killed her. She sang on, softly, steering the slung back toward the stronghold. She would enter from a different place in the wall.

And this time, she'd be alert for piles of dung with swords of steel.

EIGHT

SADO HAD ORDERED DAWNRAY'S WINDOW TO BE BARRED.
What did that matter? There was no one left to rescue her.
Perhaps God's plan was to isolate her in this palace, to serve as
His light to these despicable people. But how could she find that
kind of grace in herself when she had lost her father, her free-
dom, and now her only hope for escape?

Thankfully, she still had Carin. The maid's part in the tragedy
had gone unnoticed. She waited on Dawnray, pressing a foolish
comfort. "I heard Sado tell Ghedo that they couldn't find a
body," Carin said. "Maybe there's—"

Dawnray pressed her hand to the girl's mouth. "Don't. I can't
bear it."

Dressmakers, hairstylists, and perfumers bustled about the
sitting chamber. Alrod had left the palace again, so why were all
these people here? Upon Merrihana's entrance, the fashion mon-
gers bowed like puppets on a string.

Dawnray stood tall, shoulders straight and gaze direct. Let
them treat her like a cow—she would not act like one.

"Hair first." Without even looking at her, Merrihana pushed
her into a chair. "Here is a lock of mine so you may match it perfectly. You understand me? I expect perfection."

"Yes. And you will have it," the hairdresser said, his voice
tremulous.

"Requesting pardon," Dawnray said. "But what is to be done
to me?"

Merrihana clapped her hands. "Everyone out. Leave me with the lolly."

When they were alone, she pulled Dawnray to the mirror. "Look, girl. What do you see?"

Merrihana was the lofty royal with the long neck, high cheekbones, full mouth. Dawnray was the village girl with the clear skin and bright eyes.

"I don't know what—"

"Are you stupid, girl? You see we are nothing alike," Merrihana said.

"No. We aren't."

"I have beauty, and I have accomplishments. But when my husband looks at me, do you know what he sees?"

Almighty, you must give me the words. For I have nothing to offer this woman. "A wife who does her best to love him?"

"That's what he should see. But what he does see is barrenness. Do you not grasp the irony? The baroness and her barrenness. Now, when my husband looks at you, he doesn't see your coarse breeding or your open defiance. He sees a fertile field that needs only to be sown with his seed to make it flower."

Dawnray dared to touch her arm. "I'm sorry. I truly am. I—"

"I need to remedy that."

"I don't understand."

"Oh, it's very simple, girl." Merrihana's smile was devoid of joy. "From now on, when my husband looks at you, he is going to see me."

The stronghold of Traxx was not what Anastasia would deem as subtle.

The streets gleamed with gold. Though it was still daylight, diamond globes overhead cast brilliant light, as if the stronghold expected its splendor to outshine the sun. Wealthy shoppers draped themselves in the same gaudiness, with multiple layers of glittering jewels, elegant fabrics, and every manner of feather, frill, or mogged enhancement.

A woman with pink hair and a bulging bosom wore a dress that changed color constantly. What poor silkworm had been mogged to feed her vanity? Another woman strutted about, leading a dog with three heads that whimpered steadily. A man wore a pointed white hat that, upon closer examination, turned out to be his own skull.

Pay attention to your task, Anastasia scolded herself. *You have enough problems as it is.*

Chief of which was the fact that she had lost her pack of weapons and supplies. She had emerged from the thorns far from where she had fought the dung-soaked strong-arm. When she made her way back to where she had dropped the pack, it was long gone. So were three short blades, including her own. A bow and a quiver of arrows. Various knives, rope and twine, even a packet of Kendo's fire powder.

No armor, thank God—Brady had asked them not to bring it. They were after one length of shroud—it wouldn't do to lose a bagful. And it was a good thing Anastasia still had Niki's sword. Timothy would be furious at her for losing his—but Niki would take her head off.

Anastasia considered sending word back to Horesh, asking Bartoly to bring more weapons. But there was almost no chance of sending a message via birds from inside the stronghold. The wall of thorns was topped with cobratraps. Meant to take down strong-arms on flying mogs, the flesh-eating plants also swallowed birds on the wing.

So instead of wasting time on messages that might not get through, Anastasia decided to press on, get Niki her sword, and let her dictate the next step. First, though, she had to figure out how to get into the palace.

The other two had the perfect ruse: Niki posing as a wealthy outlander who wanted to sell the minstrel that Brady had allegedly stolen and Merrihana longed for. But no way would a commoner like Anastasia be allowed in, especially one carrying an outrider's sword.

The original plan was for her to buy some ware attractive enough to gain admittance to the palace courtyard—plus a cart big enough to sneak in the weapons. Taryan, in charge of Horesh's costuming, had given Anastasia a silk dress to help her blend in—it took her just a minute to find a hidden corner and remove the travel tunic that covered the silk.

"The orange will go well with your dark eyes and pale skin," Taryan had told her. "If you're asked, you are the servant of a Finwayan landowner. If you dress the part, people will believe you."

Anastasia was surprised to see that people did treat her differently when she was wearing the silk. A man stopped and stared, his eyes following Anastasia as she passed. Her cheeks grew hot. No one had ever looked at her like that before. She felt a strange urge to toss her head and sway her hips.

Proverbs: Charm is deceptive and beauty is fleeting.

Why had she suddenly thought of that? It was part of a childhood memory drill, a way of learning Scripture. In training, she and her comrades had recited the whole drill as an aid to concentration. As they matured in training—and their faith—birthrighters personalized the verses to fit their own calling. Anastasia's teachers had promised this drill—and the living Word—would kick in when she needed it. Apparently it had.

"Lady, stop!" A bristle-haired woman ran up to her and wrapped her in a black shawl. It sparkled with what Anastasia realized were hundreds of diamonds. "Look how it accents your lovely hair and those red cheeks. Surely forty gold pieces isn't too much to pay for such beauty."

"No. Thank you." Anastasia tried to shrug off the wrap, but the woman tied it under her neck and then held up a mirror.

Her black hair picked up the sparkles in the shawl. Anastasia liked the way it made her look.

On the Ark, people only dressed up to celebrate Resurrection

Day and the Nativity. Otherwise, everyone wore utilitarian jumpsuits, the colors meant to specify their job or student status and not to adorn. Here it was different. Anastasia liked the way men and women alike stared at her fresh skin and straight teeth. How they admired her healthy body and thick hair.

What are you doing, rook? Don't you know temptation when it seizes you?

No. Not like this. Temptation back in training meant getting Cooper in trouble or flirting with someone else's boyfriend. Temptation in the world meant wanting more people to stare at the fire in her cheeks and the shine in her hair and the grace in her walk and—

Anastasia handed the shawl back to the woman. "No, thank you. I don't need this."

Niki had drilled one phrase into her head from the first day that she collected Anastasia up on the polar ice until she left her earlier this day. *To lose focus is to fail. To fail is to die or cause a comrade to die.*

Focus—what could she buy to gain admission to the palace? She could buy silk wraps or fur slippers or copper pots or jade bracelets. What novelty was there in any of that? The privileged shopped here, lounging in carriages while their servants raced about. Nothing here was unique enough to lure the palace gate-keeper to admit her.

The heady aroma of fresh bread drew Anastasia to the farmers' market. Carts displayed abundant fruits, grains, and meats, all glowing green. Even the juicy chunks of beef and plump ducks had been mogged. And common sense said that no one at the palace would be enticed by any of this food—they doubtless had all this and better.

She walked down one street and up the next, her feet blistering and her head spinning. The Ark was orderly, with straight walls, courteous people, muted sounds. Horesh was rustic but peaceful and orderly. This world was chaotic and garish. Frightening . . . and also exciting.

She moved into the lower markets that backed into the brick wall that stood between the stronghold and its wall of thorns. The streets here were dusty, the wares ragged. Her nose protested the odor of old fish, wilted vegetables, too many rat droppings. People in tattered shirts and grimy trousers eyed her with interest. Stupid rook—her silk dress was an invitation to robbery. She slipped into a hay shed to pull her trousers and tunic once more over her dress. Yet she still drew attention.

"He-he-he. Look this way, gal-ee."

Don't! But she was drawn like a finger to damp paint. She couldn't help but look.

A craggy-faced woman in a burlap cloak pushed something into her path. "Look what I got for sweet gal-ee."

"A little boy?" The boy's eyes were huge, his ribs stark against his skin.

"Do with he as you choose. You like to paint your toes, he do for you. You like to kiss, this'un's been trained in it."

"But he's just a little boy."

"Got to earn his feed someways." The woman motioned her closer. "You like to sell among the nobles, I cain't go there. But for a gal-ee like you, good profit's made all the time in that trade."

The child stretched out his hands, bound with rough twine. "Please, miss-ee. She can nay afford to feed me one more day."

Anastasia bent down to him. "Will she let you go if she can't sell you?"

He drew his finger across his throat. "Me blood'll draw fee from sorcerers. That lot nay ever has enough for their stews. Please, miss-ee. Save me."

Horrified, Anastasia faced the woman. "How much?"

The woman squinted. "Four gold coin. The sorcerers pay more, but the boy like you."

"I'm not rich."

"You be liar then. Strong shoulders, white teeth, and—" The woman yanked up Anastasia's lip. "Red gums."

She slapped the hand away. "I am well cared for because I serve a kindly king. What I have is his provision, not my possession."

"He-he-he, gal-lee. You have bag with plenty of jingle-ee."

Anastasia instinctively grabbed her left pocket. Fool—she had just given the old hag and everyone else on the street the location of her gold. She forced haughtiness into her voice. "I can spare one gold coin. Even that is paying too much."

The woman held up three fingers.

Anastasia walked away, praying for the woman to call her back.

The woman grabbed her elbow. "Take he for two. A gift from me."

The boy clung to her leg. "Please."

"Oh, all right." After doling out two coins, Anastasia pulled the boy away. "What's your name?"

"Manny," he mumbled.

"Do you have family I can take you to?"

He nodded. "Across the way."

"The street?"

"The city."

"Across . . ." What had she gotten herself into? "Come on. We'll have to move fast."

"Wait, miss-ee," he said.

"What?"

He burst out crying. "My bro . . . bro . . . brothers."

"I'm taking you to them."

He bawled louder.

"I don't understand what you're crying about, Manny."

He pointed back down the street. The woman had another boy in front of her, a smaller version of Manny. "He's too small for the sorcerer, so if she nay sell him, he go to the butcher."

"To help in his shop?" Anastasia asked.

Eyes almost as wide as his forehead, Manny shrieked out, "Are you thick, miss-ee? They eats the ones that do nay sell."

Anastasia marched back to the old woman and emptied her bag of gold, trusting that somehow the Lord would bless this act of mercy. She bought six more boys—the youngest a mere infant, nestled in the arms of one of his brothers. Shoppers and vendors alike watched her as she marched the children up the street.

Around the corner, Manny skidded to a stop. "I know where we be! Miss-ee, should you be wanting to get on your way, I can get these'uns home from here."

"Are you sure, Manny? I don't want someone else to grab you."

"Nay, we be safe from here. I know many shortcuts, will nay need to keep you from your way any longer."

"If you think you'll be all right . . ." Anastasia didn't want to be too eager to move on, but the day was aging rapidly. She waved good-bye, tears streaming down her face as they crossed the street.

And bolted back the way they had come.

"Hey!" She raced after them, but they darted in and out of the crowd of shoppers like stinging wasps. The boys and the woman—who turned out to be a man—had such a big lead she had no hope of catching them. Manny tossed the infant into the gutter. Anastasia shrieked as a cart rolled over its head.

Until she realized it was a doll—and she had been taken for a fool.

NINE

NIKI YANKED ON THE SILVER CORD. "STOP LOOKING SO haughty. You're a drudge, remember?"

"How can I forget it, when you remind me every three paces?"

Niki and Timothy crossed under a long trellis laced with tiny lilacs. Gold and silver roses burst from trees that lined the cobbled paths of the park. Green lawns sported brilliant flower beds, marble terraces, sparkling pools. All beautiful—but Niki was alert to the danger that stolen beauty often masks.

Nobles thronged the various glens and bowers, enjoying the first warmth of summer. Women wore their gowns cut low and hair piled high. Men strutted in silk tunics, carrying long swords that had never been drawn, let alone bloodied. Lounging on leather chaises or wicker settees, they lifted their faces to the sun as if to steal its power without giving a thought to the One who spoke its grandeur into being.

"When are we stopping? It's hard to keep this tragic expression on my face," Timothy said. "Especially when I want to laugh my guts out."

Niki looked around. "I want to find a somewhat secluded spot. Mystery breeds more interest."

"Not so secluded that I won't be heard. There." Timothy pointed out a stand of birches not far from the main path. A small creek trickled through, and several smooth rocks provided a place to sit in the shade.

"All right," Niki agreed. "This will do."

Timothy slid his gittern from its bag. He had handcrafted the instrument from willow and strung it with silk. Cloth strings shouldn't reverberate, and yet the instrument always hummed as soon as it emerged from its opaque bag. At first Brady had feared that some transmogrification had been at work. Yet there was no mog glow to the wood or the silk—only pure chords that Bartoly declared must be created by angels and delivered directly to Timothy through the thing.

The gittern hummed now as sunlight splashed its strings. Timothy cradled the instrument to his chest, his right hand pressing the strings, making music by skillfully muting its constant hum.

> Forever I'll love you.
> Forever you'll see.
> Forever has everything I need . . .

A man in a white doublet and pink trousers ducked under the trees. "He has a passable voice. He yours?"

"More than passable," Niki said. "And yes, he's mine."

The man bowed, presenting a ridiculously broad forehead. The fool had submitted to some silly potion to enlarge the top of his skull. Perhaps to indicate the immense brain he obviously lacked, if he thought this modification had any attraction. He wore the gold neckband and muted sneer that signified full Traxx citizenship. "Is he for sale?"

Niki smiled. "Why would I sell such a precious lad?"

"For much gold, one would presume."

"Then one would presume wrongly, citizen. There are some things no amount of gold may buy."

"Such as?"

Loyalty to one's mate, which was why Niki had to hold the letter from the Ark back from Brady. Even now, it burned against her skin, though she had exchanged the shroud wrapping for one of cloth. Truth, which decreed she should have given it to him, regardless of the consequences. Faith, which had freed her heart only to completely muddle her brain.

"Such as beauty." On that her heart, mind, and soul could agree.

The man circled Timothy, touching his hair, even seizing his hand to examine the length and strength of his fingers. A crowd gathered, peering into the glen where Timothy sat, his hair a halo in the sunlight.

Like a gathering of buzzards, they made Niki's skin crawl. They brutalized creation to maintain their privilege. Brady would pity them, but Niki could only try to repent of her desire to kill them all.

A flash of gold caught her eye. She did not turn her head but slowly moved through the gathering, nodding to people and smiling blandly as a figure in a resplendent cloak followed her. The purple veil immediately identified the man as a sorcerer, and his pale blue eyes above it made her blood run cold. But this couldn't be Ghedo—not without the grand purple raiment of a master sorcerer.

Yet she knew those eyes, the dip of his left shoulder, the gait of his walk that made it seem as if his feet didn't touch the ground. People parted in his wake, perhaps believing that to even touch a sorcerer was to invite disaster.

She felt her grip tighten on the silken folds of her dress, and she willed her face to remain bland and friendly. It was a blessing that they had left their swords with Anastasia. Had they not, Ghedo's head would be rolling down the slope and into the creek . . .

He grabbed her arm. "Girl."

She turned and forced herself to bow. "Thank you for the kind word, for surely I am rarely mistaken for a child. You would, however, do us both a favor by addressing me as Miss."

He stared at her, his veil fluttering as he breathed. In, out, in, out, showing the outline of his mouth and chin so that Niki would recognize him whether he dressed as noble or drudge.

"I have need of your minstrel," he told her.

"As do I. He soothes my—" She almost said *soul,* but that was a word unknown in the strongholds. "He quiets my heart. Without him, I would be lost."

"I could make you another like him. I am quite skilled."

Her nails bit into her palm. How she wanted to shove his head in the water until he breathed no more. "I'm sure you are, but talent like this is so rare as to be unique."

"What price would you take?"

Niki threw her head back and smiled. "I doubt you can provide the one thing for which I would bid him farewell."

His eyes crinkled—Ghedo was returning her smile. How mild his eyes, how young the skin of his forehead. Apparently no regrets ever haunted his sleep or furrowed his brow.

"You'd be surprised," he countered. "I have great access to the palace."

Niki shook her head. "You have great boasts, but you wear novice robes. Shinier than I've ever seen, but still plain gold. Now, if you would excuse me—"

Ghedo grabbed her arm. Before she left Traxx, at the very least she would separate his grasping hand from his arm to punish his boldness. "I tell you, girl. I have great access."

She had expected to bargain with a courtier or a highly placed merchant, not Alrod's personal sorcerer. Who, she reminded herself, was either partially undercover or had fallen from favor. But Niki was here for a purpose, and so she would deal with the devil if that be necessary. She leaned in so close that her nose almost touched his forehead, for he was a small man. "How much access?"

"Almost unlimited. What would you take in return for your minstrel?"

"A solid oath that he will not be harmed in any way. Nor mogged."

"Not a problem. He may be restrained, however?"

"He is restrained now. He knows his place."

"What else?"

After a show of hesitation, Niki smiled, curling her lips as if embarrassed. "It would . . . it would be a lovely boon if I could be a lady."

"I can supply silks and powders beyond your imagining," Ghedo said.

She grabbed him, startled at the hardness of muscle in his slender arm. "I mean a noble lady. With a title and a seat at court. Have you that much access?"

"Tell me your name."

"Nikolette."

Ghedo laughed. "You shall have your silks and your circlet, Lady Nikolette. For I have connections you cannot guess at and power you cannot comprehend."

But do you have an outrider's sword?

Because once they connected with Anastasia, that would be the first thing Niki would reach for.

Anastasia wandered down the street, people's laughter still echoing in her head.

A tall youth took her elbow. "You all right, miss?"

She shoved him away. "Get your hands off me."

He raised his in surrender. "Sorry."

"Now you're sorry. Everyone on this punchin' street saw me get cheated, and no one warned me or stopped that old woman. Or man. Or whatever he was. Or she. You're all a bunch of thieves."

The boy laughed.

"What's so funny?"

"Your face is the color of raspberry jam."

She stomped away. He followed her. "I didn't mean to make you mad. I just wanted to help."

"Little late for that, isn't it?"

"If I had seen the dodge from the beginning, I would have stopped you from your—" He gulped back laughter. "—good deed."

Anastasia turned left, then spun right. She had no notion of where to go next.

"Hey, let me help you before you get into more trouble."

"Are you deaf? Don't waste your time. My bag of coins is empty."

His smiled faded. "I'm sorry. I just assumed you were one of the nobles, hanging around these streets for your amusement."

"Well, I'm not anything except lost and out all my money."

"Which is why you should let me help you."

Anastasia pushed by him, no destination in mind except to get away. "I don't even know you."

"My name is Gabe. So now you do know me."

"I'm supposed to trust you because you uttered your name? Which is probably a lie anyway. You're probably just a better-fed crook than the rest of these people."

"No. Look, I serve at the palace." Gabe pulled up his sleeve to reveal a gold band on his forearm. Anastasia had seen similar bands on shoppers in the finer markets and on servants racing around to do their mistress's or master's bidding. This band was plainer in design but set with dark amethysts.

"So what? You have an armband."

"An armband and that." He pointed to a large wagon down the street with two sturdy mules in harness. "If you need a ride somewhere, I can take you. Because you don't look like you belong here."

Anastasia turned now and smiled innocently. "Really? Are you heading back to the palace?"

He nodded, eyes eager.

"What are you hauling?"

His face clouded. "Stuff. Nothing really."

Anastasia circled the wagon. They had told her that her training would take hold when she needed it, but she still was amazed at being able to untangle a knot of aromas. "Lye. Lard. Aloe. Ester. Lanolin. Rose. Hmm, some mint and oregano. Corn syrup. Molasses. And . . ." A quick chill passed down her spine. "And something else."

"Nothing else."

"Something with a sharp edge. Like metal. But I can't quite . . ."

"It's not your concern."

"But my business is your concern?" Anastasia was dizzy from trying to navigate this situation. She needed access to this wagon and the palace, but it was not clear how she should spin this situation out.

Gabe nodded. "I'm not being nosy. I just want to help."

She had to tread very cautiously. Being jumped by a pile of dung and cheated by some dirty-faced kids were nothing compared to the trouble she could get into with a sweet-faced stranger. "Why do you want to help? I have no money, and you won't get my honor from me. Should you try, I am quite able to kill you." She stared defiantly, suddenly aware that he was very pleasant to look at. His skin was clear, his nose straight, and his jaw strong enough to give him an edge of manliness without blunting his good humor. His bright blue eyes gave a startling contrast to his thick black hair.

"I don't want anything from you. Why are you so difficult? I'm just trying to help you."

Anastasia laughed. "Do I look like a lamester—I mean, idiot?"

"No, I'm the idiot." He turned to walk away. "Sorry for bothering you."

Had she overplayed her hand? She scurried after him. "Wait! Why do you say that?"

Gabe stared down at his feet. Was this genuine sheepishness, or just too much sun? The skin at his neck was redder than that of his cheekbones, indicating the rush of blood to his face.

"Gabe, please." She touched his arm. "I was rude. Please tell me why you said you were an idiot."

"I'm just . . . there must be something wrong with me."

"I don't understand."

He smiled but the blush spread, darkening the skin behind his ears. "No one in Traxx and certainly no one in the palace feels the same urge I do."

Oh, no. I've ranked out now—tangling with some sort of pervert.

"What urge?" she whispered.

"The urge to help people."

Her heart leaped at such a notion—assuming he was telling the truth and not spinning her.

Gabe turned away. "You think it's stupid too. I thought—thought maybe you were different."

Anastasia grabbed his arm. "I *am* different. I mean, where I come from, the impulse to help others is considered a good thing."

He squinted at her. "Where do you come from?"

"I can't tell you, Gabe."

"Will you at least tell me your name?"

She smiled. "Stasia."

"I really would like to help you, Stasia—if you tell me what kind of trouble you're in."

"My mistress and the minstrel she is selling are already inside the palace grounds. I was sent to buy something special as a gift for the baroness."

Anastasia started to cry, not at all surprised that her tears were real. "I tried to do something good, and now I have no money and no gift. My mistress will rip out my hair if I return empty-handed. Which really doesn't matter anyway, because the gatekeeper will never let me into the palace courtyard empty-handed."

Gabe frowned. "I'm not allowed to carry money, so I can't help you that way."

She rubbed her eyes. "But you're at the market. How do you get what you need?"

"The vendors know to simply give me what I ask."

"Why aren't you allowed money?"

His smile lost its luster. "My master thinks I'd run away."

Anastasia grasped him by both arms. "If you had a way to gain your freedom, would you?"

He looked about in a panic. "Shush. You never talk to a drudge like that."

No one was within ten feet of them—a fact that Anastasia should have checked before she spoke. "Well, would you?"

He held her gaze for what seemed like forever before he said: "Yes."

"What if I could promise you freedom?"

He laughed. "You can't even walk down the basest street of the stronghold without getting into trouble."

"My mistress could help you get away from your master."

Gabe's face darkened. "Don't you know what this band on my arm means?"

She shook her head.

"I come to this market, walk about without being bothered, take whatever I need because"—he looked both ways, his voice again a whisper—"because I serve Ghedo, the master sorcerer of Traxx."

Panic seeped through Anastasia's skin, bringing a chill to her bones. This could be very good or very, very bad. "Him? So, do you like being his stooge?"

Though Gabe did not speak, the grinding of his back teeth supplied his answer.

Anastasia pulled him close. "If I promise to get you out of the stronghold, will you get me into the palace?"

"Not here." He motioned to the shop where his wagon was parked. The shop was shuttered and locked, but he had the key. The shadowy interior was stacked with huge clay jugs whose seals did not block that sharp-edged smell.

Anastasia hesitated by the door. This fair-faced lad could be a rapist, a drudge seller, or a thrill killer. Her training told her to flee.

But what was it Brady said? *Sometimes we just go with the gut.*

Anastasia's gut said to stay and play it out.

Gabe squeezed her shoulders, his fingers digging so deep she had to stifle a cry. "I am loyal to Ghedo and would give my life for the high and mighty ones, the crown jewels of the east, the exalted Alrod and Merrihana."

Anastasia breathed another quick prayer and said, "I don't believe you."

"And I don't believe you, Stasia. I'm not so stupid to think you are a mere drudge."

"I am not a drudge. But I am a servant."

"I am loyal to Ghedo. All the rest was useless talk. Sorry to have wasted your time."

As Gabe tried to push by her, Anastasia held him with all the force she could muster. She had either become completely a birthrighter or gone completely insane. "If you will get me into the palace—me and the sword I carry for my mistress—we will take you out of the stronghold with us when we go. We will guarantee your safe transit to a place where you can live as a free man, far out of the reach of Traxx. I promise this."

Gabe shook his head. "Even if what you say is true, I would be killed before we reached the Grand River."

She put her mouth to his ear and whispered, "Not if you're riding with an outrider."

The blood drained from his face. "What have I done to make Ghedo try me like this? Go back now and tell the sorcerer that I passed the test."

"I can prove that I'm telling the truth."

Gabe's eyes shifted back and forth as if he expected the sorcerer to jump out of the shadows. "How?"

Anastasia drew Niki's sword from the bundle on her back. "Tell me, Gabe. Is this the weapon of a Traxx strong-arm?"

"No."

"It is a fine sword, isn't it?"

"I've seen sketches. On reward posters." He ran his finger along the hilt. "Are you an outrider?"

"No. But my mistress is. Alrod has something that belongs to her, and she needs to get it back. She intends no harm to anyone."

He laughed.

"Not this time," she added. "I promise. When our business is complete, we will leave quietly. You could come with us. We don't live in luxury, but we do live free, and the people we help prize that freedom. All you have to do is get me and this sword into the palace. Will you?"

He grabbed her head, his hands burning her cheeks as he studied her. "Are you telling me the truth?"

"I swear."

"You want me to betray Ghedo by bringing an enemy into the palace. And you want me to betray him a second time by running away?"

Anastasia touched his cheek. "I want you to honor the impulse that makes you want to be helpful, even though no one else in this stronghold would even think of such a thing. I want to bring you to live with others who honor the One who gives you this impulse. Will you help me?"

Gabe shook his head. "No one betrays Ghedo and lives."

"You can be the wave breaker."

"The what?"

Anastasia smiled. "The first, my friend. You can be the first."

TEN

BRADY RODE HARD, TARYAN AT HIS SIDE. AJOBA FOLLOWED behind, her task to watch over Cooper. Though it was only his second week in the saddle, the rook hung on without complaint. When they stopped to rest however, the boy could barely walk.

Time was when rooks could be introduced to camp life slowly, learning to ride and track and fight in the world without the pressure of collections or assaults. Brady had had to press Kwesi, Cooper, and Anastasia into missions immediately. Rather than the usual three tracking crews, he had sent out six, half of which headed west to fulfill Arabah's lists.

Brady knew Bartoly still fumed over remaining at camp. But it was still the best plan. If Niki needed help in Traxx, Bartoly would be less than a day away. If the gargant awoke, the big outrider would be there to either calm him, subdue him, or—*please, Lord, no*—kill him. Bad enough that the baron had had the poor man's body mogged to huge proportions. But warping his soul with a loyalty potion—that had been unthinkable. Only time would reveal the consequences of that foul act.

"There is no evil these men will not attempt."

"Amen," Taryan called out.

Brady grinned. "I said that out loud?"

"Aye."

"A very bad habit of mine."

"But so very amusing."

Her gentle smile gave him both comfort and anguish.

Why hadn't the Ark answered his query? Couldn't they understand that the older birthrighters were wearing down without the comfort and encouragement that marriage provided? What was Brady to do with this hold Taryan had on his heart?

Things would have been different had Brady stayed on the Ark. Not inclined to physics or engineering, he would have been a hands-on worker. Maybe one of the divers who actually wrestled beams into place or mined ore or guarded the perimeter. He would surely be married by now and starting a family.

Had he chosen that life, he never would have killed one man, let alone many.

Yet as they rode, Brady drank in the rush of the wind, the pounding of hooves, the scent of honest exertion. Even with the lingering signs of environmental corruption from the wars—wasted, withered areas where nothing would grow, strangely mutated species, odd smells—these open rangelands held their own beauty. With few trees to mask the horizon, the sky seemed endless. Cattle, buffalo, and sheep dotted the plains.

A pair of squawking blue jays swooped down. Brady patted Thunderhoof to a walk, motioning the others to do the same.

"From Kendo, I presume?" Taryan said.

"Aye." Brady listened intently, trying to interpret the birds' cries. "They stopped to allow Kwesi to make his first collection. Deep in the scrub woods, he found a swamp. Lots of uncollected species, including one of the turtles on Dakota's list."

"Excellent news," Ajoba said.

Brady suppressed the urge to glare. "The locations are good, the way thus far has been clear. No sign of strong-arms, though they ducked one band of marauders."

"What's at issue, then?" Taryan asked.

"They're running out of shroud already."

Ajoba flushed. "I knew this would happen."

Brady leaped off Thunderhoof and crossed to Ajoba. "You just said five words too many."

She tugged her horse away, tears streaming down her cheeks.

Brady whistled his instructions and sent the blue jays on their way.

"I couldn't catch what you told them to tell Kendo," Taryan said.

"I said that they were to make do with what they had."

"Oh, lad. Is that truly wise?"

"Either God will provide or I'm a fool. We'll know soon enough." Sometimes it was a very fine line between steadfastness and obstinacy. Brady could only hope that he had discerned the difference.

He was ready to urge them forward when Cooper cried out. "A ferret! There. It's black-footed."

Before Brady could respond, Ajoba crept into the scrub. He dashed to her entry point, careful not to disturb the collection. Dakota had listed the black-footed ferret as almost extinct, but the location he had given them was still leagues west of here. Yet Brady trusted Cooper's sighting. Trackers were gifted with excellent eyesight and the rook had a fine memory for detail.

Cooper was so intent, he held his breath.

"Mate, you're going to burst," Brady whispered. "Remember your training."

The rook nodded, exhaling slowly. "Should I go in after Ajoba?"

"She'll signal if she needs us."

Taryan stood by, eyes closed. Praying, Brady realized, ashamed that prayer had not been his impulse. He was angry because this should have been Cooper's collection. Ajoba was so eager to prove her usefulness that she abandoned all courtesy. *Grant me mercy for Ajoba. For surely I have lost that along with any trust I had for this girl.*

Ajoba screamed.

Cooper leaped forward, short blade in hand.

Brady tugged him back. "Wait. Assess the threat."

Ajoba's scream rose to a hair-raising shriek.

"I'm coming, Ajoba. Hold on!" Brady pulled on his shroud gloves and mask, motioning for Taryan and Cooper to do the same. He dropped to his belly and carefully slashed the brush at its roots—a knot of woody branches and tiny waxed leaves. Taryan pulled aside what he cut. Cooper leaned in to drag it away.

"No," she said. "Let me do it. We can't let it touch us. Not until we know the threat. Use your blade to push it far away."

Brady could see the drag marks where Ajoba had crept in. Her screams had petered into a heart-rending whimper.

"Ajoba, I'm almost to you."

"No. Stay back. Too late." Her words were choked with fear.

He saw her back now, heaving with silent agony. Brady touched her shoulder. "I'm here, Ajoba. Let me help you."

She shook her head. Her throat glowed green. "You can't. Leave me."

"I'm going to pull you out into the open so I can see better."

"No. Too late."

"You argue with me, even now?" He forced amusement into his voice as he grabbed her ankles and dragged her out of the brush.

Taryan bent with him to see what had seized Ajoba. Eight black bumps the size of corn kernels ringed the base of her throat.

"Cooper, burn the brush you cut," Brady said. The rook hurried to set the pile of branches on fire.

"Mogged ticks?" Taryan said. "What sense does that make?"

"An easy way to bring down an army," Brady said. "Cover their blankets or sleeping mats, and the soldiers won't know what hit them. Coop! Bring me some of that fire."

Cooper lanced a burning branch with his short blade and dragged it to within five paces of Brady.

"Once I pull a tick off, I'll toss it in the fire." Brady pulled off his glove and fingered one of the ticks, which had already swollen to the size of a grape. Even when he got a good hold of its abdomen, he could not make it let go.

He punctured one with his knife and watched with dread but not surprise as the tick's shell repaired itself. Another tick let go of Ajoba's skin to chase the fresh blood. It hooked a proboscis—mogged with a barb—to her flesh and began to drink again.

She cried out with pain. "Kill me now. I can't bear to die like Tylow did. Please, Brady."

"Don't lose hope, sister." Brady looked up at Cooper. "Push that fire right next to me. Add a couple more branches so it doesn't go out."

"Are you going to burn them off?" Taryan asked.

"As long as they're hooked into her skin, they'll keep repairing themselves. I've got to lure those fellows off her."

Ajoba's hand fumbled for her dagger. Brady grabbed her hand before she could drive it through her own chest. "Ajoba, if you will ever cooperate, please let it be now."

Convulsed with fear, she bit her lip. The fresh blood drew a tick up from her throat.

Brady lanced the smallest finger of his left hand with his dagger.

"What're you doing?" Taryan said, eyes wide.

"You need to trust me too." He slashed across his finger in an X so that blood gushed freely. After smearing it on his blade, he placed it next to the tick on Ajoba's lip. It didn't move, as if it knew the steel had not supplied the blood.

"I've got to try something else." He squeezed his finger to draw more blood. "Taryan, as soon as the tick lets go of her and comes for me, flush it off with water."

Brady put his finger next to the tick. As he hoped, it let go, chasing the source of fresher blood. But when Taryan doused it with water, it wouldn't wash away.

"It's got barbs on its feet too," Cooper said.

"Only one way, then."

"Brady, no," Taryan whispered.

He laid his finger next to the tick, which jumped to his skin and dug in. Ignoring the pain, he calmly considered his options. It would be less painful to slice off the tip of his finger with the tick, but he'd bleed more and perhaps draw a flood of ticks from the brush. He would go with the cleaner option.

Brady stuck his finger in the fire.

The pain was so horrific that he wanted to howl. For Ajoba's sake, he pressed his lips together and simply moaned. Letting go, the tick fell into the flame.

Ajoba wept. "No, Brady. Please don't do that."

The end of his finger was scorched, stopping the flow of blood. The smell of burned flesh stung his nose, and his eyes watered from the smoke. Hand trembling, he cut his finger again, digging deeper to get beyond the burn. He drew another tick away and burned it. After a third time, he had cut the tip of his finger deep enough so the bone showed.

"Surely there's another way," Taryan said.

"You can let me die," Ajoba cried.

"No." Brady had to go further down to find enough flesh to supply blood. After the fourth tick, he had stripped and burned his finger past the first knuckle.

After the fifth tick, he pushed away from Ajoba and vomited.

After the sixth tick, Brady's finger had been burned down to the middle knuckle. As he took on the seventh tick, his head spun. "Cooper. Help me."

The rook wrapped his arm around Brady's waist to steady him as he burned away the tick.

Brady's right hand trembled too much to slash the last tick. "I'm growing faint. Taryan, you need to do this."

She punctured the tick. Blood flowed freely. The lemon-sized tick shrank quickly but shifted position on Ajoba's neck, following the flow. Ajoba moaned, her back arching.

"Wash the blood away so it has to come to me," Brady said. The tick was already drinking, gone from the size of a raisin to a grape in the time it took Taryan to splash water on Ajoba's neck. It had no interest in Brady's oozing finger.

"I need to offer it more blood," Brady said. "Cut me."

"I can't," Taryan said.

"Do it. Now."

Taryan slashed, and his blood came freely. After the tick bit, Brady pulled his hand away and swung it toward the fire. Cooper caught him before he fell face-first into the flames.

"I need help. Or I'll burn my whole hand."

"Cooper," Taryan said.

"He needs to support me," Brady said. "You need to do it, Taryan."

"Don't ask me."

"I'm not asking. I'm telling you. Do it."

Sobbing, she grasped his wrist and moved his hand toward the flame. She dipped it and pulled it back.

"No," Brady gasped. "It's got to stay in until the tick lets go."

"I can't."

"If you don't, I will be lost."

"It's only one."

"And it will crawl up my arm until it finds an artery and sucks me dry. I beg you, lass. Stop arguing and do what I say."

She shoved his hand into a flame, turning his wrist so the fire licked his finger but nothing else. He swallowed agony as long as he could. Then he wailed with pain.

Disguised as beggars, Alrod and Simon shuffled into the village of Luz. With his ability to change his visage, Simon was convincingly gaunt and marked with several pox. Alrod had relied on grime to disguise himself, though few commoners would ever be allowed to see him up close.

This village was further south than Alrod liked to travel without a full army. They had traveled alone, while his remaining strong-arms stood watch against Slade. The new sorcerer had promised safe passage and, thus far, he had been right.

Leaving their horses and walking into this dump of a town had galled Alrod, but he had to admit it was a sound strategy. Ghedo and Sado had successfully captured Dawnray in this same village. These people feared and hid from strong-arms but cared expansively for beggars and outcasts.

Fools. If they had sense, they would honor the strong and ignore the weak.

The streets were lined with dusty shops offering plain but abundant wares. A chubby-faced woman with bright eyes approached Alrod and Simon as they entered the main part of the marketplace. "Can I help you, sirs?"

Such formal address for a pair of beggars. Indeed, these people were simpletons.

"We come from Paz," Simon said. "We escaped a terrible fate—the only ones to do so."

Caution seeped into her gaze and her nose twitched, as if smelling something faintly disagreeable. "What did you escape from, and how?"

"Before Eli died, he begged us to flee and warn you."

Alrod did not miss the movement of her hand to her skirt, where she had likely hidden a knife. "Eli is a good man," she said. "How well do you know him?"

"Please, good woman. We are weak." Simon's voice wavered, yet something in his undertone was alluring. "We need to tell you all our tale and soon, for surely the threat is heading this way."

Concern crowded out the suspicion on her broad face. "Let me get you some water and something to eat." She went to take Simon's arm. When she touched his robe, her skin sparked. She jumped away. "What happened?"

"I am trying to tell you! Will you bring your people around so this fate may not fall on you? Eli sent us with the remedy, but neither of us has the strength to tell the story to every citizen singly."

She hurried away, disappearing down a side street. Seconds later, a heavy bell tolled.

"She's calling the village," Alrod whispered. "Listen, for the cadence tells the people either to hide, to come armed, or just to come."

"How droll. What does she tell them?"

Alrod frowned. "*Come armed.* That could be a problem, since we've only my sword between us."

"Your sword will be more than sufficient."

People appeared out of shops and huts, some armed with

clubs and others with saplings sharpened as spears. Children scurried behind the adults with miniature bows under their arms and arrows in their hands. Fierce determination marked every face, even those of the toddlers clasped to their mothers' legs.

Luz obviously thought itself a veritable fortress, though Alrod and five strong-arms could plow through such simple defenses in a matter of minutes. Still, the bravery he saw was encouraging. He would find some excellent soldiers here.

The townspeople pressed in closely, and Alrod stifled the itch to strike out. Only a favored few were ever allowed within ten paces of him, except in the heat of battle. There, the press of flesh was part of the thrill.

A heavyset man pushed to the front of the throng. With a thick nose, broad forehead, and a baker's apron, he looked every bit the peasant. "I'm North, the village elder. You have disturbing news from Eli of Paz?" Despite the flour in his beard, the man's authority was clearly marked by a confident tone and a battered sword.

Simon staggered against Alrod, clutching him for support. "A terrible fate has befallen Paz."

North's face darkened. "Traxx strong-arms?"

A woman in the crowd cursed. "May Baron Alrod choke on the vomit he spews on the rest of us."

Alrod noted her face. When the time came, he would delight in shoving those curses down her throat.

"Something far worse than strong-arms has overtaken them," Simon exclaimed.

"Yet you survived?" North queried.

Simon ignored him, scanning the crowd slowly as if to make eye contact with each person. "I can save you." The sorcerer continued speaking, uttering a string of almost-meaningless words but one clear thought: *If you just do what I tell you, believe what I say, follow me wherever I lead, you will be saved.*

The suspicion in their faces changed to hope. Alrod felt a similar hope until he saw the tide of emotion change yet again. An elderly man rubbed his ears, the confusion in his face passing to the woman next to him as if by contagion.

"You'd better listen," Alrod shouted, annoyed.

"I know that voice," the cursing woman called out. "It's the baron."

Alrod drew his sword.

Simon scowled. "Fool. I told you to trust me."

"I trust you for wisdom," Alrod said, circling in a fighter's crouch. "You should have been wise enough to realize you were losing them."

"Have I really lost them?"

"Look at their faces," Alrod said.

"Look at their feet."

He looked. The villagers were all trapped in a dark, sticky mud so thick that neither those who wanted to flee nor those who wanted to attack could do so. The same sludge hung from their wrists so that no one would be able to shoot an arrow or cast a spear. Even the children and babies were bound with mire.

"They're a captive audience. So go ahead, Alrod. Show this *unwise* sorcerer how to recruit an army worthy of one who would rule the world."

Alrod tossed off his burlap robe and assumed his most regal pose. "I am here to recruit some good men to serve with me. My men fight with honor and pride, clad in the finest armor and with the sharpest of weapons. They live in comfortable homes and wear the finest mogged fabrics: warm cotton in the winter and the coolest wool in the summer. They eat meat every day."

Someone gasped. "Meat every day?"

"They celebrate with hearty beer and spiced rum. And when they've performed well, they are rewarded with cakes."

"Better a dry crust with peace and quiet than to serve slime like you," North called out.

Beside him, Alrod felt Simon recoil.

"What?" Alrod said, confused. "Were you struck?"

"No. Keep talking while I reformulate our plans."

Our plans. Simon had refused to tell him anything, expecting Alrod to obey like a drudge. He'd show the sorcerer who held the real power. It was one thing to command bubbling vats of potions, but it took a real man to rouse other men's hearts to follow.

Alrod scanned the crowd, seeking out the few younger men. Even this far south, strong youths were hard to find, being in demand in every stronghold as soldiers. The only man with eager eyes was a scrawny youth with a pocked face. "You. What's your name?"

"Saul." The boy mumbled, his eyes cast groundward. Were he able to kick the dirt, he would.

"Do you have a girlfriend, Saul?"

The boy shook his head.

Alrod moved as close as he could without touching the mire that clung to the boy's feet and wrists. "My strong-arms have their choice of the most beautiful women in Traxx—we set the best aside for my soldiers."

The cursing woman spat, catching Alrod in the ear. Without looking, he swung his sword, pleased at the thud which meant her head had been parted from her body. The others cried out with horror or protest, but Saul smiled, showing buck teeth.

"You'd like a fine sword like this, Saul?"

The boy nodded, eyes eager.

"Come forward and be anointed as a strong-arm."

"No," North commanded. "Stay where you are."

Alrod slashed at North. The big man ducked the blow. The veins on his forearms popped out as he tried to raise his sword to fight back. Saul grinned as the mire slid from his own arms and legs, allowing him to move.

"Take the old man's sword," Alrod said. "He has grown far too weak to lift it."

Saul pried the weapon from the elder's hands.

"Don't do this, boy," North warned. "He's drawing you into great wickedness."

With a loud growl, Saul turned and spat on the man. North

saw it coming but did not duck. The spittle splashed off his brow, slipping down his face until it stuck in his beard.

Saul kneeled before Alrod, his hand trembling on the baker's sword. "I'm yours, high and mighty one."

"Lay your hand across his mouth," Simon leaned over to whisper. "And put your other hand on my shoulder."

Alrod sheathed his sword. The boy's face was cold to the touch, though the sun beat down on them. He put his hand on Simon's shoulder but could find no flesh or bone. He felt himself plunging into the sorcerer's cloak, falling into a black pit whose walls glittered with dark fire.

Change your perspective, Baron.

Simon's voice acted as a rudder, righting Alrod until he walked on those glittering walls, his footsteps a commanding cadence. A fiery power flowed into his veins, girding his bones and filling his muscles so that he wondered if he might burst.

Pass the power on, Baron. The boy will accept it.

Alrod pressed his hand to the boy's lips. Power burst from his fingertips and into the boy's mouth. Fearful of losing his hand and the power he held, Alrod did what he had seen Simon do. He shoved his hand between the boy's jaws, chasing the power down the boy's throat and further, burying his arm up to his elbow.

There was plenty of room in Saul's chest.

Do what you know must happen.

Alrod found Saul's heart and squeezed it until it burst. Though he had squeezed the heart of Traxx for his entire reign, the baron had never before known such joy and such terror until he commanded the living heart of a man.

Simon shrugged his shoulder and broke the spell.

Saul stood before them, white-faced but taller by a foot and strapped with muscle. His teeth were straight and strong, his mottled face clear of blemish. As he realized what he had become, he smiled. "How may I serve you, high and mighty?"

A woman in the throng bawled. "Saul! You get away from him. You hear me, son? He's bewitched you."

Alrod glanced her way. "That cow irks me. Silence her."

Saul pushed through the crowd, knocking over anyone in his path. To Alrod's amusement, they could not fall properly because their feet were still mired. Sword in hand, the boy—now a strong-arm—shifted his hand into position behind his hip.

"I'm your mama, boy. How could—"

With a hard jab, Saul ran the sword up under her ribs and into her heart. Alrod smiled his approval. It took most strong-arms weeks to master that move, but this common village scamp had done it after one touch from him.

Saul wiped the sword on her fallen body and bowed again. "How else, oh jewel of the east?"

"Are there any more among you that can serve as ably as this young man?"

"No!" North cried. "Don't give up your souls to him. Die if you must, but don't deny the truth."

"Silence," Simon cried out.

With veins popping and blood flowing, North ripped one arm from the mire and pointed at Simon. "I know what you are. And so I rebuke you in the holy name of—"

Simon threw Alrod's sword through North's throat just as the man shouted a name that Alrod did not recognize. The baker toppled, but somehow his words had dissolved the imprisoning mire. The villagers took flight, snatching up babies and children.

"After them, Saul," Alrod ordered.

"No," Simon said. "Call him back. He's the only useful one among them."

"So I'm to ride with an army of one?" Alrod snarled.

Simon smiled. "Baron, we are only just beginning our trip. Be patient. And enjoy the journey."

ELEVEN

"BURN YOUR CLOTHES," WERE THE ONLY WORDS BRADY had for Ajoba.

Taryan tended her wounds with a gentle touch but her frequent glances made it clear she wanted to go to Brady. He sat on the ground, his head between his knees. Cooper built a hearty fire, into which they tossed all the clothes they had worn. Reduced to their clean set of unders, Brady mumbled that they'd have to stop at the next village and buy more.

"But we don't have any money," Cooper said.

"We'll make do, Coop." Brady gave him the gentle smile he used to give Ajoba.

"Ajoba, are you listening?" Taryan turned her face to catch her gaze. "Make sure you keep these wounds clean. I think they'll heal without scarring. Be sure to apply the mold three times a day." On the Ark they had benefited from all manner of medications, with little need to apply them. Out here, birthrighters were vulnerable to all sorts of viruses and bacteria. Not allowed to take any technology off the Ark, they had to rely only on what was available in this world. Thus, their primary weapon against infection was mold grown on bread.

Ajoba stared at the blackened stump on Brady's left hand. "Brady lost his finger," she said, still stunned at what had happened. Though he no longer considered her a birthrighter, he still had crippled himself for her.

"Oh, you noticed?" Taryan's voice was edged with a rare sarcasm. "Though I would take issue with the word *lost*. He sacrificed his finger for your pride."

"It wasn't about pride, Taryan. I was only trying to do my job. It never occurred to me—"

Taryan squeezed her shoulders. "It never does occur to you, and that's your problem. I would ask you—beg you, Ajoba—to ask someone before you run off on a task like that. Or are you deliberately trying to get Brady killed?"

She yanked away. "I simply did what every other tracker in our camp does. No one blinks when you leap from tree to tree after a red squirrel or when Timothy scales a rock face to recover a condor egg or when Jayme goes down a rushing river to find a snail darter. It's not my fault that I came upon those mogged ticks. Or am I now to blame for the evil of the stronghold sorcerers?"

"You're to blame for the drama you indulge in and the role you make the rest of us play in that drama."

Ajoba burst into tears.

"Proving my point," Taryan said. "Even now, when you should be silent and respectful, you can't control the histrionics."

Cooper came to them. "Requesting pardon, Taryan. But could you get her to quiet down? Brady's biting his lip, trying to block the pain. She's distracting him."

"Didn't he chew on the corydalis root I gave him?"

"No. He won't do it." Cooper leaned over Ajoba so he could whisper directly into Taryan's ear. "He said, 'A knife's edge comes in handy in this world.' What does that mean?"

Taryan frowned. "He has a use for his pain. Thus he chooses not to dull it."

"No. Don't say such a thing," Ajoba said.

Taryan pressed a finger to her mouth. "Enough already. Thank you, Cooper. I'll see what I can do."

"He wants me to find a village, buy us some clothes. But I don't have any money." Cooper flushed so red that his face seemed to blend into his hair. "And I wouldn't know which way to go."

"I'll go," Ajoba whispered.

"Don't either of you go anywhere. Let me see if I can get Brady to at least take some of the herbal. If I know he's resting comfortably, I can ride out and get us supplies." Taryan got up, brushing sand from her knees.

As Taryan bent to Brady, he looked up like a thirsty man being offered cold water. Even in her sleeveless shirt and short pants, she was elegant—her legs slender, her form feminine, her arms shapely and strong.

Poor Cooper was still as scrawny as a boy. His hair was red, his skin as pale as the clouds. Without outer clothing and a hat, the hot sun would soon sear him. The Ark monitored the holes in the atmosphere that the long-ago bombs had ripped open. Without such instruments, birthrighters had to assume that at any moment they were receiving too much ultraviolet radiation. This was only one of the lessons that Ajoba had taught the people of the villages and wilderness—to cover up.

"Cooper," Ajoba said. "Get into the shade. Your shoulders are reddening."

He offered his hand. "You should too."

"My skin is darker."

He smiled. "Doesn't mean you can't burn too."

She and Cooper found a ridge that cast a big enough shadow to sit under. She brushed the ground carefully before they sat down to make sure there weren't any ticks hiding in the dust.

"Cooper?"

"Hmm?" He took a long drink of water and passed the skin to her.

"They say that you were right in the middle of the darkness that took Arabah."

"Who's *they*?"

"You sound like Niki." It felt good to laugh.

Cooper grinned. "That's a bad thing?"

"Can you tell me what it was like?"

He rubbed the back of his neck. "Why?"

Ajoba steadied her voice. "I let a dark creature into Horesh. I didn't do it on purpose. I thought he had been sent to advise me."

Cooper turned, his eyes wide. "You didn't recognize a demon when he came to you?"

She shook her head, stung by shame.

Cooper touched her arm. "Neither did I. When he said he was from the Ark, I was desperate to follow him. But I knew Niki would kill me."

"Maybe if I feared Brady like you did Niki, I would have been more cautious." Ajoba buried her head under her arms. "Is it true that the darkness actually swallowed the mountain called Welz?"

"Only half of it."

When Ajoba laughed this time, she felt no mirth. Only a bitter irony at the rook's innocence. "Only half, Cooper?"

"Aye. The other half of the mountain is still there."

"What's in the place of the half that's missing?"

"Nothing. Just darkness. It's like that creature somehow got its claws into Arabah and yanked it out of its rightful place in this world. Half of the mountain called Welz just happened to go along with it." Cooper grabbed her hands as if he needed to anchor himself to her. "When the darkness first came upon the mountain, it was like a sudden nightfall. But Kwesi, Anastasia, and I could feel the ground. Niki said that she used her sword like a cane and that the wolf could smell his way through the darkness.

"But after Brady and Niki fought that creature and somehow got us free, that part of Welz just went away. Nothing took its place, and there was no void where that part of the mountain had been. Yet it isn't there, not anymore." Cooper's chest heaved with silent sobs. "Arabah is in that darkness somewhere. Who knows if the birthrighters are dead—or worse?"

"What could be worse?" Ajoba whispered, though she knew the answer.

Had she continued to allow Demas into her life, and Brady not driven him off, Horesh could be lost in the same way Arabah seemed to be. That she might have brought on such a fate through her ignorance and pride was unbearable to consider.

Which is why she tried not to.

"Surely we could have waited a couple days before going on," Taryan said as she rode beside him.

"No." She did not deserve curtness, but Brady hadn't the strength to offer more.

"How's the pain?"

He forced a grin. "It would be less if you stopped asking about it, lass."

"Brady, we've got to talk."

"We are talking."

"About Ajoba."

"I have nothing more to say about her."

"But I do." Taryan's voice was low. "She wants to thank you."

Brady kept his eye on the trail. "Her silence is all the thanks I want."

"She's aware of what a sacrifice you made."

He quoted: "To obey is better than sacrifice."

Taryan turned in her saddle and gave the hand signal to pull over.

"What're you doing, Taryan? We've got to keep moving."

She smiled. "'Tis better to obey than sacrifice. So do as I say and give me your hand."

Brady stretched out his right hand. She slapped it. "You know which hand."

He slowly stretched out his injured hand. The finger was burned to the bone, and the skin that ringed it was blistered. Brady had borne many injuries and had nursed those of his comrades. Yet the sight of his left hand sickened him, perhaps because he had deliberately inflicted its wound. Or perhaps because—once again—Ajoba had put him in a position where he had no choice.

Taryan's touch was cool as she began to pray. And then the anger surged through him, once more fiery waves crashing through his blood.

Confess it, his spirit cried out. But he couldn't confess. His heart wanted to hold on to the rage because keeping it fresh was the only way he knew to ensure Horesh's safety. He must be on guard, always suspicious and raw, a stripped-down nerve that reacted to circumstances in time to protect those under his care.

"Lad," Taryan said, "you're crushing my fingers."

He pressed her hand to his lips. "Forgive me?"

She tried to pull her hand away, but he needed this touch from her, his mouth against her palm, as if he could drink in her gentle nature and thus put out the fire in his heart.

"Let go," she whispered.

He shook his head, pressing her palm to his cheek. Eyes closed, he saw a small cabin in the wilderness, a rushing stream through snowy banks, lofty pines that stretched to a crystalline blue sky. A whisper of smoke from the chimney brought with it the aroma of fresh-baked bread—spiced with cinnamon because his dear wife knew he relished it this way. He felt the weight of firewood on his shoulders, the dampness in the small of his back that spoke of honest exertion. His muscles were stronger than ever because lifting three children at once required a hearty father, and sweeping a sweet wife against his chest as they sat by the blazing fire was a joy every man should know. Peace settled on him from hard work, healthy children, a loving wife, and a world where no mogs roamed and no strong-arms raged and no princes plotted, a world where his neighbors lived in harmony with each other and their God.

"Dear one, you must let go of my hand."

He dropped Taryan's hand and, with it, any hope he had for peace this side of heaven.

"Brady, we can't do this, not with them watching. Not ever."

He followed her gaze. Ajoba and Cooper watched with almost opposite reactions—her eyes narrowed and his wide.

Brady swallowed the bitter pain that came not from the wound, but from letting her go. "You're right. It's time to move on."

TWELVE

COOPER HAD BREWED A HORRIFIC SUNBURN. BRADY HAD taken off the top of his unders to drape over the boy's head and shoulders, but burn blisters still popped up on the boy's hands and even his knees.

To see Brady shirtless made Ajoba cringe. A thick white scar ran from his right shoulder to under his left rib cage. The smaller scars and gouges must have been acquired after Tylow had woven the first birthrighter armor. Composed of wire, silk, and shroud, their armor was deliberately constructed to be porous—otherwise, the wearer would be completely out-of-time and thus no earthly good. It offered some protection but outriders lived dangerously. Their bodies bore the evidence of that.

Brady waved back at her and Cooper. "We're coming up on the settlement. Be alert."

Nestled in a small valley, Fenside was a green oasis in a parched landscape. An offshoot of the Grand, the Fens River still flowed as clean as the water that cascaded out of the Bashans. A stone dam provided the villagers enough water to irrigate the fields of corn and barley that clung to the river's bank. Spring flooding encouraged the growth of trees that provided shade and thus a haven in the dry rangeland.

Brady signaled. *Stop. Keep silent. Possible danger.* Ajoba dismounted and tugged on Cooper. She pressed one finger to her lips and then to her chest. *Quiet. Follow my lead.*

Not close enough to take cover in the brush, they crept behind a low rise. "Listen," Brady mouthed.

Cooper peered intently, as if a furrowed brow would improve his hearing.

"What do you hear?" Brady whispered, teaching even in the face of peril.

"I hear a steady whoosh-whoosh," Cooper said. "Something pushing water?"

"There's a mill on the dam. You hear the waterwheel. What else?"

"Moaning. Muffled moaning. More than one person."

Brady nodded. "What don't you hear?"

"How can I know what I don't hear?"

"Consider what you would expect in a small and thriving community."

Cooper shrugged.

"Children," Taryan prompted. "There are no children running around, no sounds of play."

"No food smells either," Ajoba whispered.

"Marauders?" Taryan said.

"Probably," Brady said. "The kind of isolation Fenside enjoys can be a natural defense—until a band of bandits or strong-arms discover it exists. Then the isolation becomes a trap."

"What do we do?" Cooper asked.

"Scout it out. Prepare for a fight. Pray to be of service. Get on your armor, mates."

"I don't have any," Cooper said.

Ajoba opened her mouth and clamped her teeth together before the words *You wouldn't let me make him any* came out.

"I know that. You'll wear mine," Brady said. "It'll be loose, but we can bind it to fit."

"What will you wear then?"

He smiled. "My sword."

"Brady—" Taryan began.

As he waved off her protest, Ajoba winced at the blackened stump of his finger. He had to be in considerable pain, yet his tone and face were composed, as if he had willed the pain out-of-time.

The only blessing was that the wound wasn't on his sword hand—unless, as sometimes happened, he had to fight with two swords.

They armed themselves quickly, their bare arms and legs contrasting strangely to their shrouded hands, faces, and torsos. After bundling various weapons on their backs, thighs, and hips, they coated themselves with dirt. They crept hundreds of paces without benefit of cover. When they reached the cornfields, they kept to their bellies. This early in the summer, the stalks were only knee-high.

"Keep your spear straight," Ajoba warned Cooper. "If it catches on a stalk, it will ruffle the leaves."

From the cornfields, they crossed into a muddy cluster of sheds, pens, and troughs. Goats and pigs hung upside down on butchering hooks, blood dripping from slashed throats. A hefty sheepdog lay panting on her side, a spear through her ribs.

All of you, stay, Brady signed.

No, Taryan argued with her hands. Ignoring her plea, he crept toward the dog, who lifted her head and tried to rally a bark. Brady rubbed her chest until she pressed her snout to his face. With a silent *oof,* he pulled the spear from her side. Though her body shuddered, she remained silent.

After coaxing the animal to chew a piece of corydalis root wrapped in dried beef, Brady cut a strip from one of their few lengths of shroud. Ajoba started to cry *no,* but Taryan covered her mouth. They had precious little shroud—how could he waste it?

After binding the animal's wound, Brady waved them forward. They followed him past manure piles and boxes of corn cobs until they could see the dam.

"Oh no." Brady pointed downriver to the mill. Men were bound to the waterwheel, their heads going under with each turn of the wheel. Some still cried out feebly in between dunkings.

"At least they're still alive," Taryan said.

Brady frowned. "Won't last much longer."

"Are we going to rescue them?" Cooper said.

"Not until we know exactly where their captors are. Or

strong-arms, if this is one of Treffyn's forays. Could be Alrod's, for that matter. He's not above traveling into outer Slade and causing trouble."

They cut back through the livestock yard and crept wide of the main street. Because trees were scarce in the area, most of the cabins and shops were constructed of clay and thatched with grass and cornstalks. A masked man guarded a grain wagon. In its bed were approximately fifty children, ranging in age from two to twelve. Every one of them was bound and gagged.

Brady scaled a roof with a running leap, landing like a cat. Moments later he slid down. "There's another wagon with the men bound and gagged. I count twenty-four horses, so count on that many marauders. But there's just one guard watching both wagons."

"Where are the others?" Cooper asked.

A woman screamed, and from a hundred paces away they heard a slap ring out.

"Having their way with the women," Taryan said, her jaw tight.

Another woman howled, a piercing shriek that made Ajoba's skin crawl.

"We have to stop that." Cooper stood. Taryan yanked him down.

Brady grabbed him by the shoulders. "To help them, you will have to kill at least one of the marauders. Maybe more. Can you do that, Cooper?"

Brady had asked Ajoba that question on her first mission. Her heart had shouted *no*. Her voice, cracking with tears, had said simply, "Yes, if that's what is required."

Cooper clenched his fists as another woman screamed. "Aye," he said.

Brady wrapped him in a hug as a father might. "I don't like it even now. But we do what we have to."

Taryan whistled softly. "I don't know, lad. It's six to one odds against us. We'd need a small army to oppose them."

"We've got one," Brady said, smiling with such ferocity that Ajoba recoiled.

If Cooper failed, the guard would shout the alarm, and the rescue would be doomed. Killing him was a task that should have fallen to Ajoba, but Brady didn't dare trust her. He and Taryan treaded water as they waited, resisting the current that would bring them into the waterwheel. Ajoba had been left huddled near the gearbox with all their weapons. She would arm the men as they were freed from the wheel. These men would be the best fighters. The ones who had resisted the marauders most fiercely would have either been slain or—for amusement—bound like this and condemned to a slow death.

"Time the rotation so you don't get caught by the blade," Brady whispered. "You'll have to leap high to catch the spoke."

Taryan smiled, her wheat-colored hair tied back for safety. The gash at her throat reddened as her skin paled from the cool water. Seeing it, Brady's fury surged again toward Alrod and his sorcerer, with a dose of anger leftover for Ajoba. Her disobedience had spawned the battle where this injury had taken place. Only Kendo's quick thinking had saved Taryan after the hoornar struck.

Ajoba's initial flight into the Bashans was something Brady had been willing to forgive. Was it Taryan's near death that had set him on edge? Perhaps, but the battle in the darkness on Welz had sealed his fury. As he fought side by side with Niki, that hell-spawned creature had snaked foul fingers into his mind, tickling his soul with ungodly temptation. He had resisted—he thought—but since then the rage toward Ajoba had burned brightly. He could scarcely bear to see her face.

That Ajoba had almost brought Arabah's fate down on their camp was unthinkable. And Brady found it hard not to dwell on it. He prayed that the builders would banish Ajoba to a sanctuary and thus remove the spur to his anger.

First, though, they needed to survive this encounter.

Taryan tipped her face out of the water to grab a quick breath and to offer him a smile. They were waiting for Ajoba to relay Cooper's signal that he had killed the guard. Until that happened, Brady and Taryan dared not climb the wheel, where they would be in plain sight.

What was taking the rook so long? Maybe Brady should have done it himself. But he couldn't be in two places at once, and this task was too dangerous to leave to Taryan alone.

More screams rose from the village. Brady's blood boiled. The bound men saw them now, hope in their eyes as the wheel doused them yet again. Brady laid his finger to his lips, but the caution was not necessary. They would wait for their rescue, perhaps welcoming the water to drown out the cries of their wives and daughters.

Ajoba waved to signal that Cooper had completed his task.

"Time it, now," Brady said. "Time it."

"Lad, stop nagging." Taryan inched toward the wheel, her head bobbing with the sweep of each blade. Should she get caught by the blade, she could be swept hard to the downstream side of the dam and dropped onto the jagged boulders below. He would have taken that task, but his strength was needed to catch the men as she cut them free.

He wouldn't have thought twice about asking Niki to do this. Was it because she was an outrider and Taryan a tracker? But that distinction blurred by the time someone was two years out of the Ark—Taryan had faced her share of battle.

Was it because Taryan was dear to him?

She disappeared underwater, then shot up and forward. Grabbing a spoke, she latched her legs over the rim of the wheel. Before she cut through the first set of bonds, the wheel swept her under the water. Brady held his breath, believing she was strong enough to resist the sweep onto the rocks. But what if he was wrong?

She reappeared, still at work even as she gasped for breath.

There were six spokes to the wheel and two men tied back-to-back on each one. Twelve potential fighters, who would help even the odds against the marauders—assuming these men were not too weak to take up a weapon.

Taryan got the first man's hands free and slashed through the rope on his feet. The downturn of the wheel took them both back under the water, and Brady realized he, too, was holding his breath.

Was it wrong, this love Brady had for this woman? His was the kind of love God had ordained from the beginning of creation, the kind that had been honored by their parents and grandparents. Six years ago, when the first-evers left the Ark, the builders had forbidden romance and marriage among the birthrighters. They had assumed the mission would be short-lived, and they thought it best to minimize distraction. But the mission had lasted longer than anyone imagined. No longer a boy on an adventure, Brady was a man.

Why hadn't the Ark answered his query? Even a *nay* would be better than this waiting. What had he said so many times to Niki? *Waiting breeds discontent, gal.*

With Taryan's hard kick to the lower back, the first man tumbled off. Brady seized him before the wheel could sweep him back into its path. "My wife," the man sputtered. "She's—"

"We'll get her. But we need to do it together, or we'll all be killed. As your friends are freed, please hold them back until we're ready."

The skin on the man's face was so waterlogged that it hung in folds. "Who are you?"

"I am Brady of Horesh."

"I'm Beck. How can I thank you?"

"Swear you'll stay put."

Beck nodded. Ajoba helped him onto the bank, motioning him to crouch so they wouldn't be seen from the main road. Brady swam back to his position in time to catch the man who had been bound with Beck.

They freed six men this way. Then a woman cried out from inside the adjacent millhouse.

Sloppy planning—Brady had assumed that the women had been taken elsewhere. He had never considered someone might actually be in the millhouse. He prayed that her tormentor would not glance out the millhouse window and see the rescue taking place a few paces away.

The woman cried again, a heart-shredding wail. With an answering cry of anguish, Beck took off for the millhouse with Ajoba frantically trying to pull him back.

Brady leaped onto the spoke opposite from Taryan. "Hurry," he said, cutting bonds with her. Clinging hard with his legs, he threw the man as far as he could, praying he had enough strength to make his own way out of the water.

The wheel took Brady under. For a moment, he longed to hold on to the comfort of this silence, this place of cool water where a youth did not have to be told to kill a man, where a headstrong girl could grow up without endangering a divinely ordained mission, where a man could dream of loving a woman in marriage, where Taryan could take his hand and put it to her lips in full sight of their comrades, who would bless their love.

The spoke came out of the water, and Brady breathed in reality. He climbed across to where Taryan was, going underwater with her, a private moment where their gaze was only for each other, and not the two bound men that separated them. They emerged from the water, and Taryan finished cutting through another man's bonds. She and Brady changed positions on the wheel, a strange dance of two rescuers and two captives.

The wheel plunged them under again, but then stopped turning—the unbalanced weight of four people was too much for it to lift. Brady saw the bubbles behind him where the water cascaded onto the rocks. *Hold on,* he mouthed to the man who had just been unbound. *Hold on until the wheel turns.*

Brady climbed up two spokes and the wheel resumed its rotation.

Panicked, the newly freed man grabbed Brady's left hand, squeezing the burned stump of his finger. Brady bit through his lip, trying to hold on through the pain. And just then the mill's bell tolled, startling them both.

Losing his grip, the captive tumbled with a scream that cut off when he hit the rocks below.

The wheel turned, and Taryan came up, gasping for breath. "They'll be coming."

"Get as many off as you can. But be ready to fight."

"All right. But what—"

But Brady was already climbing the spokes toward the outer rim. When that part of the wheel was at its apex, he leaped through the window and into the millhouse.

Beck was already dead or dying, draped over his wife's body. She was alive, squirming and hysterical. A heavy-chested man turned, trousers still partially unfastened, broadsword already in hand. Without his own sword and armor, Brady had only his dagger to fight with. He circled in a knife fighter's crouch. "Would you be kind enough to drop that sword? I don't want to have to kill you."

The man twirled his sword, showy moves meant to intimidate. "Yer not gonna kill me."

"Maybe I will, and maybe I won't. But we all die eventually."

The marauder sneered, showing yellowed teeth. "That the best you've got to offer?"

Brady lowered his knife. "What if I told you that you could live forever?"

"Wouldn't believe you."

"It's not me you have to believe. If you give me just a minute, I'll—"

The man lunged. Brady ducked, crashing his shoulder against the man's knees and knocking him over Beck's body. He dove face-first for the sword, but the man was an experienced fighter. He rolled to his feet, sword still in hand. Brady rolled too, but the man put a heavy boot on his chest, pinning him to the floor and swinging his blade back for the kill.

Brady struggled to breathe, struggled to get free. The man was too heavy and forcing all his weight—what a strange way to die. *Lord, thank you for how you've blessed me—*

Blood exploded from the man's chest. He pitched sideways, his sword catching Brady in the ribs. The man's body toppled, revealing Ajoba with a blood-smeared sword.

"Thank you," Brady said.

"The others are coming. Can you fight?"

"Of course." He pushed up, wincing at the pain in his side. Blood flowed freely, soaking his unders.

Ajoba tossed his bag at him. "Use the shroud."

"No."

"You'll use it on a dog, but not for yourself?"

"Don't start, Ajoba. I'm already more than fueled with ire to fight." Still breathless, he reached for his sword and short blade and dashed outside to join his comrades.

The rescued men, armed with the birthrighters' extra short blades, spears, and daggers, fought alongside Brady, Taryan, and Ajoba. Cooper had run to free the men in the wagon, men who had surrendered to their fate rather than oppose it. Now even they rushed into the battle, perhaps provoked by being so close to the homes and shops where their wives and daughters had been taken to serve the pleasure of the marauders. Armed with rocks and sticks, they joined in driving off the marauders.

"Are we going to let them get away?" Cooper cried as the marauders rode off on their horses.

"No," Brady vowed, but his body disagreed. The last thing he saw before the darkness took him was Ajoba standing over him, her hands soaked with blood and her face with tears.

THIRTEEN

AFTER TWO DAYS OF TRAVEL, ALROD'S NEW ARMY numbered only three. But what magnificent soldiers—three scrawny boys who under Alrod's hand and Simon's sorcery had become splendid men. Alrod smiled to watch Saul, Jary, and Jase spar, their muscles gleaming, their glances hopeful for his approval.

In years past, his strong-arms had always focused on their own gain, lusting after the gold, money, and power that came from serving in Traxx's mighty army. These three focused on nothing beyond doing their master's bidding.

The question was—who exactly *was* their master? Was it Baron Alrod, whose armbands they wore and to whose will they had sworn allegiance? Or was it the mysterious sorcerer who had somehow made them far more than their parents' breeding or their own efforts could ever hope to achieve?

"You wonder from what magical well I draw my power." Simon had sidled up to Alrod without rustling a single blade of grass.

"I would be a fool if I didn't."

Simon smiled. "It comes from you, of course."

Alrod laughed. "I'd be a fool to believe that."

"I am simply the conduit. You supply what I need, Baron. Without you, I have no outlet for this power. But you need me as well. Without me to channel your will, you're as bereft as those cowards in Luz. Remember that when Ghedo comes calling."

Alrod scratched his beard. The other sorcerer had completely slipped from his mind. "Ghedo's back at the palace."

Simon tipped his head toward the north. "So what do I hear?"

The air reverberated with a saw-edged drone. Alrod drew his sword and called out, "On guard, men." If Slade strong-arms were attacking, they would find a jolly surprise.

The tops of the cottonwood trees rustled with the sound. Not a buzz-rat—a hoornar appeared through the leaves. Alrod motioned his three soldiers back to work but kept his own sword out. Though the mogged wasps were the jewel of his strike force, Alrod disliked them immensely.

Ghedo dismounted, one hand lifted in greeting while the other kept tight rein on the mog. He hung the feed bag from the hoornar's hooked mouth parts. It chewed through a mash of ground lamb and caterpillars. A smoking pot ensured the mog's acquiescence.

Alrod had to seize control of the situation immediately. "What are you doing here? You were told to stay back at the palace."

"You asked me to manage your affairs in your absence."

"I asked you to watch out for my stronghold."

Ghedo bowed low. "I misspoke—oof!"

Simon had kicked the other sorcerer onto his face and now stood on his neck to keep him from rising.

"Simon, this is my—" Alrod wanted to say *friend*, but Simon's cold look silenced him.

"You misspoke, *what*?" Simon demanded.

"I misspoke, high and mighty." Ghedo's tone was deferential, but his clipped syllables spoke defiance.

"Baron, I would advise you to require this man to speak your full title, to ensure that he is properly aware of your exalted station."

A waste of breath, Alrod wanted to say, but somehow, his mouth spoke differently. "Speak my glory, sorcerer."

"Requesting pardon and begging for such, I did misspeak. For you are Baron Alrod, son of Elrod, grandson of Ilrod, the high and mighty one, the crown and glory of Traxx, the jewel of the east, the wise and accomplished ruler above all rulers, the hand that holds the sword and the mind that rules the heart, the great one whose will must be done, for it is high over all and mighty beyond all."

"Let him up," Alrod said.

Simon removed his foot from Ghedo's neck. "Remember your place, novice."

Alrod whirled to face Simon. "And you remember your place. Leave us."

"If that is your command, it is my heart's deepest wish." Simon drifted toward the training field, leaving no wake in the tall grass.

"Though you deserve those titles and more, the designation of *friend* is far more precious. May I still call you that, Alrod?" Ghedo dropped his veil, coming face-to-face with the baron.

"I could ask the same question," Alrod said.

"Of course. Which is why I came to tell you—"

"If you are my friend, you must support Simon's efforts."

The sorcerer flushed. "I support the growth of your kingdom and the furtherance of your glory."

"But you supply me no army with which to do it! Simon takes scrawny farm boys and makes them into men who far surpass any of our—*my*—strong-arms. Do you see them? They are incomparable. And without need of needles and potions, they are mine completely—all because of Simon."

Ghedo lowered his voice. "He appeared from nowhere. He could be an agent of Slade or Thrash or a stronghold we don't even know. How can you trust him?"

Alrod had no answer other than this: "I take his word on faith."

"I fear for you, Alrod. I really do."

"Why are you here—other than to disrupt my comfort?"

"I thought it best that I tell you personally that a woman has appeared at the stronghold. She's got the minstrel, claims to be his rightful owner."

"Merrihana's minstrel?"

Ghedo's eyes narrowed. "Brady of Horesh's minstrel."

No one had secured the outrider's body after the fall from the tower. Did he have his own wizardry to survive a fall like that? And further wizardry to take the guise of a woman and try the same stunt twice? "What color eyes does this woman have?"

Ghedo's annoyance was obvious. "What does that matter?"

"Tell me."

"Blue."

"What kind?"

"Look up at the sky above. That kind of blue."

"And who does she say she is?"

"Nikolette from Upper Finway. She claims that some bandit had stolen the minstrel from her, but she recently recovered him. The woman ranted about a romantic intrigue she and the golden-haired singer had engaged in—though I tell you, Alrod, he looked none too interested in her."

"If she loves him, why does she want to sell him?"

"Her father gave her a choice—either she sells the minstrel, or he will kill him. I say we do the old man a favor and kill him ourselves. This whole thing reeks."

Alrod laughed. "You fear a love-struck woman and a high-toned singer?"

"I fear another plot."

"Fear is a destructive emotion, Ghedo. It is caution that is wanted here. Watch them carefully, but give them room to play out whatever they intend. If the woman's story is genuine, Merrihana will be thrilled to acquire the minstrel. His sweet songs will distract her from my lolly's pregnancy."

"I don't trust this Nikolette. She looks dangerous."

He laughed. "All women are dangerous. If there's a plot involved, I leave it to you to sniff it out and deal with it."

"Alrod, I think it better if you come back—"

"I'm busy. Or have you forgotten we've got a crisis on our hands? A crisis spawned by your lack of foresight."

"Yes, we do need to replace the lost troops. But you don't have to ride off with some mysterious magician to prove me incompetent. If I admit such, will you come back?"

"Shut up, Ghedo. I won't have you nag me like a woman."

"Please—for the sake of all we've done for so many years. Hear me out."

"Go take care of my women and leave Simon and me to do the real work. Your pleading sickens me."

"I wouldn't have come here if I didn't sense there was some urgent business within the walls of Traxx that needs attending."

"Speaking of attending to business . . ." Unnoticed, Simon had returned. "Who is guarding the Mighty Gate?"

Ghedo pulled his veil back in place. "Strong-arms."

"No hoornar?" Simon's tone was that of a child, his eyes wide with innocence. "Is that the one you rode here? The one from the Mighty Gate?"

"I'll return it quickly," Ghedo said.

"You took the hoornar guarding my stronghold on this fool's errand?" Alrod said.

"It's only for a few hours. I felt you needed to know about the minstrel."

Simon's smile was terrifyingly bland. "If I understand correctly, if a hoornar travels too far a distance, it needs at least a day to recover. Is that correct, sorcerer?"

"Yes, but this was an emergency."

"The stronghold will be unguarded for a day and a half? Is that what you're telling the baron?"

"Not unguarded," Ghedo said. "The strong-arms, the thorns, the cobratraps, the rhino-rams—all these creations of *mine* are more than sufficient to guard the stronghold. The hoornar is just added protection."

Alrod ripped off Ghedo's veil and slapped him. "Go back to my lovesick wife and her skinny minstrel and leave us men to our business."

Ghedo bowed deeply and took his leave.

Taryan peered up at Ajoba. "I think there's a tear in his liver."

Brady moaned, but mercifully he did not wake up. Cooper was outside the hut, vomiting. The sight of Taryan sticking her fingers into a man's abdomen had been too much for the rook to bear.

The dog Brady had taken the spear from had shown up at the millhouse and now refused to leave Brady's side. Several grateful villagers poked their heads in, inquiring as to their rescuer's fate. "No change," Taryan said, her eyes filling with tears.

"Are you sure it's his liver?"

"How can I be sure? It's not like we're back on the—" Taryan pointed due north. Her hand was crimson with Brady's blood.

"Can't you get in there and pack it? Or sew the tear? Or—"

"Please, Ajoba. I beg you to stop bothering me with questions I can't answer. I need you and Cooper to stand guard in case the marauders return."

"Two of the men rescued from the waterwheel took on that task. They know better where to post sentries than I would. I brought Brady's pack. With the shroud."

"What for?" Taryan pressed boiled cloth against Brady's side. He jerked away from the pain. His eyes opened partway, showing only the whites.

"We'll pull thread out, stitch his wound, and use the rest to bind him up."

Taryan sat back on her heels. "No. I'm going to sew him up with cotton thread."

"But we always use shroud for that. I sewed your wrist with that in the early spring. Remember? When you fell on the ice and got that deep cut."

"Brady said no."

"No what?"

"Oh come on, Ajoba. Do I really have to repeat his words?"

No shroud except for collections. "But he broke his own guidelines. He used it on that dog."

"You dare question your camp leader?"

"So what do we do? Is it your plan to let him die?"

"I see why you exasperate Brady."

"If it were you who had been injured, he'd use shroud."

"What makes you say such a stupid thing?" Taryan busied herself with a new bandage, not meeting Ajoba's gaze.

"The look in his eye when he touches your hand. The blush in your cheeks when you touch his hair. Everyone knows, Taryan."

Taryan tied the bandage tightly, hoping it was enough to compress the wound in Brady's side. She rinsed her hands and stood. "There is nothing to know but this: Brady is our crew chief and our camp leader. His orders stand. Now go and find some way to make yourself useful to these poor people."

Ajoba stomped out. Cooper sat outside on the ground, pale and shaking. "I'm sorry."

"It's all right. Nothing to apologize for. We've all been through this."

Cooper rinsed out his mouth, spat into the weeds. "Will Brady be all right?"

"I don't know. It's deep, past the muscle. Taryan thinks his liver is cut."

"Is the hepatic vein involved? It will need to be sutured and—"

"Mate, you can't think in terms of nanosurgery and organ replacement. Out here, we can only fix what we can touch, see, and feel."

"What's to be done then?"

"If he doesn't stop bleeding, we'll have to open the wound further so we can try to repair the organ."

"Will that work?"

"It never has before," she whispered.

Cooper fell to his knees. Ajoba knelt beside him and laced her fingers through his. When they finally looked up, a crowd of children had gathered.

"We were sent to tell you thank you," a scruffy boy said.

Cooper helped Ajoba stand. "No thanks necessary," he said.

Not all the children smiled. Some faces were tear-stained, others stunned. Some had seen their fathers die and heard their mothers be raped.

Taryan came out of the hut, grim-faced.

"Is Brady all right?" Cooper said.

"While we wait and see, there are others here who need attending, especially some of the women. Ajoba, can you manage that?"

She nodded.

"Cooper, you need to help these people bury their dead. They'll want to burn the bodies of the marauders, but please ask them to do that outside of the settlement. And I need you to go through the dead men's clothes and such before that happens. See what we can learn of them."

"I don't know if I can touch the one I killed. I'm so sorry . . ."

"Hey." Taryan brushed the hair from his face. "You did what needed doing."

"His back was to me. I heard the crunch, felt the blow when I drove my short blade right into his spine. It was terrible."

"And I hope it always will be. But remember two things. You didn't bring this evil on—the marauders did. And you saved many people. Have you considered that were it not for those ticks, we'd be fifty leagues south of here? All these people would be dead or on their way to the sorcerers. You did good, rook."

Taryan gently disengaged herself from him. "You too, Ajoba."

"What will you be doing?" Cooper said. "While I'm . . . I mean, if that's all right to ask?"

Taryan laughed. "I'm not royalty. You can ask whatever you want. First, I'll see to getting us some clothes. Talk to as many of these folks as I can, find out about these marauders. Check Brady again to make sure he's stable . . ." Her voice cracked. "When that's all done, I'll ride a wide perimeter and see if any danger lurks. I'll go at least a league, so it will take me some time. I'll need to find a place to ford the river and check the other side. If the marauders haven't retreated, we need to know."

"I should go with you," Ajoba said.

"No. These people are grieving and not knowing where to go with that grief. And my gut tells me the danger isn't past—they need our presence here."

"You shouldn't go out on your own," Cooper protested. "Take one of the village men."

"I might as well take a bull with me. These men aren't trained to move like a tracker." Taryan grinned. "Stop worrying, both of you. Every hour or so I'll try to send a bird so you'll know my exact location and the status of the search. But if I miss an hour, no big event. Even if I don't check in for half a day, don't panic. I may be in a place where to call a bird would be to draw notice. If a full day goes by, send for help. I think Kendo's the closest, perhaps a day of hard riding east from here."

"Shouldn't we come find you?" Cooper said.

"It would be too late by then." Taryan grabbed Ajoba's hands. "Take care of him for me."

"I'm fine," Cooper said.

"She means Brady," Ajoba said.

Taryan pulled her into a hug and whispered softly, "If something happens to Brady and, if I don't return, conduct yourself as a birthrighter. For I believe that is what you are and will always be. Prove me right, sister."

Brady had come back to the Ark, but no one would let him in.

He must have swum here, plunged through the ice and dived the mile to the bottom of the ocean. Short of breath, his side ached, the pain stabbing from his ribs to his backbone. His fingers were blue and stiff as he banged on the hatch for what seemed like an eternity.

No one came to let him in.

Perhaps he slept and could will himself awake. And indeed, when he opened his eyes, he walked down a wide corridor, marveling at light that came not from a smoky torch or smoldering glowworm but from shining glass globes along the ceiling. The floors were polished to a high sheen and painted with lines. The Ark had grown so large that they needed the guidelines to show them where to go. It all came back to him—blue lines led to the labs, green to the training rooms, and orange to the living quarters.

He ran through the hallways, his eyes fixed on the orange line. His father and mother would still look young though his own hair was streaked with silver. He wanted nothing more than to hear Mother say that they had never forgotten him and Father tell him he could let it all go now because he was home and he was safe.

The orange line led down one hall after another. After awhile, though, the color changed to crimson, and felt wet and cold under his feet. Wet like—

Startled, Brady slipped, cracking his face hard against the floor. He tasted blood—must have split his chin. It soaked his shirt, but that was of no matter. He got up and ran faster and harder, pain ripping his ribs.

Coming to the double doors that led to the living quarters, he pushed through and found himself in the dining hall. "Yea!" he shouted, exultant to see the builders gathered at the tables, their heads bowed in sweet thanksgiving. They were silent and still, perhaps waiting for him to say "Amen!"

"Aye and amen," he shouted, but no one moved.

They turned their faces to him, and he shrieked, a denial that echoed through the vast halls of the Ark, out into the water, to the underside of the ice and back down, a resounding no, no, no. Because the faces that turned to greet him, the faces of those he loved, had all been transmogrified into the perverse visages of snakes and dragons and flies.

He stared in horror, knowing it was he, Brady of Horesh, who had done this. He who had let unspeakable evil spread from a corrupt world into the holy isolation of the Ark, where it would bring final destruction upon the birthright that the Almighty had given them to preserve.

The creatures smiled at his agony—sick twisted grins with split tongues and razor teeth that made no move to take him because they knew they had won and he had failed.

Brady howled with shame, shaking the walls with his cries until the Ark split open. He was sucked back into the ocean, icy cold gripping him as the blood rushed from his heart and he was lost forever . . .

But hope that is seen is no hope at all. Who hopes for what he already has? But if we hope for what we do not yet have, we wait for it patiently.

ROMANS 8:24–25

GABE DROVE HIS WAGON INTO THE SERVANTS' COURTYARD. Anastasia huddled in the back behind jars and boxes, spying through the slats in the vehicle's side.

She had wanted to come in yesterday, but Gabe had told her today would be safer. His master had some important business away from the palace and would be gone at least a day. So Anastasia had bedded down uncomfortably in the shadowy shop amongst the jars and the smells, worrying about how Niki and Timothy were faring and whether they'd be angry with her for losing their weapons. Finally she had drifted off into sleep, not to awaken until Gabe opened the door again and let in the morning light.

Though the service side of the palace loomed large, its ivy-laced stone walls were dwarfed by a shining marble tower. She cringed at the thought of Timothy scaling its height, only to be thrown from the top. Should she have told Brady or Niki what Timothy planned? Too much, too fast—she was too fresh from the Ark to know what to do.

Gabe paid no heed to the pecking chickens and nipping dogs that pestered his wagon. Fine linens rippled in the wind in the washing yard. At the far north of the enclosure, horses pranced in a paddock. Nearby, a man worked iron, spitting sparks with each blow of his hammer.

The sorcerer's wagon was garaged in a sturdy oak building with a copper roof and a lock on the door. Gabe closed and locked the doors before telling Anastasia to come out. His shoulders trembled as he lifted her down from the wagon.

"Hey, it's all right." Anastasia laid a gentle hand on his back, but he twisted away.

"Don't touch me there."

"Why?"

"Just don't. I . . . I have pain there. No one can touch me there. Ever."

"I'm sorry, Gabe."

"Don't be sorry. Just get me out of here. Are you going to your mistress now? When can we leave?"

"I can't go to her until I have a hot fire."

"What do you need a hot fire for?"

"I need a way to get her sword to her. I can't just strap it to my leg and walk it into the palace proper, can I?"

He shrugged. "I wouldn't know. The nearest I'm allowed to the palace court is the kitchen. If I even showed my face in the outer courtyard, where Alrod's provisioner does business, Ghedo said he'd cut it off."

"You're kidding, right?"

"My master has done far worse. Once he—"

She held up her hand. "I don't want to know. I'll need a big pot too."

"A pot?"

"Sure. Didn't I mention that before? Plus some of the ester, lard, and lanolin you have in that cart. A small knife. Oh, and the finest perfume you can lay your hands on."

He wiped the sweat from his face. "You're asking for a lot, Stasia."

"But I'm promising you so much more."

"You didn't lie to me, did you? You can get me out of here?"

Anastasia took his face in her hands and looked him square in the eye. "In the name of the Holy One, I swear that I am not lying."

"Who is the Holy One?"

"The God who made this world and everything in it. He made me. And Gabe—the Holy One made you."

He pulled away. "If he did, he made a terrible mistake."

"What? I don't understand."

"No more talk. I need to haul all this stuff down to the lair."

"I bet he's got a hot fire down there. And a big pot."

"No. You've gone too far now." Crimson splotches marked Gabe's cheeks. "I can't take you down there."

"You told me that Ghedo never comes into your storeroom. I can work there, and he'll never know."

"Stasia . . ."

"I wouldn't ask if I didn't need to do this."

Gabe rubbed his eyes. "It's crazy."

She grabbed his hands. "Sometimes we just go with the gut."

"If I do that, I'm probably going to throw up all over you."

"Freedom is worth a little sacrifice, hey?"

She laughed and Gabe joined in, a nervous chuckle from the back of his throat. "I have to unload the cart. I suppose you can help."

He unlocked another door. Beyond lay wide stairs, leading down. The walls were of the same stone that the palace was built from. "Is this the way Ghedo comes in?" she asked.

"He usually comes in through the palace."

"So, where can you go in the palace? Besides the kitchen and the outer court, I mean."

I live in the palace but have never laid eyes on Alrod and Merrihana. Yet I can travel the lower markets at will, sit in the kitchen. They're good to me there." He rubbed his eyes, the skin on his fists stretched white.

Anastasia touched his cheek. "I'd like to hear about how they've been good to you there."

"There used to be a cook. Nancy. If I was sick, Ghedo would bring me to the kitchen, and she'd wrap me in a blanket and feed me broth and hug me—she knew not to touch my back. And when I got bigger, she gave me treats and taught me songs. And then one day . . ." He covered his face with his hands.

She stroked his hair. "Tell me. Please."

"One day Nancy let me make the pudding. I was still a little boy, so this was a big treat. But I couldn't reach all the way to the bottom to keep it stirred, so it burned a little on the bottom. And the serving girl scooped the pudding without checking with Nancy."

"I don't understand. What was the problem?"

He looked at her as if wondering how she could be so thick. "Alrod ate the blackened bottom and was beyond furious. He broke every dish on the table. I could hear it all from the kitchen—all these sharp explosions as he threw yet another one against the wall. The whole time, a woman was laughing. Merrihana, they said."

"From what I've heard, that's about right. But what—"

"Nancy kissed my head and told me to step outside. The strong-arms seized her and brought her into the royal court." He sniffed, his eyes staring at something unseen. "One of the serving girls told me . . ."

Gabe seized Anastasia so tightly she could barely breathe. "They have a slab in there where they sometimes . . . for the amusement of their guests . . . I could hear her cries from out in the washing yard. I screamed so hard they had to gag me. And later, Ghedo beat me until I was too bruised to ever cry—"

Gabe shoved her away. "Have you bewitched me? Why would I tell you this?"

Anastasia pressed her hand against his heart. "That impulse to help is something good—something miraculous. Nancy showed you love, the kind of love that few know in this world. It's stuck with you, Gabe, and it calls you now. I serve that love, and the outriders serve that love, and if you can trust me and help me, we'll take you to live with people who love like Nancy loved, whose lives are an expression of that love. Gabe, please. For your sake more than mine. Will you trust me?"

He finally nodded, his eyes haunted and his shoulders hunched.

Anastasia smiled, wondering what in this insane world had taken hold of her. *Please, Lord—let it be you.*

Niki was pacing like a caged tiger. Just watching her made Timothy nervous.

Ghedo had had them escorted to this luxurious suite to wait while he arranged for them to appear before Merrihana. But that had been yesterday morning, and still he had not shown up. Neither had Anastasia.

"Where is that girl?" Niki growled.

"Her name is Anastasia," Timothy pointed out.

"Her name is *muck* if she doesn't get here soon with my—" Niki caught herself in time. It was very likely that the strong-arm at the door was eavesdropping. "My gift for the baroness." She watched curiously as Timothy shoved a heavy table against the wall.

"You gave her a tough task," he said. "Give her time."

"*I* gave her the task? You chose her for this, not me. What are you doing?"

Rather than speak, he signed the answer. *Scouting up.*

Niki nodded, understanding. They had already explored every inch of the suite and plotted every possible strategy. But not this one. Not yet.

Timothy climbed onto the table and leaped as high as he could without making a noise. On the third try he finally caught hold of the wrought-iron post from which an elegant tapestry hung and pulled himself up from there.

Good. The door might be barred, but if they could climb up into the very bones of the palace, they might get this quest over with quickly. Timothy would shove the shroud into Niki's hands, bid her farewell, and go after Dawnray.

Even as he climbed, he felt that splintering deep inside. Love was supposed to grow, to nourish other love, but Timothy's seemed to be on two diverging paths. Despite his occasional quarrels with Brady, he loved his mission, his comrades, the Ark with all his heart. Well, maybe not all his heart, because his love for Dawnray filled a large part of it. A love that wasn't just physical desire, but devotion. A determination to join their lives, their faith, their hope.

Wasn't this the pattern the Lord had decreed from the beginning? *A man will leave his father and mother and be united to his wife.* The unnaturalness of their life at Horesh was wearing on all of them, though they resisted for the sake of the mission. Truly Timothy could have resisted Dawnray, had she not been captive and so in need of rescuing.

Focus, tracker. To lose focus is to die. Not Brady's voice this time, but his own.

Niki laid her ear against the door and signaled *clear*. Timothy knocked on the ceiling. The resounding hollow tone told him that, indeed, there was plenty of space up there. The ceiling itself was plastered with ornate roses and thorns, one solid piece that he'd have to slice through with care. A shame—it was quite lovely. On the Ark, the ceilings were utilitarian, crossed with titanium beams and pipes for wiring and plumbing. Their huts at Horesh were thatched. But as beautiful as this ceiling was, it would never compare to sleeping under the open sky, with the heavens exploding in starry glory.

"I hope we'll see Ghedo soon," Niki called out. She must have heard doors opening, footsteps. He jumped down and quickly carried the table back into position.

"Lounge with me," he whispered.

"What?"

"We need to cuddle and tease. Like lovers."

"I don't know how to do that."

He shoved her onto the pillows, trying not to laugh with her as he arranged her on the settee in a noble—and therefore useless—pose. Timothy smiled. Niki was beautiful in a wild kind of way, but it took a lot for her to look at home amidst a pile of silk pillows.

"Keep calm," he told her now as he draped himself at her side. Keys jingled outside the door.

I am calm, she mouthed, squirming away from him.

He pulled her head to his, knowing that Ghedo would expect them to be in some sort of embrace. "You always look at him like you want to kill him," he whispered. "Think sweet thoughts."

"Killing Ghedo *is* my sweet thought."

They were laughing in an embrace when the sorcerer entered the room.

Timothy leaped to his feet in the custom of a servant and bowed deeply. He extended his hand to Niki and helped her up. She gave Ghedo a courteous nod, the skin of her neck flushing.

Ghedo wore the same shimmering gold cloak as before, the violet veil still covering his face up to his eyes. "The baroness will be holding court tonight. I will tell her that I have a lovely surprise for her. Until then, I'll ask you to continue to enjoy this fine suite of rooms."

Timothy looked at his feet, his dark thoughts sufficient to give him an air of humility.

Ghedo tipped his head up, stared into his face. "I can't pass this property to the baroness unless I am certain he is worthy. And that you can be trusted."

"I don't understand," Niki said.

Ghedo turned and grabbed her. Her eyes flashed and her fingers twitched. If she had been armed, the sorcerer would be missing a hand at the very least.

"I would suggest you get your hands off me, sorcerer," Niki said. "Though I'm from a small estate, my father is very fierce and has taught me to be the same."

Ghedo dug his fingers into her shoulders. "You're strong for a gentlewoman. The privileged women of Traxx do not have muscles like a man."

"Do you insult me, Ghedo?"

"I admire you, Nikolette. You are fair of face, and your form is unique. Which is why I insist you answer my question."

"When I hear a question, I'll give some thought to answering it. All I've heard so far are insults."

"Why is a beautiful woman like you built like a fighter instead of a lover?"

She giggled, stunning Timothy with her coquettish tone. "My father worries about my muscles—and my habit of spending long days training horses. Upper Finway is a harsh territory, and even those of us who have wealth are accustomed to long days out of doors. I climb mountains and swim streams as often as I dine and dance with gentlemen."

Timothy swallowed more laughter. The only dancing he'd seen Niki do was with a sword in her hand.

Ghedo ran his finger down her arm. Because Niki was not a citizen of the stronghold, the sorcerer could order her to disrobe for security reasons. That would be a disaster—she had more scars on her skin than anyone at Horesh except for Brady. Even her hands were nicked, something Taryan had tried to disguise with bounteous silver rings.

The sorcerer ran his hand along Niki's waist, snaking to the small of her back. Her fingers curled at his touch, and Timothy felt a stab of regret.

He should have nagged Brady to let him do this alone. His heart was his own responsibility, but now it throbbed with divided loyalty. Dawnray—to be taken by a wicked man. Anastasia—wandering the streets of Traxx. Niki—enduring the touch of the most despicable man in this land.

Niki held Ghedo's gaze, her head tipped and her lips in a pout. Ghedo laced his fingers through her hair. "Perhaps you'll dance with me at court tonight?" he whispered.

She giggled again, playing the role better than Timothy expected. "I thought sorcerers didn't dance."

"I'm a man of surprises, Nikolette of Upper Finway." He brushed her face with the back of his hand. "But you had better not be one."

FIFTEEN

No BIRTHRIGHTER HAD EVER SEEN THE INSIDE OF A master sorcerer's lair. Anastasia would be the first—if she lived to tell anyone about this.

She followed Gabe down the stairs. He unlocked another door and ushered her into a foyer. It looked quite ordinary, with a mat for muddy boots and hooks for cloaks.

They pushed through yet another door and into a cavern. Odors assailed her—sweat, manure, and an ancient dankness that knew no sun or breeze. Heady perfumes and bitter spices overlay the stench, doing nothing to sweeten it. Short hallways led to shadow-laden grottos. Gabe pointed to an arched doorway at the far end. "That's my storeroom. There you'll find fresh air and better light."

"It's a long way away."

Gabe squeezed her arm. "I keep my eyes on the floor every time I come through."

"How can you bear to live in such a place?"

He shrugged. "Doesn't matter where my body lives, I wrap sky and sun and trees around my mind, and *that's* where I live. Come on." Gabe took off at a near trot.

"Wait." She caught up, tapped his back.

He whirled, his hand raised to strike. "Don't touch me there. I already told you that."

Anastasia lightly stroked the palm of his upraised hand. "I'm sorry. Is there something on your back I can help you with?"

"No. Just don't touch me there and don't ask anything about it. Understood?"

Why was Gabe so sensitive about his back? He couldn't be a mog. She would have noticed the telltale green glow, even though his pullover shirt had a high neck. "I won't do it again. Promise. But could we please slow down?"

He glanced about nervously. "Why?"

"I need to look into these grottos."

"No. It's wicked, and that is all you need to know."

"Is that what you know?"

He frowned. "Of course I do."

"Who told you?"

"No one had to tell me. I just know. I've always known."

Anastasia tried to keep her voice light, though her heart thudded. "If you know that, why don't you leave?"

"Where would I go? No one would want someone like me." He tugged at her. "Come on. Keep moving."

"I need to know what manner of evil this is. So I can report it to the outriders."

"What good would that do?"

"Those who fight against evil are stronger when they know what they face. Ghedo will be gone until tomorrow, maybe later. That's what you said."

"Fine. If that's your choice, so be it. But I warn you—this place will gnaw out your insides if you let it." He took her hand. The protective gesture pleased her.

The first grotto held esters, oils, and beeswax, less reactive substances likely used as substrates for Ghedo's potions. Meat broth, sugar, and yeast were stored in the second grotto—nutrients for the cell lines to grow in. Rodents, insects, birds, and plant species were housed in the next two chambers—some alive and in cages, others preserved in jars or dried out on the wall.

The last grotto on the left was packed with glass cages holding snakes of all species, most of which were not native to Traxx. Sorcerers had their own dark commerce, trading potions, processes, and raw materials with each other.

"Does Ghedo live somewhere down here?"

Gabe laughed. "He's got luxury quarters up in the marble tower, which is fine with me. He's only down here when he's got a mog to make or orders to give. He spends much of his time plotting military campaigns with Baron Alrod."

As they walked, Anastasia couldn't help thinking about the lasers on the Ark. Used for building, they would be more than sufficient to take out every sorcerer and stronghold prince on earth. When she was a little girl, she had asked her mother, "Why don't we just kill them all?" Kwesi had asked the same question, as had Niki, Brady, Bartoly, Kaya, and every other child raised on the Ark. Regardless of who answered, the reply was always the same: *The Endless Wars solved nothing.*

The door to the storeroom was ajar, allowing Anastasia to sniff some clean air, perhaps from an underground vent. Shelves were stacked with glassware—some beakers big enough for her to stand in—and copper and iron pots. She gasped when she saw the ceiling, painted expertly to resemble a bright sky.

"Did you do that?" she asked.

He blushed. "No one else is allowed down here."

"You meant it—about wrapping yourself in the sky."

"I have to, Stasia." Gabe rubbed his face. "Seen enough?"

"Not until I see it all."

"You're difficult."

She laughed. "That I am."

A chatter arose as they approached the next grotto. Gabe pulled her away. "We won't go in there."

"I didn't see—"

"It's just two-footers. Monkeys and the like. You don't have to see—wait, I said don't!"

Anastasia ran into the grotto. Cages of monkeys, chimpanzees, and gorillas lined one wall. The other wall held cages with humans—two men and a woman, chattering in some guttural language.

Shocked, Anastasia shoved Gabe. "How could you?"

"Did you grow up under some mushroom somewhere?" he

asked, his voice rising. "The sorcerers do whatever they want. No one can stop them."

She touched his cheek, trying to calm him. "The outriders can."

Gabe snorted. "Do you see any outriders down here? It's only me, and I'm no match for the likes of Ghedo."

"You're better than Ghedo."

"Don't say that. You mustn't—"

"It's the truth. You have a good heart."

He turned to the wall, as if he couldn't bear to look at her or this wretched place. "I treat them the best I can. If I could free them, I would."

"I know. We'll get you out of here. Be patient."

"Stasia, come on. Come out of here."

"Why do they talk like that?"

Gabe dug his fingers into her arms. "Because he cut out their tongues and ripped out half their vocal cords, that's why. So they won't irk him with their pleas to be spared. I warned you, but you won't take *no* for an answer, will you?"

"No," she said numbly. She turned to the three caged people. "I'll find a way to help you. I swear it."

Gabe pulled her out into the main cavern. "Let's go to the storeroom. I'll start a fire for you."

Anastasia pulled away, suddenly drawn to a hallway on the right. It was dark and too long to see the end. She stepped in.

"No! Not in there."

"Why not?"

"That's where he keeps his potions."

She was just a few feet from the cell lines that Ghedo's father and grandfather and those before them had passed down. Potions were easily destroyed by burning—if one could just get to them.

"I need to go in there." Her lungs burned with the compulsion to brave the darkness.

Something grabbed her foot, squeezing so hard she felt her toe crack. A blade flashed by her face, and she stumbled backward, Gabe pulling her out of the hallway. She looked down and saw that an amputated hand still grasped her foot. Not a human hand but some mogged vine with grasping fingers.

"What happened?" she gasped, fighting nausea.

"Are you always this dumb, Stasia? Did you think you could just waltz in to where Ghedo keeps his potions?"

"I . . . I guess I did."

Gabe wiped her face. "The hallway called you in."

"Huh?"

"Have you forgotten who created the wall of thorns? And the siren song of the flowers?"

"The Holy One created them. The likes of Ghedo perverted them."

"Stop staring at me like I did it," he said.

"Oh," she said. "Sorry."

"You're never going to rescue me."

"I never said *I* would. My mistress—the outrider—does the rescuing. I just make all the mistakes so she doesn't have to."

His head jerked around. "Did you hear something?"

"That's my heart, about to break through my ribs." She kicked, trying to remove the hand that still grasped her foot. He jabbed it with Niki's sword and tossed it back into the hallway. A growl arose, followed by crunching.

She yelped. He pressed his hand to her mouth. "Shush."

From above, the door scraped. "Boy!" a voice bellowed.

Gabe jolted as if struck by lightning. "He's not supposed to be back today!"

"Where are you, boy?"

"Coming, master. I'm down here unloading my supplies."

A key clanked in the lock of the lower door. It creaked open, and a shining gold robe came into view. Anastasia dove into the nearest grotto and rolled under a table.

It was one thing to be in the lion's den.

Neither she nor Gabe had counted on the lion being back so soon.

Dawnray's parents had taught her that a woman's beauty came from a gentle spirit and a kind nature. With fancy clothes, dyed hair, and elaborate jewelry, the baroness had turned Dawnray into a poor imitation of herself.

Coming in with a tray of food, Carin burst into tears. "What has that witch done to you?"

"Don't. Please, you'll get me started, and I just can't. She beats me when I cry. She says it'll ruin my face powder."

Carin wailed louder. Dawnray put her hands over the girl's mouth. "She beats me but she'll kill you. You have got to stop."

"But your beautiful hair . . ."

"It'll grow back," she said, knowing she'd be dead long before her hair cascaded down her back again in its natural color. What would Merrihana do if she delivered a child with auburn hair? Would she dye the baby's hair black too?

The sound of footsteps made Carin break away and busy herself with setting out food. The three stylists hustled in.

Merrihana followed them. "We're standing at court tonight. I've yet to decide what we're wearing because you have created quite the dilemma. Your skin tone is all wrong to flatter my wardrobe. Too sun-stained, with freckles like some common garden wench."

The stylists pawed at Dawnray, holding fabrics to her neck, brushing powder across her chest where freckles dared to linger. How had she come to this? She had been happy working in the shop with her father, crafting fine silver bells and horns, when she had been foolish enough to take pity on a crippled beggar. She'd invited the hunched man into the shop and given him bread and soup. He had thanked her and shuffled away, and she had never suspected he was the baron's manservant.

Hours later, under the cover of night, Sado had returned with Ghedo and a patrol of strong-arms. The sorcerer had examined her from head to foot, ignoring her father's cries. "She's a good girl. Please don't—" His pleading had stopped when the sorcerer drove a sword into his chest. When she saw him last, he was lying on the shop floor, his eyes already glazing over in death.

Pain pierced her heart at the memory—pain mingled with hatred. Even if he hadn't killed her father, Dawnray would have hated Ghedo. She despised the sorcerers who polluted God's creation with their terrifying mogs, the stronghold nobles who sucked the villages and farms dry. And Merrihana and her friends, who paraded about as if it was their right to taste pleasure at the expense of others' agony.

Surely such hate was justified, although the way it ate her insides was sinful. She sighed. If there was some mercy to be found for these foul people, God would have to provide it, because Dawnray couldn't gather it on her own.

"This will do for tonight." Merrihana held up the dress with a tight bodice of sea-green and a skirt that flowed with green, blue, and purple ripples. Dawnray dreaded the prospect of having that mogged silk next to her skin. How the baroness could stand all this, she didn't know.

Then she realized—yes, she did know. She'd seen this much. The silk and jewels and fuss meant nothing, for Merrihana was the hungry beggar. Crippled by her own privilege, bound to a man who loved nothing but himself.

Dawnray glanced at the stylists. "Could I speak to you in private, high and mighty?"

"Why?"

She lowered her voice. "Surely servants should not be a party to your business."

Merrihana frowned. "Out. All of you. Tell the guard to be on alert at the door." They hustled out, Carin the only one to glance back with concern.

"If you've interrupted these preparations simply to whine, I'll give you something to whine about."

As Merrihana narrowed her eyes, the feline mogging that had shaped them was frighteningly clear. Her pupils were slits, the rich gold irises filling the rest of the eye. She had submitted to a sorcerer's needle so she could stand in the dark to watch her husband's infidelities. Was it a foul licentiousness that drove her to do such a thing?

Clearly the baroness deserved the cruel fate she had brought on herself. Yet something deep inside Dawnray reminded her that Merrihana was also a woman in pain. A woman scrabbling desperately for hope.

Dawnray sighed. Despite her own desperate circumstances, she had a hope that no sorcerer or baron could steal away. This grace was not her doing, but it had become her obligation. She held out a chair. "Would you sit with me, Baroness?"

Merrihana sat, still somehow managing to look down her nose at the standing Dawnray.

"May I sit with you?"

Merrihana nodded. "I trust you will not be wasting my time. The penalty will be severe if you do."

Dawnray sat, folding her hands and adopting a meek pose. "I'll do better at honoring your wishes if I understand your intentions."

"My intentions are none of your business."

Dawnray shrunk into herself, taking the pose of an animal submitting to a more vicious animal. "I am so sorry. I'm a village girl and don't express myself well. If I may try again? Baroness, I would please you better if you could explain the expected outcome of this transformation."

"Are you stupid, girl? I told you."

"You do me the honor of letting me wear your hair color and copies of your clothes because you are the rightful and only wife of the baron. He needs to remember that."

Merrihana fingered her bodice where she kept her dagger. "He does remember that."

"I also need to remember that."

Merrihana nodded.

"You love him very much, don't you?" Dawnray whispered.

"I don't know what . . ." Merrihana put her hand to her throat as if to catch the crack in her voice.

"It is hurtful for you when that love is not returned rightfully," Dawnray whispered.

Merrihana slapped her hard. "That is none of your concern."

Dawnray bent low, trying to absorb the pain. "A wife should love her husband. I will honor that love and not disrupt it in any way. I want you to know that."

Merrihana plucked at her skirt. "I'm glad to see you've learned one thing well. I'll send my maid to dress you tonight. You will stand with me at court so there will be no mistake that you are my gift to my husband. You will look pleased that I have accorded you this honor. Understood?"

"Yes. Thank you."

"I'll send some ice for your face. I can't have you blemished before my court tonight."

Anastasia cowered under a broad table. The sorcerer paced about it, slow steps punctuated by a hum in the back of his throat. *He's thinking,* she realized. *Plotting a new evil—and I've dropped myself right in the middle of it.* With each pass, she silently rolled to the other side of the table away from him.

Twice as long as she and more than an open arms'-breadth wide, the table provided a deep shadow but little actual cover. All the sorcerer would need to do is look down.

His feet turned toward the table. Ghedo's knees creaked, and he exhaled noisily. He was bending down.

Should she roll out the other side and run away? Even if she could outrun Ghedo—and by the sound of his groaning knees, she might be able to—the strong-arms would know she was coming, for he would shout a warning. Even worse, the guards would know she had come in with Gabe. She had sworn to accept any risk, but she had no right to force that peril on him.

Something scraped overhead. A drawer opened. Another drawer, a third. Ghedo slammed them shut and bellowed, "Boy!"

Halting footsteps. Gabe obviously dreaded what he would find in here. He went to one knee, his face low enough so he could see her. "Master, I didn't expect you back tonight."

She smiled, and relief flooded his face. He breathed it back so he could look up at the sorcerer with a blank expression. "How may I serve you?"

"Stand up, boy. I don't have time for this toadying about." Ghedo's voice was light and boyish. Should he sing, he might sound like Timothy.

"Yes?"

"Where are my blades?"

"I sharpened them. I have them at the stone, ready to bring in. I didn't expect you back so soon, or they'd be waiting for you here."

"Get them."

"Yes, master." Gabe turned.

"Wait. I have a question for you."

"A question? For me?"

"Refresh my memory. What is it you call yourself?"

"Requesting pardon, sir, but I don't understand."

"You've given yourself a name. I've heard the kitchen girls call you by it. What is it?"

"Gabriel. They call me Gabe."

"Why did you choose that name?" Ghedo's voice took on a strange, coaxing warmth.

"No reason. I just . . ."

"What?" The sorcerer's tone was hypnotic, a skill they had warned about in training. Anastasia searched her memory for a way to resist and found herself back to that same old childhood drill. *Genesis,* she began, *And it was very good. . . .*

"I just dreamed it," Gabe said.

"You dreamed a name? How can that be?"

"I saw a man."

"What did he look like?"

"I couldn't tell. There was so much light, I had to shade my eyes."

"And what did this man have to do with your name?"

"He called me Gabriel and told me . . ."

"Told you what?"

"He told me to be strong and to be true."

"Interesting." Ghedo's voice was laced with comfort and good will. "Some think that dreams have their own magic. Would you agree?"

. . . *Joshua: Choose today whom you will serve* . . .

"I don't know."

"Would you like me to call you by this name?"

"You may call me whatever pleases you."

"You're a young man now. *Boy* no longer fits."

Gabe's feet tap-danced.

. . . *Isaiah: The people walking in darkness have seen a great light* . . .

"I have kept you apart from court to keep you safe, Gabe. Do you understand why?"

"The exalted ones would be offended by my appearance."

Ghedo laughed. Anastasia wanted to laugh with him, because his merriment promised more fun, a sweet place, a great pleasure. *Focus, tracker. Jonah: you brought my life up from the pit* . . .

"The truth is, Gabe, they are not worthy of you."

Gabe took a step back. She risked a glance, saw the horror on his face.

Ghedo laughed again. "I've confused you. Come here, Gabe."

"I . . . um . . . I'll get your knives for you."

"Come here, Gabriel."

Gabe moved slowly around the table. The sorcerer closed the distance until they were toe to toe. "I've been hard on you, Gabe."

Gabe breathed noisily, as if something were caught in his throat. Anastasia recognized fear warring with pain—of course the sorcerer had been hard. The man's heart was as much without light as the inside of a rock . . . *Romans: The creation waits in eager expectation . . .*

"Have you no comment?"

"It was your . . ."— Gabe cleared his throat—"your right and your due."

"When no one else wanted you, I kept you and fed you. I clothed you, gave you a place to sleep, employed you in worthwhile labor. Is this not true?"

"Yes. Thank you."

"I have no son, Gabe."

Gabe was silent, but the shifting of his weight to his heels told Anastasia he wanted no part of the sorcerer.

Ghedo reached for Gabe.

Anastasia reached back carefully for Niki's heavy sword.

Should the sorcerer attempt to harm him, she'd go for the femoral artery. If she could find his thigh under that robe, hit the mark the first time, perhaps the sorcerer would bleed out before he took revenge on Gabe. Ghedo would get her, of course, but if Gabe could be safe, she would have served Birthright well. For Gabe might not have recognized the figure in the dream, but she knew who had named him.

"You had been cast on the trash heap," Ghedo continued, "but I saw your promise and rescued you."

Anastasia felt strangely touched. The man had indeed done a noble deed. No, not true. Ghedo had the use of any strong-arm he pleased. He had grabbed Gabe for his own use. *Galatians: love, joy, peace, patience. Kindness . . .*

"Thank you," Gabe was saying.

"I did not flinch at the deformities."

She heard Gabe's breath catch. He was bitterly ashamed of whatever marred his back. How bad could it be?

"I accepted you into my lair. Gave you shelter, protection, training. You have access to most of the stronghold, most of the palace. Everyone defers to you because you serve me. Surely you recognize your privilege."

"I do."

"You look like something's on your mind."

"No. Not really."

"It's fine, Gabe. Tell me what you're thinking."

"It's just that . . . I've always wondered."

"Wondered what?"

"Who my parents are."

"Your parents?" Ghedo's voice lost its veneer. "Who put that question in your mind?"

"No one. It's just . . . I always assumed that you . . ."

"That I what?"

Gabe spoke in a trembling whisper. "I always assumed that you made me."

Ghedo moved closer. "But now you're not sure?"

Anastasia risked a glance. The sorcerer held Gabe in a loose embrace. Fear radiated from the boy's skin in salty waves.

"Gabe, you live because I willed it. You serve because I have allowed it. Few have had even this privilege."

"Um . . . I am . . . honored."

"What if I could give you greater privilege?"

Gabe tried to pull away. "What would you do to me?"

"I would make you high and mighty. Would you like that, boy?"

First John: God is light, and in him there is no darkness at all.

Gabe stood silent, his breath coming so fast as to be almost a pant.

"I expect an answer. Would you like to rule?"

"Um . . . if that would be your command."

"Not only would it be my command. It would be my greatest pleasure to give you a throne."

"A throne?" Gabe's voice was a raw whisper. "What throne?"

"Why, the throne of Traxx, of course."

Gabe ran from the room to the music of Ghedo's laughter.

Revelation: Amen, come soon, Lord. For I'm in deep trouble here . . .

Sixteen

Ghedo bowed low. "Thanks for seeing me, high and mighty, the gracious star of the east, the glory of the—"

"Stop. I choke on all the groveling. Sit, and chat with me while I work." Merrihana sharpened a dart against a whetstone. While other privileged women did needlepoint, the baroness preferred pastimes that involved razor-sharp edges. Ghedo was well aware that she kept a number of deadly objects concealed on her person at all times.

He poured himself a glass of ale, which he lifted to her. "To the most beautiful woman in all the lands."

"Ghedo—"

"This is a truth to be spoken and not flattery to be doubted, Merrihana." He used her given name strategically, wanting to remind her of their long relationship.

Ghedo had negotiated the marriage of Alrod of Traxx and Merrihana from the far-off stronghold of Rushika. She had been a flower that none could match, a prize many sought. What a sorrow that the very fire that made her so desirable had led her to an irreversible mistake. Still, she was fortunate. Other princes might have executed a wife who destroyed her own child-bearing capacity. Alrod had shown mercy in letting her live. Either that, or a certain pleasure in watching her suffer.

"My beauty buys me nothing." Merrihana jabbed the dart into the table, ruining the fine edge she had just honed. No matter. She'd whet it all over again, simply for something to do.

Ghedo dared to take her hand. "Though your beauty is unsurpassed, I suspect it may be the least of your talents."

Her eyes narrowed. "What nonsense are you pushing?"

"I have long suggested—nay, urged—that Alrod involve you in governing. You have a quick wit, a deep wisdom, a grasp of politics. Perhaps your beauty does play against you in that your husband is so infatuated he's never understood all you are capable of."

"If my husband is infatuated, he shows it poorly. When he's not chasing battles, he's chasing lollies. That is no way to charm one's wife."

Ghedo shook his head, summoning a tone of sympathy. "He's not well, Merrihana. Hasn't been for some time now."

She leaned forward. "What makes you say that?"

He stood. "I apologize. I shouldn't have said anything."

"I trust you to serve Alrod's best interests. You swore that in blood."

Ghedo was well aware of that fact. The scars around each of his wrists and his neck marked his fealty. Why had he borne all the pain and Alrod the glory? He mustered a wistful tone. "We came into the world just two days apart, you know—Alrod and I. Running and learning and planning, our allegiance sworn to each other since we were small boys."

He shook his head, as if shaking off a reverie. "I'm sorry, Merrihana. I bore you."

He bowed and headed for the door. She came after him and dug her fingers into his arm. "Show me your face, Ghedo. I have never seen it."

"Why haven't you asked before this? It's your right. Yours and Alrod's only."

Her tone was muted, her eyes thoughtful. "I took you for granted."

"As you may." He unlatched his veil, let it drop.

Merrihana touched his cheek. "Why, you look almost young enough to be Alrod's son."

He smiled. "I've kept myself from entanglements."

"Now tell me: Why do you say your baron is not well?"

Ghedo forced a flush up his throat. His father had trained him in body control by forcing him to view both atrocities and delights. By calling on the appropriate mind picture, he was quite able to produce a genuine response. Humility was especially difficult for him. To achieve it, he pictured Nikolette of Finway inspecting him as he had her.

"Ghedo. Please."

He lowered his gaze. "If I speak my mind, you'll attribute it to jealousy."

"The new sorcerer?"

"This Simon appeared out of nowhere, and within five minutes, the man was the master sorcerer of Traxx. How can Alrod not be bewitched, at the very least, to yield control so quickly?"

She nibbled her lower lip. "That is a concern."

"Of greater concern is Simon's taking him off on some fool's adventure. No strong-arms, few weapons, no indication of where they're going—who knows what mischief this Simon has in store? I couldn't bear . . ."

Merrihana fingered her throat. "Bear what?"

Ghedo pictured the slaughter of his mother—at the hands of his father. No imaginary image, but a stony memory. A tear came, the first since that horrific night when he was but four years old. That fool Alrod got to keep his own mother into her old age.

"I couldn't bear for him to be lost."

Sorcerers were denied such comfort, the better to bond with the men they served. Shouldn't there be loyalty in return?

"I know." Merrihana was a hard-shelled woman with an easy cruelty but, with proper handling, she could be mustered to sympathy.

"Worse yet . . ." Ghedo again reached for the door. "No. I've said too much."

"What?" She pulled him to her, her eyes searching his face.

Unused to such close inspection, Ghedo shuddered, enhancing the effect he had worked to achieve. "I can't bear for Traxx to fall. Should he keep up these insane adventures with Simon, I fear it will."

"What can we do?"

"I'm working on something."

"What? Tell me."

Ghedo shook his head. "Too early. But I do have a special surprise for you, my dear. Something to amuse you while we work through this situation."

She smiled. "Really? And that might be . . . ?"

"Tonight, at court." He bowed, put his veil back in place, and left her to simmer in what he had brewed.

Niki and Timothy stood with Ghedo in a gilded hallway, awaiting their audience with the baroness. A scuffle behind them turned their heads just in time to see a strong-arm dragging Anastasia toward them.

"Hold up there!" he bellowed. "This'un claims to belong to Nikolette of Finway. Says she has a gift for the baroness."

Ghedo raised his eyebrows at Niki. "This girl is your property?"

"I sent her to buy a gift to present to Merrihana. Looks like she found trouble instead."

Anastasia prayed that the gift she had made in the sorcerer's own lair would pass muster. "It took me quite some time to find something unique, mistress. I'm sorry for the delay."

"Get up, girl," Ghedo said, "Show me this gift."

She unfolded the length of silk and showed them what she had made with the sorcerer's own esters and lanolin.

Ghedo frowned. "Soap? Shaped like a sword?"

Niki glared. "This is supposed to please the baroness?"

"Well, I was thinking more the baron. You see, I found this reward poster." Anastasia quickly unfolded the one Gabe had given her. "And keeping in mind that you said to get something unique—well, I know the baron and baroness already have gold and jewelry and silks and furs and art and sculpture and—"

"Get to the point, girl," Niki said.

"Well, you see, mistress"—Anastasia dropped into a curtsy—"And you also, your greatness—"

"*Sorcerer* will do," Ghedo said dryly.

"It occurred to me that the high and mighty ones would enjoy having a life-sized soap made in the likeness of an outrider sword." She poked the paper for effect. "Like that one."

Niki looked about to explode. "Whatever for?"

"Why—"Anastasia turned to the sorcerer, injecting as much innocence into her smile as her revulsion would allow "—so they can watch it dissolve into bubbles. They could toss it into their bath. Or I've heard there's a fountain right here at court. Her high and mightiness could amuse her guests by putting it in there and watching it just melt away. For surely that is the fate of any who dare cross the rulers of Traxx. Is it not?"

"Merrihana will love this," Ghedo said, laughing so hard his robe shook. "I may just buy this little drudge from you, Nikolette. She's odd-witted, and that amuses me."

Niki glared. "The girl is a trial. I will not sell her because I plan to personally tan her hide when we get back home."

If we live to get back home, Anastasia thought.

In the three weeks since Timothy had last been here, the royal court had changed. The inside wall that had sparkled with diamond and topaz dust now featured rose petals and butterflies in a continuous flow, lending a sweet scent to the air. The gold-filigree chandeliers had been replaced with jade. The grey granite floor remained in place but was covered with lush carpets of real grass.

The middle of the chamber was terraced, with blooming rosebushes on each step. The pool that once held bioluminescent fish now featured three beautiful women and one handsome man. Their legs had been mogged into glistening fishtails, like the mermaids and mermen of yore. The fountain in the middle sprayed high, cooling the air of its summer heat.

The change was disorienting. Timothy turned to Ghedo. "If I may, sorcerer?"

"What?"

"When that horrible man brought me here awhile ago, everything was different."

Ghedo looked at him sideways. Remarkable how the man could show disdain solely with his eyes. "That concerns you?"

Niki pulled his ear. "Answer the man, for he is kind enough to spare time for us."

"It confuses me."

The sorcerer waved dismissively. "Constant change is necessary, or the people who frequent this place grow peevish. Should you please the baroness, you'll see some impressive—but useless—affectations."

"Of which my minstrel surely is one," Niki said.

Ghedo raised his eyebrow. "I thought you had fondness for him."

"I change affection as the royal court changes its décor." She fluttered her eyes, making Timothy almost burst with laughter. "Such change often comes with great passion."

Ghedo was clearly taken aback. Groups of courtiers parted as they passed, each unwilling to even let the sorcerer's cloak touch them. It was unheard of that a woman would actually flirt with a man as feared as he. Timothy couldn't wait to get back to Horesh and tell their comrades how skilled Niki was at wooing.

But would he be returning to Horesh at all? Dawnray wouldn't be welcome there, and Timothy was coming to believe he couldn't live anywhere without her. Would he see her tonight?

The sorcerer led them to his private alcove, raised above the general seating and separated from the crowds by snakelike ropes. Except these really were snakes, six feet long, mogged very thin, and twined to form a bizarre cord.

"Wait here. I'll go to the baroness and tell her that tonight's entertainment has arrived." Ghedo pointed at Timothy. "Do not sing until I return. Merrihana will not be pleased if you favor these people before you honor her."

"He'll be quiet," Niki said.

"Good."

"You won't be long, will you?"

Ghedo touched her cheek. "Does the décor of my alcove frighten you?"

Niki laughed. "I like snakes."

The sorcerer's only reply was *hmm*. He left, the nobles and wealthy once again parting to make room.

Timothy nudged her. "Laying it on a bit thick, Niki?"

"Hey, I'm like these fools. Easily bored." She whirled to Anastasia. "As for you . . ."

The girl reddened as Niki pulled her close. "Where's our weapons, rook?"

She mumbled something.

"What?"

"I lost them," Anastasia said. "Not lost—I got attacked and had to jump back into the thorns. And when I came out, they were gone."

"All of them?"

Anastasia held out the silk-wrapped soap. "Except this."

Niki's eyes bulged. "My sword is actually inside that stupid soap?"

"Shush, Niki." Timothy turned to Anastasia. "You lost my sword?"

She nodded. "I am so sorry, Timmy."

"Serves you right," Niki said. "You wanted her, *Timmy*. I wanted to bring Kwesi."

"It'll work out," Anastasia said.

"Are you insane?" Niki pressed her fists to her head. "Or are you just intent on driving me crazy? How do I get the sword out of that soap without everyone at court—including Ghedo—seeing it?"

Anastasia grinned. "I have a plan."

Niki collapsed into a chair. "You might as well tell me. Sit down. On the floor, you fool. You're a drudge, remember?"

While Anastasia whispered to Niki, Timothy slipped his gittern from its bag. He pressed his hands over the strings with a light touch so that he alone could hear its music. People stared over at them with interest. Carin had told him that Ghedo almost never came to court. Did these people know of the sorcerer's demotion? Surely they did—if only from his altered costume. If there was only some way to let Brady know. It was harrowing to be inside this stronghold and not have birds who could carry a message.

Ghedo entered on the dais, with Merrihana on his arm. A dark-haired girl followed them, strangely dressed in the same outfit as the baroness. Timothy squinted—the girl walked like Dawnray, but—what kind of game was this? She was Dawnray, her hair cut and dyed in an imitation of Merrihana's. He leaned forward, trying to catch her eye. But her gaze was flat, her despair having dulled to apathy.

Was she already pregnant? He had to grit his teeth not to groan at the image of Alrod touching her.

Ghedo left the baroness and made his way to the alcove. They sat in shadow until after the court herald cried out Merrihana's superlatives and bid the evening begin. The baroness let her hand fall toward the sorcerer while her gaze remained forward, feigning indifference.

The sorcerer grabbed Timothy by the arm and brought him before the throne. Niki followed, with Anastasia in her wake. "I have to tell you about a promise I made," Timothy heard the girl whisper.

"Are you insane? Later."

"But Niki . . ."

"Sing," Ghedo hissed.

Timothy released the strings, and a sweet hum filled the chamber. He pressed the strings deftly, calling forth chords that stirred Merrihana's interest.

He began his song.

> *Living life is easy when you're playing your own game.*
> *You are your destiny . . .*

At the sound of his voice, Dawnray jerked as if a puppet tugged by a string. She turned to him, her face ablaze. She stepped toward the edge of the dais. Mercifully, before she could cry out, her eyes rolled back. Timothy leaped forward and caught her in one arm before she fell from the dais to the hard marble.

"Well, the girl does make a spectacle," Merrihana said, clearly miffed.

"If I may?" Timothy handed the gittern to Niki. He hoisted Dawnray—still unconscious—up to the dais so that she sprawled at the baroness's feet. "Since she is such a pallid imitation of you, high and mighty, I suggest she is best left where a shadow belongs."

Merrihana laughed, clasping her hands with glee.

Niki handed Timothy the gittern and he resumed his song, his gaze rapt on Merrihana, his heart beating for the woman who lay crumpled at her feet.

SEVENTEEN

MERRIHANA CLEARED THE COURT, BUT ORDERED HER personal guard to remain.

Niki heard every breath each of the six took, felt every shift of their feet as if it were her own. She knew the weapons they carried, which hand they favored, what the best escape routes from this court were.

Timothy would have made the same observations and would know what to do if they were challenged. What of that pebble-brained rook? Could Anastasia keep up with them if they had to run for their lives? And what good was a sword encased in soap?

The flush on Merrihana's throat hinted at her eagerness. She seemed oblivious to the poor woman who lay crumpled at her feet. At least the girl was alive, though what purpose her copycat hair and dress served, only an idiot would waste a thought on.

Niki needed to stay alert for the impending interrogation. She had threatened to pull Anastasia's teeth out if she uttered a word. It would be tricky enough to get Merrihana and Ghedo to buy their tale. At least they didn't have Alrod to contend with, though his whereabouts were yet another worry. Niki knew well enough that the baron prowled like a lion, leaving carcasses in his wake.

"Welcome back, minstrel," Merrihana said.

Timothy bowed.

"And your . . . mistress, is it?"

Niki bowed, remembering too late to drop into a curtsy as

Anastasia had. "Nikolette of Upper Finway. Thanks for see-ing me."

"This minstrel belongs to you?"

"To my father."

"Do you have the right to sell him?"

"If I don't sell him, my father will kill him." Niki rubbed her eyes, wiping away pretend tears.

Merrihana leaned forward. "And why is that?"

"Baroness, if I may?" Ghedo stepped forward. "Before we hear Nikolette's tale, we need to clear up some previous business."

"Ah, yes. My sorcerer reminds me that this minstrel came into court last month under very nefarious circumstances." Merrihana raised her eyebrows at Timothy. "Before you and I negotiate one whit, Nikolette, I need to hear why he went flying out of a palace window with that criminal."

Timothy looked at Niki. "May I?"

She nodded, amazed that he always kept his composure—something she'd never be accused of.

"High and mighty, it's a complicated story. You see, my mistress Nikolette has been very kind to me. In her father's eyes, too kind. He sold me to this man without telling her. And that's how I came to court."

They had agreed to let Merrihana pry their cover story out of them. Should they supply too much information up front, Ghedo would realize that they deliberately anticipated his suspicions.

Ghedo studied his nails, pretending to be bored. "And the man's name?"

"He said it was Moses."

"Moses? Are you sure?"

"I'd never heard of such a name either. But I've never been out of our mountains, so how would I know?"

"Strange name. Are you sure that's what he said?"

"Strange name to fit a very strange man. Perhaps he made it up."

"Do you know why he was interested in you?" Ghedo's tone was flat.

"He said he knew a woman who would pay a good price for my fair voice." Timothy pretended to risk a glance at the baroness. "Said she'd treat me well."

Merrihana looked about to jump off her throne. "Ghedo, perhaps—"

The sorcerer touched her arm. "Another couple of questions, and then he can sing for you in private." He jumped off the dais and grabbed Timothy's ear, his voice suddenly rough. "Why did you run away with him?"

Timothy shrank into himself. "He had my gittern."

What good frauds we are, Niki thought, proud and ashamed at the same time.

"Your what?"

Timothy motioned to his instrument case. "It's worth diving out of a window for, because it's unique. He held it for ransom. Threatened to stomp it to bits if I didn't do exactly what he wanted."

Ghedo opened the case, jumping back as the hum rose from the gittern's strings. "Is this magic?"

Timothy shrugged. "I don't know."

The sorcerer glared at Niki. "Do you?"

"A gypsy heard him sing, said he needed to have the gittern. It's been in my father's house for four years, never caused harm." She glanced up at Merrihana. "And it has brought much pleasure."

Ghedo handed the gittern to Timothy. "Where did this Brady go after you went through the window?"

Careful, Niki signed. *Trick.*

"Who?" Timothy said, brow furrowed.

"Brady."

"I don't know who—oh, do you mean Moses?"

"The man with the blue eyes."

"No. Moses had strange brownish-green eyes. Everything about him was strange."

"How did you leave the stronghold?"

"We didn't."

"We searched it from top to bottom."

Niki brushed her hair back, risking the *take care* signal again.

"I'm ashamed," Timothy said, his head low. "Do I have to say in front of the ladies?"

Ghedo glared openly. "Yes."

With his gaze locked on the baroness, Timothy spun around. "I've bathed since."

The sorcerer backhanded him. Timothy went to his knees.

"Enough of that," Merrihana whispered.

"There will be more if I don't get answers when I ask," Ghedo said. "I didn't ask about your bathing schedule. I want to know how you stayed in this stronghold undiscovered."

"A manure pile," Timothy said. "But I've bathed and bathed. Had to dig cow dung out of my ears for days."

Anastasia snorted, disguising her laughter with a coughing fit. Merrihana smiled.

"A manure pile?" Ghedo was not at all amused.

"He held me there with him. Said I was too valuable to waste. We breathed through corn stalks for a full day." He looked up at Merrihana. "It was dreadful. Very hot, because manure brews, you know."

"I did not know that," she said, gracing him with a smile.

How strange, Niki thought. This murderous woman is absolutely smitten with Timothy.

"How did you get out?" Ghedo said.

"In the dead of night. On the garbage wagon. No one noticed us because the smell made us fit right in."

"And you didn't cry out, or try to escape?"

Timothy wiped away imaginary tears. "He said no one would want me after being in the manure pile. That you'd skewer me and throw me on the fire, and my gittern with me. I'm sorry, mistress Nikolette. Now that they know, they'll not want me here."

"A manure pile." Ghedo paced. Suddenly, he stopped and got

in Niki's face, his veil fluttering with hot breath. "And how did you get him back?"

"Once I found out what my father had done—and it took almost a week—I jumped on my best horse and aimed for Traxx. The outer lands know that the baroness is a lover of the arts, especially music. Timothy was on his way back to me by then. I met him on the main thoroughfare, singing for food."

Ghedo whirled to face Timothy. "How did you escape Brady?"

"Who? Oh, Moses. I didn't. He just . . . let me go. He had desperately wanted to sell me here at Traxx and then, suddenly, he didn't want me. I asked why he didn't just leave me for the baroness, and he said something nasty."

"What?"

Timothy winced. "Please don't make me say it in front of her. She's a beautiful lady. I've never seen anyone like her."

Ghedo rolled his eyes and motioned Timothy to whisper again.

"Tell me," Merrihana said.

"You tell her," Timothy said. "Please sorcerer. Don't make me."

"He said you were a black-hearted witch and didn't deserve him," the sorcerer said.

Timothy rushed to the dais. The strong-arms moved forward but Merrihana waved them back. He pressed his face to her slippers. "He said it—but it's not true. And I know I don't deserve this second opportunity to brighten your day, but I'm so grateful for it. Thank you, high and mighty. Thank you."

Niki fought a sudden wave of fury. It wasn't right that they should ever have to bow before these . . . these swine. She felt Anastasia touch her hand—she hadn't even known it was balled into a fist. With great effort she relaxed it and pushed her lips into a smile.

"Enough," Ghedo said.

"I need to speak to Nikolette," Merrihana said.

"Yes, we'll hear from her now," Ghedo said.

"Alone."

"Wait!" Anastasia jumped up.

Niki wanted to strangle her.

"A drudge speaks?" Merrihana snapped her fingers at the guards. "Get her out of here."

"Please, Baroness. She only wants to present the gift we brought for you," Niki said.

Merrihana glanced at Ghedo. "It will make you smile," he said. "Take a look."

She waved Anastasia forward, laughed when she saw the soap cast as a sword and heard the explanation of what it represented.

"Shall I put it in the pool, high and mighty? It can float and bubble while you talk."

"No. We'll save it for my husband. He'll love it."

"We don't know when he'll be back," Ghedo said. "You should enjoy this mockery of the outriders."

"Oh, all right."

Anastasia ran to the pool, soap held over her head. She tossed it in. The spray from the fountain roused bubbles immediately. Niki prayed that this empty-headed plan of Anastasia's would work. Not that they had much choice at this point . . .

"Now, can we clear the court?" Merrihana said. "I need to speak with this woman alone."

"Not until I am sure she's not a threat," Ghedo said.

"Sorcerer!" The baroness stood, every inch the terror of the lands and not the lovesick patroness of music.

Ghedo bowed. "We'll wait in my alcove so you two can speak privately—but I want to keep you in sight."

"Fine."

"What about her?" He pointed to the unconscious woman.

"The lolly? Leave her—she amuses me like that."

Anastasia scurried forward. "Requesting pardon?"

"Now what?"

"May I remain at the pool and stir the bubbles? It's far away. I won't eavesdrop."

Merrihana rolled her eyes. "Just go." She waited for the others to retreat, then motioned Niki to join her on the dais. This time Niki remembered to curtsy.

"You have considerable trouble with your drudges," Merrihana said.

Niki laughed. "I do—but I cause considerable trouble as well. I come from a troublesome people."

"Will you cause trouble for me?" the baroness said. "Am I to consider you a rival?"

"Truthfully?" Niki said. "A week ago, perhaps."

"And now?"

"I've seen the bigger world outside my mountains. And I've enjoyed those I've met." Niki glanced at Ghedo, a quick flick of her eyes.

The baroness caught the gesture and smiled. "Even those others might fear?"

Niki imagined how lovely it would be to rip that veil off Ghedo's face and slap him soundly. "Especially those."

"Why was your father threatened by the minstrel?"

"Baroness, I will admit to you, woman to woman—I am a tad headstrong. Our minstrel is extremely pleasing, especially to the eyes and ears. But he was merely a dalliance—until my father told me no. Then I absolutely had to have him. Since we're not nobility, I could by law and custom buy out his indenture and marry him. Papa yelled, I yelled louder, he threatened, I threatened louder and"—Niki laughed—"before I knew it, my poor father was flagging down strangers on the road, seeking to sell the minstrel."

"Will he try to follow you back home?"

Niki glanced sideways. "You tell me."

Merrihana extended a tiny mirror from her pocket. Niki knew the reflection would show Timothy gazing directly at her with puppy-dog eyes.

A huge splash interrupted them. From across the court, Anastasia waved from the pool. "I'm all right. Don't worry about me."

"We can only hope she drowns," Niki said.

Merrihana laughed.

"Maybe I should sell her as well. You could use a court jester."

"My interest is only in exquisite music, not clowns. What if the minstrel dissatisfies me or if I tire of him?"

"I already told the sorcerer my one condition of sale. I only ask that you not kill him. Sell him, set him free, put him in the kitchen. But such a talent is so rare that we all have an obligation to preserve it. Will you swear, high and mighty?"

"Nikolette, you have nothing to fear on that account."

"But your husband—he is known for his strength and . . . and . . ."

"And his ruthlessness?"

Niki nodded. "I would have liked to meet him."

"Be assured, miss. Whatever pleases me very much pleases my husband."

Niki sighed. "Men are a trial, are they not, Baroness?"

"I couldn't agree more." Merrihana laughed, her hand on Niki's arm.

Niki pasted on her smile once more, praying fervently for patience because she had had just about as much of this place as she could stand. She had thought men like Alrod and Ghedo were the ones most responsible for the horrible state of the world. But truly, weren't the Merrihanas even more to blame?

Alrod and Ghedo sought power to rule lands and people. But Merrihana just wanted to be amused. And so people starved and suffered and wept, species were profaned, creation was mocked—all so Merrihana and her ilk could have a spot of entertainment.

Niki hazarded a glance over toward Anastasia and the fountain. Merrihana and Ghedo would not be amused to find that the entertaining piece of soap the rook pushed about in the water covered a razor-sharp blade.

Nor would they be pleased to discover that Nikolette and her minstrel were equally sharp—and dangerous.

"You've brought me a great gift, sorcerer."

"The only gift I bring is the burden to decide the minstrel's fate. Consider carefully if you should go through with this, Merrihana," Ghedo said. "Alrod wants the minstrel dead."

"He thought he was in league with that Brady of Horesh."

"I'm still not convinced he wasn't."

"You're sounding as paranoid as my husband."

"Am I?"

"Yes."

Ghedo paced. "Perhaps I am."

"Paranoid?"

"Alrod is on the edge, and perhaps I've gone there with him. But I'm starting to believe this all has gone too far."

Merrihana said nothing, but her breathing accelerated.

"Paranoia is dangerous," Ghedo whispered. "A fear of what is not real."

"I know."

"He's been obsessed for so long. First with besting Treffyn. Then with the outriders. Now he's off with this sorcerer, a fraud who could be anyone—a spy from Holt or even from Slade."

"No," she said, considering. "He's something more than just a spy."

"My point is that Alrod, paranoid about what's not real, has nevertheless let a very real threat right into his confidence. And then he traipsed off with the man after knowing him for just a couple of days."

"I know, I know."

"What more can I do? I searched out the baron, found him training three farm boys. He claimed they were his new army. Yes, they were good-looking and strong, but what can any leader—even a great one—do with only three soldiers? He chased me away. I begged him to come with me, but he said he didn't need me, that

Simon was building him a powerful army." Ghedo exhaled dramatically. "I'm afraid for him, Merrihana. I really am."

"I am, too, Ghedo."

"What should we do?"

"You said you had an idea."

Ghedo resumed pacing. "Perhaps I spoke too soon. I don't want to act precipitously and put something into action that could hurt more than help. But I also don't want to wait until the kingdom falls down around our ears. I believe I need to take action to protect Traxx. And to protect you, Merrihana. Alrod may have forgotten—but I have not—that you are also the rightful ruler of this stronghold."

She nodded slightly. "I appreciate that."

"Merrihana, thank you for listening. This has been a tremendous burden on my heart."

"Mine, as well."

"We'll hope for the best."

"Yes, we will." Her skirts rustled as she stood. "But we won't wait forever for the worst."

Ghedo waited until she left before he smiled.

EIGHTEEN

THE FIRST HOUR, A ROBIN HAD COME. IT SANG A DETAILED description of where Taryan was.

A finch came the second, another robin the third.

There was no fourth bird.

As the day wore on, Ajoba searched the sky. Cooper's gaze turned inward, his eyes haunted from picking over six marauder bodies and then burying them. Ajoba tended to as many of the wounded villagers as she could.

She soon learned that the wounds were not just physical. The citizens of Fenside had always been hardy and self-sufficient, traveling to the bigger world only to sell their grain and corn oil. They knew about marauders, mogs, and strong-arms, but had imagined their isolated location would keep them from such evil. Now they struggled not only with their natural grief and pain, but with a crippling fear that such an event might happen again.

Sixteen women had been terrorized, six actually raped. One of them—a woman named Hannah—was nearly inconsolable over the loss of her husband, Beck. After many words, Ajoba just took her in her arms and sang the lullaby that her own mother had sung to her. *Close your eyes and sleep, dream of wishes sweet . . .*

Brady had not awakened. At first, Cooper and Ajoba took turns pressing their hand against his wound. Eventually, she enlisted children for the task. There was just too much to do in the settlement—such as figuring out a way to fend off another attack should it come.

Cooper was too inexperienced to advise how to set up defenses. Ajoba too was stymied until she imagined herself as Brady; then she began seeing opportunities with every glance. Low-hanging trees made perfect cover for hiding rocks that could be dropped on invaders. The branches were close enough that children could move from one tree to another and escape capture. *What kind of a world was this where children must . . .* But she didn't have to finish the thought. She'd made transit a year ago, and since then she'd seen a lifetime worth of horror.

Ajoba taught the older children how to hollow the middle of their plentiful cornstalks, fill them with the alcohol made from their grain, and bind them as firetraps. A single burning arrow could explode them in sequence and trap a dozen men. She tested for the two best archers and set them to making perches from which they could strike.

She took the strongest fighters, mostly men but some women, and sent them scrounging for weapons. Shovels and picks had not driven off the marauders the first time. At the very least, they needed to add spears and slings to their weaponry.

Ajoba puzzled over how to make spears with the paucity of saplings in the area—the trees that protected Fenside could clearly not be spared. An enterprising grandmother showed her the way—split a cornstalk, sharpen its end, tamp it with clay, and bake it in a slow fire. A cornstalk spear would last for only one blow, but could be quickly replaced. The supply of dried corn-stalks was almost endless—the roofs were thatched with them. Better to live without roofs until harvest than not live at all.

In the middle of the afternoon, Cooper returned from burial detail, his face smeared with mud and streaked by tears. Ajoba washed his face like a mother would. "You all right?"

He shrugged. "How's Brady?"

"Let's go check."

A starling perched on the roof of the hut where Brady lay. Cooper brightened. "Must be from Taryan."

"Shush. Let me listen. It's from Dano. They've been collecting steadily, making good progress with their lists. But they only have two pieces of shroud left. He's asking what he should do."

"Oh. Hmm. What will you tell them?"

"That's not my place to say."

She went in, Cooper on her heels. The sheepdog Brady had rescued still sat watchfully at his side, eyes fixed on the unconscious man. Katje, a little girl with a freckled nose, dutifully held her hand against Brady's bandage, stained bright red. A boy not much older than a toddler dabbed his brow with a damp cloth.

"We're doing the best we can, lady," the girl said.

"Thank you. Could I get in there for a minute?"

Ajoba lifted the bandage, saw that blood still seeped around the stitches. She pressed on Brady's stomach, thankful not to feel fluid under his skin. Blood could be pooling under his back. But he was too heavy for her to roll, and there was no remedy to offer anyway.

His face had a gray cast, and the lines around his mouth were pronounced. Her throat clenched at the sight of the scarred stump where his finger had been. She pinched the back of his hand. The skin stayed tented. He was dehydrated from loss of blood.

Forbidden to take anything off the Ark—including simple medical supplies like intravenous needles and lines—birthrighters often improvised. But she hadn't Kendo's skill to carve a chicken bone into a needle tiny enough to feed fluid into a vein. If she could wake Brady, perhaps she could get him to drink.

"Brady. Can you hear me?"

The bird had followed them in, squawking.

"What's it saying?"

"It's not messaging. The bird feels Brady's distress. They love him, you know, even the ones that don't nest at Horesh."

She lay her hand on Brady's chest, dismayed to feel the stutter of his heart. If he had been wearing his armor, he would not be lying here. What would have been lost to let her spin new shroud and make more armor?

"Cooper, how far away is Dano's crew?" Her head for numbers was weak, but the rook had a real gift for coordinates and locations.

"He's a two day ride to the west."

Ajoba touched Brady's cheek. "I know you're weary, but could you wake up for just a minute? Dano is almost out of shroud. What should I tell him?"

His only answer was a rasp in his throat.

She put her mouth to his ear. "Taryan is missing. Should I go look for her?"

He moaned and threw up his arm with such force that the stitching in his side tore, causing another crimson gush. Ajoba pressed the bandage back into place.

She couldn't let this go on. Brady was too necessary to the Birthright Project to let him die from his own stubbornness. "Get me his pack. I need some shroud."

He looked inside. "But there's only one piece left."

"Give it to me."

"He said . . ."

"Would you deny Brady the chance to live?"

He shook his head.

"Give it to me."

It was a small square, suitable for a mouse-sized collection and nothing more. The cloth stung her hand, a familiar comfort. One hand, burning with shroud. The other hand, burning with blood.

Horesh depended on Brady—his wisdom, courage, boldness, creativity. His humor and thoughtfulness lifted their every care. His deep love for God helped keep theirs strong. Surely it was right to do everything in her power to save him.

One hand, burning with shroud. The other hand, burning with blood.

This was simply a matter of switching hands and stuffing the wound with shroud. The bleeding would stop, suspended out-of-time until Taryan returned.

The starling took flight, squawking its leave. If no one answered it, the bird would fly back and message "no answer." Maybe that was for the best. Let Dano worry about how to handle his shroud shortage. Though Ajoba rode with a crew, her role as a birthrighter was officially suspended. Perhaps she'd never be one again. Who was this bird to demand an answer from her?

Who was she to allow Brady's blood to flow through her fingers? Wouldn't it be an act of mercy to do the best she could to save him?

Ajoba brought the shroud to his side.

Behind her, Cooper's breathing sped up. He wanted this for Brady as much as she did. The bird swooped one last time and made for the door.

Horesh depended on him. But on whom did Brady depend? Surely not Ajoba. And though the shroud was heaven-sent, he didn't even depend on that.

"Wait," she whistled. Ajoba wet her lips and spoke as clearly as she could. Starlings were good mimics and thus good messengers, but she wanted no mistake as she spoke her instruction. She added a blessing and whistled the bird away to deliver her message:

Make do with the shroud you have, Dano.

She gave the piece of shroud back to Cooper and pressed a clean cloth to Brady's side.

The flow of blood slowed. But it did not stop.

The new army of Traxx grew slowly but nicely. Ten young men had been converted into ten fierce fighters, with bodies of iron and wills unformed and malleable, subject to Alrod's whim and pleasure.

Dusk fell. Alrod's men built a cooking fire and cleaned the deer they had killed with their bare hands. Simon had vanished midafternoon and only now appeared at Alrod's side as he whetted his dagger. He had shed his traveler's disguise in favor of his sorcerer's robe and veil.

"Where have you been?"

"Roaming about."

"Doing what? Take that veil off so I can see your blasted face."

Simon removed his veil. "Better? Or should I remove my cloak also?"

Alrod had never seen the man's body. He could be some complex mog, some foul creature foisted on him by Prince Treffyn. Why had he not insisted on the customary exam before accepting the man's offer of service?

Because somehow Simon had dulled his every caution and stirred his every passion.

"Yes. Take off your cloak."

"You seek my secrets."

"And if I do?" Alrod stood.

"You only needed to ask. My only condition is that we need privacy." Simon threw something into the fire, and a wall of flame rose up to surround them.

"How do you do that?" Alrod whispered.

"Are you a slow learner? I've already told you. It comes from you."

"Show me what you've got under that cloak."

Simon gazed at the wall of flames, and they arched up and over, sucking the air out of this burning sphere and yet pumping something into Alrod that he had lusted and fought and lied and killed for. And so when his sorcerer shrugged off his cloak to reveal what lay underneath, the baron did not flinch.

Simon's ribs and arms and spine were not made of marrow and bone, but somehow stacked with rings of noise—cries of desire and loathing and fear and jealousy that broke through as individual voices now: *Give me . . . pleasure me . . . fear me . . . worship me.*

Alrod recognized his own as the strongest and most pure of the voices, one refrain over and over: *I will reign over all.*

"This does not explain where you go in your frequent absences. And why you think it is fitting to leave me." Alrod had to shout to be heard over the clamor of the sorcerer's body.

Simon pulled his cloak back on, silencing the din. "It is fitting because I serve you wherever I am. As to where I go, I have many strongholds I must tend to. When a crack in the door develops, I need to rush off and block it."

"I thought you served only me."

"I serve you, even when I serve these others—for you will reign over all that I sustain."

"Show me."

"Not now." Simon wiped his brow in the first gesture of fatigue Alrod had ever seen in him.

"Now," he insisted.

"In time."

"I will not add my glory to your intrigues, Simon, unless I see the others."

"To see, you must touch my shoulder."

"I touch your shoulder each time we commission a soldier."

"Without the cloak."

"I . . ." Why was he hesitating? It showed weakness.

"Not weakness. Wisdom," Simon said, answering his unspoken thought. "Will you see what you will rule, or will you trust me?"

"Take off the cloak."

Simon tossed it aside. The flesh on his hands roiled, each tendon and joint singing its own refrain. The left hand shouted every possible synonym for rape, while the right screamed with every variation of murder.

Alrod stepped toward Simon, his left hand outstretched.

"Your sword hand. Otherwise, you're leading with weakness."

Alrod placed his right hand on Simon's naked shoulder. And fell down the same glittering hole. But this time, it spoke to him—*Take*—and sang to him—*Enjoy*—and shouted at him—*Destroy!*

Suddenly he was in Ghedo's lair, in the grotto where the man mogged smaller creatures. Ghedo spoke to a young man, something about a throne, but Alrod couldn't catch the meaning, nor could he see the face of the person he spoke to. Under the table was a bright light, as if a fire burned there. "What is he saying?"

"You trained Ghedo well," Simon said. "He schemes as well as any I have enjoyed."

"What? You don't serve him."

Simon laughed. "No. He serves me, and he will yet serve you, Baron."

"Who is the boy he speaks to?"

"What boy?"

"Don't you see him?"

Simon grasped Alrod and turned him into a whirlwind of screams, pleasurable at first but of such tenacity that he became bored. They were in the streets of a stronghold. "This isn't Traxx," Alrod said.

"You don't recognize Slade?"

"I've never been here."

"I offer it to you." Simon bowed low.

"Now?"

"In time. If you want it."

Alrod straightened, taking as regal a pose as possible with his hand somehow glued to the sorcerer's shoulder. He walked through the streets, stunned not to see the same riches that adorned his own stronghold. Shops and houses were orderly but utilitarian. People dressed plainly and moved with purpose.

"Look more closely at them," Simon whispered.

"Why? Are they mogs?"

Simon laughed. "Treffyn doesn't use potions to build himself an army and ensure its loyalty. Look closely, even at the women."

Alrod stepped into a crowd, pleased that no one challenged his presence. *They don't see me,* he realized. *What an amazing power to have.* No one seemed to be older than their mid-twenties, though plenty of children ran about in the only purposeless action on this street. All had upturned noses, dimpled chins, and strawberry-blond hair. And there was something odd about them.

It took him a minute to figure out just what it was. "They all look like Treffyn. Did he mog them such?"

A current of fire passed through Alrod, so fierce he thought his heart had erupted in flames. *Listen when I speak to you. I won't repeat myself because of your refusal to pay attention.*

"My apologies." Alrod chewed the side of his tongue, refusing to show his agony. The fire relented.

"Speak intelligently," Simon prompted.

"If they are not mogs, which you already assured me they are not, they must be related to Treffyn."

Simon smiled. "Indeed. The crafty prince of Slade, whom you dismiss as a dandy, has embarked on a traditional route for making a loyal people."

"He bred them?"

"Each one."

"But Slade has been populous for generations. Before we became hostile, the ambassador came to my father's court. His hair was black." A spark lit his eyelid. "No need, Simon. I'm just thinking aloud. No one here seems to be older than thirty. Which implies that the older generations have been eliminated."

"Don't use pretty words with me," Simon snapped. "Treffyn held them in camps and leeched their blood, one by one, to feed the wall that surrounds his stronghold. After a generation of his hard work—and hard pleasure—only his sons and daughters survived in this place."

"Brilliant."

"Is it? What of variety of experience and craft?" Simon said. "These people are of little use to me. You'll defeat them easily."

"When?" Alrod felt that familiar urge—he had coveted Slade since he ascended the throne. Control of Slade meant control of the Grand River and all the rich territories downstream.

"In time. Shall we return to your troops, Baron?"

"No. This is like taking me to a garbage dump or the drudge

town. I demand you show me something of value. Show me everywhere you have been, everywhere you go."

The fire raced through his veins again, but Alrod was ready for it. "You dare resist?" Simon said.

"You need me as much as I need you, Simon."

The fire died. Simon bowed. "I will be happy to comply. But you had better hold tight, because few could survive this trip."

"Don't try scare tactics. I insist on seeing it all."

"Not scare tactics, Baron. I am telling the truth."

"Now, Simon."

Simon wrapped his arms around Alrod, and together they fell into that glittering pit. So long, so dark, so cold, though fire licked through star-sized holes. Somehow Alrod knew there would be a time when all would be gathered into this pit and shaken like diamonds in a jar until a fire like none other blazed.

As they fell, the world sped by, scenes playing out as if pictures on ruffled pages. But no book could make one's skin ache with craving, one's tongue long to taste and drink and consume.

Alrod was startled to see his father driving a knife into a woman's heart and handing a baby to his mother—confirming Alrod's lifelong fear, that he had been born of a lolly.

He watched his grandfather beat a boy so viciously with a stick that the boy's flesh hung in strips from his back. The boy was his father, who had willingly passed the pain along to Alrod.

And so they flew backward in time—Alrod thinking that Simon's magic must be long-lived and very powerful. Alrod grasped the sorcerer's ribs, ignoring the screams that leaked through his fingers because there was much to see, much to know, and he would have it all.

He saw sorcerers under trees. A beautiful horse tied to the ground with needles in its eyes, its ears, being mogged to serve in battle. Strongholds growing up among villages. The wall of Slade, constructed not of stone but of millions of mogged skulls, bone hardened to be impenetrable and nearly unbearable to look at. Nearly. Alrod looked at it with admiration.

"The first sorcerer," Simon whispered, and Alrod beheld the man. Tiny and cramped, skin crusted, perhaps from toxland exposure. Breaking through a door in the side of a mountain. When it finally opened, the old man wept with joy. Alrod followed them in, finding a cavern almost incomprehensible to his eyes—gleaming steel shelves, glass and steel vials, too many things that he could not recognize. Something wailed and lights flashed, but the man ignored all because the walls were lined with thousands and thousands of narrow glass vessels, each one marked with old wording that Alrod deciphered: *Shark. Alligator. Bone. Growth inhibitor.*

"The potions?"

"Yes. I drove the man to bash the door, though it took most of his life."

"Where did the potions come from? And why were they locked up?"

"Hold tighter, for I will withhold nothing."

The world exploded backward again, the toxlands spitting up fireballs, then taking back green grasses and flowing rivers and many houses of fine quality and soaring towers—which meant the myths had been true. Birds flew, but so did men in metal ships with wings. People raced around their bounteous strongholds in beetle-shaped wagons with no ox or horse to pull them. Men killed other men with streaks of light and explosions of blood.

Alrod and Simon circled the world, and it was the same everywhere, though the means of killing varied. Huge explosions of fire folded back into what had been before. Starving people with flesh stretched over bones watched while soldiers guarded piles of food. Time turned back and those same people were babies born to bright-eyed mothers. Would those mothers have choked their children at birth had they known what lay ahead?

Massive, shining buildings rose from a slash of fire. More fire, scattered in smaller bursts, yielded to structures of brick and ships that sailed a broad sea that Alrod had never seen. People crammed into a building, dying from a poisonous air. More of the same, cooked in ovens, yet somehow that strange light into which neither Alrod nor Simon could look surrounded them.

As they flew backward, Alrod saw that it became harder to kill people. Bayonets pulled out of men's chests and the men hid behind a tree, waiting for their opportunity to do the same. Piles of bodies marked with plagues were dragged off, the pox disappearing from the cities until one man walked a street, slapping at his calf as a flea bit him.

Light-skinned men in heavy armor fought darker-skinned men on fast horses, breaking apart, riding back leagues and oceans until they plotted in their own huts and tents and palaces.

Now an odd sight—people whose faces could not be seen because they were filled with light. He watched them conquering kingdoms, escaping mouths of lions, walking backward out of torture—but that meant, in this reverse tangle, that they had really walked willingly into torture. More of these people flamed like candles but with a light that wouldn't be snuffed—facing jeers and flogging, put in chains, stoned, shimmering blood flowing from a saw as a man came back together, his face so bright that Alrod covered his eyes.

They stopped on a high hill where three crosses stood.

"Behold, the place of my greatest triumph."

Alrod tried to look but was blinded by a light so brilliant it seared his brain. Someone whispered his name, but he couldn't bear to answer, didn't have time because he had a world to conquer.

They continued back, passing through cities and villages that looked much like Traxx but for the lack of mighty thorns and crushing mogs. Yet people still killed and people still died, some with faces of light and some with faces eaten away by worms.

They stopped. "Behold, Alrod—the site of my greatest triumph."

"But you said . . ."

No fire punished Alrod's question. Only a slow slither about his heart, a delicate satisfaction as they watched a woman chewing a succulent fruit, the meat going back to the fruit so the skin glistened. Her mouth slowly closed in the reversal of her first bite, the shimmer in her eyes showing only the fruit and nothing of the glory that glowed about them.

"If you're the man I think you are, Alrod—you will find the point of no return and savor it with me."

Surely no woman had ever been this lovely. She wandered back into a garden that was the sum of all gardens, her voice calling for a man that Alrod knew would be the sum of all men.

"Ready yourself. For we'll move forward into the moment. Find it and cherish it."

Time jerked forward, and the woman scanned the trees—so plentiful and bursting with fruit, but she sought only one. In the middle of the garden, a tree with that lustrous fruit. She wandered to it, and Alrod was there with her, between her and the tree she so earnestly sought, so he could see her face, feel her breath, read her eyes.

And then he saw it—the *sigh* that turned all time on its head. A flicker at first, but as it grew, it found its own joy and its own life.

Doubt.

Fueling this first doubt like water to a seedling, Simon whispered, "You will not surely die . . ."

The world spun forward again, and Alrod saw that flicker of doubt kill every man and woman who had ever lived, and he drank in the power of their spilled blood, singing his own tune to the screams of agony and pleas for mercy.

Until it all skidded to a stop. That hill again, blood and water running from a slumped form on a cross.

"The site of my greatest triumph," Simon crowed again.

A lone voice broke through the endless curses: *I AM THE WAY.*

Caught between life and death, triumph and failure, not knowing which was which and how one could be the other, vowing to know nothing but the one thing he did know, Alrod had only one response.

"I choose my own way."

In the same way, the Spirit helps us in our weakness. We do not know what we ought to pray for, but the Spirit himself intercedes for us with groans that words cannot express.

ROMANS 8:26

NINETEEN

AJOBA SAT IN THE DARKNESS, WHISTLING FOR HELP.

No bird had come from Taryan in almost a day. Brady's condition was grave. Taryan was missing. Ajoba had to send for Kendo. He was loyal and resourceful—he would know what to do. But how could she reach him if no bird would answer her?

Had there been some catastrophe? The toxlands were smoldering reminders of bombs that had chewed through the very essence of matter, swallowing everything in their path.

Dano's bird had gotten through. But it had come for Brady, not her.

Perhaps the birds no longer considered her a birthrighter. Ajoba's stomach soured at such a loss. She was still a woman of faith and had an obligation to serve the best she could. Should she go after Taryan? Take her horse and ride east to find Kendo? Stay and nurse Brady?

"What're you doing?" Cooper's words were thick with fatigue.

"Is Brady all right?"

"I checked. He's hanging in there."

"Good. But don't say 'hanging in.' It's jangle."

"Oh. Right. Sorry."

"Hey, it took me half a year to stop saying stuff like that. Changing the way you talk is a jam punchin' thing to do."

"Yea. I mean, aye. What're you doing?"

"Still trying to whistle down a bird. I don't know where they all went."

"I saw doves nesting in the rafters of the millhouse."

They walked across the settlement, signaling with enough frequency to keep from taking an arrow through the ear. Ajoba was pleased that Fenside had taken her warnings seriously. From inside a hut, Hannah still sobbed. Someone started up the same old lullaby. *I will be with you for always.*

They took great care in approaching the millhouse. The marauders had made their advance on the village by braving the rapids under the wheel, the noise and whitewater sufficient to mask their approach. To avoid such a sneak attack, Ajoba had set guards all about, pairing men with boys. The men would stay awake, and the boys would see more ably in the dark.

When they received the *all clear* signal, they went inside. The windows were now covered with cloth. Two men and three women worked by candlelight, reinforcing the main door and making shutters for the windows. The stone walls and slate roof made the millhouse a formidable fortress. If they could not fight off an invasion, they might be able to barricade themselves in here until help came.

The surviving village elder, a man named Curt, greeted them. His obvious look of respect took Ajoba aback. He thought her a military genius, but she had only done what Brady might have done.

"We're looking for doves," she said.

"Hmm. Haven't heard 'em for some time." He grabbed a dried corncob and flung it into the rafters. Nothing.

"Maybe I should climb up there," Cooper said.

"They would've scattered at that. They're gone."

A drowsy voice piped up from a corner. "Da, they flew off midafternoon. I worried they's expecting trouble."

Ajoba suppressed the urge to bite her fingernail.

"Were you hungry, miss? That why you're looking for a dove?"

"No, thanks. Keep on with what you're doing. We'll help tomorrow."

She and Cooper went back out into the night. "Now what?" Cooper said.

"Pray for me."

"I do."

"Right now."

Cooper bowed his head. Ajoba stared into the sky, counting the stars that crowded the heavens. She loved their silence, so vast compared with the chaos in her heart. Painful memories kept sounding in her ear. Kendo barking out, *You can't obey even the simplest request.* Brady as he sacrificed part of his hand for her, his voice cracking with pain, *You argue with me, even now?*

Taryan, with one last instruction. *Conduct yourself as a birthrighter.*

Ajoba had done all she could here to fortify Fenside's defenses, to see to Brady's wound, to soothe folks and offer hope.

Conduct yourself as a birthrighter.

Birthrighters do not abandon their comrades. Someone needed to find Taryan, and since she was the most senior birthrighter still standing, the job fell to Ajoba.

She loaded a bag with some food and added cloths in case she needed bandages. She strapped on her short blade, sharpened her dagger, and filled her water bag.

"Are you leaving me alone?" Cooper said.

Ajoba smiled. "You know better than that."

"But what . . . I've never . . . I don't . . ."

"Shush. You'll be fine. Keep up with the patrols, gather weapons where you can, watch the far side of the river. And take care of Brady."

"What if you don't come back either?" Cooper rubbed his arms so hard that Ajoba feared his sunburned skin would spark.

"Then you must persuade these people to leave. They keep refusing, but Cooper, you'll find the words. Follow the water upriver—not down, because of the toxlands. As soon as the birds return, send to Bartoly, Kendo, Dano for help. And take care of Brady."

"You already said that. Besides, I'd rather he took care of me."

"Conduct yourself as a birthrighter, mate." After hugging him,

Ajoba hopped onto her horse Lacey and headed to the site where Taryan had last reported from, studying the moon and the stars from horseback to locate the coordinates. It quickly became clear why Taryan had deviated so quickly from her planned circular route. She must have crossed a fresh track—from the marauders perhaps—and followed it. Ajoba prayed that Taryan had marked her own trail with signs only a birthrighter would look for.

By daylight, Ajoba had picked up a trail near Taryan's last report. Horses had come this way, carrying riders. She scuffled in the dirt, trying to exact a count. Ten, maybe, or a couple more? The marauders had numbered almost twice as many. Had they split up or was this yet another troop of bandits?

She scanned the area carefully, looking for a marker from Taryan. Finding none, she decided to track the horses for a little while. Within a league, she spotted a pile of rocks on a huge boulder. She counted the rocks and paced that many steps due north. Under some brush, she found the scratched code that indicated what Taryan had gotten into. *I'm following the riders southwest until I know who they are. I don't dare call a bird until I'm high enough that I can check the surrounding area, make sure there are no outlying guards. Take the same care, Ajoba, and don't do anything stupid.*

Ajoba? How did she know? Logical thinking. Even if Brady had regained consciousness, Taryan knew he would be in no shape to come after her.

It wasn't until hours later that Ajoba was able to climb to higher ground and get a good look at this territory. The rangeland would get drier and browner the further south she traveled. Through her spyglass she spotted a whirl of dust on the southern horizon. She could cut them off in a straight line, catching up in perhaps a couple of hours. But if Taryan had followed their trail, she might miss her.

Every few leagues, Ajoba found another marker from Taryan. Her coded scratchings took on a wry tone. *You're not supposed to be here.*

Further on, the tone changed. *If you're here, I'm in real trouble. Thank you, sister, but please pray—ask if you should go back.*

One last one read, *They're coming for me. I'll try to hide, but my tracks are as easy to read as theirs. I would have messaged all this, but where are the birds?*

The horsemen had made camp for the night. Ajoba decided to scout it out and see if they had captured Taryan.

She left her horse without tying her. If she suffered the same fate as Taryan, she didn't want Lacey trapped out here. She was well-fed, strong, and valuable. Someone would find her and take care of her.

Ajoba waited for darkness to fall before she approached the horsemen's camp. Guards were posted. Despite their strong faces and fierce stares, they seemed inexperienced. She crept past them, going slowly to keep from perspiring and thus keep her scent down.

She would creep and stop, creep and stop, just as Bartoly had taught her only a year ago. It seemed like a lifetime. Was it no wonder that after six years, Brady's hair was threaded with silver and Niki was snappish?

She passed four slumbering men. More handsome faces, but they slept soundly when they should be alert for danger. Were these nobles playing at being bandits?

Creep and stop. More men sleeping like babies.

A tent was set up across the way. It was plain cloth, certainly nothing a noble would camp in.

But there was something in the air. A scent. Two scents, in fact, that Ajoba knew well. One was Taryan—*Lord, please let her be untouched*—and the other was a scent that turned her stomach.

What was Baron Alrod doing this far south?

Which led to an obvious question—who were these men? Certainly not Alrod's usual soldiers. Traxx strong-arms were much better trained and coarser of face.

Ajoba found Taryan bound and gagged near the horses, with

no guard posted nearby. She slipped off Taryan's gag and sawed through the ropes on her hands.

"You came," Taryan whispered. "You weren't supposed to."

"Shush." Ajoba slipped her dagger between Taryan's ankles to cut through the rope. Taryan gave a silent scream, her mouth open wide.

"What? What's wrong?"

"Alrod broke my ankles."

"Both?"

She nodded, her face contorted with pain.

"That beast. I have to get you out of here. Where's your horse?"

Tears rolled down her cheeks. "Supper."

"They killed Sammy? Were they hungry?"

Taryan shook her head. "They did it to mock me. Made me watch as they butchered him. Tried to make me eat, but I kept vomiting."

"Let me think." Ajoba scanned the campsite. The guards kept their faces pointed in one direction—probably the one they had been told to watch. She could use one of these horses to take Taryan, but it would be easily spotted. Taryan couldn't ride well without use of her legs—she'd need to sit behind Ajoba. A horse carrying two riders would not outride these men.

If she could get her out of the campsite and to Lacey, they could gain a big lead before she was discovered missing.

"I need to tie your ankles back together. So they won't bounce as I carry you."

Taryan shook her head. "Call for help."

"No birds."

"Try anyway."

Ajoba warbled and waited. Taryan whistled. The sky remained clear of birds. They were almost to the strip of toxland that bordered Brennah. Perhaps birds steered clear of here. Or had something else scared them from the sky?

Ajoba ripped the legs of her trousers—a gift from the Fenside folks—and wrapped each of Taryan's ankles in a makeshift splint.

Alrod had smashed them with the flat of his sword. "I'm sick of being ill-used by you outriders," he had said.

Brady would kill him—if they survived to tell Brady.

If Brady survived to hear their tale.

She helped Taryan get her shirt and trousers off. She stuffed them with brush, using dried grass to approximate her hair. The dummy might pass as Taryan for a little while, at least in the dark of night, gaining them time. She tied Taryan's ankles together, wrapping the rope over the sticks that formed the splints.

"How can you carry me?" Taryan whispered. "I'm bigger than you by far."

"God will provide." Ajoba braced her feet, bent her knees, and put her shoulder into Taryan's midsection. She lifted, her back screaming with pain. She pushed with her thigh muscles, straightening up with Taryan slung over her back.

She'd have to carry her at least three hundred paces—a hundred to get past the guards and another two hundred before she could deposit Taryan and go get Lacey.

The first step was horrific. The next was no better.

Ajoba reached the guard perimeter at the end of her strength. Despite her precautions, Taryan had fainted from pain. The guards were closer together than Ajoba remembered. She'd need a significant distraction to get past them. She tried to bend so she could pick up a rock. Her knees wobbled. She couldn't bend down—she'd never get back up with Taryan on her back.

She could toss her dagger through a guard's back, but that would alert the camp to an intruder. Instead, she used the blade to cut off one of Taryan's splints. With a whispered prayer, she threw the stick as far as she could.

"Hey. What's that?"

The nearest guard left his post to investigate. She ran forward, praying her steps would be muffled and Taryan would not wake and scream with pain.

Somehow she made it all the way back to Lacey with no one

the wiser. Ajoba resplinted Taryan's ankle before splashing her face with water to bring her to consciousness.

"Thank you," Taryan whispered.

"I don't think they'll notice you missing until morning. They seem rather stupid."

Ajoba took off her armor so she could slip off her outer shirt and drape it over Taryan. Her own dark skin wouldn't suffer as much from the sun when it came up. She was ready to lift Taryan onto Lacey when she realized something. "Where's your armor?"

"Oh, no. Alrod took it from me."

Ajoba collapsed into the dust, her head in her hands. "Niki went into the stronghold to retrieve the piece of shroud he took from me. Their work will be worthless if he keeps your armor."

"Brady will get it back," Taryan whispered.

"No."

Taryan clutched her hands. "Please, no. He can't be . . ."

"He's alive. But he's too injured. I need to get it now."

"How?"

"I'm going to load you onto Lacey, and then I'm going back in."

"No."

"Yes."

She dressed Taryan in her own armor and lifted her onto the horse's back. "If you hear me scream or if I don't return by sunrise, conduct yourself as a birthrighter."

"What?"

"Get out of here as fast as you can. And take good care of Lacey for me."

Ajoba checked her short blade, hefted her dagger, and set her face for Alrod's campsite.

Alrod hadn't slept, of course. He lay awake, knowing someone would come to retrieve the shimmering clothes the girl had worn. He had left her out where she could be found with no guard nearby to interrupt the tearful reunion.

He had expected Brady but was not disappointed to find the girl with the exotic eyes—Ajoba, that was her name—sneaking into his tent. Keeping still, he let her poke about, impressed at how someone with as unfettered a mouth as hers managed to move silently.

Her protracted exhalation signaled that she had found the burning clothes. Alrod also had been trained to be silent, and so he was able to pin her arms before she realized he was awake.

"Miss me?" he whispered.

"Madly. How've you been, Baron?"

"Exceedingly irked. And you?"

"Exceedingly irksome."

"What are you doing here, Ajoba?"

She leaned into him, her back fitting against his chest. "You know the answer to that quite well. The question is, what are *you* doing here, Baron?"

"I do not answer to you, girl." He wrapped his arms tighter about her and squeezed.

Even with the air pressed from her lungs, she managed to speak. "You will . . . answer to . . . God. Might . . . as well practice . . . with me."

Alrod laughed and relieved some of the pressure. "I don't know who God is."

"I could tell you."

"And I don't care to find out."

"Could I turn and speak to you, face-to-face?"

He loosened his grip further. As she turned, her eyes searched out his. He pushed hard with his legs, rising up and knocking her onto her back. Laughing, he climbed on top of her as if she were a lover and not a nuisance.

"Don't," she whispered.

"You asked for it."

"Not this."

"You haven't earned *this*, so I suggest you shut up before I give you what you *have* earned."

"Alrod, please. I beg you to let me tell you about God. The love He has, even for you."

He searched her eyes now and saw what she lacked—that doubt that Simon had showed him, that doubt that had soared through the ages, through the plagues and fires and screams. That doubt was the crux of Simon's power. That she lacked it made her of little use to him. Unless . . .

"Tell me the truth, girl."

"What?" She glared with a ferocity that pleased him.

"Have you ever been with a man?"

She curled her lips into her teeth. Trying to come up with the answer least likely to get her into trouble. Alrod yanked her hair. "The truth."

"No. I have not."

"You're quite annoying, but with your mouth taped shut, you'd be very attractive. Why haven't you? There must be men deaf enough to put up with you."

"It pleases God that I remain pure as long as I remain unmarried."

Alrod laughed. This girl was a full-blown idiot. "You expect to marry?"

"I expect to be blessed by God. Whether that includes my marriage in the future or my death in the next moment, I trust that blessing."

He put his mouth to her ear. "Your leader does not trust you. How does that make you feel?"

Her breath quickened, which meant his guess had been on target.

Interesting—Brady of Horesh was still vexed by this girl. Perhaps there had been some punishment meted out or some other kind of rift. Perhaps she chafed at his anger. There must be a way he could use this to his advantage.

These were two weak women on their own—one who couldn't

walk, and one who could vex the sting out of a nest of hornets. The other one was likely a virgin also, and even better looking. Dawnray was his chosen vessel, but if she turned out to be tainted, he could use these two. Or perhaps he could adopt Treffyn's practice of spawning as many heirs as his energy would allow. The other one had a sweet beauty, and this one was just begging to be tamed.

"You're drooling," Ajoba said.

"What?" He automatically raised his hand to wipe his face, and she kneed him in the groin. Pain exploded behind his eyeballs, but he managed to grab her. She swung around, the heel of her hand aiming for his nose—a mortal blow that would send the cartilage into his brain. But he ducked it, catching her hand on the side of his eye. A bone cracked, his cheekbone and perhaps her hand, for she yelped aloud this time. Somebody stirred outside the tent.

"It's nothing," he called out. "Just entertaining that woman." It wouldn't do for his soldiers to see him boxed about by a woman. Besides, he was enjoying himself.

Ajoba leaped for the door but he caught her ankle and twisted. She went down, kicking and flailing, but small enough so he could grab her by the hips and bring her back under him. "Enough games," he growled. "My pleasure will be your bitter pain. When I'm finished, you filthy cow, you'll be cursing the day you were born a woman."

She raised her right hand for another blow. Instinct drove him to dip his head to his own right as he caught her hand midpunch and snapped her wrist. But then something hot touched the side of his face, something in her free hand that he hadn't seen coming—the burning cloth that, covering his face, put him in a horrific place of pure darkness and nothing else but his own self.

A figure moved in the darkness, a slender and broken figure whom Alrod disdained and would not ask for help. Instead, he clung to himself. Somewhere distant, he felt rope about his ankles and his wrists. But as long as the burning cloth covered his face, he couldn't get beyond his own self. Finally, the girl ripped the cloth away from his face.

"What did you do to me?" he gasped.

"Tied you like the stuffed pig you are."

He glanced at his hands and feet. Indeed, she had bound him very competently.

"What do you want, Ajoba?"

She put her dagger to his face. "I want to see you dead."

"You don't have the nerve."

She smiled. "Oh, but I do. What I don't have is God's permission. So I will leave that task to Brady of Horesh. Unlike me, he has been entrusted with such tasks."

"Wait. What is that cloth?"

She looked back at him. "Will you hear about God?"

"I don't care about God. I want to know about the cloth."

She dug through his personal gear with her left hand, her right pressed to her ribs. "I may be foolish, Alrod, but you're the fool. All right, here's something suitable."

"What?"

She jammed his dirty unders into his mouth and used his own stockings to gag him. Before leaving the tent, she pulled on the shimmering shirt, mask, and gloves. As she sneaked out, it struck Alrod that he had indeed been a fool. The man who had scaled his tower had been hidden under the same kind of mask. He had assumed him to be Brady, but now he realized the intruder could have been anyone.

Even a woman—or a golden-haired minstrel.

Alrod had to get back to Traxx before these cursed outriders wreaked any more chaos. But first he had to cut the rope that had, indeed, bound him like a pig.

He would not forget what Ajoba had done to him, nor would he wait for some make-believe God to grant him permission before he made her pay.

TWENTY

BY THE TIME AJOBA AND TARYAN RETURNED TO FENSIDE, Cooper was out of his mind with worry.

"Two days," he cried. "What's wrong with your hand? What happened to Taryan? What's going on?"

"Shush. Just shush." Ajoba was exhausted to the bone. She had stayed awake, holding Taryan when she was unconscious, distracting her when she came to. Lacey had been a trouper, carrying them straight back without stopping for anything except water breaks.

Curt wanted a report, but first she had to check on Brady. Cooper followed, carrying Taryan. Her face was pinched with pain but she encouraged the rook with a confident smile. *Gracious always*, Ajoba thought. *I could do well to emulate her.*

Brady was no better but no worse. Hannah had taken over his care, finding relief from her own grief. "He spiked a fever. We bathed him in our corn alcohol and prayed for him. It went away."

Ajoba smiled. "You prayed?"

"Cooper taught us how. Talking to the Holy One has soothed many of us."

Ajoba hugged Cooper. "Well done."

They settled Taryan on a mat near Brady, gave her some cory-dalis root to chew while Hannah splinted her ankles with air-filled bladders made from sheep's hide.

"Get me sticks to use as crutches."

"You can't be thinking of moving around," Ajoba said.

"Alrod will come here. You know he will."

"I took Lacey over enough hard ground and through enough brush to cover our trail."

"He has ways of knowing these things," Taryan said. "Get me something to use as a crutch so I can fight."

"You can't put any weight on your legs. It won't work."

"Then Cooper will lift me into a tree. I'll drop rocks with the children."

"No."

"Ajoba, don't shirk on me now. A battle is brewing. You feel it—"

She did feel it, a gloomy stirring in her bones. Their mission to gather original species and to give the gospel was one of peace and grace. Yet they were commissioned to act against violence when it found them or those they were called to help. These days, it seemed, it found them with more and more frequency.

Cooper had brought a message from the Ark that had been reported to all at the gathering-in: *The seams are loosening.* Surely the soul of this creation had so many cracks that darkness and violence were leaking in everywhere. Such a sorrow, for this world still held much beauty and many souls who hungered for the truth.

"We need to prepare," Taryan said. "We've got a day, no more."

"We tried to hide away." Hannah said. "But evil has its way."

"We don't mean to bring more on you," Ajoba said.

Hannah clutched Brady's limp hand to her heart. "You brought help and the Holy One. Don't regret either one, miss."

"What should we do?" Cooper said.

"Take me out to the trees," Taryan said, struggling to sit.

"No. Sleep first. We'll take you out before nightfall." Ajoba covered her with a blanket. Taryan's eyes were already closed as her hand sought out Brady's.

"You should rest too," Cooper whispered as they left the hut.

"No. Yes. After I check out the fortifications, talk to Curt, make sure there's enough food and clay spears stored in the mill house, tell the mothers that their children must nap, for there will be a battle coming, see to Lacey."

"Shush," Cooper said, guiding her to sit near the river, where the breezes ran cool and gentle. The leaves in the grove of trees uttered a soft song, a lullaby that lulled her as she leaned her head back, prayed for Brady and Taryan, the people of Fenside, her comrades near and far.

And herself as well: *Lord, give me rest for I am sorely beyond myself.*

Simon had tracked down a band of marauders who would make excellent soldiers—if they didn't kill Alrod before he could sway them to his side.

"I offer you riches beyond imagining. Fine horses and finer women. The finest mogged weapons, for my sorcerer is the best in all the lands."

"Mogs?" The leader of the band, a man named Nomad, spat to one side of his horse and then the other—a gesture of contempt among commoners. "Who be you to claim to have mogs?"

Alrod snapped his fingers, and Saul stepped forward. "This is the high and mighty one," he parroted, "the great Baron Alrod, the crown jewel of the east, the exalted hand that makes the sun rise from his kingdom."

Nomad laughed. His men joined in.

Alrod moderated his tone so not to reveal his anger. "What amuses you?"

"The Baron of Traxx—he be a man we admire. But yer no baron."

Simon stood by, silently watching without offering to help. Judging perhaps if Alrod was up to this challenge.

"Why would you say I am not?"

"Where be yer standard bearer and your strong-arms? Ye be

just some little man playing at being the high and mighty one, surroundin' yerself with pretty boys that couldn't fight if they had to."

Alrod dismounted. "Shall I prove who I am?"

Nomad laughed louder. "With that fancy sword of yours? Yer a scrawny man, not able to lift such a weapon."

"You're right. The sword proves nothing." Alrod unstrapped it, dropped it in the dust.

The marauder shifted in his saddle. "What ye be doing, man?"

"As you demanded. Proving my merit."

Alrod leaped, knocking Nomad off his horse. They tumbled in the dirt, the marauder on top as he had planned it. Alrod jabbed his dagger up under the man's ribs and, with a brutal twist, killed him.

The other marauders shrank back, transfixed, as Alrod hoisted his knife over his head with a roar. Nomad's blood ran over his hand, soaking his sleeve, filling him with a raw power never to be found inside the walls of his own stronghold. "Does anyone else doubt me?"

Silence.

"Do any of you dare serve me? My offer of glory still stands."

One man stepped forward. Then another and another, until they crowded the baron. Alrod glanced at Simon for the signal to begin.

Do it without me. You have earned the right and gained the power.

And so he would. "One at a time, kneel before me."

The first man knelt. Alrod put his right hand to the man's mouth, the fingers of his left hand itching for Simon's shoulder— but the sorcerer had said he had the power. And so he jammed his hand into the man's mouth, his free hand raising the blood-ied dagger to warn the others back.

Alrod felt teeth and tongue, but where was the power to change this man? He knew that power, had tasted it in that fruit, swallowed by a throat that had spoken no evil until after taking the first sweet bite, until after that flicker of doubt tainted her perfect eyes. Indeed, it was this doubt that wormed into the heart of the ages, that spoke rebellion and greed and violence, that Alrod needed to reach for.

He saw it now, a coal in the middle of this man, notched with the maidens he had raped, the men he had killed, the children he had sold into drudgery. This was a heart suited to Alrod's purpose, and so he embraced it with his hand, feeling the man change about him, feeling the pop of bones as they strengthened, the stretch of scars into unblemished flesh, the filling of muscles with the will of the high and mighty one of Traxx who had proven he was a man worthy to be followed.

When he had grasped that smoldering coal and set it aflame, he pulled his arm from the man's mouth. The face and form were familiar but the eyes darker, the gaze fiercer, the smile more grateful.

"What say you, soldier?" Alrod said.

"How . . . how can I serve you?"

The others pushed to be next. The making of Alrod's army was the most blissful afternoon he had ever spent. As the last of the men took on his strength, his thoughts wandered to his future heir. Should Dawnray be untainted, he would have her as soon as he got back. A child would be born. Then perhaps a second or a third, or as many as she could bear before she was too worn.

Would the seeds of his loins come into the world with his will already burning in them? Or would he stick his finger into their tiny mouths and breathe this life into them from birth?

Simon had promised—indeed, given—a power far more potent than transmogrification. Alrod's skin burned with this power, his mind like a fine crystal that saw into the future where the banner of the hornet flew over every corner of this world, its stinger curved to strike.

Only one thing stood in his way. The cursed outriders. Men or women, they were a force with which to contend. He grabbed

Simon's arm, not flinching at the chorus of screams that rattled through the bones of his own hand. "We need to talk."

They walked, finding quiet away from his new army. As now required, Simon removed his veil, just as Ghedo always had when they were alone.

"What do I do about the outriders?" Alrod said.

Simon laughed. "Did you think you were forming this army to take on that fool who rules Slade? Once the outriders are dead, even Merrihana could take down that stronghold. Your army has a mightier purpose."

"To put me on every throne on earth."

"Beyond that."

"What is greater than ruling every land?"

"This world has a deep secret. One the outriders know."

"Do you know it, Simon?"

"Yes."

"Tell me then."

Simon exploded in the same burst of light that Alrod first saw him in. When he settled back, his eyes were serene, but the two snakes in his cloak had strangled each other. He snapped his fingers, and they revived. But they had changed. Each now bore a scarlet stripe down its back.

"Remove that. Scarlet is not a Traxx color."

Simon turned his face away. "I cannot."

"What?"

The sorcerer grabbed Alrod, frosting his heart by his touch. "There is a mighty secret, hidden deep, and guarded with a magic so powerful that I cannot speak of it. Should you discover this secret, your power would be beyond what you can imagine. The outriders and their comrades know it."

"Can they speak it?"

"They can. If they will remains to be seen."

"How can I go where you can't?"

Simon smiled. "You are not bound by this magic. In fact, of all the stronghold princes, you alone are best able to destroy it."

Alrod nodded. "I'm ready. Where do we start?"

"The men you just commissioned suffered a defeat at a settlement to the northwest of here. Such wouldn't have happened without the help of Brady of Horesh."

Alrod smiled. The blissful afternoon had just become sublime.

Brady had built this cabin with his own hands. He'd hewed the logs and stacked them, cut the slate and shingled the roof, even blown the glass of the windows. He'd chosen the spot next to the rushing river, where the music of the water invigorated him by day and soothed him by night.

Taryan worried about the children, so close to the water, but he had built a sturdy fence that contained the toddlers. The older ones he had taught to swim. Niki was more fish than girl. While her brother Kendo also swam well, he preferred to build rafts and bridges.

Brady's days were filled with hunting meat, tending crops, and raising his children. His nights were filled with studying the Holy Scriptures and loving his wife, just as the blessed Lord had designed. He saw God's hand in the abundant sunshine and lofty mountains, felt His touch in the hugs of his children and caress of his wife, knew His voice in the cry of the raven and the whisper of rain.

This was a summer day and, though he sweated and the sun stung, he kept digging. This was a glorious creation but not heaven—not yet—and so Brady had to contend with the bothersome corn borers that wormed inside the young green stalks. He would have no such worry with his children, because he had moved them far away from the borers that wormed into men's souls.

He jammed his shovel into the rich brown dirt and brought up a stink.

He stood, unmoving. Listening to the laughter of his children, the cry of their newborn and Taryan's sweet lullaby. Feeling the sun on his face, too far away to be destroyed by the hand of man, though some had tried. The wind at his back had cooled him while he worked, but was insufficient to block this rancid odor that seeped from the very ground under his feet.

Brady could cover it up. Shovel the dirt over it, turn his back on whatever rotted in the heart of his garden. He could pack up his family and move further upriver. He was trained in survival, as was Taryan. They could live almost anywhere if need be.

A tremor passed under his feet. Taryan paused in her lullaby, but only for a moment. She resumed singing, trusting him because she always had, just as his children always had. The Lord had given him this trust as a gift, and he had built a cabin for it and tended a garden for it and sweated and ached for it.

But Brady was so tired. His side hurt where he rested on his shovel. He turned his face away to breathe in the air as it rushed with the river, to catch the fragrance of his children—milk and honey and play.

Something moved under his shovel. He could jam it hard and kill whatever foul thing lay there. But like the corn borers, some things just kept coming. A bird fluttered about his head, singing simple words that he understood, though how a farmer who lived by a river could understand birdsong was as distant as the memory of trackers and training and thick ice and cold water pressing down on a clean place that allowed no corn borers.

But that was not true, because even inside a place called the Ark, a savior was needed.

The bird sang again, telling him to wake up.

Come play, Niki called.

The baby wants you, Taryan said.

Let me carry you home, the river sang.

Wake up, the bird shouted.

I'll help you, Taryan said.

The baby was gone, the children a dream, but her hand was real and warm.

Yet *he could not let go of the shovel, not until he finished what was required. He looked into the hole he had dug and saw a world of evil. He let that evil wash over him and flow into the river that could wash even this clean. What remained was what he would have to bury—and bury deep before he could awake.*

Brady dug the shovel into the dirt and covered his dreams.

Then he woke up.

TWENTY-ONE

TARYAN SNATCHED AWAY THE SWORD BEFORE BRADY could strap it on. "No," she said. "You can't even stand up."

"Neither can you. But you're going out there."

"Ajoba has a plan that includes me."

"Ajoba?" He turned toward the younger tracker, even this motion draining the blood from his face.

Ajoba smiled, trying not to show the dread that gnawed at her stomach. Brady was the outrider of this crew, the leader of their camp, one of the vaunted first-evers. Ajoba no longer knew what she was. Teacher? Tracker? Or still an outcast, soon to be exiled?

"If I may speak?" she said.

"Go."

Ajoba told him what had transpired since he had been wounded. "And then I found Taryan, both her ankles broken."

He turned back to Taryan, resting his face against the wall because he was too weak to even sit up without assistance. "How?"

"How did she find me? She's a good tracker."

"How did your ankles get broken? You've been dancing around that since I came to."

Taryan glanced across the hut at Ajoba. "I fell off my horse."

"Hmm." Clearly he hadn't bought her tale but at the moment was unable or unwilling to press. "Continue," he told Ajoba.

She finished laying out her plans. Two days ago, it had all made sense. Now clay-hardened cornstalks and children dropping rocks from trees seemed ridiculous.

When she finished, though, Brady had only one word for her. "Good. What can I do to help?"

"You can't even stand, lad." Taryan tugged on him as if to illustrate that very fact.

"Neither can you, but"—He grinned and, for the first time since he collapsed, he looked like the Brady they knew—"we don't want to go round that whirlpool again, do we? Prop me up somewhere. I can shoot an arrow."

"With your hands shaking like that?" Ajoba said gently.

He met her eye, the iron in his gaze something that had always daunted her; at the same time it encouraged her. "When the time comes, my hands will not shake."

Hannah mopped his brow. "I can stand with him, brace his arms if I need to."

"We'll move you to the millhouse then," Ajoba said. "I've got a perch set up in the upper vent."

"Good. Cooper can continue to wear my armor. Ajoba, you should use my sword."

"I can't."

"You refuse?"

"I'm not strong enough."

"You will be."

"Not with a broken wrist." It hadn't hurt until she acknowledged it, but now sharp pain snaked through her elbow and into her shoulder.

Brady's eyes burned. "When I get my hands on Alrod—"

"I told you he'd know," Ajoba said. "He always does."

"I can fight," Taryan said, "but I'll have to use my short blade. Let's give Cooper your sword."

Brady shook his head. "He's not ready—not with a sword. You've at least trained with Niki and Bartoly."

"When the time comes, Cooper will know what to do."

He sighed. "I can only hope."

"We'd better get in place. I expect Alrod to show up shortly. He's got about ten men—though they seem rather dim to me."

"Don't underestimate him."

"Believe me, I don't. Taryan, we'll move you outside, but we won't lift you into the tree until we get a signal. That way you won't be too uncomfortable."

"What happens when she's discovered? She *will* be discovered." Brady's face poured sweat. Even speaking exhausted him. Fresh blood still stained his bandage, though not as much as before. "She'll be an easy target."

"I may not have legs that work, but I've got arms. Strong ones," Taryan said. "I'll hoist myself along, follow the children through the trees to the mill, if need be. At the very least, I'll have my bow. Men will die before they pull me out of any tree."

"Hannah, could you bring one of the men to help you move Brady to the millhouse?" Ajoba said. "Have them bring him his bow and plenty of arrows."

"Giving orders about me, Ajoba?"

"Even now, you argue?" She kept her tone light.

He leaned back, drained of all color. "Just remember one thing."

"What's that?"

"Bless your troops before you send them to fight for their lives."

Ajoba went outside to let the night hide the tears streaming down her cheeks.

The next hour went by in a flurry of activity. Ajoba roused families and made sure everyone ate before moving to their assigned places. Elderly and pregnant women took the babies and toddlers into the millhouse. Brady waited in the loft, though Hannah told Ajoba he had passed out twice as they hoisted him up there. Taryan waited under the trees, encouraging the older children with tales of valor, assuring them they would fight with honor.

Ajoba raced from post to post, making sure everyone had

weapons, knew their roles, knew the signals for retreat. She prayed for each person, some of whom had embraced faith and others who squinted as if she were insane. Once again, she wondered if she should have pressed harder for them all to flee Fenside. These folk had refused her urging, even after the death and torment at the hands of the marauders. This was their home, and here they had lived free. Even traumatized, they would not give that up lightly.

Cooper, guarding downriver of the millhouse, was her last stop. He was alert, but his eyes were troubled. "What is it?" she whispered.

"I don't know if I can do it again."

"Do what?"

"Kill someone."

When the time comes, she wanted to say. But he hadn't been out of the Ark long enough to trust fully what that meant. "What specifically is worrying you?"

He shook his head. "I don't know."

A hundred tasks pressed down on her, but she sat with him, shoulder to shoulder, looking into the dark under the dam. The tumbling water made visibility difficult and hearing near impossible, but Cooper had sharp senses. They would have to trust that they wouldn't be surprised via the river again. The sharpened rocks she'd had set in the shallowest section should help ensure against that.

"Try," she said.

"Brady knows, and Kwesi and Stasia. But no one else knows that I was awake during transit."

"Were you? That must have been scary."

"Yea. Fright time, if I can say."

"Yea, this once, a-okey." The jangle from training sounded strange coming from her own mouth. Yet just a little over a year ago she had still been in training herself, speaking the strange slang and making up more.

"Not just that, but I stayed awake in the darkness, even when Kwesi and Stasia fell asleep."

"That I knew."

"But no one knows what I'm about to say."

"I'm honored to listen."

"When I was caught in that darkness on the mountain called Welz, I just kept singing 'Glorious' because it kept that creature at bay. Then someone asked me to stop."

"A demon asked you?"

"No. It was an angel. I'm sure of it."

"Why?"

"I can't say. That part of the story belongs to someone else."

"Oh." It wasn't a big leap to understand he spoke of Niki. Sent to bring home the rooks from transit, she had come back a different person. Still snappish and bossy, but there was a light in her eyes. A peace had settled on her.

"I got taken to this place," Cooper said. "Kwesi and Stasia were there sleeping. But apparently I—don't know if it's a curse or a gift—I don't sleep when I'm inside shroud."

"Really?" On occasion they'd wrap an injured comrade partially in shroud while they performed some primitive surgery or to set a bone.

"But before that, I was walking in a garden."

"Oh, Cooper."

"I never told anyone because it . . . it . . ."

"It was a blessed privilege."

He shook his shaggy red head. "I can't tell you, because I don't have the words."

She brushed his hair from his eyes. "Thank you for telling me this much."

"The thing is, after being that close to our real home, I—it's just that killing is really hard for me," he said. "I know we fight righteous battles, but to walk on ground that has never been soaked in blood . . ."

Ajoba grabbed his hands. "That *you* were able to walk there was bought with precious blood."

He hung his head. "I know."

"Cooper, listen to me. It's hard for all of us, even if we haven't glimpsed heaven. You have to know that even Brady, who has never shirked a fight, finds it hard to kill. If you ever stop hating that you swing a blade, then it's time for you to stop being a birthrighter."

"I'm sorry."

"You've got nothing to be sorry about."

"Not for me. For all of us. For this jam-punchin' world."

Ajoba wrapped her arms about him. "Eya, mate. So am I."

Brady sat on a high stool, his chin resting on the windowsill. Hannah had insisted on putting out a towel to cushion his chin, a good thing because it kept his jaw from trembling. He had been injured many times, but had never been so weak. He was getting old. The kids in training took bets on how long he, Kendo, and Niki would live. Three of the first-evers—still active and serving.

"See you in a couple of years," the builders had said when they left the Ark.

But no one on the Ark had remembered the world being this big. How could they? The great-great grandparents who had sunk the Ark under the ice had long ago gone to their rest. None of the builders alive now had ever walked in this world. How could anyone who lived in peace imagine an opposition so wicked, a terrain so dangerous, obstacles so nearly insurmountable?

Yet when the directive came—*It's time to go out and gather*—what choice had they but to send their children? The vision had come to every person on the Ark at once, to some in a dream and to some in other forms. Even small children had heard the call and understood that the young and strong would be the ones to go out. They would be the birthrighters.

Almost all the twelve-year-olds on the Ark had volunteered for training. Only four had completed the first training class successfully. Those first four birthrighters—Brady, Tylow, Niki, Kendo—had gone forth with no one to meet them above the ice, no established camp to join. But God had provided. Clothes, dogs, short blades, food, a sled were all waiting at the exact spot the whale spat them out.

Over the past six years, twelve camps had been established to serve Birthright. If Arabah was lost forever, there were now eleven. More were being planned. *The seams are loosening*, the prophetic message had said. But had the seams ever been tight this side of Eden?

Birthrighters had been in the world long enough to become full-grown men and women. Bartoly was bigger than anyone expected, Niki taller, Kendo smarter. Dano, Jayme, Leiha, and Kaya were all of senior status, having passed their twentieth year. And Taryan . . . He felt his thoughts slipping in a familiar direction. In quiet moments, did the need to be joined to a wife or husband wear on them too? Or was this Brady's personal weakness, one of those good things laid in his path to tempt him?

He mentally kicked more dirt on that dream.

He had little hope of surviving this attack, not when defended by a tracker with two broken ankles, a disgraced teacher, a tormented rook, and stunned villagers who hadn't seen such violence in a long time. He prayed that some of the children would survive. They should have been hidden across the river, but Ajoba was too inexperienced to think of that. If he had the strength, he could swim them across now, in the dark of the night.

Brady tested himself, nearly toppling off the stool.

"Would you like to lie down for a spell?" Hannah whispered.

He shook his head, grasping the wall to keep upright. What hope had they against Alrod? Ten soldiers, Ajoba had said. Fenside outnumbered them, but Alrod's men would have full health, dark hearts, and excellent weapons. Only a fool would think that Fenside's river wouldn't run with blood.

The plan to barricade this millhouse was good, but it had depended on being able to send for help. Where were the birds?

The birds' presence and help had always been a tangible and comforting sign of the divine presence. Had God now lifted His hand from them?

"Are you in pain?" Hannah whispered.

"Hmm. No. Why?"

"You're crying."

"Oh."

"Now you're smiling. Why?"

"For the past few years, I've been too weary to muster tears. Consider these a good sign."

Hannah smiled as her own tears wet her face.

Brady continued to lean, unable to stand. *When the time comes . . . may Your grace be sufficient for me, Your power made perfect in weakness.*

TWENTY-TWO

"Dawnray, wake up."

"What? Is it time to leave?"

Merrihana had her by the shoulders. "What do you mean, leave? Where do you think you'd be going?"

Dawnray rubbed her eyes, trying to bring order to her slumber-soaked mind. "No place. I was dreaming."

Though it was the middle of the night, Merrihana's hair was combed and her eyelashes waxed. What was she doing here? Had Timothy's plan to rescue her been uncovered? Had Alrod returned?

Dawnray tried to push up from the sheets, but Merrihana sat on the blanket, pinning her by the shoulders. "Stay."

"I need to pay you proper respect."

Merrihana smiled. "Instead of royal and drudge, why don't we chat as friends?"

The baroness had continually found opportunities to denigrate her verbally as well as to punch, pinch, or slap her. To even suggest they could be friends was insane. Yet Dawnray had an obligation to treat this woman with as much grace as she could muster.

"What is it, high and mighty? How may I serve you?"

Merrihana brushed the hair from her eyes, a maternal gesture that Dawnray found oddly touching. "Call me Merrihana."

"If that's your wish." Dawnray waited, trying to resist the notion of cowering under the covers.

The baroness turned her gaze to the barred but unshuttered window. The night wind blew the curtains about, bringing in the sweet scent of the Wall of Traxx. Though the mogged blossoms served as a deceptive trap, the grace and loveliness of their original forms still lingered in the fragrance.

The pupils of Merrihana's eyes contracted in the candlelight.

"Thank you," Dawnray answered.

"For what?"

"For lighting a candle. It was considerate of you to remember that I can't see in the dark as you can."

"Must you remind me of my failure?"

She should have just kept her mouth shut. "No, of course not. I just . . . wanted to say something nice to you."

"You can breathe easy, lolly. I believe you." The baroness wrapped icy fingers around her own. "You spoke of love yesterday. Why?"

Dawnray pushed up in bed so she could look Merrihana straight in the eye. "Because I think . . . I mean . . . you seem to have a great capacity for it."

"And you seem to think that is a good thing. Why?"

Lord, if ever you would give me words . . .

"Because love is a gift from our Creator, a shadow of His regard for the people He made in His image. Our love is usually imperfect, sometimes even hurtful." Dawnray dared to squeeze the baroness's hand. "But it's a force more powerful than wind or—"

Merrihana pressed her hand to Dawnray's mouth. "I don't want to know about such fanciful notions. Tell me about a woman loving a man, a man loving a woman."

Dawnray took a long breath. "What did you see in your mother and father?"

The baroness tented her fingers, pressed them to her face. "A useful political alliance."

"Was there regard for each other?"

"There was suspicion. Mutual interest. A carefully cultivated image presented to a hostile world."

"And that is what you and your husband experience?"

She nodded, her mouth tightening.

A tremendous sympathy raced through Dawnray, her heart

aching for a woman who, for all her cruelty, had never been much more than a pawn.

"Merrihana, my mother made it her life's work to provide a warm and healthy home for my father. My father would have died for my mother." Dawnray wept, hot tears falling on their clasped hands. "And the night I was taken, my father could have made bags of gold by simply selling me to Ghedo. Instead, this man who had never thrown a punch or jabbed a knife fought to the death trying to protect me.

"This, Baroness, is love. Love is not proud or boastful. It is not self-seeking or easily angered. And Merrihana, please believe that love does not delight in evil." Dawnray dared to wrap her arms around the woman's shoulders and hold her as a mother might a child. "It always protects, always trusts, always hopes, always persists. It is a gift . . ." She hesitated. "A gift from a Creator so gracious that He died for us so that we could share in that love."

Merrihana pushed her away. For a flash, Dawnray saw—or perhaps imagined—the clear-eyed bride who had come to the castle, not the jealous wife who wore the eyes of a cat.

"Please," Dawnray whispered. "Let me help you know the God who loves you."

"Sorry to bother you."

"Please . . ."

Merrihana blew out the candle, leaving Dawnray in the darkness.

"A sorcerer's assistant?" Niki couldn't believe her ears.

Anastasia just nodded.

Niki had to jam her fist into her own mouth to keep from yelling. "What sorcerer?"

The rook pointed straight down and mouthed, *That sorcerer.*

"Are you insane?"

"The opportunity presented itself."

"Which means that either you panicked and this oily mutt saw his opportunity to get a young girl alone, or you panicked and this dodgy associate of you-know-who saw an opportunity to get close to us. Either way, it's a disaster. *You're* a disaster. I swear, if I had known how much trouble you would stir up without even trying, I would have left you up on the ice."

Three weeks ago, this tirade would have brought on the trembling lip and brimming tears. Now Anastasia stood there and took it. "Are you done yet, Nikolette?" she shot back. "I don't want to rob you of the opportunity to rank me out."

"Watch yourself, Stasia," Timothy said.

Niki got right in her face. "You want to jangle, rook? Listen up, joe, because it's your dime that's steamin' here."

Anastasia's eyes bugged. "Whoa. You know how to punch it."

Timothy laughed. "Who do you think invented the training slang, eya?"

"Shove that hot air back in your lungs," Niki said. "This is serious, tracker."

Anastasia stood on tiptoes to get nose to nose with her. "This is a boy whom God has called. If you'll only meet him, you'll see that's quite clear."

"The master butcher of Traxx raises a little boy to be a godly young man? Shove that stupid notion back in your head—apparently there's plenty of room up there. Don't you understand how you endangered all of us by telling this boy that I'm an outrider? You know the price on my head. This Gabe could buy himself a small kingdom with the gold Alrod has offered."

"It was the only way I could persuade him I was serious."

"About what? You being the biggest idiot this side of the arctic ice?"

"Serious about rescuing him from Ghedo and taking him to a sanctuary. He wouldn't believe I could do it. And he's right—I can't. But an outrider can, and he knows it."

Niki went to the window. The sky was still dark. Three hours until sunrise would give them plenty of time to escape this trap. "We're leaving. Right now."

"No," Anastasia said. "It's not necessary."

"No," Timothy echoed. "We don't have what we came for yet."

Niki grabbed each of them. "Will you not be satisfied until *I'm* hanging on the wall next to that blasted mogged bat of Alrod's?"

The image must have filled their minds as well as hers, because Anastasia sank down to the floor and Timothy went sheet-white.

Niki felt her own knees go watery, though not from fear. She would gladly hang on that wall in Brady's place. She would do anything to ensure his safety, which was why she'd held back the letter from the Ark.

The problem was, nothing she could do could ensure Brady's safety . . . or her own . . . or Kendo's or Taryan's or Timothy's or this infuriating rook standing there in front of her. They all lived lives of extreme peril and would die far too early. Even if the sorcerer's assistant represented no threat, escape from this palace was not guaranteed. And if they did escape, some other danger was bound to be around the next corner. The life of a birthrighter was short, and an outrider's life was shortest of all . . .

The next thought hit without warning, and Niki shook her head at the strangeness of even thinking it. *Who am I to deny Brady what little happiness he seeks, simply to buy him another week or month?*

Timothy touched her arm. "Take Anastasia and go back to Horesh. I can handle this from here."

Niki grabbed the girl by her elbows. "Does this Gabe wear sorcerer's robes?"

"No."

"Does he mog? Tell me the truth, rook. Does he use the needles?"

"No. He hates all of it."

"And he doesn't leave because . . . ?"

"He's not allowed. Niki, he has no concept of anything outside of the stronghold. Ghedo tells him terrible things, like people would kill him."

"You said he had a sweet face. A kind nature. Why would he believe Ghedo's story?"

"He's . . . got something wrong with his back."

"A hump?"

"No. Nothing I can see. But he won't let anyone touch it. And I heard Ghedo say something about it too."

"You heard Ghedo?"

"He came down when I was there. In Ghedo's lair."

Niki paced the room, letting the howl inside her lungs seep back into her blood. And trying a tactic that still felt unfamiliar to her. *Father God, help me here, even though I don't deserve any help because I lied to Brady and I'm furious with this girl and there's something in Timothy's eyes, some music I can't hear.*

Even as she prayed the words, a peace settled over Niki, the kind of rare calm she had known only at Horesh, with the river rushing by and her comrades at her side. This was a peace she couldn't rouse on her own, one she didn't deserve, yet it held her now like her mother's embrace. And with the peace came this thought—that though she had been hotheaded and obstinate, God had reached through her fury and made her heart something she could never make it. His purpose was far greater than she could ever imagine.

"Do you really believe this Gabe is called by God?" Niki finally whispered.

Anastasia nodded.

"If you believe it, rook—speak it."

"I'm not a total fool," Anastasia said. "Well, perhaps I am foolish. But Niki, Timothy—I don't just believe God has called Gabe. I know it."

"Ask him if he knows where the shroud is," Timothy said.

"How would he—"

"If he's Ghedo's assistant, he must have seen it."

"Ask him," Niki said. "Do you have a way to contact him?"

"He's not allowed in this part of the palace, but I can ring his bell from down in the kitchen. We have a code, you know. I'll meet him down in the yard. You can ask him."

Niki stood, unable to take that step of faith that could catch her up to Anastasia's leap.

Anastasia hugged her. "It'll be all right. You just need to meet him, and you'll know."

She shook her head. "Rook, those are very famous last words. Now go."

Anastasia went out into the hall and asked the guard's permission to go down to the kitchen. Her footsteps faded away.

Niki poked Timothy's chest. "*She* was your idea."

"Niki, if bringing Stasia was a mistake, we have to trust God's redemption."

"Been there," she said. "Finally done that."

"I don't mean just once. Every day."

"You preaching to me, tracker?"

He smiled. "Brady's not here. Someone's got to."

Niki smiled back ruefully. He was right, though she still found it hard to trust anything but her own sword hand. She had just submitted to a rook's judgment, yet even her own was questionable. It had definitely not been her place to make the decision for Brady about the letter. Niki wasn't jealous of Taryan—she loved her like a sister. Perhaps she loved Brady more, but that was no excuse to usurp the Ark's authority.

No excuse to play God and determine the course of Brady's heart.

If Niki survived, she'd get the letter to him. She would enjoy his joy as he read it. If he married Taryan, she would bless them both.

And she would trust God to redeem her broken heart.

Calling through the grate on the door, Sado stirred Ghedo out of a deep sleep. "The baroness requests the pleasure of your company," he said.

"Now?"

"She's been drinking, sorcerer."

Ghedo pulled on his cloak and veil before admitting Sado into his sleeping chamber. "What concern of that is yours?"

Sado raised his hands in appeasement. "I provide this information to assist you in serving her. Nothing more."

Ghedo had always enjoyed Sado, especially the stories of his and Alrod's fathers and grandfathers. He couldn't stand to look at the man anymore. The manservant's youth and health were an affront to Ghedo's skill as a sorcerer—though he would wager anything that this transformation wouldn't last. The red in his eyes had begun to turn brownish, like dried blood. And was that a hint of a line across his forehead?

"How's your back, Sado?"

"Fine. Why should it be otherwise?"

Once the decision was irrevocable, the first person to die would be Sado. It would not do to have such a loyal servant left alive. Alrod had likely left him here to spy on Ghedo. Yes, soon he would die.

Ghedo found Merrihana with her face tear-stained and her hands clutching a mug of wine. Without bothering to ask permission, he straightened her robe and wiped her face.

"What's troubling you, Merrihana?"

"I had a dream," she said. "Many dreams. So troubling."

As Ghedo had planned. These dreams were of his making. He had given her a sleeping draft in her tea, spiked with a serum to make her mind malleable. After she dozed off, he had come back in and waited for her eyes to flutter. When he was sure she was in dream sleep, he had whispered deep imaginings to her.

"The baby is breathing, Baron," Ghedo had said in his own voice.

"What's wrong with his leg?" he answered himself in Alrod's voice.

"Extra toes, that's all."

"He's a monster."

"Alrod, his face is perfect. His body is strong."

"Kill him."

"Don't ask me to do such a thing." Ghedo had injected ample sympathy into his pleas. "Let his mother see him and help decide. Though I think Merrihana would love him."

"Give him to me, sorcerer. I'll do it if you can't." How easy it had been to fake the razor edge of Alrod's voice.

Ghedo had warbled an infant's cry, watched Merrihana jerk at the sound, though she hadn't woken. She couldn't—not locked by his draft and his drama.

"Baron, no. Let him—"

When Ghedo cracked a chicken bone, Merrihana had cried out, her arm flung to her face.

When the draft wore off, Merrihana had wandered the royal halls. She'd ended up in the lolly's suite—such a dramatic departure that Ghedo knew his efforts had had an effect.

She looked at him now with haunted eyes. "Did my husband kill my babies?"

Ghedo looked away, willing a flush to rise into his cheeks. "Why would you ask such a thing?"

"Did he?"

"High and mighty, I am sworn to silence on this topic."

Merrihana dug her fingernails into the back of his hand. He winced—they were sharp as daggers. "I also rule this kingdom. You said so yourself."

Ghedo got up and paced, repressing the urge to smile. "Alrod did what he thought was best for you."

"And I had no say in it?"

"He felt you had borne enough pain with the births. To see live children that were imperfect—when you yourself are well nigh perfect—would kill you. At least that's what Alrod said."

She slammed the mug of wine against the wall. It shattered, leaving a blood-red stain. "Eight times. And each time I was told the child was born dead. How many of my children actually survived birth, only to be killed by their father's hand?"

"Don't ask me. Please . . ." Ghedo allowed himself a tiny crack in his voice. More than that and she'd be suspicious.

She sagged against him. "Maybe he did spare me."

"Maybe," Ghedo whispered.

"You said that was the truth. That he wanted to spare me."

"Yes. That's"—a slight hesitation—"what I said."

"What other reason would there be?"

"None. He loves you."

She shoved away from him. "How do you know?"

A construct of human emotion, love was a foolish attempt to dignify lust. Perhaps the illusion was necessary for men and women to elevate themselves above the animals. Ghedo knew better—he had wreaked death and shaped life. And he knew they were all doomed unless he could unlock the secret of creating life and defeating death. Alrod's temper tantrums, his conquest fantasies, and especially this new sorcerer were serious impediments to that noble goal.

"Ghedo, I asked you a question. How do you know Alrod loves me?"

"He chose you to contract in marriage. He could have had others."

"As I could have."

"You were pursued by half the world, Merrihana."

She leaned against him, her heart beating twice as fast as his own. It was inappropriate that she should be in his arms, and of course he had no interest in her. But until she came to the desired conclusion, he needed her in a vulnerable state.

"Alrod prizes his family heritage." Ghedo brushed back her hair. "You know that."

Her breath caught. "Yes."

"He felt that he honored you by allowing you to . . . how did he say it? Oh yes, participate in the fine line of his family. Mix your blood with his."

Merrihana tensed. "That's why he did it."

"Did what?"

"He killed my babies because they weren't perfect."

"He wanted to spare you."

"He had no interest in what I wanted, no stake in a mother's heart. He wanted to protect his family line."

"Merrihana." Ghedo held her close. "Dear friend?"

"What?"

He put his mouth to her ear. "What if—and this is just another dream—but what if someone felt you had the right to your son? What if that someone told Alrod he would kill the child but actually took him away, placed him with a decent family. Made sure this son was protected, clothed, fed."

"What are you saying?" She tensed, her breath like fire on his neck.

"What if someone had spared for you . . . a fine son?"

Her body trembled, a leaf in the wind he had conjured. "I'd want him. Right now."

Ghedo closed his eyes, letting the corners droop in apparent sorrow though he knew she couldn't see him. "Alrod would kill such a son. If he existed."

"Why?"

"Though his imperfections are so minor as to not be visible, nevertheless the baron would consider him damaged. Not worthy of bearing his blood."

She pulled away from his embrace and grabbed his face. "Then you must kill Alrod."

Ghedo shrank back, projecting appropriate shock. "Merrihana, how can you imagine such a thing? I've served the man my entire life."

"And yet you risked your life to countermand his orders. To save a son for me."

He looked her directly in the eye, an unsettling experience. He disliked cats. The creatures could not be controlled and thus were dangerous to have about. That Merrihana saw the world through cats' eyes was something that spooked Ghedo, even after all these years.

He took her back into his arms, holding her like a parent might, stroking the side of her face, dabbing her tears. "For your sake, Merrihana," he whispered. "I risked my life for your sake. And your son's. Every day is a risk for him and me, but I willingly took this on. For your sake, dear one. But how can I bring the two of you together with Alrod in the way?"

Her eyes narrowed. "You said yourself that Alrod is unstable. In the clutches of that sorcerer none of us know anything about."

"Yes."

"Chasing invisible outriders."

"Yes."

"He should be here, governing his kingdom."

"Yes."

"Abandoning Traxx like this is not only irresponsible . . ." She paused, on the brink of what they both knew was treachery. The politic thing to do was to turn it on another, and so she did. "Abandoning the stronghold is close to betrayal, is it not?"

Every nerve ending in Ghedo's body sparked. "It might be considered so."

Merrihana went to the window, her gaze distant on the horizon, where the crimson glow promised a new day. "How imperfect is this son?"

"If he did exist, you would find him very handsome. Because he resembles his mother, with thick black hair and wonderful blue eyes. He's sweet-tempered and obedient. And his . . . imperfection has lessened as he has grown.

"What was—"

"He was born with tiny skulls on his spine. Unsettling at birth, but they have flattened to mere nubs as he's grown. Under his shirt, no one would ever see them."

"That's all? I want to see him. Now."

"Remember, high and mighty," he warned. "We're talking a dream. A possibility. A what-if . . ."

Merrihana fumbled for the bodice of her nightgown. Even asleep, she kept her favorite dagger near her skin. "When you kill Alrod, use this."

"Are you sure you know what you are saying?"

"Will you swear to support my—my son's rule?"

"Baroness, it is you who are the rightful ruler."

"Ruler?" Her eyes were uncomprehending. She was so caught up in the idea of having a living son that she could not see the implications.

"Rulers, actually. The Baroness of Traxx and the Baronet. That is," he added carefully, "if the dream of a son turned out to be the truth."

She fixed him again with that feline stare. "Is it the truth, Ghedo?"

He paused dramatically, building her anticipation, then bowed toward her. "Fifteen years ago, I served you by sparing your baby. That is not a dream but the truth—truth that will become a great joy."

"Kill the man who tried to rob me of him."

Ghedo bowed to hide his smile. "As you wish, Merrihana."

"When you're done, bring me my son."

"It will take me days to retrieve him."

"I've waited a lifetime," she said. "I can wait a bit longer."

TWENTY-THREE

THE SIGNAL TO ARMS CAME IN THE GRAY OF DAWN. Ajoba stood with the guards at the outer posts when they heard a frenzied barking coming from the millhouse. Brady's dog— giving warning. The next instant she spotted the cloud of dust, advancing with terrifying speed. Somehow Alrod had acquired an army far larger than his ten men.

The signal was silent as planned. They knew they couldn't hope to meet this threat head-on, but would have to hide and wait for opportunities to strike. Ajoba waved the guards to retreat to their fighting positions, taking it upon herself to ride along the perimeter and warn the others.

The one blessing—the only blessing—was that Alrod was not coming from across the river. If the Fenside force could kill a goodly number before the enemy penetrated as far as the millhouse, perhaps those barricaded inside could survive. They had floated coded messages downstream in empty jars, hoping they'd reach Dano, who was to the southwest.

Where were the birds? Even now she should see them fluttering from the brush as Alrod's army thundered toward Fenside. But none took to the sky.

After sounding the alarm, Ajoba secured Lacey at the outskirts of town, where Brady's and Cooper's horses were corralled. She winced to remember why Sammy wasn't there with them. The thought of Taryan's smart, loyal pony being butchered for Alrod's amusement caused her throat to tighten. Wasn't that just the perfect picture of what this world had become?

Ajoba ran to her position, south of the first firetrap. Curt held the north position—together, they were the vanguard. He was about twenty paces from her, close enough to communicate, but hopefully far enough to draw the attackers between them. She loaded tinder into the firepot, thankful to see the flame rise up.

Ajoba nocked one of the prepared arrows, its cloth head stuffed with straw. The combustible cornstalks had been set up at the edge of the village, along the main road leading into town. Furniture, corncobs, straw, and other flammable items were strewn about. It should look as if the villagers had made a quick retreat along the road. Hopefully the riders would slow for a closer look.

Wait for my arrow, Ajoba had told Curt.

She felt the ground shake, heard the battering of hooves. She dipped her arrow into the jar of alcohol and then into her firepot.

The flame went out.

Panicked, she sniffed the head of her arrow. One of the older women had set out a jar of cooking oil instead of alcohol, and it had smothered the flame. Ajoba should have checked, but she had assumed her orders would be followed exactly.

Just like Brady had.

"Curt," she called out, praying that Alrod wasn't close enough to hear. "My fire went out. Shoot when you think best. I'll try to draw them into the center of our fuel piles."

He popped his head up, waving *no*.

"Do what I say!" she shouted.

The horde came into sight, Alrod riding in the second tier, with four of his soldiers before him. These stupid men believed it an honor to precede the baron, when their position was simply to trigger any traps.

The men behind him made her blood run cold. Alrod had somehow met up with the marauders and convinced them to do his bidding. The force of ten they expected numbered at least thirty—most of whom, she knew from experience, were extremely dangerous. Fenside had neither the weapons nor the experience to fight off such a force.

Alrod pointed for the group to split. Why had she thought

they'd ride into the center of town? She had archers and spear throwers around the perimeter, but they'd only take down three, maybe four before being spotted. She had to draw Alrod this way, where their main defenses had been set.

She raced to Curt's hideout. "No matter what I do, don't shoot until you have at least five or six men in the fire circle. If I'm in there with them, so be it."

"Miss . . ."

"It all depends on you. Do it."

He opened his mouth, closed it again. Then simply said, "Aye."

Ajoba darted across the way, deliberately not looking at Alrod's troops. Let them think she was trying to hide. She raced back across the road, toward the houses, casting a panicked glance behind her and pulling on one door after another.

She crossed into the open again, cheese for the rat.

Alrod and half his men headed her way. She shrieked and ran for the town center. They came at a trot, alert for danger. She ran faster, praying Curt would hold his arrows until he could get enough of them in the ring of fuel to do damage. Even with the dust stirred by the horses, she smelled the alcohol when he lit the fire. A moment later she heard the phtfft sound, followed quickly by two more and a series of small bangs as the alcohol-filled cornstalks exploded.

She risked a backward glance. Alrod, sensing a trap, had hung back, but some of his men were caught. Horses reared in panic, and her heart ached that the helpless animals should reap the consequences of the baron's evil. She counted five men go down. Two more turned and tried to run away, but were cut down by Alrod's sword.

The smoke provided cover but robbed Ajoba of breath. The smell of burning flesh and the frantic screams sent her to her knees. She breathed fresher air with the dust.

"Forward," Alrod growled, picking through the waning fire with his head up and his eyes vigilant.

Ajoba signaled for the archers and spear throwers to let loose and rolled out of the way. More men were struck. The first villager was hit, cut down by a stray arrow from his own comrades. As he fell, their positions on the roofs of the huts were easily revealed. Alrod signaled four men back to the fires, where they took burning wood and set the huts ablaze. Each villager was cut down as he leaped from the fire.

The noise was intense and horrific—men screaming, flames roaring, horses shrieking, men cursing.

The children! Ajoba hadn't anticipated that they would see their fathers killed. If even one cried out, Alrod would set the trees ablaze. But maybe not. The leaves on the trees were summer green, the limbs filled with sap—they would not burn easily. The children would have time to get out and race for the millhouse, their mothers and older brothers acting as a shield—assuming they did not lose their nerve. But could Taryan make it? And would they be safe even there?

Ajoba used the conflagration as a screen from which to shoot her arrows. She moved frequently, hoping her pesky shots were considered to be from a troop and not a lone girl without good aim. She took three soldiers down, but her arrows bounced off the baron. His armor, she remembered, had been fashioned from the skin of a mogged crocodile. Flexible and light, the kind reserved only for the most privileged of nobles, it deflected the arrows easily.

When Ajoba exhausted her supply of arrows, she hurried to join the gauntlet of fighters that stretched between the trees and the millhouse. From here, she could hear the sounds of fighting in the outer reaches of the village. Fenside's men, wielding their shovels, picks, and clay-corn spears, fought hard for the lives of their families as some of Alrod's men worked their way toward the millhouse.

Directly in front of the millhouse, the fortification warriors—mothers and older children—huddled behind piles of dirt and corncobs fortified with flat stones taken from the river. A horse might be able to leap such a barrier, but would be made to pay, so the baron and his men would most likely approach on foot, which meant they could be engaged face-to-face.

But Lord willing, few would survive the stoning and make it here. To think that their lives depended on children in trees. Children and Taryan.

Alrod regrouped the rest of his men, their forms sharply outlined by the fires behind them. Ajoba gasped as she got a closer look at the marauders. She remembered them as being scarred and coarsened, with legs bowed from rickets. These were definitely the same men. She recognized their horses and their clothes and even their faces. But looking at them now, they all seemed clear-skinned and powerful of limb. Was it danger that shifted her perception, or had Alrod foisted some change on the men?

No time to ponder that—she had to lure them into the trees. Again, she would be bait—this time as planned. And rightly so. She wore armor and could take punishment that a villager could not.

"Be ready," she told her warriors. Many faces were tear-stained, some hands shook, but the determined gazes and set mouths told her that the mothers and brothers understood what was at stake.

Fenside's children—ready to stone a stronghold prince.

Their babies—trapped in the millhouse.

She risked a glance at the upper window. Brady waited, his face white, his eyes strained. His heart would be breaking, not to take part in this.

Ajoba raced for the trees, calling up to the children. "I'm bringing them. Be ready. Don't worry about hitting me. Just bomb away."

Overhead, a boy asked, "What's a bomb?"

Weapons, plagues, terrors, wars . . . and it still goes on. I commend these children to Your care, Lord.

She screamed at the top of her lungs, "Alrod!" Twice more, before the ruckus in the village quieted. She crept to the edge of the trees where she could be seen. "Send those men away. Let's you and I fight it out."

The children gasped. "Shush," Taryan hissed. "It's a trick. Be ready."

Alrod pulled his horse to where he could see her. He kept men on both sides of him, ready to block a sudden arrow. "A stupid girl challenges me? I know it's you, Ajoba. Even that shining mask can't block that big mouth of yours."

"Aye, and that big mouth just offered a big challenge. Are you man enough to accept?"

"I'm man enough to offer you surrender."

"I do not surrender."

Alrod laughed. "No, you talk men to death."

She faked a hand motion to the tree side of her hip. "There!" A marauder pointed to where her phantom troops waited.

"Circle round," Alrod said. "Half after her—the other half go the long way around." He had gathered about twelve of his men to him. The others—by the sound of it—were still engaged in fighting at the outer reaches of the village.

Ajoba prayed the baron's half would come after her. He seemed to start her way, but a man walked to his side, a tall man in the robe of a master sorcerer. Not Ghedo, though. Why hadn't she seen him before? And what was that awful smell?

Alrod leaned over to take the sorcerer's counsel. The man turned, looking straight at her. But he had no face, only a well of darkness, and Ajoba's heart convulsed as she realized how Alrod's troops had been transformed.

She scurried back into the trees. "Wait until you have them under you," she whispered.

Six men on horses came into the trees. She had expected them to be on foot—their heads were almost in the leaves. Would they see the children, and sound the alarm? The first did look up briefly. But the children were very high, leaves sewn to their trousers as cover. She darted about in the middle of the grove, acting like a frantic woman, hoping to distract the soldiers. She stripped off her gloves and shoved them under the top of her mask, hoping the extra layers of shroud would prevent her skull from being crushed should she take a bag of rocks to the head.

"Now!" Taryan yelled, and rocks rained from above.

Men ducked, only one suffering an immediate fatal blow. The horses reared and screamed. Another man went down, but wasn't injured enough to stay down. She rushed at him, feeling a blow to her own head from rocks, thankful that most of the force was shuttled to out-of-time. The fallen man stared with astonishment that she had survived a boulder to the head. His astonishment died with him after she ran him through, left-handed, with her short blade.

"Hey, good one." Curt had joined her, his face black with soot, putting Taryan's sword to good use.

None of Alrod's six made it out of the grove alive. But the other half of the band was closing in, and all their rocks had been used.

"Retreat!" Ajoba shouted. The trees rustled, leaves giving away the location of the young attackers. Arrows flew, the leaves and branches blocking mortal blows until one of Alrod's men realized where the children were heading.

He cut down the first boy to drop out of the tree. A girl took an arrow to the thigh. One of the mothers at the fortification screamed. She took the third arrow. Brady let his arrows fly from the millhouse, providing enough cover to kill two men and drive the rest away.

"Are they gone?" Curt asked. "Did we win?"

"They'll be coming around the other side. We need to get everyone inside the millhouse."

Brady had disappeared from the window. She feared he was trying to come out and fight, but Hannah shouted that he had fainted.

"Taryan!"

"Back here." She had only advanced halfway.

"Quick." Ajoba found her, opened her arms. "Jump."

"I can't. My legs will shatter."

"You must. Wrap your armor over your feet. The shroud will help, and I'll try to break your fall. Hurry. Aim for my chest—more shroud there. Trust me, sister. But hurry."

The impact rolled them both to the ground. Taryan screamed but stayed conscious and was able to pull herself onto Ajoba's back. Ajoba limped toward the millhouse.

The first enemy rounded the corner of the building and rode straight at Ajoba and Taryan. Ajoba tried to run, could barely keep staggering toward the door. She saw his furious eyes, his wide-open mouth.

Just as the man raised his sword, he toppled. Brady had regained consciousness and was hanging halfway out the window so he could shoot sideways.

Ajoba had no breath for praying, but she heard Taryan whisper a *thank you* near her ear.

Now the mothers and surviving men from the village were surrounding them outside the door, heaving rocks at the attackers coming from the side. Ajoba struggled inside and dropped Taryan into the waiting arms of two women.

"Everyone in," she yelled.

Brady provided cover while the rest returned to the millhouse.

"Close the door," Curt cried as he rolled in, an arrow sticking from his shoulder.

They leaped against the door, slamming it and sliding the various bars into place. Ajoba panted, and someone poured water over her face, then helped her drink.

She looked around, icy fingers snaking into her ribs. "Where's Cooper?"

TWENTY-FOUR

"Is your throat sore?" Merrihana asked.

"No, m'lady. I could sing forever." Timothy had spent the early morning hours with the baroness, cloistered in her private garden, and he marveled at the change in her. Eyes that just last night had been touched with sorrow were now merry.

Had his music provoked this mood shift?

Or was she so unstable that she could be burdened one day and dancing the next?

His task was to keep her occupied while Niki and Anastasia continued their search for the shroud. According to the sorcerer's assistant—whom he and Niki had yet to meet—Ghedo had taken off from the stronghold yet again, giving them the opportunity that they needed.

The baroness kept Dawnray at her side as well. She had apparently given up the ridiculous attempt to dress and paint the girl in her own image. Even so, Dawnray looked troubled, as if Merrihana's burdens had somehow slid onto her shoulders.

"What shall I sing for you now, Baroness?"

"Walk with me, Timothy." With a flick of her hand, Merrihana made it clear Dawnray was to remain where she was.

They strolled through the garden, a sanctuary on the top of the marble tower. Though draped in ivy, the spikes that protected this pinnacle from flying mogs were still unmistakable. This was the nature of noble life—beauty crowned with violence.

"Are your parents still alive?" Merrihana said, linking her arm through his.

What a strange question. They hadn't developed their cover story this deeply. He'd answer with the truth. "Yes. I haven't seen them in over two years, but I'm told they're well."

"Are they also drudges?"

"They're servants." *Of the living God,* he added in his mind.

"Did they sell you?"

He laughed. "No. I volunteered for this."

"To be a slave?"

"To sing for the pleasure of others."

"Do they love each other?"

"Who?"

"Your parents."

Timothy smiled. In an uncertain world, this was an assurance he often clung to. "Very much. And they love me the same way."

"But they let you go?"

"They wanted what was best for me. If a life of service would allow me to sing, they blessed that service."

Merrihana stopped, turned to face him. "Can you love as they have?"

Timothy willed himself to not look back at Dawnray. Merrihana was a beautiful woman. Troubled, given to violence, but he couldn't think of that—not when she studied every blink of his eye. And he could answer this particular question truthfully: "Yes."

"What if I were to ask you to love me like that?"

"High and mighty, you're married."

"By contract, my husband is allowed his lollies, and I'm allowed consorts."

"I don't understand," he said, though he understood perfectly. How desperate could this woman be, to demand love from a near stranger?

Merrihana brushed his cheek with the back of her hand. "I can buy your voice, your music, your constant presence," she mused. "I can command your respect, your obedience. But your love—that would need to be given willingly. Could you do that, Timothy?"

There were many lies Timothy had told for the sake of Birthright. But this was one lie he could not. Nor could any birthrighter. For if they were not true to love, they could not be true to anything.

"Love is grown, not given," Timothy said. "It takes time to take root."

She nodded. "Thus, it is a challenge."

Timothy laughed. "Aye, love is a hard thing. But worth pursuing, is it not?"

Merrihana traced his lips with her finger. "It surely is, minstrel."

Minstrel. For the moment, at least, it sounded like a name he could live with. Not tracker, not birthrighter. Just a minstrel, someone who lives to sing—to give pleasure. Being here, on top of the world, was a temptation. Shielded by spikes, surrounded by flowers, in the clutch of a beautiful woman—any man would be captivated by all this.

But he was not a minstrel. Not really. And his heart was elsewhere.

A pain seized Timothy, so sudden that he had to grasp his chest.

"Are you all right?" Merrihana's face filled with alarm.

"Yes," he told her, slightly breathless. "Heart just skipped a beat, that's all."

His heart was elsewhere. Timothy thought he had made his choice—that his heart had made the choice without him. He had the will to serve Birthright, but the passion to love Dawnray. He must not fail either one.

Niki and Anastasia huddled in the wagon shed, having sneaked in here before the light of day. Niki fumed as they waited, one hour turning to the next, their stomachs growling for breakfast and then for lunch.

The sorcerer's assistant finally crept in after high noon. Anastasia stood to greet him. "Ghedo needed me, but now he's gone—probably for a full day," the boy said.

Niki stood. Gabe's eyes widened. "Who are you? Are you the outrider?"

She frowned. "The question is—who are you? *What* are you?"

He kicked the dust. "Depends who you ask."

"I'm asking you."

Anastasia opened her mouth to answer. Niki waved her silent. "I'm waiting."

"I don't know."

"That's not an acceptable answer."

Anger flashed in Gabe's eyes. "All right. I'm a deformed reject. I don't know who my parents are, or even if I had any. Taken off the trash heap by the master sorcerer of Traxx. Raised by cooks and maids and gardeners—when they were in the mood to put up with me. Trained by the sorcerer to haul supplies, measure oils, clean his messes. Forced by my own weakness not to look at the horrors he spawned but to pretend I was somewhere else, to deafen my ears to screams of agony or cries for mercy. Provoked by something inside me that I can't name to look at the blue sky, sailing clouds, cool rain, and to dare dream that there is something greater than Ghedo's needles or Alrod's swords or my own fears. Seized by my own longing to go beyond the wall of thorns and cobratraps and see an eagle soar free and a horse run like the summer wind and to find freedom in the far-off mountains.

"In short"—he turned to leave—"I'm a freak of nature."

But Niki grabbed his hand. "Nice to meet you, Gabe of the trash heap." She grinned. "I'm Niki of Horesh."

"Niki of the reward posters? This is what you look like without the mask?"

"Afraid so."

"You dare to come here?"

She laughed. "I dare too many things. I understand you'd like to leave this place."

"Yes," he said. "Please. Get me out of here."

"We'll do our best," Niki said. "But we first have a mission to attend to. I need to find a shining cloth that—"

"The burning cloth? About this wide?" Gabe motioned with his hands to show two paces by three.

"Have you seen it?" Anastasia asked.

"Alrod gave it to Ghedo. He's supposed to be figuring out its secret, but he's been busy with Merrihana. And you, I guess—if you're the one that brought her the minstrel."

Niki groaned. "Dare I ask where he keeps it?"

"With his potions."

"In the lair?"

He nodded.

"What are we waiting for? Take me there."

"You don't understand—"

Anastasia clutched Niki's arm. "He guards his potions with mogs."

"So?"

Gabe squeezed Anastasia's hand. "Make her understand."

"What would be more precious to a sorcerer than his potions? He's got vile mogs to protect them."

"So?"

Gabe put his mouth to Anastasia's ear. "Why doesn't she understand?"

"She's an outrider," Anastasia whispered back. "They're thick sometimes."

Niki laughed. "We may be thick, but we're not hard of hearing. As for you, Gabe of the trash heap, you take me into that hole where Ghedo works his demented magic, show me where my burning cloth is hidden, and let me worry about the rest. You do this, and I will help you become Gabriel of the far-off mountains. Got it?"

"Got it," Gabe said, finally daring to smile.

Timothy flopped onto the pillows next to Dawnray. "I've only got a minute. She's gone to find her stylists and tailors to have some new clothes made for me."

She smiled. "Lucky you."

"Are you all right?"

"Don't worry about me. Just be careful, Timothy." She lowered her voice. "Even now, she could be eavesdropping."

"We'll be leaving soon. Maybe even today."

"Be careful," she repeated.

"I know a safe place in the north. We can be married there."

"What? I didn't say anything about getting married." Dawnray clutched her throat, ashamed that she had led him to believe this was an immediate possibility. "I can't—I mean, I would like that, but I can't promise . . ."

His eyes were wounded. "I came for you."

"Thank you, dear one. Thank you so much." She pressed her hand to her heart. "But we can't just jump into marriage. It's not . . ."

"Not what?" His eyes swam with tears.

"Not right. You know it's not, Timothy. We need time to get to know each other first."

"I thought, under the circumstances . . ."

"That I would be grateful? I am, incredibly so. That I would be drawn to you? Tremendously so. But you see what passion does to these people—filling their appetites, only to leave them hungry for more."

Anger clouded his face. "You think I'm like Alrod? Wanting to satisfy some physical need?"

"Shush—keep your voice down. Of course not. I'm just saying that I have been raised to respect a certain propriety."

"And I haven't been?"

She squeezed his hand. "I'm sure you have been. Which is why you have to agree that love cannot be spoken again until friendship is formed."

A cackle of voices—Merrihana's stylists—echoed from the hall.

"I love you," Timothy said hurriedly. "And because of that, I will honor you."

He picked up the gittern and launched into a song about Merrihana just as she came back into the garden.

Dawnray watched him as he sang, putting the same passion into his song that he had just spoken to her. And knowing, though he couldn't say it, that he was really singing for her.

She sighed quietly. She wanted to love him. Maybe she did love him. But to leap into marriage because Timothy was her rescuer would be a huge mistake.

If God was merciful—and she knew He was—they would have time for all that soon enough.

TWENTY-FIVE

"I MADE A MISTAKE IN MAKING YOU A TRACKER," BRADY said.

Ajoba studied her feet. A battle had taught her what four years of training and a year of serving had not—how important it was to respect authority. Well-meaning people like the woman who had filled her jar with oil instead of alcohol. Or even Curt, who had questioned her orders with Alrod bearing right down on them. "I'm sorry. I—"

He cut her off with a laugh. "I mean, you should have been an outrider. Well done, mate."

It all crashed in on her then. Smoke and fire, blood and bowels, screaming attackers and crying children, flying spears and slashing swords. Two children dead, four injured. At least five men dead. Two mothers, one grandmother.

Cooper missing.

Ajoba wept, Brady's hand on her head, Taryan's arm over her shoulder. So much to mourn. Tylow dying a year ago, a vine in his boot snaking to his heart. Arabah gripped in darkness. A world brought to the brink of no return, should the seams loosen further. Weapons, plagues, terrors, wars—the Endless Wars so many years ago had only been the beginning. Horses and flowers and men transmogrified to what their Creator never intended, the sorcerers and stronghold princes hurling the ultimate insult against mankind and God in their lust for power. And to fight it all, only a faithful remnant huddled under the ice and a desperately small band of young people sent back to do what they could.

What would they do should the seams loosen further?

Still she cried on, for the slash in Taryan's throat and her friend the gargant lying in a coma outside Horesh. For her arrogance and pride, which allowed her to be deceived so easily. For her anger at Brady's anger, for her determination to prove her worth when she needed to prove her humility.

And for the forgiveness of a merciful Lord and the restoration of a blessed Savior that even now held her so tightly Ajoba could not be ripped away. Not by her own grief or her impending death or any failure. She marveled to realize that even now, with her heart broken, she knew that. Even now she felt the mercy flowing like the river rushing under the wheel of the millhouse, washing away her transgressions, promising an eventual end to tears and pain.

Until then, she would do as she was told. Even if that meant riding north into exile, or walking out that door to face Alrod, her hands empty but her heart firmly grasped.

"Ajoba. Sit up, please." Brady grasped her elbow and urged her to straighten.

Ajoba stood. "I'm sorry."

"Shush. I've heard enough." Brady reached out to gently touch her face. "Ajoba, you need to know—I never sent the letter to the Ark."

Her eyes widened. "You didn't?"

He smiled. "Oh, I wrote it. And I almost sent it—you know how angry I've been. But something held me back. Something told me that when the time came you'd conduct yourself as a true birthrighter. And you have. Welcome, sister. Welcome back."

Her heart soared. "Thank you," she whispered.

"Now," he continued, "we still have work today. Can't leave Cooper out there." Brady left unspoken what would be odious to give voice to. Even if the boy were dead, the armor he wore had to be recovered before Alrod got it.

"I'll go," Ajoba said.

Brady struggled to stand. "No. I will."

"You can't."

"True. But I will. The time has come when I must."

"Wear my armor," Taryan said.

He laughed. "A mite small, wouldn't you say?"

"You're not well enough," Ajoba argued. "I'm going."

He turned, his eyes boring through her. "I said that I will. Don't argue."

"We're surrounded. You need some protection."

"You can cover me from the loft up there. That will help."

"I mean—maybe I could spin some shroud." She looked down. "If I'm allowed."

Brady lifted her chin. "Mate, I'll give you my blessing. But the spindle is at Horesh, remember? Where it belongs."

"What about the last piece of shroud in your bag?" Taryan said.

"Toss me my bag."

Curt dug through the pile of spears and bows, came up with the leather bag, and handed it over. Brady peered inside. "Mouse-sized."

"At least put it to your wound," Ajoba said.

"Yes," he said. "That I'll do."

Taryan's sword was light, but in his weakened state, it was all Brady could carry. Cooper had his sword. He could only hope it had served the rook well.

Taryan had bound his side, placing a patch of shroud against his wound and relieving his pain for the first time in three days. He had hoped that their supply of shroud would multiply to fill their need, just as a few loaves and fishes had once sufficed to feed a crowd. But that even the one small piece remained was something to give thanks for. His wound was bound, and Cooper doubtless needed his armor more than he did anyway.

Taryan put her lips to his ears and whispered, "You can't feel the wound, but that doesn't mean it's not there. Act accordingly."

"I will, lass. I will."

"Come back to me, lad."

He could only smile and, in his heart, bid her farewell.

Ajoba stood by as he slipped on Taryan's mask and gloves. "What's your plan, outrider?"

"Quite the little commander you are."

She quirked a smile. "Got to watch out for my troops."

"You're a pest."

She squinted at him.

"It's a gift," he whispered. "Use it well."

Ajoba laughed. "I use it often. Don't know about well. But I keep wondering why the rest of Alrod's men haven't attacked. What are they doing out there?"

"We took out too many of his men for him to manage a direct assault," Brady said. "So they're going to wait us out—just bide their time until we run out of food and water."

"So what are we going to do?"

"Right now," he said, "I'm going to find Cooper."

Ajoba and Curt guided him up the steep stairs and into the loft where he had earlier stood. The window was small and, at the moment, barred with lumber. Brady's lungs ached with the mere effort of climbing the stairs. "Cooper was guarding the downstream side of the dam, right?"

"Yes."

"I'm going to sneak down there and try to find him. Chances are he's simply keeping low so the troops in the front of this place don't see him."

Curt scratched his cheek. "We just hoisted you up here only to have to take you back down?"

Brady smiled. "Not exactly."

Ajoba put her hand to her mouth. "You can't."

"Mate, as long as I'm awake, I'm the commander of your crew. So don't tell me I can't."

"I meant, you can't pull it off."

"Probably not, but it's the best chance I have of getting out of here alive."

Curt snorted. "You folks are all addled, aren't you?"

"Aye, you got that right," Brady said, laughing. He slipped Taryan's weapon into its sheath and laced the top tightly. He would not relish diving through this window only to fall on her sword. "Help me up."

"Wait." Ajoba put her hand on his arm. "You told me to bless the troops before I sent them out to fight." She pressed her hands to his eyelids since his forehead was covered by the shroud mask. "May the Lord bless you, keep you, strengthen you"—her voice broke—"and bring you and Cooper back to us."

"Amen," Curt said.

"Thank you. Now get me up into that window."

Ajoba pulled the bars out while Curt helped Brady onto the high stool where he had sat before. The sky had gotten dark. Too dark for early afternoon. "Do you get thunderstorms here, Curt?" he asked.

"What? No, never."

Brady understood it all now. This was why there were no birds in the sky. Why the marauders had become mighty warriors. Why Alrod felt comfortable traveling without his usual army.

Why the man in the master sorcerer's robes—the one Ajoba had seen with Alrod—was not Ghedo at all.

The coming darkness was the real reason he had to go after Cooper.

He scanned the ground on the village side of the river, where what was left of Alrod's troops had gathered. The fires in the streets still burned, as did most of the homes. No one paid much attention to the millhouse. Awaiting orders, most likely.

Alrod was not in sight. A bad sign. He probably wasn't killed in the battle, not while wearing his mogged armor. He wouldn't have left either. He knew Brady was inside, along with others. He was likely scouting a means of entry into the millhouse.

Brady squeezed into the tiny window until he was almost falling out headfirst, waiting for power to gather in his legs so he could spring.

It didn't come.

"Ajoba, run down and warn everyone not to panic when they hear what I cry out. But it would help to have someone screech or shriek in response. With some crying to follow."

She scurried down the steps.

"Curt, I need you to toss me out of this window. Hard enough to clear the foundation and gear house and make the water."

"Man, I am just not that strong."

"You will be. On my count of three. One—two—three!"

Brady flew from the window, his scream not faked because this was truly insane.

The water met him, cold and still except for the steady pull of water toward the wheel. He kicked up, his head coming out long enough to cry for help, praying that his warning was heeded and no one inside the millhouse took him seriously.

He pretended to paddle away from the waterwheel, kicking just enough not to be drawn in until he was ready. Arrows rained about him, striking the side of his head and dazing him, though the birthright armor took part of the force.

He felt the turn of the waterwheel, the sucking sound as each blade cut into the water and spun it downstream. When he rescued the villagers before, he climbed the wheel and rode it. This time he would have to brave the blades themselves, timing his dive perfectly so as not to lose his head.

"Auuuuugh!" He slid under the water, kicking hard on legs that barely worked. The blade cracked against his shoulder. He shot back up, not having to fake flailing this time, letting his pain come out in another howl.

Under the water again—holding back a split second—and this time he got between the blades. He hung on, managing to drape himself in such a way that he wouldn't be crushed as the wheel made its turn. He rose out of the water, faking a broken body. Screams sounded from inside the millhouse, so fervent that he worried they believed his death. They might not be too far off if he didn't exit the wheel more competently than he had gotten onto it.

Brady took a second turn on the wheel, hanging partway off the blade so it would not surprise the attackers if he was not to be seen on the next turn of the wheel.

Chilled, he was trembling too hard to get off. He huddled deep into the blades on the next turn, hoping he would not be seen while he rallied more strength. He needed to get out of the water as soon as he could or he'd lose all his strength through shivering.

One more turn, and he would push out from the blades, hoping to tumble in the wheel's downswing and not be crushed on the rocks. He curled into a tight ball, back facing outward, holding his breath and waiting until his part of the wheel was at its lowest point.

Almost there. Ready . . .

The wheel stopped.

Someone must have jammed a log into the gear. Brady was stuck underwater, caught between two blades and the rock bottom. He gave a violent kick against the blade. It splintered but held. He was at the end of himself—his strength, his air, his hope.

Brady reached beyond for one last kick. He cracked the blade open and tumbled with what little water leached through the dam onto the rocks below.

He huddled on the rocks, listening to cries from inside the millhouse, even shouts of concern from the marauders, as a heavy darkness moved across the sky from the east. He knew that darkness. He had experienced it on Welz less than a month ago, had fought in it with Niki. The demon was spinning a void, perhaps with the power of Alrod's lust and the marauders' wickedness. Brady confessed his own anger, not willing to contribute to this darkness, taking forgiveness on like a cloak.

He rolled off the rock, grateful that, with the wheel stopped, there was no violent flow to contend with. He used Taryan's sword as a support for legs that wanted less than ever to work.

Ajoba had set sharp rocks in this part of the river as yet another trap. He picked through them with care. None of the troops even bothered coming to the downstream side of the wheel to see if he had survived. They were more interested in downing their victory ale than gawking at yet another dead body. But Alrod should be interested. Where was he?

When Brady cleared the dam, he stopped. Listening, sniffing, waiting.

Then he saw it—Cooper outlined like a candle flame on the far bank. He stood with his sword out, staring into some sort of dark tunnel . . . and singing, his voice holding strong though his shoulders sagged. Somehow Brady summoned the energy to climb up and take his place at the rook's side, his sword also out. Now he recognized the song: "Glorious."

Alrod stood across from Cooper, a creature of darkness at his side. Its foul stench hovered all around them.

"Ah, Brady of Horesh," the creature said.

"I don't think I've had the displeasure," Brady said, vaguely aware that strength was returning to his legs. Not his own strength—he had reached its limit in the river. But a power he knew he could depend on.

"Feel free to call me Simon."

"The master sorcerer of Traxx," Alrod added, like a petulant child who feared being left out.

"Baron, I thought better of you," Brady said. "How have you let yourself come to this?"

Alrod smiled. "I'm not the one trapped."

"Think again, Alrod."

Alrod's eyes shifted to Simon, but he maintained his confident pose.

"I can't get to them," Cooper said. "But they can't get by me."

"Good work," Brady said.

"Do you want your sword?"

What could he do by himself that he and Niki hadn't been able to do back on Welz? Yet for the sake of all these people, perhaps he should try. He reached for the sword—

Not yet, son.

—and waved away Cooper's offer. "No. You keep it."

"Will we fight?"

"Yes, Brady," Alrod sneered. "Will we?"

Brady wanted nothing than to rush Alrod and plunge his sword into him. Surely Alrod wanted to do the same. But for some divine purpose, each was being held off.

"Cooper, come back into the millhouse with me."

"Retreating, Brady? I thought better of you."

"Baron, I would truly suggest you do the same."

Alrod laughed. Simon stared, flesh melting from his face. Seeing the truth, Cooper faltered.

"Mate, it's all right. Let's go into the millhouse, have a bite to eat."

"The marauders . . ."

"Pawns. Mere shadows on this tent that Alrod and that sorry lump of sorrow are pitching. We've nothing to fear from them except sloppy insults and a bad odor."

He took Cooper's arm and turned him, hoping he was right. If not, Alrod's sword would find its way into both their backs. One step, then another. Alrod could not follow. This was a stalemate, then. The Lord's stalemate, for His good purpose.

"Brady of Horesh!" Alrod called out. "I know your secret."

Brady inhaled deeply, trying not to show the dread that fell on him. He looked over his shoulder and forced a smile. "I have many secrets, Baron. I expect you do as well."

"Not the kind that could drive every kingdom and every land into my hands. Hidden deep, but not too deep for me to uncover."

"He knows," Cooper hissed.

"Quiet, mate. He's fishing," Brady whispered before turning back to face Alrod. "You're deceived, Baron. There is no secret grand enough that will make you the king of all kings. Isn't that true, Simon?"

The creature shook, splattering shrieks like drops of foul sewage. One splashed Alrod's cheek but, inured to such horror, the baron didn't notice.

"What's he talking about?" Alrod said.

"Are you so easily swayed?" Simon crossed his arms over his

chest. "Never did I imagine I'd echo an outrider. But I thought better of you."

"Answer my question, Simon," Alrod demanded. "Did you lie about there being a splendid secret?"

"I did not."

Brady laughed, half-expecting the baron to stick his tongue out like a child. "You ask the sorcerer the wrong question."

"Is it your ploy to prolong your life with blather, Brady?"

"Ask your sorcerer if you will be the king of all kings."

Alrod spat. "I don't intend to contribute to your nonsense."

"Chicken?" Cooper made a pecking motion with his head.

Light exploded, nearly blinding Brady. Cooper cried out, "What was that?"

"Ignore Simon. Focus on Alrod."

"You ignore me at the peril of that which is hidden on the mountain called Welz, outrider." Simon smiled, his teeth reflecting faces Brady once had known—friends named Maya and Chad and Lin and others who had left training after him.

Brady kept his gaze on the baron. "Alrod, I advise you one last time, in the only act of kindness I will ever show you. Ask Simon if he can indeed make you the king of all kings."

Alrod turned to Simon. "Will you?"

"Yes. If you will discover their secret, yes."

"How will I do that?"

Simon smiled, his teeth now showing the faces of ones Brady loved dearly. Niki and Kendo and Leiha and Kwesi and Kaya and Bartoly, shifting the faces until even Magosha and Manueo and Niki's wolf passed through the creature's mouth. Brady steeled himself to ignore the images but Cooper huddled against him, appalled.

"So simple, my dear baron," Simon hissed in answer. "Now that you have trapped Brady, find yourself an outrider—preferably a woman, just to make it fun—and torture her until she speaks. Or he speaks for her."

Alrod's laughter echoed in the tunnel of darkness.

"I've heard enough. Let's go." Brady wrapped his arm around

Cooper, feeling the strength drain out of his legs once again. They helped each other across the river, up the bank, and into the front door of the millhouse without one spot of challenge from Alrod's soldiers.

"Simon lied," Cooper said. "Didn't he?"

Brady nodded. "He's very good at it. Now, come on, lad. I'm suddenly hungry enough to eat a horse."

TWENTY-SIX

THE HISTORIES TOLD OF ANCIENT AND ASTOUNDING weapons. Of bombs that could fly through a window no bigger than Niki's back and blow up a city block.

Surely this was a time for such a bomb. With one well-placed explosion, Niki could rid the world of a great evil. Ignite a bomb in the middle of this great cavern, and its mighty blast would make a crater big enough to suck the whole palace into it. *Surgical strike*, the histories called such a thing.

Those bombs were a great evil, her father had said as he helped her study her histories. A harsh necessity, her mother had countered, thus igniting debate.

The old sayings of *fighting fire with fire* surely applied to this place. No one could argue this lair and its poisons out of existence. It would take Niki's sword, driven into the heart of Ghedo's universe. Surely the Lord had put this sword in her hand when He called her to serve the Birthright Project.

Yet her life had not been redeemed with a sword, though she had tried desperately to make it so.

Niki fell to her knees, desperate to tell the Almighty how sorry she was. Sorry for the horrors of Ghedo's lair. Sorry for Gabriel, who looked about to explode with fear. Sorry for how hard she had been on Anastasia.

Sorry that there were times—too many times—that the sword in her hand was still necessary. And that she sometimes burned just to swing it, no matter what.

May your grace reach even here, Niki prayed, hoping that

Anastasia was right and that God's grace had found a home in a boy whose only home was a sorcerer's lair.

She stood. "I'm ready."

"Go in peace," Anastasia said.

"I'm not going anywhere."

"You can't be sure of that."

"I don't know how far the chamber of potions goes. Don't know much, actually," Gabe said. "Only Ghedo goes in there. Anastasia learned that lesson the hard way."

"She learns all her lessons the hard way." Niki turned to Anastasia. "Don't you dare try to help or rescue me or anything else unless I ask. Are we clear?"

"Yes, but what if—"

"Hey! Do I need to tie you up to make you obey?"

Anastasia bit back her pout. "No."

"All right, then. Keep your ears and eyes on alert for the sorcerer."

"He's not due back until late tonight," Gabe said.

"You going to argue too?"

"Sorry, outrider."

Anastasia had said the chamber of potions could draw someone into its clutches the same way the flowers on the wall of thorns could. Niki stuffed mint leaves into her mouth and smeared lard over her nostrils. "Get me the rat, Gabe."

Niki released the rat at the entrance to the chamber of potions. A stunned look came over its little face and, clearly with no notion of why, he was drawn in. They watched as mogged pumpkin vines snaked up through an iron grate in the floor and squeezed the life out of the poor little fellow.

"Get me those mats, the ones where the boots are. And I need another rat." Niki tossed the mat into the hallway and covered the grate. Then she released the next animal.

"Is that it?" Anastasia whispered. "Did you take care of the trap?"

"Do not talk to me," Niki snapped. "I already told you that."

"Sorry."

"Apologizing is still talking. Shut up."

The second rat penetrated deeper into the hallway before a horde of flying beasts descended on him. Miniaturized vultures—mogged with a thirst for warm blood, judging by how quickly they ripped the animal apart. Though their bodies were the size of butterflies, their beaks were sharp and strong. Perhaps some piranha had been included in their transmogrification.

When the little birds had finished their meal, they receded into the side grate from which they had come. Whatever triggered their release had also triggered some powerful lure to call them back.

Niki looked back at Gabe. "You say that Ghedo waltzes in here and nothing attacks him?"

He nodded.

"I don't have all day to defuse his little traps, and I'm sure he doesn't either. There must be tripwires along the way that he knows to avoid. Or maybe there's a master switch he throws that closes all these grates. What have you noticed?"

"Nothing," Gabe said. "I mean, I haven't seen anything. He sends me into the storeroom. He says it's so nothing will get me if they get loose. I'm sorry."

"You never even peeked?"

"I learned very early not to disobey him."

Anastasia raised her hand.

"What?" Niki said, irked. "We're not in school."

"You said not to talk, so—"

"What!"

She pointed across the cavern. "Perhaps the prisoners might have seen something."

Niki's heart ached to see human beings in cages. They rattled the bars, choking out sounds that she couldn't decipher.

"They can't talk," Anastasia said. "Ghedo cut out their—"

"Don't. They know what's been done to them." She went to each of the captives, introducing herself and grasping their hands. "I swear, we will get you out of here."

One of the men banged his fist against the door to his cage.

"I can't. Not yet," Niki said. "You'll want to run away. I understand that, but that would be dangerous for all of us."

The woman wrapped her arms around her knees and sobbed.

"Look, if we unlock your cages, will you swear you'll wait in here until we tell you it's all clear?"

They nodded.

Niki hesitated another second, then turned to Gabe. "Do it."

While he unlocked the cages, Niki sought a clear line of sight for the entrance to the chamber of potions. She found the vantage point in a cage where a ginger-haired man sat.

"Sir. Please look with me." She helped him sight down her arm. "Have you seen the sorcerer enter there?"

He nodded.

"Did he do anything right before going in?"

The man uttered incomprehensible squeaks.

"Can you write it down?"

He shook his head. Few people outside the strongholds could read or write unless a birthrighter teacher taught them.

"Will you show me?"

He nodded.

"You can't run for the stairs. Understood? You have to stay down here until we tell you it's safe to leave."

He nodded again. Niki looked at the others. "You've given your word. If you run away, we'll all die. So if you try to leave before I tell you it's all right, we will have to kill you. Do you understand?"

They nodded, eyes stunned.

Niki pulled Anastasia aside and gave her one of Alrod's knives. "If anyone tries to run, kill them."

"What?"

"You heard me."

"You meant it? How could you?"

"They run out of here, the guards will catch them, we'll be discovered, we'll all die. Terrible deaths."

"Can't I just—I don't know—cripple them?"

"Not unless you intend to carry them through the thorns on your back. Or would you leave them like that for Ghedo? Grow up, rook. This is a very hard world. We walk a fine line between necessity and compassion."

Anastasia turned the knife in her hand, her fingers so lax she almost dropped it.

"Can I trust you to do what is right?" Niki said. "Not what is mushy and cute, but what is right?"

Anastasia straightened. "Yes. You can."

"Good." She motioned the ginger-haired man to follow her. "Come on."

The poor man could barely shuffle. His back was bent, his legs balky from being cramped in the cage. His gaze shifted continuously as if he expected Ghedo to jump from the shadows.

Niki finally lifted him in her arms and carried him across the main cavern. He felt like a child, his ribs and shoulder blades prominent.

"Does the boy hurt you?" she whispered.

He shook his head.

"Does he use needles on anyone or anything?"

He shrugged, mouthing *don't think so.*

Niki glanced back to ensure they were out of Gabe's earshot. "Does he take good care of you?"

Tears sprang from his eyes as he nodded emphatically.

Niki breathed a quick prayer of thanksgiving. When they had crossed the cavern, she said, "Can you show me now?"

He motioned for her to put him down. Niki lowered him carefully to his knees. He picked at a slate tile on the floor. She pried it up to find a heavy iron lever. She yanked it to the opposite position and was rewarded with the echo of clanks from within the chamber of potions.

Grates being closed. Many grates—which meant an army of mogs had awaited her.

"Thank you." She helped Ginger-hair stand. He nodded and

waved away her assistance. With his head held as high as his broken posture would allow, he shuffled back to the grotto that had served as his prison.

She signaled Anastasia. *Going in now. Pray.*

Niki unsheathed her sword and stepped into the heart of Ghedo's dark lair.

Dark thoughts. Ghedo was supposed to foist them on others, not be consumed by his own.

A distant loyalty had driven him to the sky early this morning. He had vowed to try one more time to appeal to Alrod on the basis of friendship and shared experience. A waste of time—the sorcerer now headed back to the stronghold on the weary hoornar, convinced any reconciliation was a lost hope.

He still wasn't sure what he had seen. A village by a river, so distant as to be strategically worthless, so poor as to offer little but endless rows of corn. Simon and Alrod had somehow constructed a net of black . . . *black what?* . . . over most of the place.

Some kind of black, incomprehensible void.

For his entire service as sorcerer, Ghedo had wreaked terror. This was the first time terror had ever been incited in him. The magic Simon spun was incomprehensible and frightening.

By telling Merrihana that she had a son, Ghedo had left himself no choice but to overthrow Alrod. Now he worried what he was up against. What weapons could he bring against that which he could not understand?

Sanity. Yes, that was it. What Simon and Alrod had done to that village was insane. What Ghedo had observed from his hoornar was madness given form.

Surely cold cunning could cut through this bizarre construct. Merrihana was capable of such, if Ghedo could rein in her emotions. Between the minstrel and the boy, she'd be exactly where he needed her. This could yet turn out to be a glorious day.

He'd need to stop at the barracks outside the stronghold to let the hoornar rest. There he'd announce that Merrihana was dissatisfied with her husband's treatment of his troops and that she was doubling their wages. Ghedo would award each battalion a pair of lollies from his own private harem in appreciation for their loyalty. He had no desire for these women but kept them simply for show . . . and for uses like this. The promise of continued favors would help ensure their allegiance to the sorcerer of Traxx, regardless of the head on which the crown rested.

Ghedo would check the stronghold's defenses, order extra food for the thorns, send spies out to monitor the mad baron. Once he spun the story, it would sweep through the stronghold quickly. *Alrod's gone insane.*

When all that was accomplished, he would give mother and son what they had longed for their whole pitiful lives.

The cavern that housed Ghedo's treasures was divided into a consecutive series of grottos. The first grotto seemed to be some sort of trophy room. Unlike Alrod's mummified trophies, Ghedo's prizes were stored in giant glass jars. Each jar was labeled with a scroll that detailed how the victim had allegedly transgressed against the sorcerer and the manner of the victim's death.

The labels were detailed and alarming. Ghedo clearly did not know mercy, nor did he know moderation.

The victims were stored chronologically, the most recent in the front. It was dated less than two months earlier. The oldest dated back more than twenty-two years, before Niki was born. Ghedo was surely no older than forty, which meant his first victim had been slain when the sorcerer was younger than the rooks.

More chilling was the name of the victim.

Father.

Niki knew that Alrod had ascended the throne of Traxx on the death of his father. To keep pace, Ghedo must have killed his own father so he could seize the robes of the master sorcerer and keep pace with his childhood friend.

Niki found the shroud tossed on a table in the second grotto. Apparently Ghedo had little interest in unlocking its secrets, at least not recently. Gabe said he had been spending a lot of time with Merrihana. A love affair? Doubtful. The baroness was clearly smitten with Timothy. Was the sorcerer planning a palace coup?

"Should've bribed the staff," she muttered to herself, "found out why Alrod left the stronghold. Ghedo too."

Brady would have had the presence of mind to process peripheral information while remaining focused on the mission. She had to pay better attention. In fact—

Her eyes widened as another thought struck her. In her haste to grab the shroud, she had almost overlooked a valuable opportunity.

Niki stuffed the shroud into her shirt and went in deeper, in search of Ghedo's potions.

The closed grates rattled with the screeching and slamming of mogs bred for the sole purpose of ripping her to shreds. The further in she walked, the larger the grates became. And while imagination had never been her strong suit, it didn't take much to consider the horrors Ghedo might employ to guard the cell lines that were the source of his power.

The third grotto in was stuffed with scrolls—detailed instructions on potion nourishment and application. Successful and failed experiments were also carefully recorded. Niki noted three separate handwriting styles in the parchments. Most parents left their children with a good character, maybe a portion of land or a carefully taught skill. The sorcerer's heritage was these potions, the skill to use them, and the lack of regard for the creation he transmogrified.

Niki wrapped the scrolls in the shroud and raced out to the main cavern.

Anastasia brightened to see her. "You got it."

"Can we leave now?" Gabe said.

"I need a fire."

Gabe signaled her to follow him into his storeroom. The place where he lived had a different feel to it—hope. A massive iron stove provided warmth, dispelling the dankness and rot that stank up the rest of the lair. They were deep enough underground to benefit from this heat, even though it was summer above.

Gabe opened the door and showed her a small fire. When he realized what Niki had wrapped in the shroud, he cried out. "You can't!"

"You don't want me to burn his scrolls?" she said.

"I do," he said, breathing hard. "I'm just . . . I can't believe that this is happening. That someone can undo a sorcerer's life."

"Say the word," she said, fixing him with her eyes, "and I won't do it. We'll take the cloth and leave you to your life."

"This is my word." Gabe grabbed an armful of scrolls and tossed them into the fire.

When they had finished, Niki said, "I need a torch. That one?"

He pulled it from its wall bracket. "Are you going back in for the potions?"

"If I can find them."

"You will," he said, his voice full of admiration. "You can do anything."

There had been a time when Niki believed that. No longer. "Gabe, whatever I do for good is only through the grace of God."

"The Holy One Stasia told me about?"

"Yes."

"Will I meet him?"

She smiled. "You already have."

"But I . . ."

"I'll explain later. Come on."

Niki urged the prisoners to be patient a bit longer. She hugged Anastasia. "I'll be right back. But if I'm not, get these people out of here."

"You'll be back," she whispered.

Someday I won't. She prayed this wouldn't be that day.

Niki checked the lever before going back into the chamber of potions. Still in place. Even so, she kept her sword ready in her right hand, the torch in her left. Eons after the last bomb had fallen from the sky, she would be the bomb. Hers was the surgical strike that would cut out the cancers that the Traxx sorcerers had blighted the world with.

The last grotto was a cavern in its own right, thirty paces wide and forty deep. Lined with glass bottles, clay jars, covered plates—all on shining white planks—the chamber of potions stank. Some of the stench was attributable to the meat broth in which the cells grew. Some was the outright rot of genetically engineered bacteria stewed in the throats of pigs, in the stalks of wheat, in the caps of mushrooms. The live media were also caged on the white shelves, adding to the smell.

There must be a thousand potions here, Niki realized. Everything was stored behind some sort of translucent veil, perhaps similar to that with which Alrod had mummified his enemies and loved ones.

It was warm in here, perhaps at or above Niki's own body temperature. The rest of the lair, apart from Gabe's heated storeroom, had been chilly. Where was this heat coming from? She saw no stove or fire pit.

Niki couldn't fret about that now. She had at least three lifetimes of work to destroy.

She tried to part the veil with her sword. The fabric didn't flow; it felt as solid as glass.

She poked it with the point of her blade. It gave but didn't break.

She whacked it with the hilt, hoping to see it shatter. No luck.

How did Ghedo go about getting to his own potions? She turned to head back to the doorway, thinking that perhaps she had missed some opening in the veil.

The door was now covered with the veil.

Niki had walked into a trap.

Something splashed against her cheek, burning like a fire-tossed spark. Fluid—clear, but stinking like vomit.

It became suddenly plain to Niki, like a swift punch to the gut. The veil that surrounded her was not static material but living tissue, the smooth muscle of a stomach. The potions were stored outside the stomach. The shining white planks and shelves had to be bone—ribs, most likely. The dripping fluid was acid, provoked by hunger to digest a morsel.

And Niki was the morsel.

She had always expected to die in battle, rescuing a child or busting up a mog laboratory in the forest. Not like this—without comrades, swallowed by the very evil she opposed.

Literally in the belly of a mog.

Worse of all, Ghedo's potions were within her sight but out of her reach.

Niki jammed her torch against the veil. It convulsed, a spasm that almost crushed her. The torch flickered, its fire sucking up the little oxygen left now that the entrance was closed off.

Years ago in training, Niki had paid ample attention to swordsmanship but little to biology and chemistry. Yet she had to pass exams to leave the Ark, and that knowledge was inside her somewhere. Desperately she searched her memory.

Meanwhile, all she saw were the potions. All she felt was a brutal loathing for the sorcerer. All she wanted was Brady.

But there was only one thing she needed to do. One thing she could do.

She fell to her knees, her skin burning as the acid pooled. *Lord, I give myself up to you. I give him up to You. What more can I long for than to want You more than him or anything else?*

Her mind cleared, and she took stock of her situation. She was kneeling in hydrochloric acid, or something like it, and hydrochloric acid was nonflammable. But when mixed with metal, the chloride became salt and the hydrogen became gas—and hydrogen was quite happy to flame.

If Niki were to die, she could at least destroy Ghedo's potions along with herself.

Alrod's daggers, still hidden on her body, were highly-polished steel. They wouldn't react to the acid. But her knife was raw iron, not even cast with a paint. She tossed it into the biggest puddle of the acid.

Nothing. She thought harder. And remembered about catalysts.

She needed some catalyst to provoke the chemical reaction—something like high pressure or high temperature. Her torch was not enough. What—

Spirit, you need to be the catalyst.

Niki waited, her breathing labored and her torch almost out. Did she see something in the puddle—a couple of specks? Or was the fading light and lack of oxygen making her see things that weren't there?

No, the puddle was cloudy with salt crystals.

Niki kept the torch behind her, hoping not to spark the hydrogen until it had gathered in sufficient quantity, praying what little oxygen was left would not bind with the hydrogen and become water. Her chest burned with a physical reminder of her shame, the letter she had withheld from Brady, dishonoring her friend and depriving him of what he so desperately longed for.

But the letter was bound to her back, not to her chest.

It was the shroud burning her, stuffed under her shirt. The shroud Ajoba had crocheted and Alrod had stolen. One side in this time, the other side out-of-time.

The shroud was small, meant to cover Ajoba's body—she had made it to slip through the thorns of the gargant pen before the battle of the Bashans. Niki was much taller, her shoulders broader, her legs longer. If she couldn't bind herself completely in it, the explosion would snake inside and take her as surely as if she were unclothed.

She unfolded the piece of shroud and pulled it over her head, knowing it was a foot short. And shroud never stretched. Yet as she tugged, this piece somehow stretched to fit over her.

Niki fumbled for the torch. It glowed orange. Was there enough oxygen left to feed the fire? Enough hydrogen—the basic element of God's creation—to form a much bigger fire? Enough shroud to cover her?

It's all right, Lord. I'll take whatever you have in mind for me.

She tossed the torch near the puddle. It flared, tasting its first whiff of hydrogen gas.

With the shroud wrapped under her body, Niki cowered inside as the fire passed over with a mighty roar.

TWENTY-SEVEN

IT WAS LIKE THE END OF THE WORLD.

Anastasia couldn't hear it—the first mighty roar had deafened her. Yet like the howling of some massive creature, she felt it in her skin. Gabe and the captives were knocked back by the concussion, covering their heads in real fear that the palace might come down on them.

Fetid smoke poured from the chamber of potions. "They're burning," Gabe said.

"And Niki with them," Anastasia cried out as she ran into the haze. She couldn't see or hear anything, but she could feel the heat, smell living tissue burning—*please, Lord, not Niki.* She stumbled over debris, choked when she tried to call for Niki. For once, she resolved to keep her mouth shut.

Forty paces in, Anastasia stumbled over something that burned her leg. She jumped away, frantic that she hadn't brought a rope or laid a trail of rocks to find her way out. She couldn't do this, shouldn't be here, too young, too stupid, too scared, too—

I can.

She knew the voice. *Jesus, I'm so scared. I don't know the way to go.*

I am.

Anastasia's mind couldn't grasp what her heart did—that the burning against her leg was not fire, but shroud. She had been wrapped in it, spat out onto the ice in it. Niki had opened the shroud and welcomed her to this world. She fumbled at her legs, finding the bundle of shroud, wrapped tightly from the outside so Niki—*please Lord, let it be her in there*—couldn't release herself.

Anastasia plunged her hands onto the shroud, into some other time, and pulled Niki into the here-and-now. She came out gasping for breath, mouthing words Anastasia couldn't hear.

She tried to explain. "I'm sorry. My ears—"

Then she realized with astonishment that the outrider was asking her for help.

Leaning together and using Niki's sword as a cane, they found their way out to the main cavern. The smoke had dissipated into the vents that ran up the sides of the walls. Anastasia took long gulps of air, noticed Niki mouthing something else at her. She knocked at her ears, hearing whispers and whooshes. Her hearing seemed to be coming back. "What did you say?"

". . . strong-arms . . . coming down to see what happened."

"Maybe not. It's pretty soundproof down here. Because of the"—Gabe's face clouded—"the screaming and all. And even if they did hear it, they would assume it was something Ghedo had caused."

"Let's get those folks out of here. They won't be able to walk. Gabe, we'll put them in your wagon. Once you get to the thorns, we'll see if we can rustle up an extra slung and drag them through."

"The thorns?" Gabe's eyes went wide. "The slungs?"

"Outrider stuff, eya?" Anastasia smiled. "Wait a minute, Niki. What do you mean 'when *you* get to the thorns'?"

"I'm not leaving," Niki said. "It was one thing taking the shroud, but blowing up Ghedo's life's work? The sorcerer won't take kindly to that, and it won't be a big jump to figure out that Timothy's involved. You two leave, take these people—I don't suppose you could go out the main gate, Gabe?"

"The gatekeepers have orders not to let me."

"The thorns it is, then. Anastasia knows how to do it."

They helped the two men and the woman onto their feet.

Ginger-hair was already showing more flexibility. The other two had begun to stretch and move about stiffly.

As they approached the foyer, Niki stopped them. "Stasia . . ." Niki had never called her that before.

"I have something that belongs to Brady." She reached up the back of her shirt and brought out a thin, cloth-covered bundle. "Give this to him. Tell him I said I'm sorry for not getting it to him sooner."

"What is it?"

"None of your business. Gabe, you go up the stairs first, in case someone is poking around up there."

He nodded and took the lead. Anastasia hadn't noticed how many stairs led to above ground, not until she helped someone else make the trip. As Gabe neared the top, Niki tapped his back. He stiffened but didn't protest.

"Wait." Niki stepped between Gabe and Anastasia and took hold of the dark-haired man that Gabe had been guiding. "I need you to check beyond the door. Don't peek out and look furtive. Act natural. We'll be about ten stairs behind you, just in case."

Gabe nodded, rattling his keys. He unlocked the door, pushing it open.

"Gabriel! Good afternoon."

"Sorcerer! You're back early."

Soundlessly, Niki pressed against the wall, hand close to her sword. Anastasia fingered her knife but pressed against the wall next to the terrified captives. How could Ghedo not see them?

Shadows—he didn't expect to see anything.

And grace. *Thank you!*

"Big plans—of which you're a very big part." Ghedo's voice dripped with good cheer. "I've come to bring you into the palace."

"The palace?"

"Big plans, Gabe. Big plans."

The captives trembled so hard, the stairs began to rattle. Gabe stepped out and slowly pushed the door almost closed behind him. He probably wanted to slam it and run. If Ghedo knew that his potions were destroyed, he'd skin each of them and tie them out in the hot sun to bake. Still alive.

"Let me lock up and I'll come with you." Gabe's muffled voice came through the crack in the door.

"Yes," the sorcerer told him. "Good boy."

The door closed completely, and Anastasia breathed relief as Gabe pretended to lock it but did not. Niki pressed her ear against the door. "They're gone," she said, her face pale. "You'll have to take these people out alone, Stasia."

"We promised Gabe . . ."

"This is an order."

"Ghedo will be merciless when he sees what you've done. He'll know Gabe had something to do with this."

"You need to trust Gabe to me. Take this." Niki pressed the shroud into her arms. "Listen to your orders. Are you listening, rook?"

"Yes. I am."

"Get the people and this shroud through the thorns. As soon as you're out of reach of the cobratraps, get a message to Bartoly. Tell him to come, bring armor and weapons. Hide these people in a campsite, take one of the mules, and go retrieve our horses. Timothy's too. You and he are to wait for me."

Anastasia searched for the cool place in her mind where she could store all these orders.

"Send a message to Brady, find out where he is. Warn him that Alrod could be heading his way. Oh, and tell Bartoly to bring my wolf. He probably won't obey Bartoly, but if he waves my blanket or something, the wolf will come."

"Armor, Brady, wolf . . ." Anastasia stocked it all away. "But what about Gabe?"

"I will take care of Gabe and Timothy. You will not—under any circumstances—do anything other than what I have just told you. If I see you back inside these walls without permission, I will carry you to the ends of this earth and leave you there. Do you understand me, rook?"

She grabbed Niki in a hug, surprised that she allowed it. "Yes, Niki. I do."

"He's for real," Niki whispered.

"Timothy?"

"Gabe. You did good, rook."

"Not me."

"I know. Now get going."

Anastasia didn't need to be told twice.

He was his mother's son.

Any doubt was erased when the stylist cut the boy's hair and dressed him in royal silks. The boy trembled to be in the heart of the palace—a place Ghedo had decreed off-limits for the fourteen years since the boy learned how to walk.

He had allowed Gabe to have privacy in his bath so no one would see the deformities that marred his spine. They were certainly grotesque—one skull with eyes that blinked and another that actually rotated on its stalk. At least they had not grown in proportion to the boy himself. At birth the seven skulls had been the size of walnuts, making it a treacherous birth for Merrihana, though he had ensured she would sleep through it. As Gabe had inched toward manhood, however, they had remained small.

Had Ghedo the capacity to shear them from his back, the firstborn son of Merrihana—and rightful heir of Baron Alrod—would be spectacularly handsome. He had his mother's eyes—her original eyes, that startling blue of a rare sapphire—as well as her finely formed nose and black hair. Alrod's contribution was the strong jaw and wiry physique. The boy would never be large, but he was tightly muscled from lugging about supplies.

It was his character that concerned Ghedo. Sensitive as a woman, given to kindness for those who never required it, such as the washwomen or beggars in the street. Fortunately, his courage was as watery as his will—Baronet Gabriel would remain firmly under the thumb of Merrihana. And she in turn, distracted by her newly acquired son and her newly seduced minstrel lover, would be easily controlled and manipulated.

The only remaining problem was explaining to Merrihana why he hadn't killed Alrod. The truth was that Ghedo hadn't dared risk exposure to the black insanity. He'd tell Merrihana it was better that Alrod survived so there could be no talk of an assassination, no countermeasures from the few troops that were still loyal to the baron.

With tears in her eyes, Merrihana could explain to her court that her husband had gone starkly insane, wandering the lands with strange people and bizarre notions. Once Ghedo had a firm grasp on the Traxx army and had bolstered it with fresh mogs, he'd take on the crazed man he had once called a friend.

Friend. Ghedo allowed himself a disdainful sniff. Loyalty had proved a bitter waste of time. But foresight—careful and cunning foresight—had brought Ghedo *this*.

Spiffed and shining, Gabe stood near the window as if he was about to jump out. He hadn't the guts to, of course. Nor would he want to, once he learned of the honor and luxury that were about to be his.

Ghedo guided him to the table and motioned for him to sit. "You're disoriented."

"I'm . . . confused."

"I want no more hesitation in your speech. Speak clearly and forcefully."

Gabe nibbled on his index finger. Ghedo went to slap his hand away, thought better of it. This transfer of power needed to go smoothly—he didn't need Merrihana seizing control of her son and leaving her sorcerer out in the cold. Gabe had to be as dependent on Ghedo as she was.

He sat across from Gabe, poured him an ale, and bade him drink. The boy sipped, too fearful not to obey. He choked on its tartness. Ghedo smiled and mixed in water and sugar to lessen the sting. "I did the same thing when given my first taste of ale."

Not true, of course. Ghedo and Alrod had snuck ale from the army's storehouse as often as they could. How he missed his friend, and how he despised the fool his friend had become.

Gabe clamped his hands over the cup. "Requesting pardon, sorcerer?"

"You never need to request pardon from anyone ever again. Except, of course—your mother."

The boy leaped from his chair. "I really have a mother?"

"I'm not so skillful that I could conjure you from thin air." *Not yet, anyway.*

"She's alive?"

"Yes. And she's readying herself to receive you."

The boy ran to the window, hanging out so he could see around the curve of the tower and into the servants' courtyards. Ghedo yanked him back. "Whatever are you doing?"

"Is she the lady who cleans the silver, perhaps? She's always been kind to me."

He laughed. "You are looking in entirely the wrong direction."

Gabe squinted. "I don't understand."

"Soon enough you will. For now, know this: When your father wanted you killed, it was I who saved you. You owe your very life to me."

Ghedo bowed with intentional formality.

"When you come into your kingdom, Gabriel, remember me."

Timothy was stunned by the request. "You want me to . . ."

Merrihana clutched his face, her eyes fixed on his. "Give me a baby."

He glanced at Dawnray—an instant of weakness that betrayed him.

"It's her," the baroness hissed. "The lolly?"

"What?"

"You're here for her. Not for some political intrigue that my sorcerer conjures up or for some mercenary motive that Nikolette spouts. It's my husband's lolly, isn't it?"

He laughed, forcing as much bravado into his expression as he could muster. "A spectacular woman like you is jealous of a lolly?"

"You covet her."

"Don't be silly. I don't even know her."

"Fine," Merrihana said. "In that case, I'll have her killed right now. In your full sight."

Timothy took her hands into his, begging his heart not to burst and betray him. How could he distract her, change her mind when fear roared through him like this?

Flirtation was one discipline that had not been included in birthrighter training. Timothy understood romance, having seen it in the grateful touch of his father's hand on his mother's back.

Seduction was unnecessary on the Ark because love was patterned after what they saw in the Scriptures and the faith they clung to in their hearts.

"Dear one," Timothy attempted in a lyrical tone. "I looked at the lolly because they said your husband is going to get her pregnant. If I make you pregnant, which child is heir?"

"She is not pregnant and will not be unless I will it. In fact . . ." Merrihana studied him, clearly planning some trap. He would have to take great care. "Perhaps I will have you impregnate her. Would you like that?"

Timothy kept his gaze on her face, projecting as much adoration as he could with revulsion ripping through his gut. "I would prefer the high and mighty to the low and common," he said, brushing his lips to hers.

His first real kiss—and Timothy felt like vomiting. Yet he found he was also stirred by the baroness's sweet scent, her striking beauty, her lush lips, the aura of power. To his surprise he found himself wondering what it would be like to possess this woman and all that came with her.

She kissed him back, trailing her mouth along his jawline,

pressing her face to his neck. Timothy looked over her head at Dawnray who looked away, disgust plain on her face. Timothy felt a stab of irritation. Couldn't she understand he was doing this for her? Their duty carried a blessing but also many curses ... though Timothy wondered if Merrihana's hands roaming his back qualified as a curse.

No matter. His body ached with weariness and his mind felt clouded. And he knew there was a part of him that craved a gentle touch from anyone.

The truth was, more than two years of hard service had worn him down. It had been nice to sleep between silk sheets, on soft down. What harm had eating tender meat done? At Horesh, stone-beaten meats were boiled because stews went further than chops.

At Horesh, everyone sang with him, drowning out his voice. It was nice to have an audience thirsty for his music.

Timothy had never thought for a moment that Dawnray wouldn't jump at the chance to marry him. She called it "time to get to know each other," but he knew it to be rejection because of the pain it stirred. If Merrihana did not hesitate to love him, why did Dawnray? If he was worthy of royalty, why was he not worthy of a village girl?

He sighed in confusion, not knowing what to do next.

Lord, save me from myself, he prayed. Because for all he didn't know, Timothy did know this:

He was not sufficient to save himself.

The ceiling exploded with a pop and a shower of plaster. Timothy watched in shock as Niki leaped to the floor, her outrider's sword in her hand.

"Guard!" Merrihana squealed.

The strong-arm didn't even get his sword out before Niki bashed him with the butt of hers, knocking him cold.

The baroness fingered her bodice, apparently unafraid. "Unorthodox entrance, Nikolette."

"Get your hands where I can see them," Niki said.

Merrihana smiled and extended her fingers. They glistened with jewels, her wrists hung with diamonds. "What exactly do you want?"

"I'll keep this simple. The deal's off. I'm taking my minstrel and getting out of here."

"May I ask why?"

Niki laughed. "I'm a woman. Subject to changing my mind."

Timothy motioned to Dawnray. "Come on."

"Timothy, what are you do—" Niki's words were cut short by the door opening.

"Baroness, I am so—" Ghedo exploded. "What's going on in here?" His gaze fixed on Niki's sword.

Merrihana took advantage of the distraction to grab Dawnray and force a manicured finger to the girl's throat. "You're not going anywhere, minstrel," she whispered. "You move, and she dies."

"What?" Timothy whispered. "What are you—"

Then he looked closer and saw the tiny vial with the needle-sharp tip. He'd seen one like it in the Bashans, near Alrod's camp. It was the kind of needle sorcerers used to apply potions.

The baroness read his mind. "No, not a potion," she said with a small smile. "You might be surprised to know I'm quite good with poisons."

Timothy froze, eyes fixed on the needle. Niki didn't notice his inaction. She had her own task to attend to—keeping Ghedo at bay.

"Are you armed?" she asked the sorcerer sternly.

"I am not."

"Prove it," she said to the sorcerer. "Disrobe."

Ghedo laughed. "And you plan to make me—how?"

In a flash, Niki sent a dagger flying past his face, slashing the tip of his ear. "Next one comes through your heart." From across the room, she glanced at Merrihana. "And you, Baroness, need to hold still. Be assured those cats' eyes make a striking target."

"Ghedo, where is . . ." The baroness's voice trailed off.

"Safe," he said.

"Then send this odious woman out of here and get on with the business of governing."

"No," Ghedo said. "We need to clean up this mess before it spreads."

Niki whipped another knife, taking off the top of his ear.

Timothy kept a wary eye on Merrihana's hand. If she were startled, that needle would go into Dawnray's jugular. She stood under the baroness's hand, white-faced and stunned.

"You're good, Nikolette," Ghedo said, blood running down his neck. "So good that you must be an outrider."

"You're a piece of garbage," she said. "Don't think you'll exhaust my supply of knives before you exhaust my patience. Disrobe, you filthy swine. I won't ask again."

Ghedo shrugged off his cloak. He wore a sleeveless tunic and trousers. Underneath, his form was lean, his shoulders narrow.

"The veil now."

"I will not."

Niki pulled out yet another dagger. "Then I'll nail it to your brain."

He dropped the veil. His face was boyish, his chin weak.

"The clothes now."

"Absolutely not."

Niki raised the knife.

"Why would you do this to me?"

She laughed. "I don't have time to list the millions of reasons. But the practical one is that I don't want a needle or dart coming my way. Undress. Or, if you'd prefer, I could just kill you."

He pulled off his shirt. His skin was pasty white, and his chest wrapped with a cloth that likely held his hidden weapons.

"The trousers next."

"In front of the women? That's hardly—"

"Take them off, or I'll nail them to your—"

"Fine, fine."

"What do you want, Nikolette?" Merrihana said. "Will you kill him?"

"Would you like me to, Baroness?"

Timothy watched her eyes, where some cold calculation took place. "I'd prefer you didn't," she said.

"If he continues to irk me, I'll leave his head on your doorstep," Niki said. "The undershorts now, Ghedo."

"Is that what you really want, Nikolette?" the sorcerer said.

"I'm not barking to hear my own voice."

"Think long and hard, outrider."

"You think short and fast, sorcerer. Because my patience is at an end, and my dagger is ready to fly."

"I can forgive all that has gone before," Ghedo said, "but this I will not forgive. I will hunt you down and make you pay. And not for minutes or hours—your torture will be exquisite and close to eternal."

Niki laughed. "For a scrawny piece of scum, you make nice threats. On the count of three, you lose those trousers or you die. One . . . two . . ."

Ghedo dropped his pants. Everyone in the room gasped . . . one at a time, so that the moment was stretched to breathlessness.

Underneath the trousers, Ghedo wore skin-tight shorts that left no doubt that the sorcerer had kept a very deep secret.

"A woman?" Niki said. "You are a woman?"

"You, of all people, should understand what power women can hold," Ghedo said. "But only in a man's guise."

Merrihana's hands began to shake. "Does Alrod know?"

"Baroness, please," Timothy said, but she ignored him, the needle bouncing against Dawnray's skin, a shiver away from piercing it.

"He's too stupid to know," Ghedo said.

"How did you pull it off?" Niki asked.

"My father was disappointed to have spawned a girl, so he

dressed me as a boy from the time I could walk. I had younger brothers, but they were stupid and disposed of accordingly. I alone had the intelligence and quick hands that a master sorcerer needs. Father's first plan was to find a way to make me a man. He experimented with many commoners but could not work the proper potion. As I neared puberty, it became harder and harder to disguise my true nature."

Niki snorted at those words, but Ghedo continued: "When Alrod and I were twelve, his father died, and he took the throne. My father approached Alrod to ask if he would allow him to take a woman on as an apprentice sorcerer." Ghedo took a deep breath and looked pointedly at Merrihana. "Alrod said women were good for one thing only. I trust I need not spell out what that was."

"That dog." Merrihana's hand began to clench.

Ghedo, caught up in his own tale, ignored them both. "Fearing repercussions from his deception, my father planned to banish me before my womanhood came into full bloom. He wanted to apprentice one of the sorcerers from Outer Traxx. I had a simpler solution."

"I'll bet you did," Niki said.

"Don't provoke him," Timothy said.

Ghedo shrugged. "I killed my father and took on the robes that were so able to conceal my woman's body. You're a strong woman yourself, Nikolette. Surely you've understood how powerless a woman is in her own right."

"I've heard enough," Niki answered. "Timothy, shut your eyes."
"No."

"Then turn toward Merrihana for a moment. I need Ghedo to unbind hi—her chest and drop all her hidden weapons."

"You're going to accord that scum modesty?" Timothy said.

"Yes, I am. We won't sink to her level."

Timothy turned his back to Ghedo. A stupid thing to do, perhaps, but maybe Niki was right—they could not sink to the mire these people traipsed through.

Merrihana leaned close to him and whispered, "You leave with her, the lolly dies."

Dawnray stared up at him, her face a stark white.

"How do you know Niki won't kill you?" he whispered.

"If she was going to kill anyone, it would have been Ghedo."

"She still may," Timothy said. "You don't know her."

Merrihana laughed. "I think I know her better than you do. She won't kill a powerless woman. But I will, minstrel."

He glanced over his shoulder, but Niki didn't hear, so intent she was on disrobing—and thus disarming—Ghedo.

"Niki won't let you keep me," Timothy said.

"She will if you tell her that it's your choice." Merrihana pressed the needle hard enough to made a little dent in Dawnray's throat.

"No," Dawnray told him. "Leave me to die. It's better this way."

"Can you protect me from Ghedo?"

"She'll suspect you of being an outrider like she is, but I'll swear you are not."

"And in return?"

"First of all, the lolly lives. Second, you live and live well. I'll be generous. You entertain me, amuse me, love me. Not only will I not harm the lolly—I'll even carry through on my original offer."

"I don't follow . . ."

"You can make her pregnant."

"I'd rather die," Dawnray said, the words piercing Timothy's heart.

"All right, Timothy," Niki said. She had bound Ghedo's hands behind her back and covered her with a quilt. "Tie up the baroness."

"Touch me and the lolly dies," Merrihana whispered.

"Niki, go on without me." Timothy motioned quickly—*I'll explain later.*

"Hurry it up. We have to leave now, before the guards check in."

"I need to stay," Timothy said, his skin becoming ice. He

couldn't trust Merrihana to keep her word and protect him, but he could trust her to kill Dawnray.

Niki slapped her sword against the wall, commanding his attention, but he would not obey. Could not obey. He felt himself falling into a black hole with no bottom. "No. Niki, I'm not going. I need to stay here."

"Why?" The catch in her voice broke his heart.

"Because . . . I . . ."

"Is she holding you here against your will? Tell me, Timothy."

"Convince her." Merrihana's voice was low and deadly. Out of the corner of his eye, Timothy saw her put her other hand to Dawnray's neck, a second needle popping from her ring.

"I've never lived like this." Timothy mustered a boyish smile for Niki. "I like it."

"You can't be serious."

"He feels it," Ghedo said. "He's been touched by power, and he wants it."

"That's not true. I only want to sing, that's all. I never wanted anything else."

Niki looked at Ghedo, then back to Timothy. She had her hands full, caught between the two most dangerous women in the stronghold. She wouldn't be able to wait much longer to leave.

"I'm leaving," she finally said. "You can follow or you can rot, Timothy."

He gave her a weak smile. "'Bye, Niki."

"Tracker . . . please . . ."

The door opened.

A dark-haired boy, about Anastasia's age, stuck his head in. "A troop of strong-arms are com—" He stopped midsentence, his gaze locked on Merrihana.

Her hand trembled and, for a hasty moment, Timothy thought she had driven the needle into Dawnray's skin.

"You're him," she gasped. "My baby."

"Get out of here, boy," Ghedo growled. "It's not safe."

"Come to me, Gabe," Niki said.

"No!" Merrihana said. "Don't harm him."

Timothy caught the baroness by the wrist. "She won't unless you hurt Dawnray."

The boy obediently stood with Niki, flushing as he stared at Merrihana.

"Merrihana, tell your strong-arms to grant us safe passage," Niki said.

"Yes. Of course. But don't hurt him."

"I won't if we're not hurt."

"Will you keep him?" Merrihana said.

"That's up to him," Niki said. "Will you come with me, Gabe? Or do you want to stay with her?"

Timothy felt trapped in the middle of a vortex. So many things going round—a man who was a woman, a baroness who was a mother, a woman who held his heart without giving hers in return. All spinning, with him in the silent center—as if somehow the strangeness of this encounter had muted the voice of the Lord. Though that couldn't be, so it must be that his ears were stoppered. Even the phantom voice of Brady had been silenced, so that all Timothy knew was the beating of his own heart.

"Child, stay with me," Merrihana was saying.

"You already know what you'll get with her, Gabe. You'll be free with me," Niki said. "Free and decent and loved."

"I love him!" Merrihana cried. Again the needle bounced against Dawnray's throat.

"I never had a mother," said Gabe.

"I never had a son," Merrihana said. "It's not too late."

"It's not?" Gabe's voice was a mere whisper, but it resonated through the chamber. Timothy was not the only one in the middle of a vortex.

The baroness released Dawnray and reached for Gabe. "I can give you a kingdom. All that you ever wanted is right here."

"But I've never wanted any of this." He clutched Niki's arm. "Let's go."

"How can you?" Merrihana cried. "You're my son."

Gabe raised his hands, reaching toward Merrihana, but then turned his palms out as if to push her away. "Even if I am," he whispered, "I am nothing like you."

"But my baby . . . my Gab—"

"I'm sorry, but I need to leave." He said it with a gentle courtliness, almost as if declining a cup of tea, though his eyes registered pain and longing.

The baroness howled, a heartrending shriek that rattled the window. Looking to vent her rage, she lunged for Dawnray. Timothy dashed against her, knocking her away. Merrihana went down, hitting her head hard on the stone dais that held her sumptuous bed.

"Run, Niki," Timothy called.

"Come on!" Niki called back.

Timothy grabbed Dawnray, about to follow, when he saw the needle sticking in her ear lobe.

"Timothy, now!" Niki urged.

"Leave me," Dawnray begged him. "Please."

For days now, he had teetered on the edge of decision. Now, one look at her pale face determined his choice. He had to act now or Dawnray would be lost.

"Go on without me." He couldn't even look at Niki as he said it.

He felt rather than saw her hesitate, start to argue, then shake her head. "May God have mercy on your foolish soul." Then the thump of boots on marble told him she and the boy had left.

Timothy felt a rending deep in his spirit. This was the moment he had longed for and dreaded—being torn from Horesh. But he couldn't mourn now—or celebrate. He had mere seconds before the poison did its work.

There wasn't even time to sterilize a knife. He grabbed one of the daggers Niki had thrown, prayed Dawnray would forgive him, then sliced off the bottom half of Dawnray's ear. She cried out sharply as the needle fell away, but her grateful eyes told him that she understood.

"We've got to get out of here," he said. "Can you walk?"

Dawnray nodded, both hands clutched to her bleeding ear.

"Minstrel," Merrihana said, barely able to lift her head. "You would leave me too?"

"May God have mercy on you," he told her. "For it's His love you need, not mine."

Timothy stuck the dagger in his belt, bent to retrieve his gittern, and then wrapped his arm around Dawnray's waist to help her from the room. She pointed him toward the servants' stairs. As they hurried toward freedom, his heart surged with a strange mixture of emptiness and exhilaration. A sense of having set his course.

Niki would be heading back to Horesh, but he would take Dawnray and Carin northwest, perhaps to the sanctuary in Chiungos. He would work hard to make Dawnray love him—and work hard to forget he was once a tracker, called by God to serve a noble mission.

Besides, he thought as the gittern bounced gently against his leg, he had another calling, another way of serving. One he could follow no matter what happened.

Perhaps Dawnray would never consent to marry him.

Perhaps his comrades would never forgive him for abandoning the mission.

Perhaps he wouldn't even make it out of the palace alive, though Ghedo was literally unmanned and Merrihana seemed to have no interest in pursuing him.

So much was uncertain, but one thing he knew.

No matter what the next minutes or days or years held, Timothy still would sing.

And we know that in all things God works for the good of those who love him, who have been called according to his purpose.

ROMANS 8:28

TWENTY-EIGHT

BARTOLY AND NIKI RODE HARD ON THE TRAXX SIDE OF the Grand, ignoring the feeble protests of the border guards. As Ghedo consolidated forces, what remained of the border guards posed little threat.

The wolf kept up easily, rustling the deep grass like a swift-moving breeze. As they headed south, they passed a battalion of Traxx strong-arms moving north. Niki and Bartoly ignored them. It was more important they get to Brady and fast—once they figured out where he was—than worry about their own safety.

"So what are we waiting for?" Bartoly said.

"For the scout to find us."

"I've never seen the fellow."

"I have. Brady introduced us." Was that really just a bit over a week ago?

"Doesn't make sense, mate," Bartoly said. But he rode on, grinning, as the wind swept back his unruly black hair and beard. He was clearly thrilled to be back in action, though he worried about the circumstances that sped them south.

They both were worried. Somewhere deep in her heart, Niki knew the circumstances were dire.

All crews except Brady's had reported in with regularity. Collections were going well and, though they were short of shroud, somehow there always managed to be enough. They were discovering, as Niki had discovered, that faith stretches shroud. No doubt Brady was discovering the same thing.

By now, Anastasia would be back at Horesh. Bartoly had met them with Manueo and a wagon, since the rook was not likely to be able to handle the three rescued captives, a wagon, and finding her way through the caves.

And Gabe—Merrihana and Alrod's son. What a world.

Gabe—somehow, improbably, a child of God. *What a God.*

But what had happened to Timothy? Niki's brow still furrowed in confusion over that. Why hadn't he followed her out? He had made some noises about wanting to stay with Merrihana, but he'd seemed more interested in the poor girl forced to shadow the baroness.

None of it made sense. But she couldn't worry about Timothy right now. She'd hand that problem over to Brady—once she found him.

She'd hand over the letter from the Ark, too, or die trying. Before hugging Anastasia good-bye, Niki had taken it back and bound it once more to her back.

And then, once the wagon had headed off for the Narrows, she had called for Dakota.

The wolf growled when Niki buzzed as Dakota had shown her. Bartoly stared as if she were insane. "He said he'd come if I needed him," she said, praying her call wasn't just empty air.

They couldn't wait for him to show up, though. Niki and Bartoly, armed heavily, had jumped on their horses and headed south. They'd been riding for hours when Bartoly slapped his neck. "Blasted wasp."

Niki laughed. "Don't let the trackers hear you calling a honeybee a wasp."

They followed the beeline, meandering along until Dakota stepped out of the brush. He sent the bees off on their scouting mission, and half a day later they had their answer. The scout studied the elaborate dance of the worker bees, somehow understanding their directions.

"They're on the Fens River," he said. "Though I don't know why your birds couldn't have found them."

Dakota buzzed the bees away, but they swarmed back—thousands, a hundred thousand coming from all sides and descending like a storm cloud. Where had they come from?

Bartoly panicked and tried to swat them away.

"Don't move," Niki said. "They're showing us something."

More bees, a million perhaps, formed a huge canopy. Daylight diminished, the bees increasing in number and tightening their swarm until they were covered in a darkness Niki knew and dreaded. Someone took her hand—Bartoly, she assumed. But no, this hand was smoother, more slender. Strong, though, and she welcomed Dakota's strength.

The swarm lifted and Bartoly shouted, gleeful to again see the sun.

"It's bad," Niki whispered.

"I'll ride with you," Dakota said.

"But you're a scout. You fellows are . . ." Bartoly met Niki's eyes, and he understood her meaning: *Scouts are weird.*

"Yes. We are rather different." Dakota tipped his head, his bald scalp an odd contrast to Bartoly's bushy mane. "But I'm still part of Horesh."

Bartoly slapped his back. "You bet, hey."

While Dakota saddled up, Bartoly sent a bird to Kendo, telling him to meet them by the Fens. They resumed their ride south.

"What do we do when we get there?" Bartoly asked.

Niki glanced at Dakota. "You're the leader," he told her.

"We pray," she said.

After three days inside the millhouse, the people of Fenside were suffering. Food was ample but water scarce. Because Alrod had commanded his troops to break down the dam, the water level was too low to come through the pipes and far too low to turn the wheel. After the second day, the river had ceased to flow altogether—Alrod must have somehow diverted it upstream.

The millhouse was almost treacherously hot. The black net that Alrod's sorcerer cast made the temperature soar inside. With no water for cooling and no breezes, they would all suffocate or cook to death when the last chink in the darkness closed. Brady and his comrades had tried to pray a way through the darkness but, as on Welz, it was solid and unbreakable.

Why, Lord? Why can we not? Brady prayed, but he received no answer.

Alrod stood beyond the darkness, calling out taunts to Brady and terrorizing the people with threats that the birthrighters knew were not empty.

On the second day, Brady had made an offer to Alrod. "If I come out, will you let these people go?"

Alrod had laughed. "I don't need to make bargains. But your people fought well. So if any wish to serve in my army, we will give them safe passage out."

Two men and three boys had left to join Alrod. Brady had watched from the roof through one of the last remaining holes in the darkness. With the creature at his side, Alrod had stuck his arm down their throats and wreaked a frightening change in them. The men became straighter, the boys became men.

The seams of this world were loosening, and an army of darkness was being raised.

On the third day, birthrighters and Fenside folks clustered together, drawing strength from familiarity and, for many, newfound faith.

"Tell us another story," Hannah said. This was how they had passed the time up to now—retelling stories from the Scriptures. Cooper had told the villagers about Noah's ark, Taryan of Naomi, Ajoba of Stephen. Brady was wondering which story to tell now when little Katje piped up with a question.

"Will he make us drudges?"

"Will who make us drudges?" he asked her.

"That man outside."

"Baron Alrod?"

"The one in the purple cloak. He keeps threatening to."

Brady glanced at Taryan. They hadn't heard any threats from the sorcerer, but somehow a child had.

He tousled Katje's hair. "God has a special place in his heart for drudges. Because a long time ago, God's people were drudges in a land called Egypt."

Brady launched into the story of Moses and the plagues. The children's faces glowed from sweat—it was well above body temperature in the millhouse—but their eyes shone with wonder. Brady had just finished telling about the plague of locusts when he stopped midsentence.

"What happened then?" Katje asked.

How had he forgotten which plague came next? "My mouth is too dry. I need to stop."

"Please don't. It keeps them from being scared." Curt passed him the waterskin. There was precious little left in it.

Brady waved away his offer of a drink. "The plagues yet to come are disturbing. Maybe children shouldn't hear them."

Taryan squeezed his hand. "Lad, the Scriptures are holy. Let them do their work."

As Brady told about the plague of darkness, these dear people and their children clung closer to each other, even though their faces were a deep red from the heat. One elderly woman had been finding it hard to breathe. A tiny baby boy hadn't roused for hours now. The poor sheepdog lay on her side, her tongue as dry as sand but her eyes still fixed on Brady.

This was not how Brady had expected to die. His comrades wouldn't even know where to look for them or why four birthrighters never returned to camp. He would never see the Ark sail. All his hard work, and for what? To break the hearts of his parents?

In the role of camp leader, Niki would be the one to write to them: "Your beloved child and our treasured comrade . . ."

"No!" he shouted.

Cooper jolted. "What!"

He would not let this darkness seep into him. "Yet all the Israelites had light . . ." Brady went on with the account, the coming of the plague of the firstborn. Salty tears poured down his face, though he couldn't spare the moisture from his body.

"They put blood on the sides and tops of the doorframes of the hou—"

Brady stopped, mouth open.

Taryan wiped the sweat from his brow with her sleeve. "You all right, lad?"

"And the destroyer will pass over you," he shouted. "The destroyer will pass over because of the blood on the doorframes!"

"What's he talking about?" someone muttered. "Has he gone mad?"

"I know the way through. Blood on the doorframes made the destroyer pass over Israel. We'll reverse it—pass *under* the darkness by divine means."

"What divine means?" Cooper mumbled.

"Shroud." Brady struggled to his feet, ripping off the bandage that bound his side. He pulled off the piece of shroud that covered his wound, and the blood again began to ooze. He stretched and pulled, but the shroud would not multiply or increase to fit his need.

Brady knelt, face to the floor. *Why not?*

Forgive and restore, son. It's time.

But I— He started to argue. Then he understood.

He looked up, seeking Ajoba's face. "Forgive me," he said.

Her brow wrinkled. "For what?"

"For not forgiving you."

"But you said—"

"It wasn't enough. I was willing to give you some credit. But my heart was still too hard to fully forgive. I could fight alongside you, let you fight for me, but I wasn't ready to bless you. Or to let you fill the role God called you to."

She knelt beside him, pressing her cheek to his.

"We needed you," he said. "You kept trying to tell me that,

but I didn't want to listen."

"Because I jabber too much. I need to learn to be still."

"You will." He smiled. "Come with me. We need to sit next to Taryan, because she can't stand."

"I don't understand."

"I do," Taryan said. "I will not do this sitting. Cooper, help me stand." Cooper lifted her and held her upright, keeping her weight off her legs.

Brady cupped his hands over Ajoba's head. Without Niki, it fell to Taryan to lay her hands on his. He prayed—not a prayer of anointing, because Ajoba had already been anointed, but simply a prayer of blessing, that God would bless her and them through the gifts He had given her. When he was done, he hugged her. "Welcome back."

"Thank you. Oh, thank you."

"No tears. We have too much work to do."

"I don't understand."

Brady grinned. "I need you to spin us some shroud."

Alrod paced around the campfire. "Why don't we take Brady? I don't need the rest of them."

"Do you think he'll talk once they're free?" Simon said. "But watching those little ones cook like little birds in a pie will make him sing. Trust me on this."

Alrod nodded. Of course he would trust the sorcerer. Hadn't he already done things beyond imagining?

Saul—now the army commander—splashed across the stream. To keep it from diverting into the millhouse, his men had dug a bypass. They had complained of the hard labor until Alrod punished the first one. Since then, his soldiers had been completely compliant.

"High and mighty, high and mighty," the commander called.

"What is it?"

"The waterwheel. It's turning."

Alrod looked at Simon, who said dryly, "I don't see how it can."

"Has the water resumed its course?" Alrod asked.

"No," Saul said.

"Of course it hasn't. My measures are in place," Simon said. "Those fools must be turning it manually for some ridiculous reason."

"It would be too heavy for those people to turn without water, especially as weak as they must be." Still, Alrod's heart thudded. He had seen what these outriders were capable of in the Bashans. Should he see it again here, Simon's head would roll.

Don't you ever threaten me, you sorry lump of sod.

Alrod felt a hideous pain in his neck, and suddenly the sky sped by. He screamed when he realized his own head had been tossed up high, spinning until he couldn't comprehend up from down. Then he saw sharp rocks rising up to meet him, driving through his skull with a pain so intense as to have no beginning and no end. He longed to drop into that cool water and be done with it. But he was stuck on this rock, forever in torment.

Will you threaten me again?

"No. I won't." He grabbed his ears to ensure that his head was still his. The pain lingered, a blistering inside the spine.

"It's not the men turning the wheel," Saul said. "It's something . . . I don't know . . . it's like fire making it go round."

Brady said it would work. And Ajoba, rather than arguing, had obeyed.

Glint now danced over her palm and through the crack they had opened between the shutters. She watched in amazement as two men ripped the shutters completely off so all could watch as the sparks flew onto the waterwheel and made it turn.

"See?" he said, grinning.

"We don't have a spindle," she whispered.

"Oh, but we do." Brady led her into the basement of the mill, where the driveshaft from the wheel fed into the gears. "The gears drive the millstones on the main floor," he said. "This long bar which transfers power from the gears to the millstones is called—"

"A spindle?"

"Aye, mate. It's a spindle. I'll send Curt down to cut an opening in the wall so you have access to the wheel. I need you to keep spinning, fill up that spindle."

"But how will we weave? My loom is back in camp too."

Brady pushed her wet hair back from her face. Like everyone else, she was soaked with sweat she couldn't afford. One child had fallen into convulsions, another panted shallowly. The adults had not drunk water since last night. "How did you do it in the Bashans?" he said.

She looked down, ashamed. "I took a crochet hook with me. I don't have one here."

"So, we'll make crochet hooks."

"Brady, we'll die before I have enough shroud crocheted—"

"You might be the only one who can spin shroud, but we have a mill full of women who know how to crochet. I even learned how to do it in training, eya? We'll do this."

Ajoba's only duty was to hold her palm up and let the glint pass across it to the wheel. Six hours later, her arm felt like it would break off. Dehydrated to the point of fainting, she struggled to keep on her feet.

People clustered about her, crocheting patches of shroud. They had been afraid to touch the burning thread until Curt picked up a hook, formed from the core of a corncob, and made a few loopy stitches. One by one, the rest had followed suit.

They had all moved down to the lower room, where it was just a little cooler. Every once in awhile, a child would venture to the opening that Curt had cut and gaze longingly out at the broken dam and the muddy bed of the river Alrod had somehow stolen from them. Brady's dog couldn't even lift her head. Taryan had clipped its fur short to cool it but had slapped Brady's hand when he tried to give the dog his own ration of water.

"Brady . . ." Ajoba's arm fell to her side. The glint rolled down her leg and dissolved. "I can't hold my arm up."

"Katje. And Jules. Come here." He set two children under her arm.

At his side, Taryan motioned him to her face so she could whisper. "What happens when we pass through? Alrod's still out there with his soldiers. We're half-dead now. We can't fight them."

"I just have to believe we'll have help on the other side. Otherwise, it's all for—"

"Ouch!"

Jules slapped his neck. "A hornet got me," he complained.

"Lad, a hornet *thinks* he's got you," Brady said, laughing. "But this is a honeybee that's found you. It stings for now, but the honey's on its way."

"I could break him with my bare hands," Bartoly said.

"No. It's got to all happen at once," Niki whispered. "If we act before they're ready, they'll be trapped."

Bartoly spat, as if he could make the half league between them and the millhouse with the force of his breath. "You don't know that for sure."

"Maybe she does. Do you, Niki?" Kendo said, swinging upside down from a tree limb. At least he had the courtesy to frame his doubt as a question.

"She does," Dakota said quietly.

"How do we know when they're ready?" Bartoly asked. "Or do you already know that too?"

"No. I don't. I . . ." She glanced at Dakota, who gave her one of those strange smiles in which his mouth barely moved. "I think maybe when the wheel stops spinning."

"It's a miracle that it spins at all," Kendo said. "And that we can see it."

The darkness was solid to the touch and to sight. They couldn't see the millhouse, and they hadn't been able to see the wheel—until glint started to turn it.

"What's a miracle," Bartoly was saying, "is that your wolf smells like fish rot and I haven't strangled him." He made a face and fanned the air in front of him. "Can you get him away from me?"

The wolf responded with a low growl and Niki laughed. "I should probably protect him from the likes of you. You're no flower yourself, mate."

"Here." Dakota patted his leg. The wolf went to him and lay his head on his thigh.

"Either you're a better man than I, mate," Bartoly said, "or you have no sense of smell."

Niki waved him silent. "Now, troops. Let's make sure we have everything ready."

Alrod had thirteen very able-bodied strong-arms and one creature of darkness. To oppose him, they had three outriders and one scout, one scruffy wolf, and a swarm of bees. But the fact that they were all over the age of twenty meant they had plenty of experience—and plenty of years beating the odds of survival. Then again, their advanced age as birthrighters might mean their luck was about to run out.

It's not luck, child.

"Thank you," she whispered.

"Amen," Dakota said.

"You don't know what I'm talking about."

He gave her that strange smile that told her he knew so much more than he ever said.

Kendo jumped out of the tree, his spyglass still in hand. "The wheel's slowing."

TWENTY-NINE

THEY MADE IT AN ADVENTURE.

"Hide-and-seek," Brady said. "A fun game where we hide you from the bad guys by wrapping you in this shiny cloth."

"What's the seek part?" Katje asked.

"You're going to seek sweet dreams," he said.

More than one parent insisted on trying out the shroud first. "It's weird but fun," Hannah said.

Taryan absolutely refused to be wrapped. "I can fight."

"You can't even walk," Brady said.

"She can ride on my back," Curt said. "We need as many fighters as we can get."

Brady hesitated, knowing he had no right to value Taryan's life over any of the others in his care. It hurt to feel his love for her— *Lord, it was a good love*—being ripped out of his heart. "Do you have enough arrows to make yourself useful?" he asked.

"When I run out of arrows, I'll use my fists," Taryan said. "Preferably on Alrod."

Brady couldn't begin to worry about what that creature of Alrod's might bring against them. He had tried to warn the people—including his own birthrighters—about the power of temptation, but they had looked at him blankly.

"If swords won't work against that creature, what will?" Ajoba asked.

Cooper supplied the answer. "Back on Welz, I just sang 'Glorious,' over and over. It kept that one off me." As they wrapped the children and prepared to leave, he taught the song to their parents and grandparents:

You're one who heals the wounded.
You can calm the storm at sea . . .
Glorious! You are glorious! . . .

Carefully they reviewed the plan. Six women would raise the canopy of shroud. The fighters would run under it first, moving out into the darkness to take on whatever force Alrod had waiting. Those not fighting would rush the bundled children under the canopy, run downstream of the darkness, and toss them into the river. That way, if Alrod managed to kill all the adults, the children would eventually be brought to the Ark—the eventual destination of all shroud-wrapped collections. If their parents survived, they could retrieve the children and bring them home.

Brady was fairly sure the shroud canopy would get them through the darkness and fairly sure his comrades would be waiting on the other side to fight with them. Though he did not look forward to facing the demonic creature again, he hoped it would take on him and not Ajoba or Cooper. He doubted it was interested in any of the Fenside folks, other than as pawns.

And what was its interest in the birthrighters?

Alrod had said something about a secret. A splendid secret. The Simon creature knew about the Ark but couldn't speak that truth. He wanted Alrod to wrestle the information out of a birthrighter. And then?

He sighed. No point in speculating about that now. He had a battle to fight.

Brady raised his hands, asking for quiet. He should give a fiery speech, say something to encourage fighters and bearers alike. But when they all fell silent, all he could think was to sing again his favorite part of the song they had just learned. He croaked it hoarsely, out of a dry throat, his voice gaining strength as he sang.

As it was in the beginning,
it will be for ages yet to come.
You're The Lord Almighty.
You're the One and Only Son.

"Amen!" Cooper yelled.

"Aye and amen," Brady said.

Ghedo sat in Alrod's chambers, staring at the baron's wall of trophies.

Choices, choices.

She had confined Merrihana to her room, telling her strongarms that the baroness's ravings were due to her head injury. That fall was a distinct advantage—no one believed the baroness's babbling claim that Ghedo was a woman. Merrihana would forget soon enough herself. Ghedo had dosed her liberally with herbs that robbed one of recent memories. Perhaps she'd even forget about the minstrel.

Ghedo would not. She would find the minstrel—who clearly was with those outriders—and she would hunt down Nikolette of Finway, who must be Niki of Horesh that the reward posters proclaimed. Both would suffer excruciating deaths, if indeed Ghedo decided to kill them. Perhaps years of agony would be more fitting.

Choices.

The most significant still loomed: Merrihana or Alrod? Merrihana was in position to rule Traxx. Once stripped of this ridiculous notion that she needed to be loved, she would be suitably ruthless for Ghedo's purposes while remaining nicely malleable.

Yet there was a more intriguing prospect, one whose irony made Ghedo smile even in her utter fury.

Merrihana could not bear an heir for Alrod because she had submitted to transmogrification.

But Ghedo had never gone under her own needles.

How absolutely lovely it would be to seduce Alrod, bear him a son, and then use her considerable magic to work her own purpose. That cow Nikolette had blown up the potions here at the castle, but Ghedo had plenty more in secret lairs scattered throughout the Bashan mountain range. With faster, more devious mogs, Ghedo could eliminate both Alrod and Merrihana and then claim the throne for her own child.

Ghedo sighed as she taped her breasts back up. It was a shame that Nikolette had also blown up her trophies. Alrod's head would have looked so perfect in a jar next to her father's— the only two men she had ever loved.

Brady was the first out of the darkness, sword flashing, singing loudly.

"Now!" Niki yelled when she saw him.

Bartoly bellowed and rushed to the left of the hole that had been made in the darkness. Niki went to the right. Kendo and Dakota were staged halfway around and would be taking on the strong-arms stationed there. The wolf would go for someone's throat—he would know who was friend and who was foe.

Brady looked like a shrunken version of himself as he battled. "Hey, gal."

"Hey, pal," Niki said, "Do I always have to bail you out?"

"Only when I'm not bailing you out."

As they fought, women ran through the tent of shroud carrying large bundles. They ran down to the place where the diverted river returned to its banks and tossed them into a fast-rushing stream. A sheepdog ran excitedly behind them to track their passage.

Within minutes the battle was over. Alrod's remaining strong-arms had been cut down like butter. Yet the darkness—solid now except for the shroud-covered tunnel—would not yield.

After riding the perimeter, Kendo reported, "We got 'em all but the baron and his friend. They're nowhere to be found."

"It was too easy," Brady said quietly, looking around.

"We were too good," Bartoly said. "They're all dead, I tell you."

"It's not about them," Niki said. "It's about us. My crew is all here. Who's missing from yours? You had Cooper, Ajoba, and Taryan—"

"Cooper went downstream to help recover the children," Ajoba said.

"Where's Curt?" Brady said.

"He fought well, but one of the Fenside deserters killed him," Ajoba said, shaking her head. "I thought someone brought Taryan back here."

Brady's legs gave out, and Bartoly had to catch him. "Alrod's got Taryan. Simon told him we have a secret—that he needs to get it from a birthrighter. That's what he's after. They'll be long gone by now."

Niki rushed to him. "Are you hurt?"

"He almost died on us a few days back," Ajoba said. "Been fighting wounded since."

Brady struggled in Bartoly's grip. "I have to get to her before Simon starts on her."

"How many?" Niki looked around. "There's six of us, not counting Cooper. Even with all of us tracking, it'll be hard to find them in the dark."

Kendo was reaching for his saddlebags. "I brought some of my fire powder."

Niki shook her head. "I know this darkness, Kendo. I doubt your gadgets will make much of a difference."

Dakota touched her arm. "Tell me about her."

"What's he talking about?" Bartoly said. "Mate, you're not bringing those hornets down on me again, hey?"

"She's got light hair—sort of like ripe grain, straight to the middle of her back," Brady said. "Slim. Blue-green eyes . . ."

"Two broken ankles," Ajoba added. "Alrod broke them."

Niki gripped her sword, and Bartoly cursed.

"She . . ." Brady panted.

"She has a good heart," Niki said. "Can your bees measure that, scout?"

"No," Dakota said. "But our Lord can."

They moved into the darkness, following a line of bees, assaulted by shadows that had no substance except for accusation.

Ajoba felt her heart being stretched, her mind soiled. Close beside her, Bartoly's eyes bulged, his head turning continuously toward Niki. Dakota rubbed his head so hard Ajoba expected him to wear through his skin.

Kendo rode in circles three times until Niki grabbed his horse and righted him. Ajoba caught a glimpse of his intense features as he rode by her, sword slashing left and right in confusion.

They all have secrets, a familiar voice whispered in Ajoba's mind. *If you knew their secrets, you could help them.*

"Demas. Be gone." But doubt already inched its way under her skin, making her grasp on her short blade more tenuous than her broken wrist mandated. It was Demas who had caused her trouble in the first place, who'd deceived her and led her astray. But Brady had driven off the demon weeks ago, before the battle in the Bashans. Had the fallen one been tracking her every move since then, waiting for an opportune time to strike?

Strike? Child, it is not my intention to harm you, but to raise you to higher service. Surely you understand that your leader Brady is not perfect. He has many secrets and has made many mistakes.

Ajoba cast about, searching for Brady. But it was too dark, and he crept too expertly for her to find him. All she had to guide her was the buzz of the bee line and a brush of air as they flew past.

Your friends—they suffer so. Don't you want to help them?

A flash of light blinded Ajoba, causing such pain she had to drop her short blade so she could cover her eyes.

Look. See what you allow.

She peeked through her fingers, stunned to see a holovideo of her comrades playing out before her. This was technology left behind on the Ark, but somehow Demas or someone had the same capacity to show scenes in living, breathing moments.

Private moments that only One should see.

And what does that tell you about your privilege? The honor shown a tracker who became a teacher, a teacher who became an outcast, an outcast who became an outrider, only to be accorded the highest honor of a second anointing. Look, child. See how they have suffered.

Brady leaned over the bank of the Grand River, his head underwater. Steam rising from the back of his neck, so consumed with anger and frustration he was.

Kendo bent over the dirt floor of his shop, sketching high towers and motored vehicles in the hard clay. When he finished, he smiled. Then he rubbed it out with his heel, tears streaming down his cheeks.

Niki lay on her back under the night sky. She stared at the stars, her lips moving as she counted them. Her face was composed, but her fingers dug into the cold soil like iron claws as she tried to fight some deep longing beyond the stars.

Taryan bowed her head in prayer, at sweet peace until a muscle in her jaw twitched.

The images swirled faster, one comrade after another cracking open so their fears and longings spilled out like disemboweled guts, ugly things that were so unworthy of their calling, base desires that someone was bound to indulge eventually because they were so frail and so human, and then *Watch out, because it's going to get ugly—*

"Enough! In the name of the Blessed One, get behind me."

Ajoba picked up her short blade, not really surprised to feel it lighter. Of course they were human—but a provision had been made for their failings, a cleansing and redemption and restoration, and *that* was what moved her into the darkness.

"You okay?" Brady asked from somewhere near her.

"What?" Ajoba was startled to find he had been nearby this whole time.

"We're all fighting it. Singing helps." He drew in a breath, singing out the first notes of "Glorious." But his voice was silenced when a black void rose before them. From somewhere in its center, Taryan cried out.

Brady rushed forward, screaming, and something monstrous seized him—or he seized it. Ajoba, at his side, gagged at the stench that floated around her as they struggled. The man in the purple cloak had become a gargant, not of flesh, but of everything foul that flesh spawned. He shook Brady like a doll but Brady wouldn't let go. Instead, he swung his sword, casting sparks with every blow that struck the creature.

Someone rushed by—Niki, leaping high into the air, her sword going into what would be the creature's neck. She twisted the blade with one arm while grabbing for Brady with her free hand. Ajoba was astounded at the strength that must take.

She studied the creature, seeking a way to aid her comrades. It was vaguely human in form but with a hundred eyes and a mouth big enough to swallow someone as small as Ajoba whole, should she be foolish enough to approach.

"With Your help . . ." She gripped her short blade, searching for an opening.

But Niki and Brady seemed to be gaining on the creature, battering it backward. Bartoly was at its feet, swinging his sword with two hands like an ax, as if he could fell it like a tree. It staggered backward and Bartoly shouted in triumph, rushing in to deliver more blows.

Then Taryan screamed.

A scream not of fear but of horror—it pierced through Ajoba like a shock of foul lightning. And Brady, too, for he dropped his sword. He battered the creature with his right fist while he went for his short blade, but the creature had found new life.

Especially when Taryan screamed again.

Ajoba crept forward, resolved to join Bartoly if she wasn't called elsewhere. To her right she spotted Dakota trying to get around to the back of the creature. The creature spit fire at the scout. He blocked it with his sword but it clung like a burning fungus that Dakota had to hack free of with his knife.

This isn't working, Ajoba realized. But was that the truth? Or was Demas or the creature or any of the dark things flying about her head casting doubt again?

No, it was the truth. As long as Alrod had Taryan, the creature would have a hold on Brady.

There had to be another way.

Ajoba went face-down in the dirt and sniffed. Alrod's scent wasn't hard to pick up, especially mixed with Taryan's fear. While Ajoba's comrades wrestled the creature, keeping it occupied, perhaps she could track right past it.

She crept in the dirt, cheered to smell human scent and earthly odors instead of the rot of the creature. She moved past him, sensing a comrade nearby but not seeing him. Kendo? She marked a trail for him by cutting off strips of shroud from armor. Whoever he was, the other birthrighter would know how to read it.

She wormed along in the darkness for what seemed like a long time. Here, far from the river and any tree cover, the stars at least should be visible. But the creature had cast a pall over this territory too. Not the impenetrable darkness it had cast over Fenside—but a shadow heavy enough to make sight difficult.

"Now faith is being sure of what we hope for and certain of what we do not see." She quoted the verse out loud, her face to the dirt, thinking about the first command of Almighty God to "let there be light" and understanding why light came before all.

Something flickered ahead.

Easy now to smell wood burning in the campfire. But even stronger was the tang of blood and the heady odor of exaltation. There was no doubt which belonged to Taryan and which to Alrod.

Ajoba found them behind some boulders, the monster of darkness far behind her now, though the sounds of battle—her comrades' cries and prayers—still clung to her.

Alrod had bound Taryan to a stump. Her hand bled copiously. She was missing the little finger from her left hand. *The same finger Brady sacrificed for me,* Ajoba noted with a pang, though she breathed a prayer of thanks that Taryan's torment had just started.

Alrod grabbed Taryan's other hand but pressed the blade of his knife flat against her cheek. "Tell me the secret."

"God is light," Taryan said. "In him there is no darkness at all."

Alrod brought the knife down, and Taryan screamed, but with no sound this time. She must have heard Brady bellowing in the darkness and was trying to spare him.

Ajoba crouched low, gathering her strength, looking for the right spot in Alrod's armor to aim her short blade. She'd have one try, no more than that. She braced her splinted right hand with her left, breathed a quick prayer.

And leaped.

He caught her reflection in his knife and whirled to meet her. In a practiced motion, he kicked away her weapon, kicking again with his other foot to the side of her knee to drop her to the ground. Ajoba tried to roll away but Alrod came down with a victorious shout on her broken wrist and she screamed.

He laughed and raised his knife, knowing not to go for her armor but lower, kneeling backwards on her torso so he could go for the major arteries in her legs. She tried to throw him off her but he was too heavy and too furious, so when she saw his knife flash overhead, about to fall, she prayed that someone would save Taryan.

Then suddenly, Alrod jolted sideways, and his knife went flying. Ajoba, stilled pinned, craned and twisted to see what had happened.

Kendo!

The outrider had hurtled out of the darkness, knocking the knife out of Alrod's hand. His forward momentum kept him going, so now Kendo tumbled over and over through the clearing. By the time he got to his feet, Alrod was already flying toward him, aiming for his face in a move Kendo hadn't anticipated. Ajoba could only watch as Alrod's blade drove into Kendo's eyes—

Please, Lord, no—

And Kendo was falling, falling—

—into Your hands.

Ajoba got up, found her short blade, swung it hard with her good hand. It clanged off Alrod's armor. He laughed and came at her, knowing to go for her eyes as he had with Kendo because the armor wouldn't protect her there.

She curled her shoulder and threw herself against him. He toppled backward and she swung again with both hands, this time going for the one place she knew she'd get him, cutting that sword out of his hand by cutting through his wrist, her own wrist screaming in pain as she did so.

He gasped in shock before bellowing in rage. A moment later, he ran for his horse and rode off into the darkness.

"Coward!" she screamed as she rushed toward her fallen comrade.

Ajoba saw the worst, but reminded herself that Kendo now saw the very best.

She turned her attention to Taryan, cutting more shroud from her armor so she could bind her comrade's hand.

"I didn't tell him," Taryan mumbled.

"He wouldn't have believed you anyway," Ajoba said. "It's too wonderful for the likes of him."

She helped Taryan to sit, secured the shroud bandage, and went back to Kendo. He looked impossibly small lying there, bereft of his valiant and trustworthy spirit. Ajoba fell on her knees, her heart breaking, barely noticing that Taryan had joined her at his side.

And then the darkness lifted. Alrod had been the creature's anchor—with him run off, the others must have easily vanquished him.

Overhead, the stars shone in blazing glory. So clear and seemingly so near that Ajoba raised her hand to touch them. All she felt was the cool night air . . . and a sure peace that Kendo saw far more now than distant stars.

When Brady, Niki, and the others arrived, the stars gave them little comfort.

Ajoba withdrew, sitting with Dakota while the others mourned.

"It's hard to walk a solitary path," he whispered.

"But we all do."

Dakota nodded and lay back on the ground, staring up at the stars. She sat beside him, praying for her own grief but more for the others, who had known Kendo so much longer.

After awhile, she glanced down at the scout. Dakota's eyes were open and his face peaceful as he gazed into the heavens.

But his fingers dug into the ground like iron claws.

Ajoba bowed her head and prayed for him too. The next thing she knew, Cooper was shaking her by the shoulder. The sky was gray, with a blush of pink in the east where morning would soon be born.

"It's time to go home," he said.

Amen, she thought. *Aye and amen.*

THIRTY

NIKI STOOD AT THE DOOR TO BRADY'S HUT. "CAN WE talk, pal?"

He looked up from his work. He had been confined to his hut at Horesh by Bartoly and Niki until that gash in his side finally stopped bleeding. After a day, he had persuaded Bartoly to help him go see Jasper the gargant, who finally showed signs of waking. This morning, he'd asked Cooper to walk him down to the river and sit there with him.

After almost dying of thirst, he would never take water for granted again.

"Sure, gal," he told Niki now. "Come on in."

Niki's face was mottled, her eyes sunken. She couldn't stop crying, it seemed. He still couldn't get used to her this way—as a woman who wept—though he knew the change was for the better.

Perhaps his own tears would flow more freely once he got hydrated.

When they had found Kendo's body, the others had known to leave Brady and Niki alone with him. Together they had carried him to the Fens River and buried him there.

Now, together, they mourned.

Six years ago, four young people had come off the Ark for the first time. Four had become three. Three had become two.

"You all right?" she asked.

"Trying to be. You?"

"Trying to be."

She didn't look in any hurry to sit, so Brady stood. "What's wrong?" he asked.

"I have . . . I . . ." She shoved something into his hand. "Here."

"What's this?"

"It's a letter from the Ark. From when I did the transit."

A flush went through him, hope and dread. "You found another letter?"

Niki met his gaze. "I'm sorry."

"For what? I'm glad you found it."

"I didn't find it. I kept it back."

A chill came over Brady. "What do you mean?"

"I read it and didn't like what I read. So I decided not to give it to you."

This dizziness was not from his injury, but from his world turning upside down. Niki would never do such a thing—but here she stood before him, telling him she had.

"What didn't you like?"

"Read it."

"I want you tell me."

She kicked the dirt. "I didn't like that it gave you permission to marry."

"Me?"

"Are you deaf, man? Why do you keep repeating things?"

"I asked for all of us. Not just me."

"Fine. Any birthrighter of senior status."

"Why didn't you want me to know this?"

She turned away.

"Nik?"

"Don't call me that," she whispered. "I beg you."

Brady turned her to him. He tipped her chin so she had to look at him. "You've never done anything like this before. I don't understand."

Niki grabbed his hands. "I don't want you to understand. Take the letter, do what you want with it. But please, just accept my apology and leave me be."

He studied her face—his best pal, his comrade, his right hand, his guardian, his sanity. He had always known he was all this to her as well. But had he missed something? Had his own regard for Taryan made him insensitive to a woman he would give his life for? Had he crushed something in this woman who was so precious to him?

What a fool he had been, not seeing what had always been so obvious.

Brady held her face in his hands, willing her to forgive him but not able to ask for such forgiveness because that would reveal he knew her secret. *Sometimes,* he thought, *pretense is a mercy.*

"Thank you for watching out for me," he said.

"What? What are you talking about?"

"This marriage thing is a distraction. We'll deal with it eventually, bring it to the elders and hash out a policy. But first, we've got to get the crews back, figure out what we need to do about Arabah." Brady brushed the tears from her cheeks. "Thank you for exercising good judgment."

"What good judgment? I lied. Lied and disobeyed."

"You took care of me," he said gently. "And . . . I think you're right. It would be wrong for me to marry. Not for you or Bartoly or Ken—oh—" Brady's heart broke all over again, and he reached for Niki. "I forget he's gone."

"Me too." She folded him into her arms and laid her cheek against his so their tears could mix. Then, after a minute, she whispered, "You're an idiot, you know."

"What do you mean?"

"I've always trusted your heart," she said. "Now you need to."

Brady stepped back so he could study her face. "What are you saying?"

"I'm saying God didn't give you this love so you could be a martyr."

"But—"

"Go to her. Tell her what she already knows."

Brady wrapped his hands around Niki's, then pressed them to his chest. Looking into her eyes, he saw that she meant it. Then he realized: "I'm afraid." The words released in him a river of fear, filling him with adrenaline, making him want to run.

But Niki held him tight, her hands on his shoulders. "Afraid of what?"

"Tylow's gone. Kendo's gone. What future can I offer to anyone?"

"So you withhold love so the one you love doesn't have to lose it? That makes no sense, pal." Niki smiled—the same smile as on that first day on the ice.

Fresh from the whale, Brady, Kendo, and Tylow had huddled under an open sky they'd never even imagined. But Niki had stood straight, her smile as wide as the world she opened her arms to. On that day, six long years ago, her courage had helped her comrades to stand and face the unknown.

"Get going or I'll toss you out of here," she told him. "I can do it, you know."

"I know." He kissed Niki's cheek and, with a quick glance back, stepped out of the hut.

Outside, the river roared. But the sound was nothing like the pounding of Brady's heart as he took off, running, for Taryan's hut.

THIRTY-ONE

A BUSH DIDN'T HAVE TO BURN TO BE ALIVE WITH THE glory of God.

Ripe raspberries clung to green branches. Sure, there were thorns, but one must expect to be scratched when reaching for sweetness. A mouse scurried under the roots while a rabbit hopped around it, wiggling its whiskers as it sniffed out low-hanging berries. Finches twittered deep in the underbrush, safe from the hawks and feral cats that wouldn't dare the mass of briar and thorns.

Dakota didn't mind being caught in this tangle. Here he had shade and he had sun in abundance. Birdsong from the cotton-woods and a creek trickling somewhere in the grass. A deer had come by, but when he raised his head, it had hopped off, a delicate explosion of power and grace.

He could lie here forever, but night would fall and then the leaves and then the snow. *Forever* had no meaning in this world, but one day he would gaze at a sky that had no need for a sun or a moon and yet would burst with beauty beyond any of the heavenly host. He closed his eyes, willing sleep, but it would not come. He had put off a distasteful task for a day, and that was a day too long.

This letter was Brady's to write. But without a word passing between them, Dakota had taken on the task. So he scrounged up pen and paper from his leather bag, using his knee as a writing desk, summoning words none of them had ever expected to say. Words that would rip at the heart of all those on the Ark, just as they tore at his own heart.

A comrade has betrayed us . . .

He filled in the bare facts about Timothy—as much as they knew—leaving it to Brady to sort out details in the next few weeks. He wrapped the letter in shroud and left it for the hawk. The letter would make its way to the Ark through the air, the river, the sea.

Even now, Dakota did not take such blessings for granted.

Something rustled behind him. He reached for his knife but stayed his hand as he sniffed the air. He knew the scent of the wolf, sorted through it to find the scent of its mistress.

"How did you find me?" he asked.

Niki sat next to him. "You've got your bees. And I've got—"

"A loyal friend." The wolf sniffed at his leg, then curled up next to him.

"He likes you," she said. "He doesn't like many."

"I'm grateful."

They sat a long time together, listening to birdsong. *She knows silence,* Dakota thought. *I hoped she would.*

Niki didn't speak again until the colors of sunset stretched overhead. "Must a scout always work alone?" she finally whispered.

Dakota reached for the raspberries, plucked the choicest ones, and offered them to her.

"Perhaps not," he said.

Glorious

Can you hear the distant thunder?
Can you feel the tremble of the earth?
Can you see His Spirit moving?
Let us sing the power of your word.

As it was in the beginning,
it will be for ages yet to come.
You're the Lord Almighty.
You're the One and Only Son.

Chorus:
Glorious! You are glorious!
We sing your praise in all the earth!
Glorious! You are glorious!
We sing your praise in all the earth!

People come from every nation.
Gather 'round and let your spirits rise.
Raise your hands, a mighty chorus.
Lift it up and shout it to the skies!
You're one who heals the wounded.
You can calm the storm at sea.
Every knee will bow before you,
for you have set the captives free!

Victoria James
©2004 V. James

You're Everything to Me

Living life is easy when you're playing your own game.
You are your destiny.
Loving, losing, winning, everything's the same,
all the same to me.
Everything was nothing until you came my way.
Now everything reminds me of you.
Never could've seen this, never could believe
you're everything, you're everything to me.

Chorus:
Forever I'll love you.
Forever you will see.
Forever has everything I need 'cause
You're everything to me.

Laying in the darkness, I fall asleep at night.
All there is is me.
Never had a vision or dream fantasy,
but where's reality?
Gone are all my senses. I find I reminisce memories of
*   being with you.*
Can I still be dreaming or can this really be?
You're everything, you're everything to me.

I'm never looking over my shoulder.
I'm never getting stuck in today.
You're on my mind all the time.
These arms want to hold tomorrow and every day.

Victoria James
©2005 V. James

For Always (Hannah's Lullaby)

When the birds of spring come alive to sing
in their golden wonderland,
I will dance with you under skies of blue.
'Cause I will love you forever and I'll be here, with you,
    for always.

And when geese fly by in the autumn sky,
gliding above the earth in her lunar glow,
I will bring a light to your darkest night.
'Cause I will love you forever and I'll be here, with you,
    for always.

When you're tucked in bed and all your prayers are said,
and you wait with joy for a brand-new day,
close your eyes and sleep, dream of wishes sweet.
'Cause I will love you forever and I'll be here, with you,
    for always.

Victoria James